The Holding

By M.A. Newhall

The characters and events in this book are fictitious. Any similarity to real persons or events is coincidental and not intended by the author.

ISBN 13: 9780997433623
ISBN 10: 0997433620

Copyright © 2017 by Ormus Publishing

Cover design by Eddie Vincent/ENC Graphic Services

Ormus Publishing
Taunton, MA
ormuspublishing.com

Publisher's Cataloging-In-Publication Data
(Prepared by The Donohue Group, Inc.)

Names: Newhall, M. A., 1985- author.
Title: The holding / M.A. Newhall.
Description: Taunton, MA : Ormus Publishing, [2019] | Title from cover.
Identifiers: ISBN 9780997433623 (paperback) | ISBN 0997433620 (paperback) | ISBN 9780997433630 (ebook)
Subjects: LCSH: Human trafficking--Fiction. | Man-woman relationships--Fiction. | Kidnapping--Fiction. | Loss (Psychology)--Fiction. | LCGFT: Psychological fiction. | Erotic fiction. | Thrillers (Fiction)
Classification: LCC PS3614.E5845 H65 2019 (print) | LCC PS3614. E5845 (ebook) | DDC 813/.6--dc23

10 9 8 7 6 5 4 3 2 1

Prologue

Adrien leaned back in his chair, propping his feet on the balcony's railing as he thought about his latest business interaction. He took a deep drag from the joint in his hand, allowing the sweet smoke to seep and burn before exhaling it slowly.

Cherub, he had called her. It was not a term of endearment but rather a mere descriptor—something to call her during her training. It was fitting, though, he must admit. She couldn't have been more than 19, her cheeks round and full as though she had never lost her baby fat. Like most of the Americans Adrien dealt with, she had been visiting Costa Rica on spring break with the hopes of getting wasted and laid. And, like most Americans he dealt with, she had been difficult. Entitled even. It hadn't taken long to change that. Adrien snorted at the thought, flicking the ashes before taking another deep hit.

His upbringing in France had given him a propensity to despise the modern American attitude, which is why he found it so much more interesting to work with American girls. His father had warned him against it, and had even gone so far as suggesting it would be too hard to train them…to break them. But Adrien liked a challenge, and his father quickly recanted his position when Adrien's training yielded results. The family business flourished more than ever. Customers from all over the world were vying to get their hands on an American girl. Even Adrien's brother had begun accepting a few Americans to train here and there.

Adrien's mind wandered to his last moments with *Cherub*.

"She's ready?" Frederic, Adrien's father, asked. He spoke in French, knowing the American wouldn't understand. As his question hung in the air, his eyes surveyed the girl as though there may be some physical clue that she was not, in fact, ready.

"Of course," came Adrien's reply, as he shoved her forward and she stumbled toward Frederic. She glanced back at Adrien and he caught a distinct look in her eyes. He recognized it as the same look she gave him the first time they met. He hadn't seen this emotion from her in quite some weeks, but here it was nonetheless. *Terror.*

Adrien smiled at the memory. He flicked the joint over the balcony, satisfied with it. He was beginning to feel the familiar tingle as the weed worked its way into his system.

They had met in a predetermined spot, as these things always went, for the hand-off. This time, the spot was along the side of a dark road leading from Costa Rica toward Nicaragua. Their client was a wealthy Nicaraguan politician who had agreed to meet them in the anonymity that came with the dark, Central-American night sky. Only the stars would witness their indiscretions.

Technically, Adrien's presence wasn't needed. He had done his part; he had trained the girl to be obedient, willing…pliant. But he always attended the hand-off for two reasons. First, he had convinced his father long ago that it was best for customer satisfaction. While his father made it his business to know their clients' deepest desires, Adrien made it his business that he alone knew whether the girl would be a good fit. His father agreed it was a good idea. Adrien figured ensuring the girl's master was a right-fit was the least he could do for her. He wasn't a monster, after all.

But it was the second reason that most pulled Adrien toward attending the hand-off. It was that final glimpse of the women that he had trained—the look of utter disbelief as they were handed to their new master. The pleading in their eyes, as though they couldn't believe Adrien would let it happen. Despite all he had done to them—the way he terrorized them into submission, humiliated them until there was nothing left but a shadow of their former self—they still had the audacity to think that maybe he would stop this. That maybe he cared.

It's amazing, he thought, *the human capacity for hope.*

———————————————————

I

____

"Another drink, miss?" The waitress's voice startled Sophie from her latest reverie. The woman's accent gave her away as a Costa-Rican native, the sound of the word 'miss' landing on Sophie's ears as 'meese.' For a brief moment, Sophie thought of a child mistaking the plural for moose.

She squinted up through her sunglasses at the petite woman standing on the beach before her. Sophie lay sprawled on the chaise, her body facing the deep aqua ocean while the sun remained hot in the sky. She nodded, offering a quiet "Si, gracias" before handing over her empty, plastic cocktail cup while simultaneously jiggling her wrist to inform the waitress of her all-inclusive status. The woman nodded, scurrying up the beach toward the cabana bar. She didn't even have to summon the memory for it to re-surface. It was already there, awaiting her as she closed her eyes.

"Get your ass in here!" Josh called from the edge of the pool. Sophie looked up from the novel in her hand, shielding her green eyes from the glare of the sun on the resort's crystal-clear pool water.

Josh looked at her expectantly from where he clung to the edge, a coy smile plastered on his face. His blonde hair was wet and hung limply, his brown eyes looking at her expectantly.

"I'm in the middle of a chapter!" she called to him from where she sat on her chaise, hoping that her explanation might trigger some empathic patience from him. She should have known better. Sophie shrieked as the cool pool water splashed her legs.

"Don't make me come up there! I'll throw you in if you don't get over here, Kingston!"

"Fine…I'm coming," she grumbled as she folded the page to mark her place. She set the book down on the chair next to hers and made her way to the edge of the pool. She sat down on the grainy concrete, sticking her feet over the edge. The water cooled her feet and legs, hot from the Mexican afternoon sun. "You suck, you know that?" she said as she leaned back, propping herself on her hands.

"You love me," Josh offered, doing a push up on the edge of the pool to bring his face close to Sophie's. "Admit it."

She smiled, and that was all he needed for an answer. He gave her a quick kiss on the cheek, wrapped his arms around her waist, and pulled her into the pool.

"Miss? Miss…" the waitress hesitantly prodded. Sophie opened her eyes, shaking her head as though she could dispel the memory from her mind. She took a deep breath and grabbed the piña colada from the woman's outstretched hand.

"Gracias," she said, staring at the pineapple-speared straw. It taunted her. *Be happy!* it screamed. She removed it, throwing it toward the water to be consumed by the ocean.

"I hope you were zoning because you're super relaxed and enjoying this amazing vacation, and not because your mind is wandering to its usual things," Sophie's best friend interjected from the chaise next to her. Sophie didn't have to look at Megan to know her eyes were inspecting Sophie, waiting for her lie.

She gave it to her, offering as much of a smile as she could muster.

"I just dozed off for a minute. All this sun is doing me in." Sophie glanced over, seeing if Megan would accept the line she fed her. It seemed to satisfy, as Megan readjusted herself in her seat to allow the sun to focus its rays elsewhere on her tanning body.

"I just worry about you. You know that," Megan said after a moment's silence. Sophie could feel Megan's eyes drift over her again. She had every right to be worried, Sophie knew that. It was the whole reason the two of them had gone on this vacation. "You just haven't been the same since…you know…"

You know. Somehow, it had become this unspoken thing, so sensitive that it didn't even get the courtesy of being named. It was true, though. Sophie wasn't the same.

"I know," Sophie admitted quietly. A wave of guilt swept over her at the thought of causing her friend to worry. Megan had worried so much, that she had convinced her wealthy parents to pay for an all-inclusive resort for the week. Despite being 25 years old and having her own career in fashion design working for a women's apparel company, Megan had no qualms with asking her parents for favors. Equally, they had no qualms with giving Megan anything she wanted. The idea of it usually made Sophie feel uncomfortable, but she couldn't help but be grateful for this most recent handout. She herself was a mental health counselor. On giving up her love for art after undergrad, she obtained her master's degree in psychology counseling. Despite holding a degree of higher education, the field paid a meager salary. She would have never been able to afford this type of vacation on her own. The realization caused Sophie to feel even guiltier for not being able to snap out of her reveries, if only just for the week.

But a week was a long time to ask for, given that Sophie hadn't been able to snap out of it for the past thirteen months. It's not like Sophie didn't want to snap out of it, to feel normal again. To feel *anything* again. And while her grief slowly wrapped itself around every inch of her heart, Sophie couldn't seem to find a way to shake the monster that had taken residence, coiled in her being.

"I know how much you must miss him," Megan's voice reached Sophie's ears again, "but you have to find a way to be happy again." Sophie took a sip of her drink in reply. She knew this, too. Of course she did. And yet…

Her grief was different this time. It wasn't the same type of grief she felt when her parents had died. The type that, despite the heaviness that threatens to pull you down, you know you'll be okay. *This* grief…*this* was omnipotent, devastating. It gave no indication that anything would ever be okay again.

Josh's death had taken something from Sophie and she didn't think she would ever get it back. This realization had begun to seep into her consciousness when, after six months, Sophie was still drowning in loss. Her memories were an escape, at first. She would willingly allow herself to reconnect to the times she shared with Josh, indulging in the recollections. But, after a while, Sophie no longer needed to summon them. They came without invitation, invading her mind, ripping her from the here and now. As a mental health counselor, Sophie knew this was not the typical experience of grief. But she was helpless to stop it. Its effects assaulted every aspect of Sophie's life. It became hard to sleep, hard to eat, hard to *think* about anything other than the loss. She was unable to stay focused at work and, when clients started complaining to her supervisor that Sophie appeared not to be listening (which, really, was the *only* requirement of her job), there was only so much consideration her agency was willing to give. They let her go last month, recommending she seek help while wishing her the best.

"Let's stop talking about this. I'm trying to forget about it for once." Sophie offered another lie. Megan seemed to accept it willingly.

"Fine, missy. But if I catch you zoning again, I'm going to make you do shots with me!" Megan warned, sitting up in her chair to grab the SPF 30. Sophie rolled her eyes at her friend. "Hey, wanna hit up the bar tonight and then head to the casino? I overheard people in the pool saying they've been winning big-time on the slots there."

The thought of the casino—the noise, the crowds—caused Sophie's chest to clench. She swallowed it down, compelling herself to relax. "Um, sure, I guess." Sophie took another sip of her drink.

"Come on, Soph. Have some fun while you're still 25 and hot. It's not gonna last forever, you know. Things start to droop after like…age 30." Megan smiled and awaited Sophie's response like a test proctor, ready to gauge her friend's ability to reply with a shred of normalcy.

"Ugh…fine!" Sophie forced a laugh, hoping she'd passed.

Sophie brushed her long hair in front of the bathroom mirror of their hotel room. She had just finished blow-drying her golden-brown locks, which now fell in waves down her back.

"Promise me you'll never cut it."

These moments were the worst. Moments where his voice echoed in her mind, making her believe that he was there. That she was really hearing him. The first few times it happened, she caught herself looking around, searching for him, on the off-chance she wasn't crazy.

He isn't here, she reminded herself. *He's dead.*

Allowing the memory to fade, she gazed at her tired, green eyes in the mirror and proceeded to apply some makeup with the hope of concealing the dark circles that had taken permanent residence beneath them. Her gaze fell to her wrists then. Faded marks from the darkest moments of her grief tattooed the delicate skin. She quickly smeared some concealer there, too.

"Let's go, bitch!" Megan called from the other room. Megan's crassness didn't faze Sophie. Their friendship had begun with these same words their freshman year at MassArt in Boston, as they waited in line to get their photos taken for their student IDs. Sophie was attending school for fine arts and photography, while Megan, Sophie would soon learn, was there for fashion design. Sophie was ahead of Megan in line, but clearly not paying attention when the queue began to move. Sophie instantly took a liking to Megan's boisterous nature, so unlike her own, and the two quickly asked for a transfer to share the same dorm room.

They became even closer during January of their sophomore year, when Sophie heard the news that both of her parents had died in a car accident while navigating an icy New England road. Having no siblings and only her mother's sister and brother-in-law to call family, Megan quickly became Sophie's biggest support. Megan stayed by her side at her parents' funeral and stayed up with Sophie at night while she mourned the loss of her childhood and the future of her family. And, after graduation, the two moved into an apartment together in Boston while Sophie pursued her master's degree.

"I'm ready to get my drank on," Megan appeared in the doorway of the bathroom wearing a short, black, A-line dress that hugged her natural waist, flaring from her mid-belly down. Rail-thin and flat-chested, Megan was not graced with the same sultry curves as Sophie, but her background in fashion and design guaranteed she always knew what clothing would be most flattering on her body type.

"Almost done," Sophie replied, absentmindedly brushing some blush on her high cheekbones. She quickly applied some mascara and stood back from the mirror, catching Megan's eyes in the reflection. "Am I good to go?"

Megan scrutinized her for a second, stepping into the bathroom. She pinched at the excess fabric of Sophie's aqua-colored, halter-style dress. "Aside from needing to put on a little weight? You look great." Only Megan could admonish Sophie while simultaneously doling out a compliment.

"All right then…let's go, bitch!" Sophie had become a master of sorts, an actress for a captive audience, putting on fake smiles, injecting the sound of excitement into her voice. It was an exhausting necessity, this existence on a perpetual stage.

"That's what I like to hear!" Megan laughed and followed her to the elevators. Sophie pressed the call button. The arrow lit up and the doors opened. Megan and Sophie stepped in, surprised to be the only passengers.

"So, what do you think about getting wasted and hooking up with some hot Costa Rican tonight?" Megan raised her eyebrows and smiled in Sophie's direction.

"I think that's a great idea…for you. Not me," Sophie emphasized.

"I think it's a great idea all around. Come on, Soph. You just need to get back out there."

Is that what people think? Sophie wondered. *That I just need to get laid and it'll fix everything? I'll just forget about Josh, forget how much I loved him, how much I wanted to marry him?* Sophie shook her head at the thought, tears stinging behind her eyes. "It's not that easy."

"I know. I'm sorry. I didn't mean it like that. But maybe it will help you get your mind off things and maybe, if you can get your mind off the sad stuff, you can start thinking about happy stuff again."

The words hit Sophie's ears and, willing them to soak in, she thought about what it would mean to start moving forward. So many times she had tried…but so many times she found that she couldn't. It was as though she had lost the very instinct to live.

Megan offered a sympathetic smile as the elevator dinged, indicating they had arrived at their destination.

The sound of music playing in the room reached their ears as the doors opened to reveal the expansive, high-ceilinged, 'adult-only' section of the resort. A bar was situated on the far-left side of the wide room while small tables and comfy leather chairs dotted the forefront of the space. Glasses clinked as cocktails were shaken and expensive wood-scented scotches were poured and given to their eager recipients. Piano music drifted through the lounge for those enjoying the bar while the faint sounds of a heavier beat came from the dark entranceway of the resort's casino situated past the bar.

"Wow, this place is huge!" Megan exclaimed as she and Sophie exited the elevator. "Let's get a drink!" Megan grabbed Sophie's arm, tugging her to the bar. Sophie allowed herself to be dragged through the crowded room, distracted by the stimulation to her senses. Sophie glanced toward the casino entryway, the fluorescent lights from the slot machines assuaging the darkness of the room in which they sat.

"Come on, baby, I just need a few hundred dollars," Josh pleaded with Sophie, his hand gripping hers as though, through osmosis, she

would absorb the 'yes' that he needed to hear. "I promise I'll pay you back."

"Josh, you haven't been able to pay me back for the last couple hundred you borrowed. And the couple hundred before that, and…well, I'm running out of money here. We can't use my entire inheritance on a few poker games. We need that money for other —"

"What the fuck, *Sophie?!" He all but threw her hand back at her. His pleading demeanor quickly morphed into one of anger. Sophie shrank back. She hated when these dark storms washed over him. "You're gonna do this now? Right as I'm about to pick up my game and win, you've got to go throwing old debts in my face? I didn't think people who love each other did that to each other. What about unconditional support? Isn't that what you're always talking about? Huh? Where is that now, Sophie?" Josh's eyes burned into hers, his brow knit with anger. She didn't answer. "That's what I thought. Thanks for nothing." He grabbed the car keys from the kitchen counter and slammed the door on his way out.*

"Hello? The man isn't going to wait all night, Soph. What do you want to drink?" Megan snapped her fingers a few times in front of Sophie's eyes, effectively bringing her back to the moment, where a tall and impatient bartender stood waiting for her drink order.

"Um, dark and stormy, please," Sophie breathed as she showed the bartender her all-inclusive bracelet. *Dark and stormy. Like Josh.* Despite the harder times, she was comforted by the idea that she could somehow drink Josh in—somehow allow him to be a part of her again. Consume him, the way he consumed her.

"And can you get us two shots of tequila, as well? Jose Cuervo," Megan's voice piped up as she turned to look at

Sophie. "I was serious when I said no more zoning. Now look what you're making us do. You know how I feel about shots, Sophie…"

"Yeah, you *love* them. I'm the one that can't gag them down!" Sophie whined at the idea of taking a shot. "I'm sorry I zoned. You know I can't help it sometimes…I'm really trying here, I swear."

"Are you begging me to *not* take a shot?? And yes, I *do* love them. They're efficient and effective. What's not to love?" The bartender returned with Megan's cosmo, Sophie's dark and stormy, and two shots of Jose Cuervo with lime. Megan grabbed the two shot glasses and wedges of lime, handing one of each to Sophie. Sophie stared at them with a look of disgust before reaching down the bar to grab the salt shaker.

"On three, bitch," Megan instructed with a smile, as she prepped herself with salt and lime. "One, two, three!"

The liquid went down smoother than Sophie remembered it would, the burn arriving as an afterthought. Still, it made her cough.

"See? Not so bad! Want another?" Megan took a swig of her cosmo, and Sophie did the same to extinguish the burn that was settling in her stomach.

"Let's do it!" Sophie said with a smile, waving the bartender over. "One more round, please!"

Megan turned to Sophie, a smile on her face but questions in her eyes. Sophie knew these questions well. *Is this for real? Are you really having a good time?* Sophie had asked herself those same questions many times over the past thirteen months. The answer was always a resounding 'no.' Yet, Sophie continued to hope. Apparently, so did her friend.

Sophie shrugged, taking another sip of her dark and stormy. "Might as well, right?" Now, Megan's smile turned into a bona fide grin. Megan held up her cosmo glass, half-full, in a motion to cheers.

Sophie raised her glass and let it clink against her friend's. The noise scratched at her ears.

2

Sophie walked down a windowless hallway. She could see a door at the end of the hall, and let her feet lead her toward it. She felt a heaviness in her chest, a warning not to continue. Yet, it never occurred to her to turn back. She grabbed the handle of the door and turned. She looked in the room before her and recognized the garage of the house she grew up in. A smile spread across her face and she ran to the car that sat in the bay. She quickly opened the back door and got in.

"Hi, sweetie! Ready to go?" Her mom's singsong voice came from the front passenger seat. She didn't turn to face her daughter, but Sophie knew it was her. Likewise, she knew the driver was her dad. She didn't need him to speak or turn around—she could feel his presence.

*"Hi, Mom. Hi, Dad," she greeted them, relaxing into the seat. She smiled genuinely and looked out the window. They were driving—*when had they backed out of the garage?*—along a winding road.*

"Do you have your seatbelt on, sweetie?" Sophie's dad asked from

the front seat. "You're going to need it." He turned to face Sophie. She saw the blood trickling down his face. The gash on his forehead was a deep red.

"Dad?" She was alarmed. "Dad, you're bleeding. Pull over." He smiled in reply and turned back to the road. "Dad!" Sophie was shouting now.

"Stop yelling, Sophie." Josh's voice cut through her panic. Sophie turned to the seat next to her. Josh was there. He wasn't just here though, was he? *Sophie couldn't remember. She couldn't think straight. His presence didn't comfort her. She turned back to her parents.*

"Dad, please pull over. You're hurt."

"What did I tell you, Sophie?" Josh's voice reached her ears again. She turned back to him, her heart racing in fear. His eyes were dilated, his pupils black pools engulfing his irises. He sniffled and raised his arm to wipe his nose. His hand came away stained with blood. Sophie stared at the red that smeared his pale skin. She looked up to meet his face again.

Blood. So much blood. Pouring from his nose, his eyes. Sophie opened her mouth to scream. Instead of her own voice, she heard the screams of her parents. And then…the crash.

Sophie awoke with a start, her breath ragged as she tried to gulp air into her lungs. The sheets of her queen-sized hotel bed were twisted and tangled in her bare legs. Sophie concentrated on taking gentle breaths in an attempt to slow her heart rate. She looked at the clock on the bedside table. 5:54 a.m.

"Fuck," she muttered as she shook the dream from her mind. She looked over at Megan's empty bed, thankful to the good-looking man from the bar who brought Megan to his room instead of theirs. Thankful that she wouldn't have to answer more of Megan's probing questions about what wakes her up almost every night.

Sophie got up and went to the bathroom. Turning the faucet on cold, she brought her elbows to rest on the edge of the sink, her wrists under the streaming water. Her hands trembled as she allowed the cool water to wash away the remnants of the nightmare, as though its contents could simply ooze out of her pores and be washed away. She splashed the water on her face and looked into the mirror. Her eyes were rimmed in red. *Had she been crying?* She couldn't recall wiping any tears away, but that no longer indicated their absence. Most days she just let them slide down her face, always fascinated to find that each tear seemed to forge its own path.

Her heart rate began to slow, but the anxiety that always seemed to creep in after her nightmares started to settle over her. Her stomach twisted, bringing on a bout of nausea. *Fresh air.*

Throwing her long hair into a ponytail, she made her way out of the room. Once outside and in the mild Costa-Rican air, she quickly walked toward the beach, taking her flip-flops off in favor of walking barefoot along the water's edge. The rising sun cast an orange-yellow glow over the sand. She took deep breaths of oxygen that tasted of the ocean's salt. The nausea abated as Sophie's mind cleared.

She neared the perimeter of the resort, clearly demarked by a fence that ran from the hotel's property all the way to the edge of the beach where a hut sat, guarded by resort security and a large sign that read 'Alto/Stop.' Sophie continued past, ignoring the sign as she stepped beyond the resort's property line.

"Buenas tardes, miss. No se recomienda dejar el complejo. Is no good to leave," the guard called from the hut.

"No voy lejos. Estaré bien," Sophie called back, hoping to persuade the guard to let her go without giving her a hard time. She figured if he knew she wouldn't be going far, and she made it clear that she knew the language, he was less likely to put up a fight. The guard's look of surprise at Sophie's fluent Spanish told her she had accomplished her goal.

"De acuerdo. Ten cuidado," the guard nodded. *Be careful,* he warned.

I guess that few months in Nicaragua paid off, Sophie thought. She allowed her memories some space as she continued down the beach. She had gone to Nicaragua for very selfish reasons and had come back a completely changed person. It was May of her sophomore year at MassArt, and the end of the school year was approaching. The idea of summer terrified Sophie. She no longer had a family to go home to. She no longer had a home. When Sophie inherited the house she grew up in, she couldn't face the overwhelming feelings of loss that accompanied her whenever she stepped foot over the threshold. She sold it less than two months after her parents' death.

With the dread of summer looming over her, Sophie made a decision to spend the time away from her own life and the grief that surrounded her. She did some quick research and found the perfect place to begin healing: volunteering at an orphanage. With the money from her inheritance, she bought a plane ticket to Managua. With only a little knowledge of the Spanish language and a backpack full of belongings, Sophie moved to a small, ranch-like compound outside the country's capital city, amidst 75 children, against a backdrop of peaked Nicaraguan mountains. And this was where Sophie learned to live again.

She spent most of her mornings helping with the day-to-day chores of tending to the garden, caring for the chickens, and preparing meals for the children and workers. Her afternoons were spent doing art projects with the children during their school day, where she simultaneously gained the majority of her Spanish-speaking skills. But it was the way she spent her evenings that she loved most. Sunset soccer games, slumber parties, and laughing fits with the kids brought color and meaning back into Sophie's world. Seeing the resiliency of so many children, who never had what most children in America were afforded *and* were dealing with the loss of their only family, allowed Sophie to discover her own resiliency. If they could do it, so could she. They had taught her so much about life and what was truly important. It was this experience that steered her into a career of helping others.

Sophie sighed at the thought of the kids. *I wonder what they would think of me if they saw me now,* she wondered. Sophie had thought many times of returning to Nicaragua, but her bank account hardly afforded her basic needs at this point, much less a plane ticket. She no longer had her inheritance to rely on since everything with Josh had happened. She pushed those thoughts away in an attempt to elude one of her zoning spells.

She looked around her, realizing she had gone much farther from the resort than she had thought. The beach had winded and snaked in a way that caused her to lose sight of the little hut marking the border of the resort. Thick palms and jungle-like brush lined the edge of the sand, and the absence of local shacks was noticeable on this stretch of beach. She had come to a cove of sorts, where the only sign of humanity was a path that caused a gap in the trees. Sophie turned to leave the cove and make her way back toward the resort. She had been out for a while and didn't want to alarm Megan by being away for too long.

Sophie's feet fell silently on the sand, slowly warming from the morning's rays. She let her eyes wander down the long strip of beach that she had walked, surprised by how far she had come. She couldn't see the edge of the resort from where she stood, and she guessed she was probably over a mile away. The thought crossed her mind to jog back—something she would have done before.

"Come on, Kingston, keep up!" Josh called over his shoulder. His t-shirt was darkened from sweat along the mid-line of his back. Despite the cool April day, Josh always managed to sweat profusely on their morning jogs through Boston Common.

"Trying," Sophie gasped, pushing herself forward as she widened her gait. Her toned legs did little to help her keep up with Josh's pace, however. Physically, he was a half-foot taller than she. His six-foot frame and muscled legs had an advantage over her 5 feet and 6 inches of toned curves.

"Race ya to the finish!" Josh hollered, as they began the final leg of their usual route. Sophie noticed, enviously, that he was hardly out of breath.

"Wait! …Wait, hang on!" Sophie's distressed voice called out, causing Josh to stop and turn. She saw him slow and look back at her. She took her opportunity then and, without slowing, she reached out her hand. As he went to take it, a look of concern crossing his face, she broke into a full sprint, passing him and dashing up the path toward the gate. Arms raised, she turned in triumph to gloat her win. She jumped in place, pumping her fists. Once again, Josh's laugh rang out in the cool morning air. To anyone passing by, it was just another moment shared between two Bostonians. To Sophie, it was one of the last times she saw Josh alive.

Sophie wiped the tears from her eyes. She realized then that she had stopped walking. Mechanically, she told herself to move, forcing her legs and feet to carry her forward.

☙❧

Sophie swiped the key card in the door and quietly tiptoed

into the room. She scanned the beds for any sign of Megan's return. The shades were still drawn, giving the appearance that the sun wasn't bright and shining on the other side of the slatted blinds. Sophie's bed sheets remained a crumpled mess and Megan's bed still showed no signs of being slept in. The clock on the nightstand read 8:45. She had been up and out for almost three hours.

Exhausted, and yet wide-awake, Sophie decided to shower to pass the time until her friend returned. She let the water run cool before stepping under the droplets that fell from the sunflower-like spout. It reminded her of being outside on a warm summer day when the rain showers come so abruptly you find yourself caught by surprise. Before, those were her favorite types of days. Now? Now, her favorite type of day was the one that passed hardly noticed. Another day closer, like a notch on a belt. Sophie let out a sigh as she finished rinsing her hair of shampoo and turned off the faucet. She stepped out of the shower, grabbing a towel to wrap around her thin frame. She put another towel around her hair to soak up the water just as the door to their hotel room clicked.

"Sophie?" Megan called.

"In here!" Sophie replied.

"Ugh…I'm so hung over," Megan's voiced trailed toward her bed. Sophie heard the distinct sound of the mattress cradling Megan as she crawled in.

"So, you had fun, then?" Sophie asked as she opened the bathroom door and joined Megan in the bedroom.

"Mmmhmmm…I told him we'd go out with him and his friend tonight for dinner," Megan said from under her covers, eyes closed.

"Oh yeah? You know it doesn't actually count as a one-night stand if you see him again," Sophie pointed out sarcastically.

To herself, she thought, *God, I hate it when Megan signs me up for things without asking.*

Megan opened one eye and looked at Sophie. "So, you're coming, right?"

Sophie sighed. "Of course I'm coming. But only because I love you. And I am *not* hooking up with his friend," she added.

"If I weren't so hung over I'd hug you right now." Megan rolled over and pulled the covers over her head. "I feel like shit. How are you so awake?"

"You have to drink water before you fall asleep," Sophie offered, toweling her hair.

"I was a little busy doing other things…"

Sophie laughed. Genuinely.

"It's good to hear that sound," Megan mumbled from her hiding place beneath the sheets.

Sophie stepped into her bathing suit without responding. Pulling her cover-up on and grabbing a towel, sunscreen, and her room key, she looked at the lumpy form of her friend under the bedcovers.

"Come find me by the beach whenever you get your sorry ass out of bed," she said with a smile, putting her sunglasses on and leaving the room to the sound of Meg's grunted reply. Sophie made her way back down to the beach and found an empty lounge chair to lie on. After lathering on some sunscreen and adjusting her sunglasses, she leaned back and closed her eyes.

"Pretty please?" she begged, giving her best puppy-eyed look.

"No way. Go without me." Josh never gave in to her puppy-dog eyes. "You know I hate the beach."

"I know, but you know that I love the beach. So doesn't that mean you should come?" She smiled sweetly, hoping her logic would convince him.

"Nope, sorry. If you want to spend time with me, then no beach,"

Josh said matter-of-factly, ignoring Sophie's tactics. He smiled and leaned toward her. "What's it gonna be, Ms. Kingston? Me or the beach?"

Sophie sighed. She knew her answer already. "You. Always you."

Sophie flipped onto her stomach. She could feel the sun burning her skin, indicating that she must have been zoning for at least a half an hour. She wondered if she would ever gain control of her memories again, or if they would always wage war to seep into her consciousness, whether she liked it or not.

"There you are!" Megan's voice cut through the sound of the waves lapping the shore as she rounded Sophie's chair from behind. Megan plopped down on the empty chaise next to her, bringing her feet up and laying back. "God, it's bright out."

Sophie turned toward her friend. "Feeling better?"

"Yeah. Definitely don't want anything to do with tequila ever again, though."

"Mmmhmm, right. Give it a few hours." Changing the subject, Sophie asked, "What time do we have to meet those guys?"

"They have names, you know," came the reply. Sophie rolled her eyes behind her sunglasses. "I said we'd go over to *Alex* and *Dave's* room at like six. So, we have a few hours before we have to get ready," Megan replied, accentuating their names.

"Alex and Dave. Which one is yours again?"

Megan snorted. "He's not *mine.*"

"Right, of course. So, which one?" Sophie asked again.

"Alex is mine—I mean. You know what I mean."

Sophie almost smiled at her friend's slip-up. "What do you feel like doing 'til then?"

"This. This is perfect."

Sophie put up no arguments. She really did love the beach.

Sophie's heels clicked along the shining granite floor as she and Megan made their way down the hallway toward Alex and Dave's hotel room. Her black dress hugged her hips, without letting up, down to the hem that stopped a few inches above her knees. Thin straps led to a low V-cut neckline accentuated with a crisscross of lines that caused the eye to tour Sophie's curves. Megan had convinced her to pack the dress as a 'just in case,' although Sophie had had no real intention of wearing it. Now, she still wasn't sure how Megan had convinced her to put it on, much less leave the hotel room in it. Sophie pulled at the strap, hoping it would pull the fabric over her cleavage, to no avail. Megan slapped Sophie's hand away.

"Hey!" Sophie cried out, looking at her friend with bewilderment and pleading.

"Stop messing with it. You look hot!" Megan said, flicking her curly, dark-brown hair over her shoulder. She wore a dress that perfectly showed off her own assets.

"I can't believe I'm wearing this," Sophie grumbled, more to herself than to Megan. A small part of her hoped Megan would see her discomfort and let her go back to the safety of their hotel room and wait out the night.

"We're here!" Megan sang with a wide smile on her face. She stopped in front of a door and rapped loudly on the wood. Turning to Sophie and wiggling her eyebrows she asked, "Ready?"

The door swung open, and the man Sophie recognized as Megan's hook-up from the previous night stood in the entrance.

"Hey, Megan," he said, giving her a quick peck on the cheek. "Hey, Sophie. Glad you came."

"Hi, Alex. Glad to be here, too." Sophie's politeness took over, methodically delivering the falsehood.

Another man appeared from the depths of the room. "Dave, this is Sophie. Sophie, Dave." Megan introduced the two, clearly having met him at some point during her overnight stay. Dave stepped forward, extending his hand as Sophie offered hers as well.

"Nice to meet you." Her courtesy lied again.

"Same here. I'm just finishing getting ready and then we can head out," Dave said with a smile as he gestured to indicate that Sophie and Megan could make themselves at home in their suite-style hotel room. Rather than just the two queen beds and bathroom that comprised Sophie and Megan's room, this room boasted a living room with a couch, coffee table, and kitchenette. Two other doorways stood on either side of the living room, leading into what Sophie guessed must have been either two bedrooms or a bedroom and a bathroom. She couldn't tell, as both doors were closed.

Sophie took a seat on the plush couch, hardly noticing his absence as Dave made his way out of the room to continue getting ready.

"Want a drink? Help yourself to the mini bar," Alex said, indicating the large mini-fridge in the kitchenette. He barely looked at Sophie as he put his arm around Megan. She smiled up at him and the two began talking in hushed voices near the doorway to the suite. Sophie watched her friend turn into a giddy teenage girl in the presence of this man, wondering if she would ever experience that again. Wondering, really, if she would ever *want* to experience that again. She decided to grab something from the mini-fridge before she let herself get pulled into grief again.

She made her way over to the mini-fridge and quickly selected a Dos Equis, popping the top off and taking a swig of the cold beer. She looked out of the window in an attempt to avoid observing the happiness occurring on the other side of the room. The sun was starting to set, filling the sky with pink and orange hues. She enjoyed her beer as she noted the subtle changes the setting sun brought to the sky. *The sky will never look like this again.* The thought was fleeting, a reminder to Sophie how quickly things change. As the last of the light ducked behind the horizon, Sophie emptied her beer.

"Hey, I'm going to use your bathroom real quick," Sophie said, knowing full well she went unheard. She made her way toward the doors realizing she wasn't sure which one led to the bathroom, and which one led to wherever Dave was getting ready. She hesitated and chose one of the doors, knocking lightly. She waited with her ear to the door and, when she didn't hear a response, turned the handle.

"Hey!" Dave cried out as Sophie opened the door.

"Oh! I'm so sor —" Sophie stopped mid-apology as she took in the scene before her. She quickly recognized the small bag of white powder on the bathroom counter, where a rolled-up bill lay. Sophie's eyes met Dave's as anxiety overwhelmed her. She quickly shut the bathroom door and turned back to the living room.

Her breath quickened, heart beating rapidly, hands beginning to shake, and Sophie was no longer there.

Sophie made her way into Josh's apartment complex, using the spare key he had given her to gain access to the locked entranceway. Sophie smiled at the feeling of excitement—she had gotten out of work early after her last client canceled their session. Sophie knew that Josh would be going away this weekend for a 'guys weekend,' and she could think of nothing better than surprising him before he left to give him a proper send-off.

She flew up the stairs to the third floor and quickly made her way down the hallway to apartment 3B. She shoved the key in the lock and opened the door, greeted by music drifting from his bedroom. He always listened to music whenever he was doing anything, and she guessed he must be packing. Silently slipping out of her shoes, she pulled her sweater dress over her head. Now, in just her lacey thong and matching bra, her feet padded down the hallway toward Josh's bedroom. Not wanting to alarm him by sneaking up on him, she called out.

"Sweetie? Are you in here?" The sound of Josh's music was the only response from behind Josh's open bedroom door.

"Josh?" she called again. A feeling of unease swept over her as she moved forward. Approaching the entranceway, she rapped on the door, again announcing her presence. She looked around, seeing his shoes on the floor. A light came from the bathroom, the door left ajar. Sophie stepped into the room, calling louder now. "Josh? Are you in there?" She was met with silence. Anxiety now seized every fiber of her being as she moved into the bathroom. And then, panic.

Josh lay haphazardly on his side on the bathroom floor, sprawled near the toilet. His cheek rested on the tile floor, a trail of vomit leading from the edge of the toilet to a small puddle next to Josh's face, as though he had passed out in the midst of getting sick.

"Oh my God! Josh!" Sophie rushed to his side. She knelt beside him and pulled him fully on his side. She noticed the blood then, smearing from his nose. She quickly propped him up to ensure his face wouldn't fall back toward the floor and ran into the bedroom to call 911. She retrieved his cell phone from the bed and dialed. The operator answered almost immediately.

"I need an ambulance! Please hurry!" She rapidly stated the address to the operator.

"Ma'am, can you tell me what's going on?"

"I don't know—my boyfriend. I just found him in the bathroom. He's unconscious," she replied, the tears beginning to fall.

"Is he breathing, ma'am?"

"I…I don't —" Sophie panicked, realizing she hadn't even checked. She sprinted back to the bathroom, dropped the phone on the tile beside Josh, and brought her ear to his nose. She wept when she didn't feel the heat of his breath, deftly moving her hand to find a pulse. She grabbed the cellphone. "I can't find a pulse. I can't—" Sobs racked her body.

"Ok, ma'am, the ambulance is on its way. They'll be there in just a few minutes." The operator's voice reached Sophie's ears, but Sophie hadn't heard it. She was staring at the bathroom counter, where a bag of white talcum-like powder sat, its contents sprinkled on the counter like baker's flour. Her panic and anxiety were momentarily forgotten as a new emotion grabbed hold of Sophie: complete shock.

Sophie's heart beat wildly as she gasped for breath. She ran from the hotel room, past a stunned Megan and bewildered-looking Alex. She wrenched open the hotel door, choking in her sobs while trying to slow her breathing. Her vision blurred and darkened around the edges as she fought to take in oxygen. She tried to focus on bringing herself into the present, grasping for the wall, hoping to ground her senses in reality. She took a staggered breath in, closing her eyes. She could hear Megan's frantic voice coming from the hotel room.

"What the fuck? You didn't tell me you guys were into that shit! Oh my God…" Megan slammed the door as she entered the hallway. "Sophie!"

Sophie held up her free hand, the other still propping her against the wall. Her eyes remained closed and she concentrated on bringing her breathing back to normal.

"I'm so sorry, Soph. I had no idea they were doing that. I wouldn't have brought you here if I'd known." Megan's voice was tinged with guilt and panic.

"It's okay, Meg," Sophie gasped, then inhaled, "it's not your fault." She blew out a long breath, still shaky. "I think I just need fresh air."

"Can I come with you?" Megan asked. "I don't want you to be alone."

Sophie nodded. She pushed off the wall and the two walked silently out of the building. Sophie absentmindedly walked toward the beach. The waves lapped quietly, where the water met the sand, in an incessant reunion. Sophie took her shoes off, holding them in one hand to allow the edges of the water to caress and recede at her feet. She led them along the length of the beach toward the edge of the resort, retracing her steps from earlier in the day.

"Are you okay?" Megan's voice broke the silence between them. Sophie nodded in response, not sure how the words would sound on her tongue. She didn't want to risk it. "Do you want to talk about it?" Megan prodded.

"I don't know." Sophie finally allowed herself to speak. "I just—I can't help but wonder how I didn't know about Josh. I've known Dave for, what? Three minutes? I knew Josh for *three years* and I had no fucking *clue* that he was using drugs. How does that even happen?"

"Josh was hiding it from you, Sophie. He didn't want you to know, so he made sure you never found out."

"I'm a fucking mental health counselor, Megan. I should have seen the signs. His parents were right—I should have known. I thought it was just the gambling, but there were plenty of signs—his behavior was so off those last couple of months. And I just ignored it."

"That's not fair, Sophie, and you know it. His parents were angry. They were looking for someone to blame. You had no clue what was going on with him because *he didn't let you in*. You're not a mind reader, and he hid it really well. Of course you only thought it was the gambling—and even with that, he wouldn't take the help you were offering. It's not like you knew he was using and chose to ignore it," Megan reasoned with her.

"Then why do I feel so guilty?" Sophie whispered as the invisible weight around her tightened.

"I don't know why, Sophie. But I do know that you have no reason to feel that way."

Sophie and Megan approached the resort grounds. Anticipating the conversation with the guard, Sophie noticed the man from this morning was no longer on duty. They approached the invisible property line and stepped over. Sophie glanced back toward the hut and saw the guard watching them while simultaneously picking up the phone to make a call. *That's odd,* Sophie thought, shrugging, just relieved to avoid convincing the man to let them cross.

"Are you sure we're supposed to be outside the resort walls?" Megan asked, turning to Sophie. "Isn't there, like, drug-lord shit going on in this country?"

"I walked out here this morning. It's fine. There's nobody around, no houses or anything," Sophie reassured. Megan continued walking in acceptance of her friend's words. They were silent for a moment, allowing their thoughts to carry their minds in an intersecting path as they paralleled the shore. Sophie knew that Megan was still thinking about her and Josh. She hated that Megan had to witness her unrelenting devastation.

"I'm sorry, Meg. I'm so sorry that I can't just get over all of this. I wish I could. So many times I've wished I could just forget about it all," Sophie said, crying now, "but it just won't go away. I don't know why. I just want things to go back to the way they used to be. I don't feel like myself anymore." Sophie stopped walking as Megan enveloped her in her arms. She allowed herself to be held as her tears fell, not for the first time, on her friend's shoulder.

"Sweetie, you are one of the strongest people I've ever known. You have been through so much of your own shit. And, despite dealing with your own stuff, you're always helping others. You carry so much—your own loss, your clients' problems…you've always been so resilient. It's okay to feel a little lost, for once."

"I just feel like everyone is wondering 'why isn't she over it yet?' And I should be. I know I *should* be. It isn't normal for me to still be feeling like this. I just don't know how to fix it." Sophie wiped at the tears, now slowing, and pulled from her friend's embrace.

"I wish I knew how to make it better for you." Megan looked at her with sympathy.

"I know," Sophie said, squeezing Megan's hand, "me, too."

Still touching, Sophie felt her friend stiffen, and watched as Megan stood up straighter, eyes widening to search the nearby woods.

"What's wrong?" Sophie asked, alarmed at her friend's sudden change in demeanor.

"I think there's someone over there," Megan whispered. Sophie glanced over her shoulder. She couldn't see anything, but she held onto Megan's hand tighter and turned to go back to the hotel.

"Come on, let's go," she said, taking long strides in the sand. Megan kept her pace, and the two walked briskly in silence. Sophie looked back toward the woods every few moments, unable to detect anything but the swaying palms and rustling of wind in the jungle-like brush.

Neither noticed the two figures that had emerged from the darkness the trees provided. Their footsteps fell silently, the sound of their breathing perfectly masked by the lapping waves. Neither noticed as the two men approached from behind. Silent, practiced, the two shadows waited until they were within reach before breaking into a sprint toward the girls.

Sophie let out a gasp as she was wrenched from the security of her friend's hand. A strong hand clamped over her mouth, as she felt the prick at her neck before her body went limp and her world turned black.

3

Sound was the first thing to penetrate the haze that clouded her senses. It was like being underwater; the noises took on a bloated quality, like living in a radio constantly set to AM. Slowly, the volume returned to normal. The soft whisper of her own breathing reached Sophie's ears. It came in, steady and even. *Odd,* she thought, *considering the circumstances.* As she listened more closely, a second whisper of breath told her that Megan was near. Aside from this, echoing silence was the only sound that accompanied them.

The numbness that had engulfed her began to gradually subside. She could feel a cold, hard floor beneath her, and a similar coolness against her back. She was sitting up, her hands tied behind her, her feet stretched in front. She attempted to move her legs, only to discover that her feet had been bound together. The cold from the floor was biting against her bare feet and legs. She could feel the softness of her dress, gentle against her thighs, a desperate attempt at modesty. Feeling tautness at her mouth, she attempted to use her voice but realized an inability to part her lips. Her mouth was taped shut.

She expected her sight to return next, anticipating whatever drugs they had given her would have worn off enough for her to see her surroundings. Letting her eyelids flutter open, she was met with continued darkness. It took her another moment to recognize that she had been blindfolded.

Her memory was the last to break through the haze. The men had come up behind them so quickly, she hadn't even known they were there. She had dropped her shoes at the same time that she was ripped from Megan's grasp. But not before she glimpsed the look of pure terror on her friend's face as the blackness set in.

Terror. *Why don't I feel it?* Sophie thought. Her lack of emotional response surprised even her. She wondered vaguely if her captors had been kind enough to slip her an Ativan to ease the horror of the situation. She doubted it.

The faint sound of voices, both male, echoing from a distance brought Sophie from her thoughts. She could hear two sets of voices speaking about a third person in Spanish.

"He's on his way. He said he would be here soon."

"Did he say how many he wanted?"

Sophie didn't hear a response from the first speaker, assuming he had given some non-verbal cue to indicate his answer. It was only then that it dawned on her to wonder about their fate. Sophie had heard of the drug cartels and kidnappings happening in Central America, but she hadn't thought to pay much attention to the news. It was something she stopped doing a long time ago. Keeping up with the daily news reports, whether they were local, national, or global, Sophie felt was always so depressing. And she already had her own share of depressing news. Now, she wished she had paid more attention.

She knew, though, that money always went a long way, and ransoming Americans was becoming more common in Mexico and Central America. She didn't realize it had been happening in Costa Rica. A shuffle fell upon her ears, and a third, new voice reached them.

"Where did you acquire them from?" he asked, his tone short and clipped. He spoke in Spanish, but Sophie noted an odd accent. He was not a native speaker.

"Off the beach outside the resort area, señor." The response sounded nervous. There was a pause before the new speaker responded.

"What do you mean, 'outside the resort area?' What happened to the plan?"

"We…we thought it might be easier than trying to slip something in their drinks at the bar. You know how the bartender almost caught Gustavo last time. We thought this would be safer. We had one of the perimeter guards in on it. He let us know the girls had left the resort premises, and no one was around, so we grabbed them," the man stammered, clearly uneasy from the new man's disapproval. Sophie squeezed her eyes shut at his words and their implication—*that* was why the guard had picked up the phone and hadn't tried to stop them from leaving the perimeter.

Sophie heard a sharp intake of breath. *"Next time you make changes, you run it by me first. Where are they?"*

"Over there. One of them is awake."

He mumbled something incomprehensible before he commanded, *"Stay here."*

The sound of footsteps approaching extinguished the silence in the room. Sophie noted how large the room must be, given how long it was taking this person to reach them. *Megan.* She started, sitting up straight at the thought that Megan might not be awake yet. *Why hasn't she woken up yet?* Her anxiety grew at the thought of something bad happening to Megan. But the anxiety didn't have much time to simmer and dissipate, as the footsteps stopped directly in front of her. Sophie could feel his presence. She heard a rustle and felt a warmth radiating from him. He was so close she could smell the sweet and musky scent coming from his skin. It reminded her of ginger and lemongrass. She felt a tugging at the back of her head as the blindfold fell from her eyes. She squinted, adjusting to the onslaught of dim light.

She hastily took in her surroundings, noticing the vast warehouse-like building she was in. The walls and floor were made of concrete, and the majority of the room was empty, except for some crates along one of the far walls. Megan was slumped to the right of her, unconscious and unaware. *Lucky, in a way,* Sophie thought.

Sophie's eyes landed in front of her then, on the man crouching before her, studying her. His eyes were a gray-blue, rimmed with dark navy. There was a brightness to them, despite the darkness they escorted. His brown hair was long on top, unruly and careless. His jaw was covered in stubble, a shadow of a beard, again, giving an air of indifference. She let her eyes wander away from his face, noticing his muscled arms. For an instant, she found him attractive, recognizing and appreciating the strength of his jaw and the beauty in his features, but the idea quickly vanished—so brief was the notion, that she barely perceived its presence. Instead, her propensity toward psychological exploration kicked in—drinking him in, analyzing him, seeking the psyche behind the man in front of her. Sophie guessed he couldn't be more than a few years older than she and was surprised that someone so young and attractive could be a part of this. *Whatever* this *is.*

His eyes squinted slightly, as though evaluating her. They

held curiosity in them as he scanned her face. It was a type of disinterested amusement, like a diamond appraiser sorting through pounds of gems, looking for just the right one, knowing the diamond would never be his. He reached his hand out then, and it landed on her neck. Sophie immediately noticed the contrast of warmth his hand brought to the harsh coldness that surrounded her. She was surprised by his gentleness. He lightly pressed two fingers into the side of her neck.

Is he checking my pulse? What the fuck? Sophie thought. Just as quickly as his hand had reached for her, it retracted. As though he were trying to figure something out. And then, abruptly, he gave up on whatever answer he was trying to find. He sighed, tired, bored even. His eyes never left her face as he spoke.

"I'm going to take the tape off your mouth. Don't bother screaming. No one will hear you. And it will be worse for you if you do." His voice was soft and deep; even his English was accented—his R's came out with a slight staccato. Sophie couldn't quite place it. *Was it French?* She didn't have time to wonder, as the man's eyes bore into hers. His jaw was set in a firm line as he awaited her response. Sophie nodded to indicate she understood, and he leaned in to peel back the tape at her mouth. He did it quickly, the sting only lasting a moment. She pressed her lips together, the sudden absence of the tape feeling foreign.

Silence. He offered no indication of what was to come as his gaze continued its search.

Does he want me to say something? She knew exactly what she wanted to say, if that was the case. She quickly examined her options—don't speak and potentially never get a chance to say it, or say it and hope.

She drew in a quick breath and pleaded, "Please don't hurt my friend." It came out as a whisper, an overcompensation to avoid defying his demand. He looked at her quizzically without responding. She considered his lack of response an indication that she could speak again. Thinking quickly, she continued, "Her parents are rich. They'll give you anything you ask for as long as you don't hurt her."

He turned his gaze to Megan, as though he hadn't noticed her before. After a moment's pause, he turned back to Sophie. "And you?" His deep voice resonated in her ears. "Who will be looking for you?"

Sophie blinked. She hadn't even considered what her escape plan might be. *So much for self-preservation*, she thought. Should she already have contemplated this? She couldn't offer any of her own money—Josh had gambled her inheritance away, and she had used the last of it to help pay for his funeral expenses. Sophie's mind fled to thoughts of her aunt and uncle. She hadn't seen them since her parents' funeral almost six years ago. They didn't care to keep in touch with her, and she doubted they would care to give a large sum of ransom money to get their niece out of this mess. *Was this it then? Is this where her life would end?* It was a strangely comforting idea. The thought of not fearing for her life scared her more than the predicament itself. And even that was half-hearted.

"I see…" His voice cut through her thoughts. Her silence was the only answer he needed to make his decision, apparently. He stood up and called out to the two men, his voice echoing in the dim room, "Mira cuanto puede buscar por ella." *See how much you can get for her.*

The two men scurried from the darkness and made their way toward Megan. It was the first time Sophie was able to get a good look at the ones who brought her into this nightmare. They were both shorter than the man before her, their Hispanic descent apparent in contrast to this third man. The kidnappers' skin held a caramel complexion that was lacking in the man in front of her; though his complexion was tanned it was only skin deep. His blood wasn't in it.

She watched as one of the men approached her friend's still body. Slumped forward, Megan put up no fight when the man took her under the arms and hoisted her over his shoulder. Sophie's anxiety returned then, in a burst of new energy. Tears stung her eyes as the two men walked off with Megan. She hated not knowing if she would be all right.

"¿Le van a hacer daño?" Sophie whispered to the man in front of her. She feared the answer. His head snapped back to look at her, eyes studying her with intrigue again, this time edged with a glint of surprise. Slowly, he crouched down in front of her, the sweet smell of lemongrass and ginger, once again, invading her senses. She allowed her eyes to meet his. A slow smile tugged at his mouth as he answered her in English.

"No, they won't hurt her. Not if she's worth what you say she is."

Sophie sighed in relief, squeezing her eyes shut. Effectively, she blocked the tears from falling. She knew Megan's parents would pay any sum of money for the safety of their daughter. "Thank you," she sighed, opening her eyes to meet his.

He smiled, almost pityingly. "Don't thank me yet. You're coming with me." He placed the piece of cloth over her eyes. She welcomed the darkness.

Adrien peered at the girl through the rearview mirror, still bound and blindfolded. He hadn't bothered to replace the piece of tape over her mouth. The dose of Rohypnol he had given her while she sat splayed in the warehouse was well into her system and rendering her fully complacent. It wasn't necessary to put the blindfold on or keep her binds in place either, for that matter. There was something about the way she had looked at him, though. It made him jittery, like he was making a mistake, and he felt compelled to cover her eyes again to avoid looking into them. The binds were just easier to leave be.

Over the past ten years in this profession, Adrien had come to be an expert of sorts. He could recognize fear the way one could recognize one's own face in a photographed crowd. It was a byproduct of the world he lived in—surrounded constantly by it, creating it, he himself, the essence of a nightmare. Which was why he found his newest acquisition so curious. She seemed to lack any indication of distress. No wide-eyed crying, no incoherent sobs or pleas for mercy. Not even the terrorized request to know, "Who are you? Why me?" that Adrien considered so petulant. Petulance aside, the act showed a necessary fear. Adrien had learned to use terror to his advantage, knowing full well that terror is what breaks the human propensity toward disobedience. Fear leads to compliance, and training was much easier with an obedient subject. It was the basis of his entire training program.

Phase One: Obedience Training. The beginning of this phase included the installation of fear. Blindfold them, gag them, remove them from the safety of their creature comforts. Adrien brought them to his property, tucked far into the Costa-Rican jungle, where escape through the thick trees was an impossibility, and no one could hear the screams that might come from the large, resort-style home. He stripped them bare, placing them in a room with barely the basic amenities. With only a brief explanation to flame their fears, he refrained from providing human contact until they broke. Most of the girls he dealt with only lasted a few days in the confines of their own mind.

Part two of this phase involved teaching them all the necessary rules and commands, thus breaking any remaining resistance. Most of his customers had very specific preferences for slaves—they must be willing to follow all instructions without hesitation. The right to speak, eat, sleep, or even raise their eyes from the floor, was at the total control of their new masters. Disobedience meant punishment.

Phase Two: Physical Training. The girls were required to undergo rigorous training in his home gym. His customers had very specific tastes and sexual pleasures that required his trainees to be physically fit. Over several weeks, he built their strength and stamina in order to undergo the final phase of training.

Phase Three: Sexual Training. This was the most difficult phase, even with pure deference. Really, it was a form of psychological training; a slow, cognitive restructuring to re-associate sexual horror with sexual pleasure. Adrien was very careful about this stage—he knew how delicate the psyche could be, and delivering damaged goods to customers was never his intention.

Adrien had designed the training program himself. At age eighteen, he was bought into his family's business with a new model that changed the way the personal sex slave trade worked. Rather than the disobedient, frightened women that were stolen and immediately sold to their new owners, Adrien discovered a way to bend the women into compliant servants through his program. They no longer fought for their freedom, the spark in their eyes extinguished, resigned to their new life. Most came to him spitting, hitting, kicking for freedom, and left with only a silent tear to indicate that perhaps they never chose this fate.

Adrien's attention returned to the girl in the back seat, now slightly slumped, as her head rested against the tinted window. Her lips were slightly parted and her breath was soft, fogging the window with each exhale. Her golden-brown hair fell over her shoulders, cascading down her front. He allowed himself to appreciate her curves before wandering back to her face. Even with the blindfold and tape covering her, he had acknowledged her beauty when he walked into the warehouse.

She had surprised him—something that rarely happened—with her indifference to her situation. Rather than seeing the fear he was so accustomed to when he removed the blindfold, he was met with piercing green eyes that held…nothing. He felt the need to confirm his suspicions by reaching out to check her pulse. It hadn't quickened in the slightest. She seemed wholly unaffected by the initial stages of Phase One. *Odd,* he thought. He was reminded of *une chevrette*—a deer in headlights, not realizing the danger that was staring her in the face until it was too late.

Phase One

4

For the second time, Sophie's senses slowly returned. Her eyes remained closed as she permitted consciousness to envelop her. The sound of muted birds calling through the window reached her ears. The calls were foreign, yet familiar, in the way they comforted her. She felt radiating warmth on her body and she knew she was lying in the sun. Temptation taunted her to believe that she was elsewhere: lying on the beach or sprawled out on a blanket in a park back in Boston. *Maybe you aren't living in someone else's nightmare,* it told her. But then, she opened her eyes.

The room was a block of concrete—floors, walls, and ceiling all created by the harsh, cold material. The only softness in the room came from the rough-looking, twin-sized mattress on which Sophie lay. Above her, a transom window let in sunlight that lit the small room. A doorway to her left led to a small bathroom with a toilet, sink, and showerhead coming from the wall. There was no shower curtain and the entire room was covered in tile. Sophie was reminded of a prisoner's bathroom from those shows she used to watch with Josh, the ones that documented what it was like to live in penitentiaries across the U.S. Her heart stitched at the thought of Josh. Even here, she couldn't get him out of her mind.

On the other side of the room, Sophie could see another doorway. Again, she was reminded of a prison. *Or a dungeon,* she corrected herself. The door was made of metal with a small, barred window cut out at the top. There was no handle on the door, and the only indication of escape was a small, square pad on the wall next to the door. Squinting in the dim light, Sophie assumed it was some sort of keypad and, without the proper sequence of numbers, she wouldn't be able to leave. As she continued to stare at it, she realized there was also a pad next to the numbers, large enough for a finger to be placed. *A code and a fingerprint. Whoever this is, obviously doesn't want anyone escaping.*

Her eyes moved to the floor beside the door, where a tray with a glass of water and a bowl awaited. Sophie slowly sat up, pushing her body away from the only comfort in the room. Without sheets on the mattress, the material scratched at Sophie's bare skin. The discomfort prodded Sophie to discover that she had been stripped naked. She shivered despite the warmth of the sunlight that licked her body. Pulling herself into a seated position on the mattress, she brought her knees to her chest, hoping to generate some heat. She blinked, her head throbbing from the movement. Feeling hung-over, she took in a few deep breaths in an attempt to dissolve the drugged haze. As her head cleared, though, the questions bombarded her mind.

Where am I? Where are my clothes? How did I get here? She struggled to remember the events leading up to this moment, her body stiffening at the apprehension of the unknown. Details were fuzzy as she searched her memory.

Walking on the beach. Darkness.

Waking up. Darkness.

A tall, dark stranger talking to her. *But what did he say?* Sophie shook her head as though she could dispel the fog that shadowed her memories. Darkness.

He let Megan go. The memory shot back to her in a moment of clarity. She had asked, and he had listened. *Thank God.* Sophie's body released some of the tension. *But he took you in return.* Sophie's breath caught as the realization hit her. She had bargained for Megan's ransom but had no means of her own escape. He had taken her when he realized that he wouldn't be getting money for her release, blindfolded her, forced a pill into her mouth, and then…she had a vague memory of being carried off, put in a car. But that was it. She couldn't remember anything past that. Only darkness. Always darkness.

She squeezed her eyes shut, the aching in her head growing stronger. Her entire body felt weak, dehydrated. She looked toward the food and water that sat, waiting, across the room. She began to stand, but dizziness grabbed hold and nausea quickly followed. Deciding against walking, she crawled on hands and knees toward the door. The cold concrete was unyielding under her knees, adding to the litany of pain in her already aching body. She reached the tray and grabbed the glass of water, slipping slightly in her hand from the moisture gathering on the outside. Ice cubes sat, partially melted, in the water, and Sophie eagerly drank the cool liquid. Her dry throat screamed in pain at the sudden onslaught of fluid. She finished drinking and set the glass back on the tray, noticing the food for the first time. Rice and beans.

"Is this all we get to eat the whole time?" Josh whispered to Sophie as he swirled his bowl of rice and beans with his fork.

Giggling, Sophie replied, "Yeah, pretty much. If we're lucky we might get some vegetables." She smiled at the look of disappointment on his face.

"If I had known that, maybe I would have rethought this trip," Josh said staring at his bowl. Sophie giggled again, nudging him with her elbow.

"Come on. It's good for us to experience how the rest of the world lives. Not everyone is as lucky as us, you know," she said quietly, taking a spoonful of her rice and beans. She looked around at the children she had come to know and love, thrilled she was able to convince Josh to accompany her on a trip back to the orphanage. He had hesitated at first but was willing to come once Sophie offered to pay for the trip.

"You're right. We are lucky. I'm lucky, actually. To have you." Josh smiled at her and gave her a quick peck on the cheek. The action was met by giggles from the kids around them. Sophie smiled, happy to have Josh share this experience with her.

Sophie blinked away the memory, looking down at the bowl of rice and beans in front of her. Despite having not eaten in— *how long?*—Sophie didn't register hunger. Leaving the food, she slowly crawled back toward the mattress. Lying down, she allowed her mind to wander.

She wasn't eligible for ransom, which meant they would do something else with her. She didn't know much about human trafficking, but she knew the likelihood was high. *But what does that even mean? Will they rape me? Sell me for sex? Or maybe they'll just kill me.* The thought crossed her mind and, for the second time, it was a comforting thought. *I should be terrified. I should be fighting for my life.*

The 'shoulds.' They haunted her. They had been haunting her for the past year.

You should *be able to get over Josh.*

You shouldn't *let your grief cripple you.*

You should *start dating again.*

You should *eat, sleep, exercise, go back to your normal life.*

And now:

You should *be scared.*

You should *be bothered that they took your clothes—your decency.*

You shouldn't *let them do this to you.*

You should *fight, try to escape.*

You shouldn't *want to die.*

But all of the 'shoulds' took so much energy that she just didn't have. Not then, and especially not now. It wasn't a matter of 'should' to Sophie, but a matter of 'could.'

Could *she get over Josh, go back to a normal life?* Could *she let go of her grief?* No. She had tried and she couldn't.

And now:

Could *she fight this?* Could *she live through this?* Could *she allow her fear to give her the strength to get away?* She found she didn't really want to try. *Escape.* The thought should have crossed her mind as soon as she woke up. But as she took in her surroundings, all Sophie could think about was how much work escaping would take. And work meant energy. She had been so tired for so long. *What would it be like to just curl up inside herself?* The thought was comforting. Maybe *this*—this horror show—was her way out of the life she had been living. Maybe this would be her end. Maybe she *should* just endure whatever they were going to do to her until they killed her. And she *could* do that.

❧❧❧

Sophie awoke in a dark, cold room. She could feel her hands tied behind her back but the familiar blindfold had vanished. She looked around, expecting to see Megan next to her. She wasn't there. A shuffling noise came from across the room. Sophie's feet were free and she struggled to pick herself up.

Now, on two feet, she quickly strode toward the noise. She tried to reach it, but every step was like walking through knee-deep water. The sound got quieter, moving farther away.

"No! Wait!" Sophie began running, her hands suddenly freed from the ropes that had bound her. She moved down a dark hallway toward the noise and suddenly came to a doorway. There was a keypad on the wall, and Sophie quickly punched in some numbers.

'Access Denied.' *The screen blinked red.*

She tried another set of numbers and, miraculously, the door clicked open. She ran into the room.

Strangely, it resembled her parents' garage. A car sat in the middle of the room and Sophie found herself climbing into the backseat.

"Buckle up!" her dad's cheerful voice came from the front seat as her mom turned around to smile at her. Sophie returned her mother's smile, immediately obeying her father as she felt the car begin to back out of the garage. A feeling of peace came over her. She knew how this would end, didn't she?

The winding roads flashed by as she looked out the window, happy to be with her parents.

"What are you doing here, Sophie?" Josh's voice cut through her daydreams. Her stomach fluttered at the sound of his voice.

"I'm coming with you," she replied, smiling. He looked at her blankly.

"You can't," he replied. She frowned. That's not the reaction he was supposed to have. He was supposed to be happy that they would finally be together.

"Why not?" She could feel the anger building in her chest.

"Because you're broken. You let them use you. I don't want to be with someone who's been used." Josh gave her a disgusted look.

"Josh is right, sweetie," Sophie's mom chimed in. "We can't have that. You don't deserve to be here."

Sophie's door opened, and panic set in. She looked over the edge of the car to the road speeding past. She screamed as she felt Josh's strong hands unbuckle her seatbelt and push her out of the moving vehicle.

Sophie jerked on the scratchy mattress, the feeling that she was falling having jarred her awake. She sat up, gasping for breath as the remnants of panic from her dream invaded the world around her. Early-morning light filtered in through the small window above her. Day two of her captivity had begun.

Day one: It was hard to believe it was just yesterday that she had woken to find herself in the cramped, concrete room. After the realization hit her, she slept most of the day, chasing away the side effects of the drugs she'd been given. Aside from the glass of water she drank when she first awoke, she hadn't touched any of the food or liquid that periodically appeared by the door. She never saw who it was that came to change out the meal. An invisible presence seemed to be waiting to catch her unaware, before replacing the tray with new food. Still, she didn't touch it.

She glanced over at the door and discovered the tray was gone, taken sometime in the night while she slept. She wondered about the man she first met after being kidnapped on the beach. *Was he behind this? Or had he handed her off to yet another player in the dark?* Hope flickered behind the emotionless veil she had erected—hope that he hadn't just been someone in passing. *At least he had listened to me about Megan. But why would that matter?* His equanimity would only matter if she hoped to get out of this unscathed. And she didn't. In fact, she hoped for the opposite. *Maybe he will kill me quickly if I ask. He seemed to listen to reason the first time.* She allowed this comfort to lull her back to sleep.

When Sophie's parents died, Sophie couldn't stand to be by herself. It wasn't the loneliness that was unbearable, though, it was the fear. The knowledge that death could take her at any time turned even the most mundane things into a life threat. What if she choked on her dinner and no one was there to save her? What if she slipped in the shower, and hit her head on the side of the tub? The basement stairs were the worst. They were just waiting to trip her, eager to send her tumbling headfirst into the hard fieldstone at the bottom of the steps. It would be days before anyone recognized her as missing. She thought about this in her first days in that dungeon. How she had gone from fearing death to wishing for it. *How quickly things change.*

A beep sounded, followed by a shuffle, and a click.

When she awoke, this time from a dreamless sleep, the tray of food had returned. She could see a bowl of oatmeal and a glass of orange juice on the tray. Sliced strawberries topped the oatmeal.

Cute, she thought sarcastically as she pulled herself into an upright position. She shivered from her nakedness, the sun not yet warm enough to offset the heat of her chilly dungeon.

She walked over to the tray to grab the orange juice, uninterested in the food. There was no layer of sweat on the glass this time, and the juice was cold against her lips. She must have just missed the invisible presence. Perhaps that's what had woken her up. She placed the glass back on the tray and, surveying the food once again, briefly wondered where her hunger was. But only briefly. She had been through this before—the lack of will to eat. The only difference was that she had fought it before. She had forced herself to eat at least once a day over the past year. At least now, she was free of that. She would no longer force herself to eat. *What was the point?* The realization comforted her.

She returned to the mattress and drew her legs to her chest. She rested her forehead on her knees and closed her eyes, attempting to dispel thoughts from reaching her consciousness. The only thought she allowed to drift past, was the hope that the sun would soon warm the room. She shivered.

A beeping noise brought her back to awareness. She could hear the door opening, someone entering. Another click to indicate the door shut. She could feel a presence and wondered if it was *him.* She thought about looking up, but her curiosity wasn't enough to bring her eyes from her lap. She didn't want to feel the tug of disappointment if she looked up and realized it *wasn't* him standing in front of her—she didn't want to face the disappointment of realizing she wouldn't get her wish of dying quickly.

She heard the presence move forward, toward her. Like in the warehouse when she was first taken, the presence stopped in front of her. Ginger and lemongrass overcame her senses and a wave of relief invaded Sophie's consciousness. Only then, did she allow herself to look up.

His blue-gray eyes pierced hers like the flash of a camera in the night. She found she had to look away. While avoiding his gaze, she took in the rest of him. She hadn't realized just how tall he was the last time she saw him. At least six feet, maybe more. His hair still held the disheveled look, and the shadow of his beard was slightly fuller than the last time she'd seen him. Despite the Costa-Rican heat that was no doubt present outside of her cold cell, he wore jeans and a plain white t-shirt that hugged his sculpted body. His arms crossed, he held his hand to his chin, his thumb resting on his lower lip. In other circumstances, Sophie would have thought him attractive. More than that, she may have even been jealous of the thumb touching his lips, she herself wanting to touch, to nibble. But that was in another world. Not this one.

"Look at me." Her eyes snapped up immediately at the sound of his command. He remained standing, towering over her. The man who had previously crouched eye-to-eye with her, the man who had listened to her when she begged him not to hurt her friend, was not here. There was a harshness about him that she hadn't noticed during their first encounter. Was it new? Or had she just been too drugged to notice it before? His eyes never left hers as he began to speak.

"Listen carefully, because I'm only going to explain this once, *Chevrette*," he began, his accent allowing Sophie to register the foreign word as French. "Whoever you were before, whatever life you had, is gone. It is not coming back. From today forward, you will live for one purpose—to please your new master." He brought his hand from his mouth and crossed his arms. "For now, I am that master. If you do what I say, you won't get hurt. If you disobey, you will be punished." A flicker of amusement crossed his features. "Over the next six weeks, I will give you all of the training you will need for your new job. You are here to learn exactly what life is like as a personal sex slave. If you do as I say, this might even be easy and enjoyable."

He began pacing. Sophie's eyes were glued to him as his words sank in. "I require strict obedience in everything that I ask. That means there are rules you'll have to follow, and things you'll be told to do that you won't want to. You can do it willingly, or by force. Your choice. Either way, you will do whatever is asked of you. If you do well and follow all of my instructions, I'll make sure to find a master that is a good fit for you. If you disobey, if you fight this in any way—well—I can't make any promises that you will be sold to someone who will treat you well. Your fate is in my hands, so act wisely." He stopped pacing then. "Do you understand what I just said?"

Sophie nodded, still unable to tear her eyes from his. It dawned on her that he wasn't planning on killing her. That he was just another stop on the train, a passerby. *Maybe I can convince him to kill me before he sells me.* She doubted he would do it willingly—he was planning on making money off her, after all. *Maybe if I disobey long enough, he will kill me instead of punish me, even if by accident.* The thoughts whizzed through her mind, shielding her psyche from the crippling disappointment that threatened to invade.

The clinking of dishes and silverware brought her from her thoughts. He had moved her food, a quickly cooling bowl of soup, to sit at her feet. Crouching to meet her at eye level, his voice was soft, coaxing almost. "You should eat if you want to survive this." His eyes searched hers, for what, she wasn't sure.

"And if I don't want to?" she whispered, her thoughts escaping into the air.

He looked at her with curiosity, confusion even, at her response.

She cleared her throat, clarifying, "What if I don't want to survive this?"

The curiosity in his gaze remained, his eyes darkening slightly. His jaw ticked. Sophie was accustomed to reading people—it was part of her job to dissect non-verbal communication. She could practically feel his anger as it seeped into the air around them.

He took in a sharp breath then, startling Sophie. With no warning, his hand reached out and caught her chin, roughly, in his grip. Just as quickly, he scooped the spoon in the soup and brought it to her mouth. Using his hand that cupped her chin, he forced her mouth open with his thumb and shoved the spoon full of broth and vegetables into her mouth. He removed the spoon, holding her mouth shut. Unprepared, Sophie choked, forced to swallow it. Tears filled her eyes at the ambush and she coughed as the still-warm soup tried to reach her lungs. He took this as another opportunity and shoved another spoonful into her mouth. She was more prepared this time, and was able to chew a little bit of the food before swallowing. Still, she came out coughing. He paused, allowing her to catch her breath. He was gentler this time as he brought the spoon back up to her lips. Without fighting, she opened her mouth and took the food.

"I brought you some chicken soup," Josh said, taking the can out of the Stop & Shop bag that he had brought with him.

Sophie groaned from the couch where she lay. Despite the knitted blanket that covered her from head to toe, she was shivering. She reached for the box of tissues on the coffee table.

Josh poured the contents of the can into a bowl and put it in the microwave. "It'll be ready in two minutes."

"Thank you," Sophie managed as she blew her nose. "Ugh, I feel like shit."

"You look like shit." Josh grinned at her from the kitchen.

"Gee, thanks," Sophie replied as she threw her tissue in the wastebasket that she had placed next to the couch. She laid her head back on the pillow and closed her eyes.

"Here you go." Josh sat on the edge of the couch with the bowl of

soup in hand. He scooped some of the soup onto the spoon and held it in front of Sophie. She opened her mouth, and he hovered there for a moment before placing the spoon delicately on her tongue. She ate the entire bowl that way.

The sharp sting of pain on her cheek wrenched Sophie back into the present. Her eyes watered as she registered the radiating ache of the slap. Blurred with tears, her eyes met his. The dark navy rings around his irises seemed deeper as he glowered in anger. His hand on her chin gripped painfully, and she could see his jaw move as he ground his teeth, seething.

"Lesson number one: I am not a patient man. Wherever you just went, whatever just happened to you, it won't happen again." His voice was soft, yet laced with threat. "Now, eat your fucking food."

He waited, expectantly, the spoon poised in front of Sophie's mouth. She opened, accepting. His gentleness returned as he scooped more soup and fed her. He no longer held her chin to force her to eat, and the spoon was placed softly on her tongue as he waited for her. She ate the rest of the bowl in obedient silence.

He paced the expanse of the ground floor, away from the concrete, lower level of the house. The jitteriness returned. She had unnerved him. For the second time, Adrien was surprised by her. But now, his surprise was tainted by confusion. Never, in the ten years that he had been in this business, had he met a trainee who was seemingly without fear, who didn't appear to care what happened to her.

What if I don't want to survive this? Her words taunted him. He hadn't known how to respond—he had never had to answer that question before. He was confused. And confusion infuriated him, like a woodpecker boring a hole in a tin roof. He couldn't stand it. He responded the only way he knew how—force. She would learn quickly that he could be violent if disobeyed, but he could also be kind if she listened.

And she had swiftly taken advantage of his kindness. He recognized the dissociation as soon as the glazed look came into her eyes. Even *that* had surprised and confused him. Usually, it took his trainees weeks to learn the art of separating their minds from their bodies. It took much less time to break them of that.

But where the fuck did that come from? She has only been here two days. There was something about her that was different from his other trainees. He had noticed it the moment he looked into her green eyes. The staunch lack of emotion. He knew his customers wouldn't take well to the deadness. He would have to do something about it.

But it was the emptiness that intrigued him. He was mesmerized by it. It was a tragedy from which he was unable to look away.

He stopped pacing then and turned to look out the large floor-to-ceiling window in front of him. He had spent years learning how to break women, to instill fear, and to take away their free will. He found, though, that he had no idea what to do with someone who was already broken.

———————————

5

Day three of her captivity began just like day two. Sophie awoke, startled out of a nightmare by the sound of her own screams, shivering on her blanketless mattress. She longed for clothing, not for decency or modesty, but for warmth. The early-morning sun offered no heat from its deceptive orange glow, and only managed to act as a reminder for the birds: wake up, make noise. The exotic chirping was becoming less foreign. She couldn't recall the sound of a pigeon, so common from her old life in Boston.

She wrapped her arms around her knees and shifted on the mattress to bring her face to rest against her thighs. She knew he would come soon to bring her food. It seemed like it was the only routine she could count on—breakfast in the morning, dinner at night. Aside from that, it was a game of waiting. She knew now, at least, what she was waiting for: training. She wondered what it would be like. Her mind slowly rolled through possible scenarios of being gagged, tortured, and forced into sexual acts. She was surprised that her anxiety didn't poke at her, didn't try to squeeze the air from her lungs.

But her plan for disobedience in hopes of getting out of this kept her anxiety at bay. For once, she felt power over it. After all, he had said it himself—*he wasn't a patient man.* Maybe he really *would* kill her if she was disobedient enough. And then she could be free of the misery that this life had brought her. The thought almost made her smile. *Almost.*

Another sound, once foreign, now familiar: the click of the door, the setting of a tray. Another click to indicate her captor was not staying. Sophie raised her head from her knees to see what had been left. A glass of water and plate of toast with some orange slices sat on the tray. Her stomach growled at the thought of food. Since eating the soup last night, her appetite seemed to have miraculously returned. Ignoring it, she returned her chin to her knees.

It's hard to keep track of time when nothing is occupying your existence.

It could have been minutes, but, just as likely, it could have been hours before he returned. This time, she heard him enter the room, met with his exasperated sigh. Without raising her head from her knees, she lifted her eyes to meet his. He stood with his hands on his hips, contemplating the tray. Again, it seemed odd that he had dressed in jeans, as though he confined himself to a cool place. *Maybe he's a recluse,* she thought. *Maybe he doesn't get out much.* She almost laughed at the idea that her captor was a hermit. *He's too good looking to be a hermit.* She recoiled at the thought. How could she even think that way in a time like this? She shrugged it off with rationality: clearly it was a defense mechanism, a way for her mind to cope with the fucked-up-ness of her current situation.

The sound of the dishes tinkling on the tray brought her

back to reality. She watched as he brought the tray over, setting it down by her mattress. He lowered himself to sit close to her. He looked at her for the first time now, his eyes piercing through her.

"You need to eat." He stated it so matter-of-factly, like he thought perhaps Sophie didn't know.

"I'm not interested in eating," she stated, just as matter-of-factly. It evoked a twitch of a smile from him. She wasn't sure why.

"That may be true, *Chevrette*, but that doesn't mean you're not hungry." His words prodded her, gently coaxed her, as he brought a piece of toast to her lips. She wondered about the word *Chevrette*. Why was he calling her that? What did it mean?

"Open," he commanded, his eyes falling to her mouth. She paused as thoughts of disobedience passed through her mind. They were fleeting, and she hardly had to push them away. She obeyed for the second time, allowing him to place the food into her mouth.

Relief mixed with disappointment. *Eat. Disobey.* The two words swirled in her mind as she continued to accept the nourishment. *Eat. Disobey.*

The toast was gone. Having eaten it so willingly, she hadn't noticed how swiftly she'd devoured it. Her captor picked up the peeled orange slices, handing her one and popping one into his mouth. She watched as he chewed, his own eyes looking at her with—*what? Amusement?* He arched an eyebrow as he continued chewing. She slowly raised her orange slice and allowed her tongue to capture its entirety. It was cool and sweet, perfectly ripe. Sophie closed her eyes as she appreciated its perfection. She had forgotten the crisp tang that oranges delivered. She felt like she'd found an old friend, and sighed with content at their re-acquaintance.

"Putain, tu es belle."

Her eyes fluttered open, immediately landing on his. She had almost missed the words they had been breathed so quietly. She knew it was French but similar enough to Spanish. *Did he just call me beautiful?*

His blue-gray eyes had grown dark; the navy ring seemed a deeper blue. He stared at her lips, a flicker of emotion crossing his eyes. She felt flustered suddenly, her stomach turning into an enclosure for butterflies. His hand rose to cup her chin. His thumb grazed over her bottom lip, the softness of his touch paradoxical to the roughness of his skin. Involuntarily, her mouth parted as her breath escaped her.

A pause.

He blinked then, wrenching his eyes from her lips. Sophie wondered fleetingly if that's what she looked like when she came out of one of her trances. He leaned toward her, the smell of orange still on his breath as he quietly spoke, "Let's not make a habit of these feeding sessions. I've already told you, I'm not a patient man." His hand left her cold in its wake as he stood and gathered the tray. He placed the still-full glass next to the mattress.

"You should drink some water." Without looking back, he left.

Hot embarrassment reached her cheeks. *Why do I feel like this?* She tried to ignore the tugging notion that it was for the same reason she couldn't seem to disobey him.

Disobey. Disobey. Don't give in. Disobey. Disobey. Don't give in. Disobey. Disobey.

She had begun to scrawl the words with her finger, invisibly, like the self-induced punishment of a schoolchild. Over and over she traced the words—along the walls, the mattress, up and down her arms and legs.

Disobey. Disobey. Don't give in. Disobey. Disobey. Don't give in. Disobey. Disobey.

Maybe this way, it would sink into her skin like a tattoo, absorb, and become a part of her.

"What do you think about me getting a tattoo?" Sophie asked Josh. They were lying in bed, a lazy Sunday morning quickly turning into afternoon. The sun shone brightly through her bedroom window, bathing them in light. They hadn't bothered with the blinds.

"What, you mean like a tramp stamp?" Josh propped his head in his hand as he turned to look at Sophie.

"No! Not like a tramp stamp. Just like a…well, I don't know where I'd put it. But not a tramp stamp."

"You know tattoos are permanent, right?" Josh said with a raised eyebrow. Sophie rolled her eyes in response.

"I'm serious, Josh. I've been thinking about it for a while, and I think I'm going to do it." She hated how whiny her voice sounded. Like she was pleading for his approval.

"So, what are you going to get?" he asked. She smiled sitting up to bring her face over his.

"I was thinking of doing, like, maybe a flock of birds flying away. Maybe put it here…" she circled her chest above her heart, "for Mom and Dad."

Josh paused. "That's…nice." His tone was laced with disappointment.

"You don't like it?"

"No, no. It's awesome. It's a great idea. You should do it." False reassurances. "Tell you what. If you do that, I'll get a birdhouse tattooed right…" He trailed his fingers down his chest, over his

stomach, and along the hair that led below his pelvis, "here."
Sophie couldn't help but laugh.

She had never gotten the tattoo.

Sophie's hand rubbed the soft skin above her heart. She hadn't noticed she was doing it and wondered how long she had been zoning. Long enough for her skin to redden and feel tender under the incessant friction.

A new tray. She had also missed *that* during her zoning. She wondered if he'd been in the room, or if he had just slid the tray in without entering.

Why does it even matter? She thought. It didn't. *Right?*

She approached the tray. She knew she wouldn't eat. She touched her invisible tattoo.

Disobey. Disobey. Don't give in. Disobey. Disobey. Don't give in. Disobey. Disobey.

She was thirsty, though. Cold, damp condensation layered the glass. She lifted the cup to her lips and drank. Her grip faltered from the wetness, and she quickly readjusted to avoid dropping the glass. The motion caused an idea to sprout, its growth spurred by the water droplets, as though it were a garden to be irrigated. Greedily, she finished the water and allowed the glass to slip from her hands.

It broke but didn't shatter. Sharp pieces of glass glistened on the floor, tiny promises. She stared for a moment, contemplating the possibilities. The faded scars on her wrists screamed at her, hot with anticipation.

It would be so easy. Just two slices, long and deep. Then, wait.

She had cut herself before, a few months after Josh died. It wasn't that she wanted to die. Really, it was a morbid curiosity to see if it incited feeling. If nothing else, perhaps it would get rid of the emptiness. She had used an Exacto knife. Nice and sharp. Her blood was redder than she had imagined. The pain had surprised her.

Megan found her that day, just sitting and staring at the blood dripping on the tile floor. Silently, she helped Sophie clean up. Bandaged her. They never spoke of it, and Sophie had never tried it again.

But now…could she do it? She picked up a shard of glass, the edges forming a sharp point. She rested it on her wrist lightly grazing a path, like a practice run. If she didn't hit her vein the first time, she wasn't sure she could bring herself to try again. The slicing of skin made her squeamish.

"What the *fuck*?" His voice cut through her. She hadn't even heard the click of the door announcing his entrance. She looked up from the glass in her hand, just as he swiped it from her, flinging it across the room. The glass tinkled, shattering along with her hope of escape. He grabbed her by the arms, lifting her to face him. She hadn't realized how strong he was until she was dangling in his grasp, her feet sweeping the floor.

"What do you think you're doing?" She registered his anger first, but there was something else hidden there. *Panic.* She could see it in the wideness of his eyes, hear it in the harshness of his breath. Had she not been so familiar with the feeling herself, she may have missed it.

Panic was quickly overcome by rage. He sucked in a breath, his jaw ticking with anger. "Ça me fait chier." He practically spat the words. "Do you have any idea how much that pisses me off?" His fingers dug into her arms. "Apparently, you need to be taught a lesson. Let's go." Her feet were back on the concrete floor. He let one of her arms free, but the other still screamed in his grasp as he dragged her behind him. He quickly punched in the code and pressed his thumb to the pad. The keypad beeped and he swung the heavy metal door open.

The concrete floor gave way to cold tile. He dragged her

past a stairway and under a concrete archway into a hall. Led now into a larger room, he stopped in front of a wide door, punching in yet another code. The keypad beeped as the door clicked and he pushed her into the room.

Sophie gasped as she took in its contents. Thick cuffs were fastened by large chains dangling from the ceiling. More cuffs were affixed to the walls by large, black loops hammered into the concrete. On the far wall hung an array of items: whips, paddles, batons, crops, floggers, a knotted rope with strands that held metal balls at the end. *Is that a cat o' nine tails?* Sophie registered the room as a torture chamber. Dread filled her stomach as she was shoved from behind toward one of the sets of handcuffs dangling from the ceiling.

"Face the wall," he commanded. Her tattoo forgotten, she obeyed. It was strange how she always obeyed. This time out of sheer fear. He lifted her arm, fastened it into the cuff. She was forced on her tiptoes as he fastened the other, suddenly very aware of her nakedness as her arms stretched up, exposing her body. Meeting her eyes, he continued. "Tell me, *Chevrette,* what were you hoping for there?" He said it softly, his anger reduced to a simmer. There was something else present, some other emotion behind the question. She couldn't quite make it out, though. She swallowed, unsure what to say. He raised an eyebrow, awaiting her response.

"I just want it to be over." She whispered it, never having said it aloud before. It felt like she had told her deepest secret to a complete stranger. And, in fact, she had.

He looked worn suddenly, his eyes taking on sadness. He shook his head, ever so slightly, effectively replacing any sadness with determination. "I want you to remember this moment, *Chevrette.* If you ever think about hurting yourself again, if you ever think about wanting to die—whether it's tomorrow or ten years from now—I want you to remember how alive you are about to feel." He tugged on the chains, ensuring they were secure. "This is going to hurt." His tone confirmed the truth of his statement.

He disappeared from her line of sight as he walked toward the wall to choose an instrument. She couldn't see what he picked, and her unease heightened at the unknown. She heard him walk back toward her, stopping to stand behind her. He stepped forward then, and gently swept her long hair over her shoulder, clearing it from her back.

"Don't even think about allowing your mind to wander. I'll make this worse for you if you do."

She blinked in surprise. *Does he think I have control over when I zone?* The thought of zoning just then terrified her. In that moment, Sophie hated her memories. *They've robbed me of everything. I hate them. I want them gone.* This realization stung more than the first blow.

But then, the second strike landed. Stinging pain splayed across her upper back like licks of fire. She cried out in pain and shock. The flick of leather straps sounded as he retreated. *He's using a flogger,* she thought as she anticipated the next strike. The sensation landed in a different place from the previous two, this time feeling like needles piercing her skin.

"Oh my God," she gasped, her voice barely audible. She sucked in a quick breath as the pain subsided. She pulled against the chains in the ceiling, hoping to squirm away from the slaps of the leather straps. She could hear his heavy breathing at the exertion he expended on her.

Another blow. She squeezed her eyes shut and cried out from the pain. So much pain. Her heart pounded in her chest, her wrists hurt where the cuffs cut off her blood flow. *When is it going to be over?*

She hated him. Hated that he had taken her from her life, hated that he had stripped her naked, hated that he forced her to eat, hated that he punished her for feeling the way she did. But mostly, she hated that he had been right. She, for the first time in over a year, felt alive.

He appeared in front of her then, breathing heavy. Sweat glistened on his brow. "Have you learned your lesson yet, *Chevrette?*" he asked softly.

"Yes," she whispered.

Regret was not an emotion Adrien was used to, but he regretted the punishment almost immediately.

Seeing her knelt on the floor, quietly tracing a line on herself with the broken glass, had triggered an emotion in him, a memory, that he tried hard to forget. A younger version of himself, only seven at the time. The discovery of death, a bathtub filled with lukewarm water the color of rose petals. Adrien's mind was forever stained with the knowledge that he had been too late.

He had reacted in panic, he knew, at the sight of his trainee contemplating her wrists. He hadn't meant to get so angry. He hadn't meant to bring her to that room. That room was never meant to be seen by his trainees. He barely remembered dragging her in there and chaining her up, his anger was so blinding. And when she had admitted it, said the words he knew she would, he couldn't help but feel sadness for her. Like he wanted to protect her rather than abet her brokenness. And yet…

It had been like a light switch flicked on. Adrien recognized it the moment it arrived. *Fear.* She had been terrified. His deer, his *Chevrette,* had finally registered the danger she was in. He felt disgusted with himself.

———————

6

The softness of the mattress enveloped Sophie, the plushness of the comforter welcoming her. She wanted nothing more than to crawl under the sheets and fall into a deep sleep. But the pain wouldn't allow her to engage in such decadence. The skin on her back burned where her punishment had landed.

He had unchained Sophie, careful not to touch the tender marks on her back, and carried her, not back to her dungeon, but up the stairs to a different level of the house. She had been exhausted, unable to keep her eyes open to peek at the unexplored portion of the place she was being held captive.

He had laid her gently on her stomach in a room with a large, king-sized bed. There was an attached bathroom, where he was now. She could hear him rustling around, opening drawers, moving things. The water was running into a container. He emerged with a glass of water, approaching the bed.

"Here, take this. It'll help with the pain." He extended his hand offering two pills with the water. Sitting up slightly, she winced at the searing sting. She took them, not bothering to question what they were. She handed back the glass of water and readjusted herself on the mattress. He returned to the bathroom and, a moment later, re-emerged with a bowl of water, a washcloth, and a tube of ointment. Setting the bowl on the bedside table, he lowered himself onto the mattress beside her. He swept Sophie's hair to the side, for the second time that day, exposing her back. He dipped the cloth into the water.

"This might hurt."

Sophie almost laughed at the idea. He had already shown her pain beyond anything she had ever felt before. He had warned her then, too, that it would hurt. But that was the thing. She had *felt*. For the first time in months, she had been aware of every sensation in her body, had been wholly present in the moment, had experienced emotions—fear, anger, hate. And then…hope. Hope that if she could feel *those* emotions so strongly, perhaps she could feel happiness again.

Happiness. The idea seemed like a joke to her. Even if it were possible to find her way out of the cocoon of darkness she had constructed, *happiness* was worlds away from the nightmare she was living now. *No,* she decided, *it's better to feel nothing.*

She winced at the cool cloth against her raw skin. Slowly, he cleaned her wounds, dipping the cloth in the water every so often, now tinted with the color of her blood. Any of his residual anger was gone, replaced by a comforting kindness. She wondered about him, wondered how he could change so quickly. She was intrigued by this person. How he came to be who he was, how he came to do the things that he did.

"Why do you do this?" She asked it without raising her eyes to him, her boldness only going so far. He stopped dabbing the cool cloth against her skin.

"Do what?" Evasion.

"This." She didn't clarify. She couldn't quite figure out how to define *this.*

He sighed.

She didn't expect him to answer. But she couldn't help pondering what he was choosing not to say.

"Because I'm good at it." He returned the cloth to the bowl, allowing it to sink as he grabbed the ointment and uncapped it.

She considered his answer for a moment. "How did you get so good at it?" She winced again as he rubbed the ointment onto the hot, raised wounds.

"I've had a lot of practice." He paused. "Not everyone has the privilege of choice." It was an admission. Of what, she wasn't sure. She didn't dare ask another question, though, knowing she had gotten all of the answers he was willing to give. Silence resumed as he finished applying the ointment.

He returned the items to the bathroom, rinsing out the bowl. Her eyes followed his movement. He glanced into the mirror, his eyes capturing hers in the reflection. She saw it then; it was unmistakable, the sadness they held. She wondered if maybe he was as broken as she.

He emerged from the bathroom, made his way to the door, and punched in the code for it to open. "You should try to sleep." He flicked off the light, dousing the room in dimness. She hadn't even realized the sun had set.

"Goodnight." It was an automatic response. She hadn't even registered what she was saying until it escaped her lips.

He paused in the doorway, a look of disbelief and amusement crossing his dark features, before quietly closing the door behind him. She sighed, exhaustion taking over her aching body. Closing her eyes, she waited for the nightmares.

They didn't come.

Morning light filtered in through the window as the birds began their daily ranting. Sophie's eyes fluttered open. It took her a moment to realize she hadn't woken from a nightmare. Instead, she was caressed out of sleep by a stream of sunlight landing brightly on her pillow. She was still lying on her stomach—in fact, she hadn't moved all night. Sheets covered her legs, coming up to her waist but stopping before hitting the sensitive skin on her back. She couldn't recall pulling the sheets over her during the night.

Weird, she thought. She rolled to her side, facing the bedside table where the ointment had reappeared. *Hadn't he put that away last night?* She averted her eyes as though it would cause the answer to disappear. The thought that he had been there while she slept made her feel…well…something. She pushed the emotion away before she could register its meaning. *It's better to try not to feel anything,* she reminded herself.

Sophie took in her surroundings. She lay in a plush, king-sized bed, the billowing, white comforter a marked contrast against the black, wrought iron of the four-poster bed frame. The bed sat centered against a wall that held bedside tables on either side. The beautiful, chestnut-colored finish of the tables matched a large, wooden armoire that sat tall on the opposite wall. Sophie already knew where the bathroom was, but there was another door. *Closet,* she guessed. Huge floor-to-ceiling windows brought sunlight into the room, acting as a wall on the far side of the room. For the first time in days, Sophie was able to look outside.

She got up from the bed, entranced by the lure of the outside world. Standing at the windows, she was awed by the sight. From where she stood, the house looked like a squared "U" shape. She could see another section of the house, completely encased in glass, jutting out parallel to the section she was in. A rooftop deck with railings topped that section of the house, while another small deck jutted out from a doorway a story below. Looking straight down, Sophie realized the entirety of the house was surrounded by yet another deck on the lowest level, large enough to hold a long, asymmetrical pool. Beyond the deck was the lush, green jungle, so thick that Sophie couldn't see past the first row of trees. She didn't need to, though, to know that the house was in complete isolation from the rest of the world. If it hadn't been for the marks on her back, she would have thought it to be the perfect vacation home.

Her curiosity piqued, she moved toward the armoire. She pulled open the drawers, one by one, to see their contents. She wasn't sure what she had expected to find, but she was surprised by the contents of the first drawer. It was filled with different types of panties: thongs, G-strings, boy shorts, cuts of material she didn't even have a name for. Rows and rows of varying fabric—silk, lace, cotton—met her eyes. She began picking through the array of color, noting that they seemed to be arranged by size. Smalls, mediums, and larges. *Something for everyone,* she thought sarcastically.

She opened the next drawer. Bras, all matching the above panty drawer. Third drawer: lingerie sets, garter belts, stockings. Her curiosity grew frantic as she moved toward the closet. Pulling the door open, she gasped. Beautiful dresses, shirts, and sweaters of all colors and patterns met her eyes. She looked at the tag dangling from one of the items. Ralph Lauren. She pushed it aside and grabbed another one. Gucci. *Had he picked them all out himself?*

What the fuck kind of sicko captures women to sell for sex, and then buys them the best clothing money can afford? I was wrong. He's not broken. He's twisted.

She continued perusing the closet. *Hmmm…no shoes.* She guessed it was a way to prevent anyone from running—a walk through the thick and gnarled jungle barefoot would not be at the top of anyone's to-do list. No, escape was definitely not an option.

"See something you like?" The deep rasp of his voice cut through her thoughts, and she spun around to find him leaning against the doorframe of the closet, his arms crossed in front of him. He was wearing dark jeans and a plain, white, button-up shirt, the sleeves rolled up to his elbows exposing the masculinity of his forearms.

Her mind went blank, unsure what to say. He stood up straighter then, his arms still crossed below his chest.

"If you do well in your training, this could all be yours. You can sleep here; pick out whatever you want to wear. Enjoy a bath." He sauntered over to her then, slowly, like he was afraid she would run. His hand reached out, tucking a lock of hair behind her ears. His eyes scorched hers. "This could be easy if you just obey."

She ripped her eyes away from his, looking around the closet. *He's right.* She contemplated her options. She knew he would never kill her. She knew it the moment he began whipping her. Even in his rage, he had been controlled, never striking the same place twice, avoiding her spine or where her organs lay below her skin. *No, he won't kill me. I could obey, avoid punishment, and avoid feeling anything. I could lock myself in my cocoon and never come out.*

"So, what will it be, *Chevrette?* Comfort? Clothing? Or would you rather be naked?" Her eyes shot back to him. The corner of his mouth had turned up in a smile, his crisp, blue eyes darkening as they swept over her, drinking her in. She felt embarrassed—no one had looked at her like that in, *how long?*

"God, Sophie, you are beautiful," Josh appreciated Sophie's figure from the bed. He was lying on top of the sheets, wearing only his boxer shorts. She could see his arousal. His brown eyes continued to skim her body as she stepped out of her dress. Bending over to collect the piece of clothing from the floor, her breasts pushed against the black lace bra she was wearing. The matching black lace of the thong stretched across her ass as she bent over.

"You're killing me over here, Soph," Josh's voice whined with lust as he continued to stare, his hand wandering to stroke himself. She smiled coyly as she bent to unbuckle her strappy high heels.

"Don't—leave those on," he instructed, suddenly sitting up. She immediately re-fastened the strap. "Come here." She obeyed.

The sharp agony wrenched her from the memory. Aside from the discomfort of her hair being yanked, she was glad to have been ripped from her zoning. Grateful, even, had it not been for the sudden pain. Her hands flew up to wrap around his in an attempt to loosen his grasp. Her eyes winced in pain and fear of looking at him. She felt the anger seething from his glare.

"I don't have time for this bullshit this morning," he spat, pushing her forward, causing her to stumble out of the closet. "Let's go." He moved past the bedside table where her breakfast tray sat. He pointed at it as he walked toward the bathroom. "Eat that. Now."

She looked at the food. A bowl of Cheerios topped with blueberries stared at her, taunting her to obey his command. She sat on the edge of the bed. She knew what she was supposed to do, yet she couldn't seem to get her limbs to follow instructions.

Pour the milk. Get the spoon. Eat, chew, swallow. Repeat.

She heard the turn of the faucet, the deep sound of water filling a tub. At that moment, she realized she hadn't showered in days. She watched from the bed as he leaned over and poured a liquid—bubbles?—into the tub. She had yet to explore the bathroom but could tell by the sound of the water and the height of the raised platform that it was a deep tub. Satisfied, he turned the faucet off and walked out of the bathroom toward Sophie. Grabbing the short glass of milk on the tray, he poured it into the bowl of cereal.

"Do you have some sort of aversion to food?" he asked, impatience simmering. He lowered himself to sit next to her on the bed, bowl and spoon in hand. He cocked an eyebrow as he scooped some cereal onto the spoon and held it out for her.

Am I supposed to answer that question? She opened her mouth and allowed the spoon in, avoiding his gaze. He waited for her to swallow.

"Answer me."

"I—I guess. Sort of, yeah." She wasn't quite sure what to say as the truth swirled around in her mind. *I'm depressed. I have no appetite. Nothing seems to have taste anymore. What's the point?* He let out an exasperated sigh, causing her to look up. His eyes searched hers, his jaw set tight. She offered one, a half-truth: "I'm just not hungry very often."

He continued looking into her eyes, as though trying to decide whether or not to believe her. He must have, though, because he continued to feed her. Or perhaps he had just decided to accept that she wouldn't be completely honest with him. It was only fair, right? He had kidnapped her after all.

When the bowl was empty, he placed it back on the tray on the bedside table. Softly taking her by the elbow, he pulled her to her feet, positioning himself behind her. His hands swept her hair to her front, the grazing of his fingertips sending a chill down her spine. Goose bumps formed on her arms. She felt silly for her body's reaction to his touch.

"How is your back feeling?" There was concern in his voice.

Odd, since he had been the one to inflict the injuries to begin with, she thought.

"It looks better than it did last night. Does it feel any better?" Sophie nodded her response. She could feel the rough pad of his thumb lightly move over the marks on her back. She was surprised that she didn't feel any of the heated pain that had been present the night before.

"It feels better. Less raw, I guess." She offered him words this time.

"Good." It was almost a whisper, his thumb now drawing a soft circle on her shoulder. For a moment, she almost convinced herself that he cared for her. Almost.

"Come." He guided her by her elbow into the bathroom. It held the basic amenities but was the most elegant bathroom she had ever been in. A granite stand-up shower stood along the far end of the bathroom, the rain showerhead like the core of a sunflower. Next to the shower was a raised granite pedestal that held a deep bathtub. Steps centered the pedestal, leading into the tub. He took her hand, guiding her up the steps. The hot water hit her, simultaneously soothing and painful, as she stepped in. She submerged herself to her shoulders, wincing as the water lapped her sores. Her legs grazed a bench beneath the bubbles to sit on, the tub so deep that she had to lift her chin to keep it from getting wet. He seated himself on the steps, surprising her.

"You're staying?" she blurted out. For some reason, the thought of him watching her bathe felt more invasive than the thought of him having seen her naked over the past several days. Worse, even, than him rubbing her back with ointment as she slept unaware.

She was met with raised eyebrows, an amused expression,

bordering incredulous. "You think after the stunt you pulled last night that I would trust you in more than two inches of water?"

Oh. Right. "I could just take a shower, then."

"Do you have any idea how much a cascade of water droplets hurts after being flogged?"

She was taken aback. "No…" *Do you?*

Pointedly, he handed her the bar of soap. She took it, bringing her hand under the water to scrub herself. At least the bubbles floating at the surface covered what dignity she had. When she was finished, she handed him the soap.

"Can I…" she paused, uncertain if she could request anything. She continued anyway, "Could I use a razor?"

"Absolutely not." The answer was terse. Of course, she had anticipated it.

"I promise I won't use it to hurt myself. I just—"

"I don't allow the women I keep to use razors. *Ever.* End of discussion." The starkness in his tone surprised her—she hadn't anticipated *that.* She was good at reading people, trained by her degree in psychology and years of experience. She knew there was something behind his response. But her instincts told her not to push.

Instead, she dipped her hair into the water, grabbing the shampoo to lather. When she was satisfied, she tipped her head back, allowing the water to engulf her, to bring her under. She floated there for a moment, submerged fully in the water's peace and quiet. The heat felt good on her aches and pains as she sank toward the bottom of the tub.

She felt the stillness of the water shatter as a pair of strong hands grasped her shoulders and lifted her up. The cool air hit her face, wrenching her eyes open to meet his as she surfaced. She wiped her wet hair, still covered with soapsuds, from her eyes, utterly confused.

"Don't go under all the way." It was a command, but it lacked a certain authority, as if he was begging instead of demanding. Emotion flickered behind his eyes as he said it, like lightning, gone so fast Sophie wasn't sure if it had actually been there at all.

Something about the way he said it compelled her to respond, "I'm sorry. I won't do it again." He let go of her arm, relaxing.

She looked at him. Really studied him. And she began to fit the pieces of him together, the ones she had, at least. He couldn't be much older than she—late twenties maybe—and he had made a business of kidnapping and selling girls to others. He had alluded to the fact that maybe it wasn't a profession he had wanted for himself. *Was he forced into it?* That might explain his comments about being flogged; maybe he knew from personal experience. It seemed far-fetched. She let the assumption go, focusing on what she did know. He had no qualms with hurting women, but he was also extremely— *what? Kind? Caring?* He made sure she ate and had checked on her during the night. He certainly didn't have to do that. The clothing that he offered, too, was over the top. He didn't have to buy expensive designer clothing—fuck, he didn't have to buy anything at all. Not to mention he had chosen to listen to Sophie's request to let Megan go. He had shielded Megan from this life, had given her a chance to return home. For that, Sophie couldn't deny the gratitude she felt toward him. In fact, for the wrong he had taken part in, he seemed to be actively trying to redeem himself.

She wondered, then, whose reality was worse—hers or his. She sat, baffled, as the water around her grew cold.

There was something about her, something that he found endearing. The way she had said goodnight to him, the way she had apologized to him, as though he were someone else. Like he was a friend, perhaps even a lover.

But he was neither of those things, he knew that. He had specifically created his own set of rules and his own style of training to make sure he remembered his place as their temporary master. His father had been his inspiration. The scars on his back itched at the thought. His palm twitched, remembering the warm, leather handle of the flogger in his hand from the previous night.

He had constructed that room for himself, never intending it for anyone else. The only reason the room was sprinkled with sets of cuffs was on the off chance that he had someone there to indulge him. As it turned out, beating yourself by your own hand was a difficult thing to do, no matter how much you wanted it.

And he hadn't needed a reminder lesson in years, but he was beginning to wonder if he might. Phase One was not going as planned. *Chevrette* was beginning to blur the lines with her probing questions. And for some reason, he felt compelled to give her answers. He had never spent so much time with a trainee. He avoided it, really. It was necessary not to provide them with too much contact in the initial phase of training, yes, but he avoided it for his own reasons as well. He didn't want to get too close, didn't want to give himself a chance to get to know the girls he held captive. There was no room for emotional connection in this line of work. It was strictly business, after all.

But now, what choice did he have? He couldn't trust that she wouldn't do something stupid. *Fuck, he couldn't even trust her to eat properly.* He was incredulous at the realization. He wanted her to eat, needed her to. Buyers didn't like girls who were too thin. And she was too thin—sickly looking almost. *Why won't she eat?* That she hadn't explained herself, bothered him. He knew she was coveting the truth the moment the words came out of her mouth. Yet another act of defiance. He had met dozens of defiant women in this line of work, but this was different. It wasn't the type of defiance that he was used to. It was the type of defiance that left him wondering what the fuck was wrong with her.

And how was he supposed to fix it?

7

Sophie missed the comfort of that room already—the way the sunlight came in through the wall of windows, the illusion of calm provided by the overly-pillowed bed, the feeling of home in the closet full of clothing and drawers full of makeup and skin products (yes, she had finally snooped in the bathroom, too). He had let her dress after her bath. She took her time going through the closet and drawers, picking out a cotton, quarter-sleeve, cream shirt and blue capris. He waited patiently while she brushed her hair and deftly knotted it into a braid.

But then, he immediately brought her back to her prison on the lower level.

And now, her training began. She had made up her mind in that comfortable room. Knowing she wouldn't be able to escape, and knowing that death was no longer a viable option, she had no other choice but to obey. Obey and recede inside herself.

"You should know that you will be required to remove your

clothing whenever you're in training. I'll allow you to remain clothed for today, but this will be the last time."

Before he could go any further, she spoke. "Thank you." She hadn't realized it until she had been allowed to dress, but she really did appreciate the warmth and comfort that the clothing brought.

His brow furrowed, as though he didn't know what the words meant. Clearing his throat, he continued, "Before we begin, there are some rules that you must know and abide by. These rules are the simplest of the things you'll be asked to do, and you will be expected to do them at all times. Understood?" He paused, his gray-blue eyes looking into hers as she sat on the mattress looking up at him. She nodded.

"Rule number one: I am your master. You will address me as 'Master' or 'Sir.' No exceptions. I will remain your master until you are sold and handed to your new master, at which point, you will refer to that person as 'Master' or 'Sir.'

"Rule number two: you no longer have the right to speak unless spoken to first. If I want to hear your voice, I will tell you. When you are given permission to speak, I expect it to be with respect. Got it?" He crossed his arms, awaiting her answer.

"Yes," she replied.

"I'm sorry, I didn't hear that? Yes, *what?*" he prompted.

"Yes…Sir," she acquiesced. A smile tugged at his mouth. It didn't reach his eyes, she noticed.

"Good girl. Rule number three: eyes to the floor, unless I give you permission otherwise."

Her mouth dropped open, eyes widening. She wasn't sure why she was so shocked. It just seemed so unreasonable. Unrealistic, even.

"Do you have something to say about that, *Chevrette?*"

She managed to close her gaping mouth. "I just...I don't know if I can remember to do that. I don't—I don't know." She shook her head, eyes pleading with him to drop that one rule. He cocked his head, his expression blank, before slowly nodding.

"You'll learn. And you'll get used to it." His voice became quieter, softer. "Most of my customers have one thing in common: they enjoy power and dominance. It's best if you learn to submit here, practice, and get used to it before meeting your new master."

"What if—" she stopped herself, slapping her hand over her mouth. She had already forgotten his second rule.

"You can speak." There was amusement in his voice, like he was laughing at her. She couldn't tell, though, because she didn't dare look at him.

"What if I can't do it?" she asked quietly, keeping her eyes averted.

"Something tells me you won't have any problems." He smirked at her, but, again, she didn't see it. "But if you do have problems, I'll remind you. Like I told you already—if you obey, you'll be rewarded. If not, you'll be punished." He was so matter-of-fact, his tone devoid of emotion.

"Now that you know the rules, let's get started on the basics." He straightened, looking down at Sophie still sitting on the mattress, eyes glued to her legs in front of her. "Kneel on the floor and put your hands, palms down, on your thighs."

She moved from the mattress, positioning herself as he had commanded.

"Good. Keep your eyes down, just like that. Knees together." His shoed foot tapped the outside of her thighs, nudging her to bring her inner thighs to touch. "Back straight, bring your shoulders back."

She adjusted herself. *Why do I feel like I'm in a yoga class?* She smiled at the absurd thought.

"Something funny, *Chevrette?*" His voice had hardened, taking on an edge of anger. She quickly shook her head. "Good. Get used to this position. It's the position that your master will most likely want to see you in, any time he or she enters a room."

She? Sophie's head snapped up, completely disregarding the third rule.

"What? Did you think women were immune to the gravity of power, *Chevrette?* Eyes to the floor," he snapped.

She looked at his brown leather shoes and wondered what it would be like to wear them.

"Get up."

She leaned forward, placing her hands on the floor to push up from her kneeling position, certain to keep her eyes on his shoes while doing so.

"We'll have to work on that," he mumbled more to himself than to her. To herself, she thought, *what was wrong with the way I stood up?*

"Stand straight. Keep your feet slightly parted." He put his shoe in between her feet to indicate. "Good. Hands crossed over your chest." He took her wrists, bringing them out in front of her to help her cross them. The warmth of his thumb grazed the scar on one of her wrists. She jolted as it screamed up at her. She couldn't keep her eyes from moving to the faded pink, a Siren calling to her from the sea.

His thumb moved to trace the scar. She felt the gesture softly mirrored on her other wrist, his touch sending a shiver of electricity through her. She stole a glance at him. He was looking down, just as entranced by the marks as she. His eyes met hers, still staring at him.

"Eyes down, *Chevrette*," he whispered as he crossed her arms in front of her and placed them to her chest. She struggled to look away from him, his eyes Sirens themselves.

He continued the lesson, ignoring the charged moment that had just occurred. "This is called standing at attention. Anytime you are standing, you are to position yourself like this. Got it?" She nodded. "Good, now get back into kneeling position."

She obeyed, bringing herself back to the floor, exactly as he had shown her.

"Now, stay like that until I come back."

She waited.

The following day, he had her practice. She spent hours standing perfectly straight, kneeling perfectly still. She had begun calling him Sir, having no other name for him. Her master taught her new things, too—how to stand up without touching the floor with her hands, how to lower herself into a kneeling position without wobbling. He had her practice over and over, incessantly. Sophie's shoulders and back burned from maintaining an upright position. Even her palms ached from spending so much time flat against her thighs.

It was different from the torture of punishment, but it was torture nonetheless. The pain in her body blazed a trail for her anger to return. She hated them—the feelings. She missed her cocoon, wanted back in, clawing it open in her mind. But her chrysalis had begun to dry out, to shrivel in her absence. It left her feeling exposed.

He had kept his promise, and she was spending her first afternoon back in the comfortable room. Her training for the day completed, she showered and changed into some shorts and a t-shirt that hugged her curves. She had begun to notice the fullness of her curves returning whenever she gazed in the mirror. At every mealtime, he sat with her and fed her. Even when she willingly fed herself, he stayed to make sure she ate it all.

The beep and click of the coded door. She jumped, not expecting him so soon, and quickly arranged herself into kneeling position where she was on the bed.

"Come with me." He reached his hand toward her, beckoning. Sophie slid off the bed, her bare feet padding on the large slabs of granite that tiled the floor. She kept her gaze down as he placed his hand on the small of her back and guided her out of her room.

Stealing glimpses as they moved through the large archways, their footsteps echoing in the cavernous hallways, Sophie marveled at the enormity of the house. He led her to, what she could only assume, was the bottom level of the U-shaped house. The room was entirely open, the ceiling as tall as the entirety of the house. She was beginning to understand its layout. The main level and an upper level, plus the lower basement level where her dungeon and the torture chamber were located (for that's what that room was, wasn't it?). Her new room, the comfortable one, was on the upper level. This uppermost level of the house was reserved only for the wings of the U, which mirrored one another. Large glass windows that reached from the floor to the ceiling along the entire length of the house were the finishing touches on the awe-inspiring architectural design. She wondered what it was like to be in a room with walls made entirely of glass. *Did it feel liberating? Or did the lack of confinement leave you feeling unsecured and vulnerable?*

They arrived in the large open space at the base of the U. The space had an open floor plan, and she could see the kitchen from where she stood, raised a step from the rest of the area. In front of her was a couch that looked out the huge windows reaching the top of the ceiling. At least 30 feet, Sophie guessed. Out of the window was the lower-level deck that she had seen from her room, and she caught the glistening of the pool in the afternoon sun.

"Bring her over." An unfamiliar voice reached her ears. Characterized by a deep French accent, it held just as much authority as her master's. She wondered if this was it. If her training was over and this was her buyer. As she was nudged forward, she dared a glance at this new stranger who sat before her. He had handsome features, dark hair like her master's, but short. Cut within a centimeter of its life. This was all her glance afforded before her eyes were, once again, glued to the floor.

"Kneel, *Chevrette*," her master commanded. She did as she was told, as he had taught her, with her palms to her thighs.

"Et c'est quoi le problème?" the stranger asked. Similar enough to Spanish, Sophie quickly translated, wondering about the problem to which he referred. The stranger stood up and approached her. She kept her eyes down.

"Les yeux," her master replied. *What did he just say?* She couldn't make it out. It sounded like no Spanish word she recognized.

A hand cupped her chin. "Look at me," the new voice commanded in English. His hand was rough, businesslike. It held nothing of her master's gentleness. She didn't obey. He wasn't her master, after all.

"Raise your eyes, *Chevrette.*"

Her gaze swept upward, catching the bemused look the stranger was sending her master. Turning, she saw her master shrug, a slight smile tugging at one corner of his mouth.

"My brother calls you *Deer*," the stranger said, causing

Sophie to turn back to him. The word fell on her ears as "dear." It didn't fully register, though. She was too preoccupied with what she saw.

The man had the same gray-blue eyes as her master. He lacked the deep-blue ring around the iris, but the resemblance was unmistakable. This man was a relative.

And he was scrutinizing her in the same way her master did, looking into her eyes as though searching for something. Slowly, he nodded, removing his hand from her chin and turning his eyes to address her master. They spoke in rapid French again and she couldn't follow the line of conversation.

Until…

"Maybe what she needs is a good fucking." He said it in English, his eyes returning to hers while he reached out to caress the inside of one of her thighs. His touch surprised her, and she gasped.

She realized the blue ring wasn't the only difference between his eyes and her master's. There was coldness there, almost like cruelty.

She felt frozen. Fear and confusion enveloped her, disabling her. She didn't move; couldn't.

Her master responded in French again. She couldn't understand the words, but she recognized the tone.

Without taking his eyes from hers, the stranger said, "Come on, Brother. Look at her. That body is begging to be fucked. That mouth…what do you think, little one?" He leaned toward her, his hand slowly ascending her thigh toward the opening of her shorts. "Do you want my cock in your—"

"I said, that's enough!" A familiar hand wrapped around her waist, pulling her away from the stranger. She staggered backward as her master lunged forward, capturing the man's throat in one powerful hand. The stranger—*his brother?*—

looked shocked. Eyes widening, he clutched at her master's hand, now tightening around his throat. She could see he was squeezing, really squeezing. "Go back to your room, *Chevrette.*" It was a tone she hadn't heard from him before. Like ice. Like his brother's eyes. She immediately spun on her heels and began in the direction they had come.

"Merde—Adrien—arrête!" She heard a strangled mess of words come from the man as she exited the large room. She tried to translate, searching her mind for any similarities to Spanish.

Wait—Adrien? That's not a word. Is that a name? Is that his name?

She wasn't sure what she had been expecting, but she found she liked his name. It held complexity, like its owner—both boyish and mature in nature, gentle and dominating at the same time. She felt it suited him. Something about it warmed her. The heat of emotion suddenly reminded her that she was no longer in her cocoon. She couldn't wait to get back to the safety of her room. She needed to feel contained, numb.

Get in? Shit! I can't get in without the code!

Contemplating her options, she decided to turn around and ask for the code, the consequences better than if she had disobeyed and wasn't in her room. *Right?*

She re-entered the large room. The stranger was gasping for breath, Adrien's hand no longer around his neck. His own hands rubbed the skin where Adrien's had been. Adrien was standing in front of his brother, fists clenched, as though ready to lash out at the slightest instigation. Adrien's brother detected Sophie's re-entrance. Noticing the shift in his brother's stare, Adrien spun around. His gaze immediately softened when he saw her. His anger melted in a flash flood.

Quickly, she looked down, realizing her mistake. "Um…I'm

sorry. But I don't know the code to get into my room." *My room.* She noticed that mistake, as well.

He said something curtly in French to his brother and quickly strode toward her. His hand, once again, found the small of her back, and he guided her toward her room.

Stopping in front of the door, his fingers punched in the code, while his hand remained on her back. It was possessive, almost. The keypad beeped and the door clicked as he pushed it open, holding it for her, waiting for her to move forward. She stepped into the room and turned.

"Sir?" She didn't bother keeping her gaze to the floor.

"Yes?"

"Thank you for stopping him."

He smiled at her, reaching out his hand. She stepped toward it, welcoming his touch, so contrasting to the one she had just received from his brother. His hand cupped the back of her neck, his fingers coming to rest intertwined in her hair. He tugged, causing her chin to lift as he looked into her eyes. Something else tugged; a feeling in her lower belly, long forgotten.

There was the scrutinizing again, the searching. *What was he always looking for?* He let her go then, not abruptly but slowly, his hand grazing down her neck and over her shoulder. "You should get some rest."

He had seen something in her eyes, a flash of emotion as she leaned into his touch. It made his cock twitch. He stepped away from the door, confused by the sudden ache in his balls. Ignoring it, he made his way back to the living room.

"What the fuck was that, Etienne?" His anger returned from its hiatus in her presence.

"I could ask you the same thing," Etienne responded from the couch. He looked tense, one hand still rubbing his reddened neck.

"I asked you to take a look at her, not try to *rape* her," he growled, crossing his arms as he stood before his brother.

"Oh, sit down, Adrien. Calm the fuck down. I was just seeing if I could get anything out of her." Etienne waved him off with a flick of his wrist. Always waving him off, like the older brother he was.

Adrien remained standing. He wouldn't give his brother that satisfaction in his own home.

"She's quite beautiful, though, isn't she?" Etienne's smile returned. "Nice body. You might as well have a little fun with her while you can."

"That's not my idea of fun," he practically spat the words. "I would rather have my women screaming in pleasure, not fear and pain. It doesn't do it for me."

Etienne shook his head, his eyes alight with mirth as he looked at his brother. "How can you expect to train them properly if you don't show them what they're in for?"

Adrien shook his head. The two had always been at odds about the best ways to train women. Etienne was more inclined toward the old methods, never fully adopting Adrien's training program. "It's not about showing them what they're in for. It's about showing them what they can endure and changing their mindset about it. You can't do that when they're terrified that you'll fuck them and then beat them for no reason." Adrien knew it was a moot point, but he said it anyway.

"I disagree."

"And that's why my customers are more satisfied than yours. My girls rarely disobey. And yours? How many have been beaten within an inch of their lives for refusing their new masters? It's disgusting, Etienne."

Etienne leaned forward and rested his elbows on his knees, steepling his fingers. "Always the soft one, Adrien." The smile faded from his lips. "Maybe you should have taken up with the l'iberitage parties, with their women-worshipping bullshit, like mother did. You remind me of her, you know." He leaned back, bringing his church-shaped hands with him.

Adrien looked out the window, ignoring the memory trying to wriggle its way into his consciousness. Bathtubs and blood. "You say that like it's a bad thing."

"It is. Mother was weak." *Was. Mother was. Blood and bathtubs. Mother isn't.*

They let silence brood between them, ignoring the things they never said.

Etienne sighed, resigning, but not apologizing, "She's obedient, that one, I'll give you that. And you're right about her eyes. You have to find a way to put some life back into her, or she'll never sell." He looked at Adrien, still staring out the window. "You'll be fine, though. You're good at your job. You'll figure it out."

Adrien didn't respond to the half-hearted compliment. Instead, "You can see yourself out."

The aching in his groin had returned. Adrien had tried ignoring it, but images of her kept creeping through the barrier he had created in his mind. His brother's words flashing, taunting him. *Maybe what she needs is a good fuck.* Eventually, he gave in, wondering what it would be like to have her lips wrapped around his cock, his tip reaching to the back of her throat. He stroked himself, remembering the soft cries that she had whispered in his dungeon.

"Oh my God," she'd gasped.

It was easy to twist the memory, creating a scene of pleasure rather than pain. Adrien imagined what it would sound like to hear her moan from his thrusting cock. He came hard into his hand.

———

Phase Two

8

---

*S*ophie was in the hallway again. It was such a long hallway, with a door at the end. She reached it, opened it. Her parents' garage welcomed her. She looked toward the car where her mom and dad were standing, waiting to get in.

"Oh, honey! We're so glad you're here! We're going for a drive. Get in!" Her mom turned to her, pulling the passenger-side door open. Her dad smiled from where he was standing next to the driver's-side door. He followed suit, opening his door. Both paused, looking expectantly.

Sophie felt excited. She felt at home. But she also felt dread.

Why was she hesitating? *She hadn't seen Mom and Dad in so long.*

"Go with them." Josh's voice in her ear. She turned to look at him, smiling at her. He stepped around her and headed toward the passenger-side door. He opened it, standing back like a gentleman.

Sophie smiled at him. The dread melted as she moved toward the car, leaning forward to climb in—

She was yanked back suddenly, away from the car. Crying out

in frustration and protest, she felt strong hands wrap around her waist, preventing her from reaching her destination.

"Don't," a voice whispered. She recognized it. A deep, rasping command.

She spun around. What are you doing here, Adrien? *She hadn't spoken aloud, but he indicated he'd heard her by pointing back to the car.*

The car had changed. Mangled and broken. Shards of glass littered the floor, their counterparts still jagged in the window frames. Her parents and Josh were inside the car. Bloodied. Not moving. Sophie opened her mouth to scream and felt the arms embrace her again. They made her feel safe.

She didn't wake up screaming. She woke up perplexed. It was day six of her captivity and her body had already begun betraying her—welcoming his touch, allowing its warmth— and now her dreams followed its disloyalty. She knew she should hate him. She knew she should despise him for what he was, what he was doing. But, as it had always been with the 'shoulds,' she found she just couldn't. Sitting up in bed, she cradled her head in her hands.

She was familiar with it, worked with it, read about it in books. Stockholm Syndrome. *Is that what this is?* The phenomenon that allowed victims to sympathize and empathize with their captors, identifying with their actions, and sometimes even falling in love with them. She knew she wasn't falling in love with him, but was recognizing a propensity to distinguish his positive qualities, despite his negative actions.

But isn't this just who I am? She had always been someone who could easily empathize, always someone who saw goodness in others. It was what had made her adept at her job: seeing it in people when they could barely see it themselves.

It's also what made you blind to your own boyfriend's issues. She couldn't help the jab at herself. She shook her head, dispelling the thought, and swung her legs out of bed.

The clock by her bedside read 8:10 a.m. She had slept longer than usual, and she knew Adrien would come with her breakfast around 8:30. She decided to shower, a luxury she appreciated about her new room. Still, she made it quick, giving herself enough time to towel dry and swipe a brush through her hair before placing herself naked and in kneeling position on the floor.

The door clicked open just as she anticipated. With her eyes to the floor, she recognized his brown leather shoes as he entered and set her tray on the bedside table.

"Get up," he commanded. His voice held nothing of the gentility from the previous evening. Neither did it hold any of the anger toward his brother. It was business-like. Detached.

Sophie stood as she was told, awaiting her next instruction.

"Sit and eat and then get dressed. You have some appointments to attend."

Curiosity burned at the sound of his words. *Some appointments?* She stole a quick glance at him in hopes of gaining more information, when she realized he had turned his back to look out the large window. His left hand crossed below his chest, acting as a table for his right elbow, so his hand could cup his chin while his thumb lazily grazed his bottom lip. Sophie could see his reflection in the window. Her thoughts wandered to the thumb that traced his mouth, as it had done to her own on multiple occasions. She wondered what it would be like to allow her own thumb to plagiarize the movement across his lips.

The sting of disloyalty tugged inside her, wrenching her from her traitorous thoughts. She busied herself with eating instead. His back remained facing her while she ate her breakfast, but she could feel his eyes watching her through the window's reflection. When she finished, she set the plates back down on the tray and cleared her throat.

"Yes?" His voice sounded flat, disinterested. She wondered where the protective and caring man was from the previous night.

"What should I wear?" she asked, unsure of the nature of the appointments.

He turned then, a slight smile warming his features. "Anything you want, *Chevrette.*"

"Well…what kind of appointments are they?"

"You have a spa appointment and then a doctor's appointment."

What?? "What?" She wasn't sure what she had been expecting, but it certainly wasn't that. He smiled, allowing it to reach his eyes this time. He was clearly amused by her blatant astonishment. She couldn't help but notice how breathtaking he looked when he smiled. She couldn't look away.

"Are you staring at me for a reason, *Chevrette?*" he asked. The amusement reached even his voice. Despite the smile that still lingered, she quickly looked away, fearing she had angered him. Or, rather, afraid her actions would cause that smile to disappear.

"I'm sorry," she offered. Then, another surprise. He laughed. It infused the air with a deep, melodious vibration. The sound was beautiful in its own right. Like a long-forgotten but beloved song.

"It's fine, *Chevrette,* you can look at me." Sophie let her gaze return to his face, happy to see the smile hadn't left. He quirked an eyebrow as he said, "You have a waxing appointment. I don't allow razors in the house, and I know how…uncomfortable women can be with their hair. For training, I require a

Brazilian waxing. Anything else is up to you. As for the doctor's appointment, you'll be starting your physical training and I need to make sure you're healthy before we begin. You'll get a complete physical exam, and you'll get to select a birth control method."

Her eyes widened at the mention of birth control. *Does that mean he's going to?*—her body betrayed her again at the thought of him nestled between her legs.

"I guarantee my clients that you are on birth control that is well into your system and working properly upon hand-off. Whatever decisions your new master makes regarding your birth control after hand-off is their business."

Hand-off, she noted, *like she was an object.* Something akin to disappointment rippled through her, and the tingling that had started between her legs immediately dissipated.

"Now," he prompted, "get dressed."

He led her back through the living room. The sun shone brightly through the large two-story windows, lighting the room, making it seem even bigger than it had the previous night. A large potted tree stood in one corner, providing the illusion that the jungle reached indoors, as though the windows didn't exist. They walked across the room, entering the other wing of the house.

It was her first time in this section and Sophie was amazed at its differences. Despite being mirror images of one another, this side of the house was decorated with beautiful artwork. Watercolor paintings and ink drawings lined the walls. She recognized some of them from her time as a fine arts major. Degas's and Monet's hung, offering their impressionist aesthetics. It had been so long since she had stopped to appreciate art, and it took all of her strength not to stop to admire the colors and technical expertise that was splashed and sketched onto each of the canvases.

Adrien stopped in front of a door, grabbing the handle before pausing to open it. Sophie noticed that none of the doors in this wing required codes to open. Strange how one can miss the absence of a sound.

Adrien reached out to capture Sophie's chin, forcing her eyes to meet his. "I've never had a trainee who speaks Spanish before," he began, his voice tinged with an edge of warning. "If you're thinking about asking these women for help, don't. Don't for a minute think you can try to convince them to help you escape. I pay them more in one day than they make in an entire year working in this country. They won't help you. Understand?"

Sophie nodded. She was shocked, really, that she hadn't thought of it herself. *What the hell is wrong with me? I should be thinking of every possible way to get out of here.* She shook her head in an attempt to dispel the 'shoulds.'

"Is that a yes or a no, *Chevrette?* Pick one."

She blinked, not realizing that he was still watching her. "It's a yes. Sorry…I was…just thinking of something else and was shaking my head at that." She wasn't sure why she felt she owed him an explanation.

He opened the door, allowing Sophie to enter first. A long table, covered in cloth, sat in the middle of the room. A petite, middle-aged Hispanic woman stood next to the table smiling, clearly awaiting their arrival.

"Hola, Maria," Adrien addressed the woman in Spanish.

"Hola, Señor. ¿Cómo puedo ayudarle hoy?"

"The usual, Maria. Brazilian. And whatever else she wants."

His reply, again, was in Spanish, the translation occurring instantly in Sophie's mind.

"I have a surprise for you, Josh!" Sophie called out as she entered his third-floor apartment in the Back Bay area of Boston. He was sitting on the couch, watching TV, and eating a bowl of cereal.

"Oh yeah? What is it?" he asked, not looking away from the TV. Sophie stood in front of him, blocking his view. He tilted his head, trying to look around her.

"I think you're really going to like it," she said, hoping to get his attention.

"Uh huh, I'm sure I will. Can you move for a sec?" he asked, clearly disinterested, leaning forward to catch a glimpse of the TV. Sophie sighed, rolling her eyes.

She stepped aside, allowing Josh to continue watching his show. She stood next to the TV, looking between the two. Getting an idea, she turned toward Josh again and began slowly unbuttoning her jeans. Sashaying her hips, she moved her pants downward, exposing the lacy, pink thong she was wearing. Josh's eyes darted to her body.

"What are you doing?" His eyes were gluttonous, moving between the TV and Sophie, unsure which to choose.

"Showing you your present." His eyes returned to her body as she pulled the soft fabric of her panties down slowly. "I got a Brazilian. I thought you'd want to see."

A strong hand cupped the side of Sophie's neck, forcing her head to turn. She blinked the memory away, meeting two steel-gray eyes. Adrien's thumb forcefully rubbed the line of her jaw. To Maria, it probably looked like a caring gesture. To Sophie, it held a warning and a promise.

"What would you like, *Chevrette?*" he asked in English, the anger in his voice unmistakable. She swallowed. Twice.

"Uh…underarms and legs," she replied in English, her brain unable to access her Spanish vocabulary.

His touch turned soft for a moment before he let go of Sophie. He turned and repeated Sophie's wishes in Spanish before leaving the room. Maria looked at Sophie, indicating the table.

"I speak Spanish," Sophie offered in the language. Maria's face registered surprise, and she smiled at Sophie.

"How nice! Where did you learn to speak?" Maria asked, warming the wax.

"I took it in school and then did some immersion in Nicaragua," Sophie replied.

"Well, your Spanish is very good," Maria praised, the smile never leaving her face. "Why don't you take those shorts off? Let's start with the hardest part first." Maria gave a sympathetic smile and Sophie did as she was asked, removing her shorts and panties.

The hot wax burned for a moment, but the cloth strip that Maria placed over the spot quickly absorbed the heat.

"Ready?" Maria asked. Sophie nodded, bracing herself for the ripping pain. And when it came, Sophie gasped. The second strip was no better, eliciting a small yelp from Sophie. They continued in this manner, the pain excruciating with every pull.

She had been forced into it again, the experience of physical pain. Rather than hating it, this time, she marveled in it. She had forgotten what feeling had felt like. It was horrible, yet wonderful at the same time.

And then, she couldn't contain it.

Her laughter bubbled, spilling over. The pain was so intense, all she could do was laugh. It amazed her. And it startled Maria.

"I've heard a lot of screaming and cursing in my job but never laughter!" Maria shook her head, now laughing herself. The two couldn't help themselves. After Maria had finished her job, the two continued to laugh and talk.

"Thank you, Maria. That was the most fun I've ever had getting waxed." Sophie smiled genuinely at Maria.

"No problem, dear. That was the most fun I've ever had giving a waxing. Take care," she replied, beginning the cleanup.

Sophie headed toward the door and opened it, still smiling. Her smile vanished at the sight of Adrien leaning against the opposite wall, his hands in his jeans pockets. His brow was furrowed, giving Sophie the impression that he was puzzled. Sophie quickly looked toward the ground, feeling oddly ashamed that she had been caught smiling.

"What was so funny?" he asked.

She wondered if maybe she was in trouble for being happy. *Happy. Is that what this feeling is?*

"*Chevrette?*" he prompted.

"I forgot how much it hurts." She glanced back up, wondering if he would accept her answer or demand more. He looked confused, trying to figure out what she meant.

"Oh," was all he said. He cleared his throat, moving away from the wall. "Come on, the doctor is here." He placed his hand on the small of her back, guiding her down the hallway and into yet another room.

God, how big is this place? Sophie thought.

The room was set up like a typical physician's office, with a table in the center of the room. Cabinets lined one of the walls, and a desk with a computer sat next to them. There was a sink at the other end of the room, and Sophie noticed a table lined with jars of cotton balls and packets of antiseptic wipes. Sophie suddenly felt she had been transported back to her own doctor at home.

"Good morning," a young Hispanic woman greeted them, her English accented slightly. She smiled at Sophie. "Why don't you take a seat here?" she suggested, indicating the table. The woman walked toward the desk and grabbed what appeared to be a chart. As she climbed on the table, Sophie wondered if Adrien kept medical records of all his trainees, or if this was just for show.

"I'll be gathering some background history today, and then we'll make sure you're nice and healthy before doing your pap smear and getting you set up with birth control," the doctor informed Sophie.

Sophie's eyes wandered toward Adrien, who had taken a seat in one of the chairs by the door. He noticed her looking at him, and he returned a look that clearly said, "*What?*"

"Are you staying?" Sophie whispered, knowing she hadn't asked permission to speak. The thought of him being present for such an intimate appointment left her feeling uneasy.

Adrien cocked his head as though considering her question. "Would it make you feel more comfortable if I left?" He kept his voice low, as though he didn't want their conversation to be overheard by the third person in the room. Sophie nodded, hoping that he would acquiesce the pleading in her eyes.

Adrien was silent for a moment, his lips pressed together. Then, he abruptly stood and exited the room, shutting the door emphatically behind him.

"Es la primera vez," the doctor mumbled in Spanish, looking perplexed. *That's a first.*

"¿Qué es?" Sophie wanted to know.

Surprise registered on the doctor's face, having not expected Sophie to understand her.

"You speak Spanish?" she asked. Sophie nodded. "That's great, where did you learn?"

Sophie responded, amused and intrigued by the doctor's avoidance.

"She chose a hormone-based IUD, sir, which means she's going to need to take it easy for the rest of the day. She may need some Tylenol or a heated pad to help with the discomfort. I've gone over everything with her, so she should be all set," the doctor explained after Adrien returned.

Sophie was lying back on the table, feeling a bit woozy after getting the IUD inserted. Adrien stood next to the table, towering over her. She sensed slight irritation from Adrien at the doctor's insinuation that Sophie needed to rest for the remainder of the day. If he was irritated, though, he didn't allow it to linger.

"Are you okay to walk?" he asked gently, looking down at her. She nodded, bringing herself to her elbows. She winced as a painful cramp shot through her lower belly and down her legs. The feeling brought a wave of dizziness and Sophie's elbows no longer provided her the strength to continue her upward climb. Falling back, a strong hand caught her, gently helping her lay back down.

"Is this normal?" Adrien's voice, directed at the doctor, was laced with anger.

"Yes, sir, I assure you it is. She should be fine by tomorrow. Here, I'll give her some Tylenol now to help with the pain." The woman seemed flustered, afraid of Adrien's quick shift in mood. She busied herself with locating the Tylenol and a cup of water for Sophie, who took it, grateful for the promise of pain relief.

"Put your arm around my shoulders." Adrien leaned over her, bringing his hand behind her back and cradling the crook of her knees with his other arm.

"It's okay, I can walk," she insisted.

His face turned to hers, blue-gray eyes meeting briefly with green, before he shifted to whisper in her ear, "I expect obedience, *Chevrette*. Don't make me cause you more pain than you're already in." And with that, he carried her from the room.

———

The laughter. *Her* laughter.

It had caught him off-guard, hearing it through the doorway. His trainees had never laughed before. He'd never given them a reason to. The sound of it astonished him. He tried to ignore the way it rang in his ears. He tried to ignore the curiosity about what she looked like when she made that sound. He tried to ignore the nagging desire to witness it.

The thoughts tied his stomach in knots.

———

9

He didn't carry her back to her room as she expected. Instead, Adrien continued down the hallway, stopping in front of another door, and setting Sophie carefully on her feet. With her arms still wrapped around his broad shoulders and his hands on her waist holding her up, he asked, "Can you stand?" She nodded and with one arm still around her, he opened the door.

Sophie peered in, astounded at the sight. Rows and rows of books filled shelves that lined each of the walls. The center of the room held a couch and a large comfy-looking armchair with tables flanking either side.

A smile crept over her lips. She loved books. They had been her solace for the past thirteen months, the only place, aside from her memories, where she could escape. They offered something her memories couldn't. A reprieve from her own life.

She turned to Adrien, her smile widening. She felt like a kid at the threshold of a candy store. "May I?"

He was studying her again, his eyes watching her every

movement. His lips quirked into a smile before responding, "Of course."

Her pain forgotten, she practically ran into the room, unsure of where to start.

"The English books are along that wall. Spanish are over there," he offered. Sophie turned to him, curious.

"What about those two walls?"

"French," Adrien said, pointing, "and German."

"You speak German, too?"

He nodded.

This new information surprised her, her curiosity about his life piqued once again. "Where did you learn all those languages?"

"School." His response had a hint of sarcasm, as his mouth turned up in a smirk.

She rolled her eyes, smiling at his insolence. She regretted the action instantly.

"Did you just roll your eyes at me, *Chevrette?*" His voice cut through her. He marched toward her, causing her to back up until she was against the side of the couch. She couldn't move any farther from him without falling over the armrest.

"Tell me, *Chevrette,* is that respectful behavior?" The smell of ginger and lemongrass invaded her senses. Adrien stood over her, their bodies so close she could feel his heat warming her skin. His jaw was set in a tight line as he forced her chin up with the crook of his finger to glare into her eyes.

Sophie shook her head slightly, wishing she could rewind time. "I'm sorry. I…I forgot where I was. I forgot who I was with."

He stepped back and blinked. If she hadn't known better, she would have thought she had just slapped him. Sophie immediately felt like apologizing again.

Adrien closed his eyes with a sigh, running his hand across his forehead, stopping to massage one of his temples. She could tell he was trying to reign in some emotion. When his eyes snapped open, he had done just that, his eyes void of feeling.

"Choose a book before I change my mind."

It appeared that Adrien had his own cocoon, one that allowed him full reprieve. Sophie found that she was jealous.

Sophie lay on a lounge chair, book in hand, on the lower deck of the house. Adrien had hastily retrieved a bathing suit in her closet and allowed her to change, muttering to himself in French as he did so. She guessed he was not too happy about her day of rest. She, however, felt almost giddy.

She began the first chapter, only vaguely noticing Adrien's absence on the deck. Turning the page, she was surprised that he trusted her so close to the pool without his supervision. Or, perhaps he *was* monitoring her and she just didn't realize.

She heard the large glass door slide open, her eyes following the direction of the noise. Adrien had returned, having changed into a pair of black bathing suit board shorts and a gray t-shirt. He held towels in his hand and a bottle of sunblock. He walked toward her, Sophie noticing his lean muscles accentuated by his snug-fitting t-shirt. She was intrigued by the masculinity of his stance, his long muscled legs carrying him with an air of confidence. He towered above her chair and she squinted up at him, her hand shielding her eyes.

"Here," he said, offering her a pair of sunglasses. She put them on, thankful for the kind gesture. She smiled at him, hoping he sensed her gratefulness. If he did, he didn't seem to notice. Or, perhaps, didn't care.

"Here," he said again, this time handing her the bottle of sunblock.

"Thank you," she said softly, forgoing the smile this time. She uncapped the bottle, pouring a long line of the cream down one leg and then the other, before gently rubbing it in. Adrien sat in the lounge chair beside her and, out of the corner of her eye, she could see him watching her. Sophie continued applying the lotion to other parts of her body, his hungry gaze following her hands. She flushed, realizing that she was inadvertently giving him a show. Recapping the bottle, she decided she'd applied enough sunblock for now.

"Here, you need to do your back or your skin won't heal properly. Let me," Adrien said, grabbing the lotion from where it lay by Sophie's thigh. She nodded, having almost forgotten the flogging that had occurred the other night. Aside from a slight tightness where the skin was healing, there was no longer any pain.

He squeezed a good amount in one hand, recapping the bottle and placing it next to him. Angling himself behind her on his chair, she scooted back toward him, pulling her hair to the side. His hands caressed her upper back, their warmth sending a buzz of excitement through her body. He gently covered her healing skin with the lotion, rubbing slow circles with his thumbs. He moved down her back to where her skin was smooth, free from the scars of punishment. His hands continued rubbing, his thumbs massaging harder. He paused to retrieve more lotion and then continued at her neck. Sophie's head dropped, allowing his thumbs to knead the base of her neck, his hands laying firmly on her shoulders.

God, his hands feel so good. She let out a contented sigh.

"Does that feel good, *Chevrette?*" His voice was but a whisper, his breath tickling her earlobe. Her eyes snapped open at his words, not realizing they had even closed. It did feel good, but did she want to admit it?

"Relax," he instructed, squeezing her shoulders. She had tensed at his question and at the realization that she had permitted herself a moment of contentment. It was something she had been fighting to do for the past thirteen months—to feel anything aside from devastation or apathy, and break away from the grief-induced numbness. But now that she felt pleasure, she was confused by it. *Do I even want to feel anything now?* The question haunted her. A week ago, she would have been overjoyed by this sudden re-emergence of emotion. *But now?*

She felt guilty. Anxious. At that moment, Sophie felt Megan's absence. Her best friend wasn't able to pull her from her cocoon and, despite Sophie's desire to break down her own walls, she just couldn't. Yet, one week with this stranger and those same walls were crumbling without her even trying, even wanting it. And what would Josh think of her? Melting into the touch of a man she didn't even know. A man who had *kidnapped* her. The thought of Josh only caused the familiar anxiety and guilt to grow. And then, she was no longer there.

It was their first anniversary together and Sophie was getting ready in the apartment she shared with Megan in Beacon Hill. She had picked out a classic little black dress for the occasion, per Josh's instruction to dress nicely. He hadn't told her anything else about the evening, and the anticipation fluttered in Sophie's stomach.

She finished blow-drying her long brown waves, and bobby pinned a few strands to keep them from falling into her eyes. Next, she worked on her makeup, making sure to accentuate her eyes in a subtle but sexy way. She never loved wearing a ton of makeup, but just a little bit brought out her high cheekbones and wide green eyes.

When she finished, she slipped into her dress and located the black pumps in her overstuffed closet.

"Damn, girl. You look hot." Megan leaned against Sophie's doorframe, arms crossed and a huge grin on her face. Sophie turned, doing a little spin for her friend.

"Not bad, right?" Sophie looked down, assessing herself. She brought her hands to her breasts, hiking them up in her bra for good measure, which provoked a laugh from Megan.

"Josh will appreciate that extra primping, I'm sure. Speaking of which…something just got delivered for you." Megan wiggled her eyebrows at Sophie.

"Seriously? What is it?" Sophie couldn't hide her excitement. Without waiting for Megan's answer, she scooted past her friend. As she entered the kitchen, she detected the delicate scent of peonies. A large bouquet of light pink flowers stood in a clear glass vase on their kitchen table. Sophie let out a squeal, rushing to read the card that poked through the fluffy petals.

Opening it, she began reading:

"Sophie—I know it's only been a year, but it feels like I've known you my entire 22 years of life. I'm sending you a peony (your favorite, I know!) for each of those 22 years, and one more to honor this upcoming year together. And to celebrate, I wanted to get you something special for us to enjoy together. We have reservations for a couple's massage tomorrow morning, so get ready to be relaxed. I can't wait to see you tonight. XO"

The bright sunlight gently brought Sophie back from her spell, causing her to squint so her pupils could adjust. Blinking, she realized she was no longer wearing the sunglasses Adrien had given her and his hands were no longer moving across her back. In fact, he was no longer sitting on the chair behind her. Instead, he was sitting on her lounge chair, eyes fixed on hers.

She drew in a sharp breath, remembering his earlier warnings about his impatience with her zoning spells. She stole a quick look at his face before lowering her eyes to her lap. Funny, he didn't seem angry. His eyes, at least, didn't suggest he had lost patience with her as he had before.

He lifted her chin, forcing her eyes back to his. "Where do you go?" he breathed, pure curiosity carrying the words.

She took a deep breath as she tried to explain. It had always been difficult. The truth seemed so far-fetched, even to Sophie. "I just…I get these memories and I just kind of zone out. I can't help it and I can't seem to find a way to stop them. It just happens."

He pursed his lips, squinting. He appeared to be thinking, absorbing the information. "You've tried stopping it?"

She nodded.

"Why?"

His question surprised her. She had never been asked before. Then again, most people she told about her zoning spells understood what she had been through. She realized then, that Adrien was not one of those people.

"Um…it's complicated." She shifted uncomfortably, unsure of how much to share. His eyes flickered with amusement.

"I can do complicated, *Chevrette*. Tell me."

She sighed, not wanting to pour her heart out to this stranger, but also knowing better than to disobey. So, she settled. "I've tried to stop it because I don't like it. It keeps happening—it's been happening for over a year now—and I can't control it. And not being in control of your memories is just…it stops me from living my life. It stops me from being happy."

Had she said that out loud? It may have been the first time she admitted that to someone other than herself.

But she *had* said it aloud. And her words, she noticed, seemed to have an impact on Adrien. He stared at her with pursed lips, contemplating. It was a look similar to the appraisal he had given her when they first met in the warehouse.

And, as though something had clicked into place, Adrien nodded.

Later that evening, Adrien poured himself a scotch from the bar in his home office. Gazing out of the expansive window at the darkening evening sky, he took a sip of the amber liquor. It burned his throat on the way down, settling like embers beneath his ribs.

He had been wrong about her. She hadn't been dissociating the way his other trainees had. He recognized it now. The telltale signs of flashbacks.

He took another swig of his scotch, his mind racing with the new discovery. He tapped his glass with his forefinger, his nail making a *tink tink* sound against the cold tumbler. His gaze swept the perimeter of the forest, though his thoughts blocked his eyes from taking in the view.

He knew how to do it, how to take away the unpredictability of her flashbacks. It would require the employment of a concept he usually reserved for Phase Three of his training: cognitive restructuring. Re-associating the bad with the good. It would be simple, really. Find her trigger and provide a different association. Replace the old memory with a new, positive one. It would be simple. Easy, even. But it would require something of him that he had never done before with any of his other trainees. It would require him to connect with her.

He knew he had to do it. It was the answer he had been

looking for. But he couldn't shake the feeling that he was about to make a mistake. He downed the last of his scotch.

———————————————————————

10

The scream ripped through her, clawing at her throat. She felt it before she heard it. But it was the sound that woke Sophie from her nightmare. And even though she had woken, she continued to scream until her sobs broke through, the tears streaming down her face. Her t-shirt was drenched in sweat, causing a chill to creep across her skin.

She felt his hands on her before she realized he had entered the room. They held her shoulders, moving down her arms to softly search her wrists, then back up again. His thumb wiped away the salted tears that lingered on Sophie's cheeks and smoothed her hair from her face. His voice was equally soothing.

"What is it? What happened?"

Sophie squeezed her eyes shut in an attempt to steady her heart rate, taking slow deep breaths.

"*Chevrette,* talk to me. Are you okay? Are you hurt?" Adrien forced her chin up, bending his head close to hers to look into her eyes. Worry creased his forehead, knitting his brows.

A pang of guilt. It was reminiscent of the way she felt back home whenever she caused Megan to worry about her. Even here, she couldn't escape the guilt.

"I'm sorry. I'm fine." She drew in a shaky breath. His hands had returned to her shoulders, holding her steady and soothing her simultaneously. "I get nightmares sometimes. It's…nothing, really. I'm sorry if I woke you up." She glanced at the clock, realizing she had no idea what time it was.

2:37 a.m.

"I was awake," he answered.

"Oh." *Of course he was. That's how he got in here so quickly.*

Adrien's hands left her shoulders to run through his unruly hair. He let out a sigh, staring at her, the presence of worry still lingering on his dark features. Sophie watched him carefully, detecting thoughts flickering across his eyes as he apparently warred with himself. She noticed the moment he made his decision. His eyes became clear and his confidence returned.

"Come with me." He held his hand out and she took it, placing her small hand within his. He glanced at their hands and a small smile crept over his lips. She wondered if he marveled at her lack of hesitation to take his hand.

Is he smiling because he thinks I'm obeying? Or is he smiling because he knows I'm coming of my own free will? Is there even a difference now? These thoughts accompanied her as Adrien led her from her room and down the hall. They stopped at the door next to hers, at the far end of the hallway, a good distance from her own. This door lacked the combination pad for entry. Adrien opened the door, Sophie's hand still in his grasp.

She looked around the room in awe. It was another bedroom, about twice the size of hers. A large modern-looking bedframe sat facing the windows that served as the opposite wall.

Adrien tugged her hand, reminding her that she was not on

a tour. He was bringing her toward the window which, as she neared, she realized was a sliding glass door that led out to one of the decks. He slid the door open with his free hand, pulling her toward the opening.

A railing ran the length of the deck and there were two wooden lounge chairs facing the jungle. In between the chairs sat a short table on which Sophie could see an ashtray and a Zippo lighter.

She stepped out into the night air, allowing its coolness to soothe the residual horrors from her nightmare. She stepped toward the railing, resting her weight on its strength, allowing something else to provide support. She inhaled deeply, looking up at the clearing above the trees. She was surprised to find a starless night, the sky blanketed by a thick layer of clouds.

"Do you want to sit?" It was the first time he had asked her rather than command her. Leaning her back on the railing, she turned to face him. He looked so different, standing there in that moment, his hands tucked into his jeans pockets. There was a vulnerability palpable in the air around him. It didn't quite touch him, but it was present. She wondered if this was usually who he was; if the confidence and dominance was a pretense, or if this novelty was just a momentary fluke.

She moved toward one of the chairs and sat, and he mimicked her movement in the other chair. He faced the table between the two of them, picking something up from the ashtray. She hadn't noticed anything aside from the ashtray and the lighter before, but quickly recognized a small joint that Adrien now put to his lips, cupping his hands to block the breeze and igniting the lighter. She watched as he inhaled, taking the joint from his mouth. He held his breath, and she found herself holding hers, too.

He exhaled slowly, the smoke thick and sweet in the crisp

night air. He leaned forward with his hand outstretched, offering the joint to Sophie. She hesitated.

"It will help with the nightmares."

She took the joint from his hand, pinching the rolled paper with her thumb and forefinger. She looked at it, skeptical of its power to help her.

"It's just marijuana, right?" she asked, unsure if she should trust what Adrien offered. She glanced up to find him smirking at her.

"What else would it be?"

Not the answer she was hoping for. It didn't ease her concerns in the slightest. She took a deep breath, knowing what she was about to say was a bit bold, but hoped he would hear reason. "Well, considering you drugged me to bring me here…"

She trailed off as Adrien burst into laughter. She hadn't meant it to be funny, but the sound was contagious. An involuntary smile curled at the corners of her mouth.

"Touché, *Chevrette*. No, there's nothing else in it. It's an indica, so it will help you calm down and help you sleep. That's all." Though he was no longer laughing, the amusement hadn't yet left his face. The explanation helped to ease her worries, and she gladly accepted the medicine.

She inhaled deeply, the harsh burn making her cough as she held the smoke in her lungs. Quickly, she exhaled and handed the joint back to Adrien. He took another hit as she continued her coughing fit.

"So, I take it you're not a regular smoker?" The amusement was still present in his voice.

Sophie cleared her throat, the tingling in her lungs subsiding. "That obvious, huh?"

Adrien broke into a full grin then, handing her back the joint. "You'll only need another hit or two and you should be good."

"Okay." She inhaled again, less ravenously. The hit didn't burn the back of her throat this time, and she was able to exhale without coughing. She handed the joint back to Adrien. Leaning back in her chair she said, "Thank you, by the way." She looked at him out of the corner of her eye. He, too, had leaned back in his chair, bringing his feet one on top of the other as he smoked.

"For what, *Chevrette?*"

"For this." She wasn't quite sure what *this* was.

They were silent for a moment as the high began to creep into Sophie's bloodstream. She could feel the tingling in her lungs begin to seep through her veins. Her body felt light and heavy at the same time, and her senses felt heightened. She stroked the wood of the chair with her finger, lavishing in its roughness against her skin. She closed her eyes, taking deep breaths. The night air felt cool in her airways, warming as it entered her lungs. She imagined the little air particles being sorted into the usable parts and the waste; the precious oxygen sent to her bloodstream while the rest was discarded into the night air. Maybe she was no different, a mirror of this process. Perhaps there was some salvageable part of her that just needed to be sorted. Perhaps Adrien had already begun the sorting...

She laughed at the absurdity of it—a giggle forced out by a gust of oxygen to her lungs, or maybe the release of unsalvageable air into the night.

So, this is what it's like to be high. She reveled in the thought, wide-eyed.

"I was wondering if I would hear that sound again," Adrien's voice cut through her thoughts. She turned to him, time creeping by as her eyes re-focused.

"I'm high." Had she stated the obvious?

He grinned. "I know." Adrien stubbed the rest of the roach

out and leaned forward in his chair, bringing his elbows to rest on his knees. He peered at her, the smile still playing at the corners of his lips. "You're cute when you're high."

Adrien's smile faded as his eyes rested on her lips, then roamed from her face down her body. She watched as they turned dark when they met the curves of her breasts. Lust flickered there and Sophie's breath hitched, her nipples hardening as her own desire ignited. She kept her eyes locked on his as recognition flashed across his features. His eyes darted back to hers, then quickly back to her nipples. She allowed her own eyes to move over him, noticing the bulge in his pants despite his attempt to hide it.

She let her mind wander, aided by the pot. She imagined the feel of his mouth on her nipples, capturing them, sucking them. The heat of his tongue licking, trailing down her stomach toward a place more sensitive. The warmth of his mouth, the sensation of his tongue dipping into her and then swirling around her bundle of nerves. Her eyes closed and her breath became shallow at the fantasy. She could feel the tightening of her clit, begging for release. It had been so long since she had come. Just the thought of being touched again sent waves of heat through her, creating dampness between her thighs. She caught herself before the moan escaped her throat, her eyes snapping open at the realization of her own vulnerability, not quite believing that she had gotten so lost in her own desire.

Desire. It was something she hadn't experienced since Josh. Guilt washed over her at the thought of him, followed by shame. No longer protected by her cocoon, Sophie felt the weight of her emotions bearing down.

How could I do this to Josh? How could I betray him like this? Fantasizing and getting wet over some man who plans on selling me into a life of sex. What the fuck is wrong with me?

It left her feeling exposed in front of this stranger. She looked at Adrien, hoping he hadn't realized how caught up she had gotten in her own thoughts. Hoping, really, that he couldn't read her mind.

He had certainly noticed Sophie's sudden shift in mood. The lust she saw only moments before was replaced by curiosity.

What just happened? She could read it in his eyes, the way he squinted at her, his brow furrowed in the same way it had when he was concerned about her. She shifted uncomfortably in her chair, at the unspoken question in his eyes, hoping he didn't voice it. As if taking the hint, Adrien blinked a few times, his emotions suddenly inscrutable. Silently, she thanked him.

A light flickered in the distance, bringing Sophie's attention to the sky. A low rumble of thunder followed a moment later. Sophie inhaled, recognizing the scent of air heavy with unfallen rain that always seemed to hover before a storm.

"I love thunderstorms." The words came quietly from her lips, the insecurity from the previous moment still lingering. She wanted nothing to do with it.

"Why is that?" He allowed her to steer away from their intimate moment, and she was grateful for his momentary attunement to her.

"I like the way you can't escape it. It's something that bombards all of your senses. The way it smells right before it rains. The way the lightning looks jetting across the sky. The sound of thunder, and the way you can feel the storm in your chest when it's really close."

"That's not all of your senses. What about taste?" he asked, both sets of eyes trained to the sky.

She smiled. "Haven't you ever caught a raindrop on your tongue?"

He turned to her, his answer a simple, "No." The admission hung in the air, alongside the pre-storm scent.

Isn't catching raindrops and snowflakes a staple of a typical childhood?

Adrien was not someone who had experienced a typical childhood. She sensed this even before the conscious thought crossed her mind. Sophie was afraid to look at him, afraid to see the sadness in his eyes. Afraid that maybe he would see the sadness she felt for him in hers.

The drops started then, fat and warm, colliding against their skin with a lazy ease. Sophie smiled and said, "It's pretty simple. All you do is—" tipping her head back and sticking her tongue out to catch the drops. She looked to him and watched as another smile spread across his face. He mimicked her, tipping his head back and opening his mouth to let the drops splatter on his tongue. He squeezed his eyes shut, like the child he never got to be.

The sight made her stomach do a flip.

She heard the rain against the treetops in the forest as it began to fall harder. She squealed as the torrents of droplets engulfed them in sheets of water. She heard his laugh above the roar of the rain while she swiftly scrambled to the sliding glass door, Adrien quick on her heels.

She burst into the bedroom, still laughing as she watched Adrien scurry in behind her and shut the door. Sophie's t-shirt and shorts were drenched, her nipples hard now for a different reason. Her wet hair was plastered against her, pieces of it sticking to her forehead and cheeks. Adrien turned from the door, his own clothing soaked and his hair flopping in his eyes. He took his hands and ran them through his wet hair, sending a spray of droplets in Sophie's direction as he flipped his hair back into its usual unruly place.

He stepped toward her then, reaching out to peel a wet piece of hair from her face and move it behind her ear. The gentleness of his touch sent a shiver through her, and earlier flickers of desire returned. She recognized the look of lust in his hooded eyes as he took another step toward her. Taking a step back, her shoulders met the wall behind her. He was in front of her still, his palms now resting flat against the wall on either side of her shoulders. He didn't allow their bodies to touch, but his proximity made her squirm with anticipation. Adrien towered over her and brought his face down to hers, running his nose along her cheek and his lips lightly over her jawline.

"Is this what you wanted, *Chevrette?*" His voice was gruff, strangled, as though he were holding himself back. She swallowed.

Is it? She wasn't sure. Her body did, she knew that. But the rest of her? She needed time to figure it out.

"Why do you call me that?" she stalled.

He inhaled, pulling away slightly. "*Chevrette?*" He paused before continuing, "Because you remind me of one."

"Of one?" She remembered what his brother had said about calling her dear. *Or was it—?* "A deer? Like, what people hunt?"

He pulled away farther, studying her. Slowly, he nodded, "Yes, I suppose some do."

She bristled at the information. "Is that why I remind you of one? Because you're hunting me?"

Adrien let one hand drop from the wall, pulling himself away from her. "No. You remind me of a deer because you don't seem to know the danger that's staring you in the face." He said it pointedly, like she should take the hint. She did.

Her stomach dropped and she pressed herself against the wall, wanting space. Needing to get away from him. She hadn't wanted to believe that he was dangerous, hadn't wanted to be afraid of him. But Adrien was trying to warn her. Was she so stupid as not to heed his warning? Sudden fear clenched in her chest.

Again, he noticed the change in her demeanor. He smiled the smile he reserved for when he didn't really mean it. She recognized it by how it never reached his eyes.

"Ah, there it is," he said. He moved away from her completely, straightening his back as he continued, "I think it's time you went back to your room."

Adrien turned the cold-water faucet to the off position. He hadn't bothered to turn on the hot water, hoping the freezing droplets would wash away the remnants of the night. He hadn't been thinking clearly. He had let himself get carried away by something he hadn't experienced in a while: kindness. He wished he could expunge the memory, shake off the way it felt against his hard exterior. He hated it. It made him do stupid things.

He had almost broken a rule tonight. He had almost kissed her. And he had wanted it, wanted to push her against the wall, to let his teeth nibble her lip, his tongue to move against hers. He wanted to feel how wet he knew she was, to let his fingers dip inside her, stroke her until she came, her hips bucking against him.

He had already broken some of the rules he had set for himself and his trainees. He knew that. He could acknowledge that he would not normally interact with a trainee the way he had with her. He would not normally feed a trainee or monitor her while she bathed. He would normally have punished her for some of the rules she had been forgetting to follow. The difference was that he had broken those rules knowing it was for the benefit of her training. Because she needed to be trained differently, needed the extra monitoring.

This, though. What happened tonight was different. He knew that, too.

He wrapped the towel around his waist and stepped back into his bedroom. The rain was slowing now, the storm on its way out. Adrien looked at the clock.

5:47 a.m. Another sleepless night. It was something he was used to, his body seemingly acclimated to the lack of sleep he regularly experienced. It hardly bothered him anymore. What bothered him was the boredom that came in the middle of the night. It left too much time for thinking. And now…

He needed to get his mind off of her, craved a reprieve.

He turned on the TV, not bothering to change the channel, just seeking the background noise to clear his mind. He stepped toward the mini-bar, running parallel to his headboard on the opposite wall, and grabbed a glass from the collection on the shelf in one hand and the bottle of scotch in his other. He poured himself a tall drink, savoring the flavor as it tingled on its way down, heating him after his cold shower. The sounds from the TV slowly crept into his awareness.

"…her friend, Megan McDonald, is asking that anyone with information on the whereabouts of Sophie Kingston come forward. Sophie and Megan were abducted outside of their vacation resort in Costa Rica approximately one week ago. Megan was returned safely, but the two were separated after their kidnapping, and Sophie still remains missing."

Adrien's head snapped toward the TV. "Fuck." The word came out a quick staccato, followed by another, "Fuck! *Fuck!*"

Adrien hurled his drink against the window, the liquor splattering a syrupy trail against the glass as the tumbler shattered into pieces. Despite his outburst, and despite not wanting to, Adrien kept his eyes plastered on the television and the picture of her on the screen. Her hair was shorter, she was a bit heavier, healthier, no signs of the weariness that was ever present on her face. But there was no mistaking his *Chevrette*. She was laughing in the picture, her eyes alight with some secret shared between her and someone else. She wasn't looking directly at the lens, but at someone behind the camera. The shot was candid. Perhaps she didn't know her happiness was being recorded for others to witness.

"Sophie Kingston, 25, lost both of her parents in a car accident when she was just nineteen years old. A resident of Boston, Massachusetts, Sophie worked as a mental health counselor and periodically volunteered at an orphanage in Nicaragua. Sophie's next of kin have declined to publicly comment about her disappearance, but have said that they hope for the best. Sophie's friend Megan is pleading for her safety."

Adrien's heart pounded in his chest. It wasn't the fact that they were looking for her. Of course someone would be looking for her. If he were afraid of that, he wouldn't be in this business at all. It was the fact that now he knew. He knew where she was from, knew what she did, knew about her life. And he knew her name.

Sophie.

And the worst part? He knew what she looked like when she was truly happy.

———————————

II

He had been right about the marijuana. Sophie awoke from a dreamless sleep, thankful for the few good hours of rest. She felt surprisingly rejuvenated given the late night. She half-expected to be hung over from smoking, not quite sure of the difference between falling asleep high and falling asleep drunk. She rolled over to look at the clock.

10:30 a.m.

Sophie bolted up in bed, looking around the room for signs that Adrien had come at his usual time. She didn't see anything to indicate that he had been there, and she wondered if something was wrong. She kicked her legs out of bed, throwing off her sheet. When she returned to her room last night she had changed out of her wet clothing and into a dry pair of panties and a sports bra that had been tucked away in the closet. She collapsed into bed, too tired to process the strange events of her late night with Adrien.

Now awake, the thoughts barraged her as she stared at the woman brushing her teeth in the bathroom mirror. She knew her emotions had been heightened from the high of the previous night. There was no other way to explain the poignant flood that had occurred. She had been jolted awake by another terrifying dream, only to feel calm and at peace upon Adrien's presence. She went from feeling lustful and wanton to guilty and shameful, only to return to a state of terror again in just an hour or two. For someone who hadn't felt that many emotions in over a year, it was exhausting to encounter all of them in such a short amount of time. And then there was the nagging question: *were any of the emotions actually warranted?*

She was concerned about the unease she had felt around him at the very end of the night. She had many reasons to believe he was as dangerous as he said he was, but also had reason to believe that he had a propensity for kindness. Was the fear just brought on by the weed? Or was it possible that the marijuana was helping her think more rationally?

No. That couldn't be it. She was trained to read people, and she was skilled at recognizing what made people who they truly were. If Adrien were as wicked as he alluded to, she would know it. She would feel it.

Or not. Her mind flitted to thoughts of Josh. She hadn't known what was going on with him. Hadn't seen or felt the demons that Josh was battling. *But wasn't this different?* This wasn't about hidden demons. Sophie knew that Adrien had hidden demons, she wasn't blind. This was about what was at his core. *Was he actually someone to be afraid of?*

The click of the bedroom door brought her from her thoughts. She hadn't closed the bathroom door, and Adrien appeared in her line of sight, placing her customary tray of food on the bedside table. He approached the bathroom, propping his lean, muscular body against the doorframe.

Sophie quickly remembered herself, averting her eyes to the ground. She finished rinsing her toothbrush before assuming her kneeling position.

"It's fine, don't bother. Get up." His words were out, stopping her mid-crouch. She quickly stood up and waited for her next direction.

"Did you get any sleep last night?" he asked, his genuineness surprising her. She briefly glanced up to see if his demeanor matched his tone. Or maybe she was just trying to see through to his very core.

He stood with his arms crossed as he leaned his shoulder against the doorframe. His face was blank, his emotions masked by some unforeseen will to remain passive.

Clearing her throat, she answered, "Yes. Thank you. Did you?"

Adrien straightened, no longer leaning on the doorframe. "Did I what?"

"Get any sleep?" she clarified. "You said you were awake when you came in to get me last night. Were you able to get any sleep?"

She looked at him, not really needing an answer. She could tell he was exhausted by the dark circles under his eyes, surprised she hadn't noticed them before. She immediately felt bad for taking part in his lack of sleep.

"That's not really any of your concern, *Chevrette,*" he snapped. Her cheeks burned at his reprimand. She wasn't used to feeling ashamed for her concern over the wellbeing of another. He was right, in a way. This really wasn't the place for it.

"Eat your breakfast. You're going to need your energy today."

"Yes, Sir," she whispered as he stepped aside, allowing her to move past him to the food. Wordlessly, she ate the pancakes and fruit salad while he watched. When she was finished, he went into the closet and pulled out running shorts, socks, and a tank top.

"Put these on."

❧

He took her to yet another unexplored portion of the house, where the gym was situated. The room boasted several treadmills, an elliptical, a Stairmaster, weight machines, and free weights. Adrien handed her a pair of shoes—the first she had seen since her abduction—from a closet near the entrance of the room. As she put the shoes on, Sophie continued to survey the room, its length running a long stretch, lined with machines. It held everything her own gym had, except Adrien's included top-of-the-line equipment and a beautiful view compared to the dank, unwelcoming hangar she was used to doing her workouts in.

"You should think about losing some weight. You're starting to get a muffin top," Josh said as they lay in bed together. They were naked, having just finished making love, and his hands were caressing her back, moving toward her hips. He grabbed the skin at her waist between his thumb and forefinger. "You could stand to lose a few pounds."

She had signed up for the gym as soon as she was in front of the computer.

The tug of her ponytail brought Sophie back. Her hair was wound tightly around Adrien's hand, and he was using it to tip her head back, towering over her.

"Where were you just then, *Chevrette?*" His voice was low, laced with warning.

"I...I'm sorry. I'll try not to let it happen again."

His mouth twitched. "I appreciate your thoughtfulness, but

that's not what I asked you." Sarcasm dripped from his words, almost visible. "I want you to tell me about where you were. About that memory."

She blinked. *Wait, what?*

He raised an eyebrow, expectantly, his hand still grasped tightly to her ponytail, a reminder of his strength. He wasn't hurting her, but he could. It was a subtle message communicating dominance. She took a deep breath before answering.

"It was just a memory about my gym at home."

"What about it?" His reply was quick, as though her answer was still not what he was looking for.

"Just…I was remembering how someone told me…" her voice trailed off, eyes avoiding his. She felt uncomfortable telling him the details of her memories. Like she was splayed on a table, cutting herself open so he could examine her. She wondered if he would be kind enough to stitch her up after he was finished.

"Told you what, *Chevrette?*" His patience was running thin. She could hear it in his voice.

"He told me I should lose some weight. That I was getting fat. So, I joined the gym." The sentences came out rapid, rushed, as though time would match the tempo of her words. She wanted the conversation finished. She wanted to get it over with.

He loosened his grip on her hair, letting the strands drop. She looked up at him, as though he still held her hair and was using it to steer her gaze. She couldn't tell what he was thinking, his eyes masked by inscrutability.

"Who said that to you?"

"Um…" She felt like she was betraying Josh. That by telling Adrien, she was throwing his memory to the wolves for a feast. "My boyfriend."

His reaction was slight. Had she not been looking for it, she may not have noticed. But she did. His jaw clenched.

"Listen to me. I want to make myself very clear." He stepped toward her, closing the distance between them. His hand moved to the small of her back, pulling her closer as he looked down at her, his other hand bringing her chin up to meet his stare. "This," he waved toward the equipment, "has nothing to do with your weight. You are exercising because you need to be strong and fit for the rest of training. You do not need to lose weight. You are beautiful the way you are. Do you understand that?"

The intensity of his eyes burned into hers. She blinked, confused by his explanation, but understanding his words nonetheless. "Yes."

"Say it."

"I understand."

"No, *Chevrette*. I want to hear you say that you're beautiful."

Something fluttered in her. She tried to ignore it. "I'm beautiful."

He smiled at her, that ghost of a smile. "Next time, try to convince me that you mean it."

Sophie felt like her femurs had been replaced with jelly as she gingerly walked back to her room with Adrien. Her arms felt like bags of sand had been poured into her bones and were now sifting through her joints like an hourglass. He'd had her work out for hours. She ran miles, exhausted from her long hiatus from exercise. But he didn't let her stop. He made her use the free weights, made her lunge across the expanse of the gym floor, sweeping her knee to the ground every time. If she didn't do it properly, he made her start over. She had nearly collapsed, sure she would vomit from the strain. He had permitted breaks, ensuring she wouldn't give in to her exhaustion.

Along with the physical drills, he drilled her psyche. At every water break, he tested her.

"Why are we doing this, *Chevrette?*"

"To make me strong."

"Does this have anything to do with how you look?"

"No."

"Say the words, *Chevrette.*"

"I'm beautiful."

She had lost count of how many times he made her say it. She was bewildered by his persistence. But, then again, he had done many things that made little sense to her. Maybe this was no different. She let it be.

At the end of her workout, Adrien confiscated her shoes. They entered her room and Sophie instantly gravitated toward the bed. She looked at Adrien who was moving toward the bathroom. He nodded at her, giving permission to lie down.

"Don't get too comfortable, though. I'll get your bath ready. You're going to need to soak your muscles to relieve the soreness."

She nodded, collapsing on the bed. She must have dozed off because the next thing she knew, Adrien was standing over her, his hand gently shaking her shoulder.

"Come on." He helped her off the bed and into the bathroom. The water from the tub let off steam and the familiar medicinal aroma of bath salts. Sophie stepped out of her gym shorts and peeled off her socks. She grabbed at the hem of her shirt, attempting to lift it over her head. She was met with resistance from her muscles, too tired to even undress. She let out a feeble laugh and turned to Adrien.

"I can't—" she indicated, and was met by his amused expression. He took her shirt in his hands and delicately lifted it over her head, throwing the cloth to the floor. Next, he placed his hands under her sports bra's elastic band, touching the sensitive skin between her back and her breasts. She shivered despite the warmth and gentleness of his hands. He lifted, his hands grazing the back of her arms as the material followed suit. It was an intimate gesture, one meant for lovers rather than captor and prisoner.

She was naked in front of him, like she had been so many times before. For some reason, she felt shy this time. The numbness, her companion for so long, had begun to dissipate and, in its wake, awareness. Awareness of her body. Awareness of his effect on her. Even now, her nipples peaked at his proximity. And then, there was the awareness of her effect on *him*. The way his eyes darkened when he looked at her. It was primal, an innate reaction. She knew this. But there was something else there, some emotion that she, perhaps, reciprocated.

Adrien's warning about himself surfaced, reminding her that she should be afraid of him. *He's a wolf in sheep's clothing. And I'm his deer. Of course, I should be afraid of him.* But, of course, she was never very good at the 'shoulds.' She shivered at the thought.

"Get in, it'll warm you up." He mistook her shiver for a chill. It was those moments that confused her the most. It was the best sheep costume she had ever encountered. Unless, of course, he was actually a sheep just pretending to be a wolf. Or maybe he was raised by wolves but, in reality, a sheep. She indulged in the fantasy for a moment. But even then, she couldn't help but think of it as just that: a fantasy.

She felt his eyes on her as she washed herself beneath the water, sending little waves to the edge of the tub and over its edge to the tile below. It reminded her of the night she'd been punished.

"You know you don't need to stay, right? I'm not going to do anything to myself," she offered, more to herself than for his benefit. His heated stare had begun to have a strange effect on her already confused mind.

"Have you ever entertained the thought that I just like to watch you bathe?" he asked, still watching her. He was being playful. She saw the mirth in his eyes, but could still feel her face warm as it turned a bright red. He laughed at her reaction, tipping his head back to allow the sound to escape.

"Besides, *Chevrette,* given you couldn't lift your arms above your shoulders, I'm thinking you may need some assistance."

Sophie couldn't argue with the truth behind his statement and, when the time came to wash her hair, she let him pour the shampoo into his palm as she dipped her head back into the water. She was careful not to submerge herself. She didn't miss the flicker of alarm in Adrien's eyes as he watched her lean back to wet her hair. She was puzzled again by his reaction, but also respectful of whatever it was that held him captive to it.

He massaged her scalp as the bubbles foamed in her hair, starting at the crown of her head and moving toward the base of her scalp. His strong fingers lingered there, his thumbs massaging her neck before moving upwards with a practiced pressure that gave Sophie goose bumps despite the hot water.

"Mmm…you should have been a hairdresser," she sighed. She wondered if maybe she had made a mistake saying it. It was something she would have said to a friend, not her kidnapper. She wasn't quite sure what compelled her say it to begin with.

"Oh, really?" She couldn't see his face, but his voice was laced with amusement. "And why is that?"

She liked this side of him—the playfulness. She wanted to

hold onto it, put it in a jar for safekeeping, to bring it out whenever she wanted.

"They give the best head massages," she replied. His fingers stopped their work and he gently tugged her head back by the hair.

"Lean back." It was a command, but it didn't carry the same resolute dominance his commands usually did. It was an invitation, really. She leaned back, dipping her head in the water just far enough to cover her ears, stopping at the outline of her face. She held her eyes closed as he moved his fingers through her hair under the water, washing out the soap. His other hand cupped the back of her head; she couldn't have submerged herself if she wanted to. When her hair was rinsed to his satisfaction, he lifted her back out of the water, grabbing the bottle of conditioner.

"So, does that mean that was the best head massage you've ever had?" He was teasing, bringing her back to a conversation she had started.

"Almost. We have a lot of really good hairdressers in… where I'm from." She caught herself before she said it. *Boston.* It dawned on her that he didn't know any of that information about her. For some reason, she decided to keep it to herself. She had exposed so much to him in such a short amount of time. She suddenly felt the need to keep something from him.

"Well…maybe I should re-consider my calling." He said it dryly, tugging at her hair so that she leaned back for a final rinse.

Sitting upright in the tub, with a heightened awareness that she was alone in the water, she contemplated her response. It seemed a betrayal to herself to make light of the situation, given that his current 'calling' had landed her a one-way ticket into the sex slave trade.

Instead, she quite seriously said, "Maybe you should."

Maybe you should. Her words echoed. *Like it's that simple.*

Adrien returned to the gym in an attempt to work off his irritation. His feet pounded the treadmill as beads of sweat dampened his hair and ran down his firm chest. He already told her he didn't have a choice in the matter. Apparently, that wasn't enough for her to understand.

Why do you even want her to understand? The thought nagged at him. He increased the speed of the treadmill in response, his lungs heaving as he sprinted in place.

It was more than his heritage, the fact that he was born into a family that also happened to be one of the most prominent and prestigious slave vendors in the world. Yes, he had grown up around it, knowing that his father and uncles were taking girls and selling them like furniture to the men that came over for dinner parties after he and Etienne were in bed. But that's not why he joined the family business when he was eighteen. Had it been just about family business, he would have stepped out a long time ago. Maybe he wouldn't have stepped in to begin with.

But that choice was taken away the day he found his mother, wrists slit, body sunken to the bottom of a bathtub filled with water tinted red. He learned sometime later that it wasn't the cuts that had taken her life. On passing out from blood loss, she had slipped underwater and drowned. Since that day, Adrien always imagined the liquid that filled her lungs had left a red film that matched the pink ring around the tub—a stain that remained to torture him, no matter how much bleach Adrien's father used to scrub it.

His mother had left a note. The decent thing to do. But Adrien knew what she had written in that note was the catalyst of change for his and Etienne's fate. Their mother, it seemed, couldn't reconcile with the family business. She wanted out, and Adrien's father had refused to grant her wish. So, she found her own out. Permanently.

His father, Frederic, was outraged. His anger, at first, was directed at their mother. It was no secret Frederic believed she had acted selfishly, her memory becoming the epitome of weakness. Her inability to handle her family's profession became unacceptable. This is when Frederic turned his anger on Adrien.

Adrien was only seven, but he was always kind to the slaves that Frederic brought home before they were sold, sympathetic to, though not quite understanding, their plight. It was these acts of kindness that reminded his father of their mother. And Frederic couldn't—wouldn't—stand for it. He punished Adrien with all of the tools that Adrien now carried in his own home. Frederic forced Etienne to watch, his lessons learned through osmosis. For years, Adrien endured these beatings, molding him into the person his father wanted him to be.

Despite the beatings, there were moments Adrien dreamed of a different life for himself. A life where he could study at a university, pursue a meaningful career, meet a girl, fall in love, lead a normal life. At one point, he indulged this fantasy. Adrien only made that mistake once.

He had met a girl, had really begun to fall for her. It was puppy love, but it was really the only affection Adrien received during his youth. He was seventeen at the time, still in high school. One night, he brought his girlfriend home to meet his family. It would have been such a normal thing to do, if not for his father. A week after, she went missing. Adrien didn't have to wonder what had happened to her. It was meant to send a message, and Adrien received it loud and clear. There was no hope for normalcy in Adrien's life.

He knew Frederic had taken and sold her. Frederic's soul was as calloused as the scars on Adrien's back.

And now, Adrien wasn't his mother. He wasn't weak. He had proven that when he stepped into the family business. But, then again…

Maybe strength wasn't defined by his ability to handle the family business. Maybe it was defined by his ability to get out.

12

They fell into a routine. In the mornings, he would come for her. As expected, she would wait for him in kneeling position, her palms pressed against her thighs, knees together. Naked and exposed, she would keep her eyes down until he gave her permission to do otherwise.

Sometimes he would feed her, sometimes she ate willingly. Either way, he supervised until her plate was empty. After breakfast, she would dress in her workout clothing and he would bring her to the gym. The workouts always started lightly—a ten-minute, slow-paced jog on the treadmill or elliptical, followed by stretches. This is where the routine varied. Sometimes he would have her do weights; sometimes he would bring her back to the treadmill. But always, the workouts left her exhausted, her limbs like rubber.

She could feel herself getting stronger, though, and could see that she was putting on weight. Her muscles regained their toned physique. When she looked in the mirror at night, she began to see the woman she had once been. She no longer needed Adrien to remind her that she was beautiful, no longer needed to say it out loud. She believed it. And he must have known, because he stopped commanding her to say it.

He did other things, however, that Sophie thought odd. She would zone and he would bring her out of it by softly prodding, always asking her what she had been remembering. Most of the time she acquiesced, although she omitted many details about Josh. Sometimes, she omitted him altogether. Usually, Adrien would simply remind her of where she was, in the here-and-now. But on occasion, he would do things so gentle and sweet that Sophie simply forgot what she had been remembering.

Then, there were the nights. Sometimes, she was so exhausted from the workouts that she slept through until morning. Other times, her nightmares ripped through her, wrenching her from sleep. Adrien always came for her.

And nighttime was different with Adrien. With the sunset there seemed to be a shedding of roles, as though with the end of the workday Adrien no longer needed to play the part of dominating master. The change was subtle. It wouldn't have been obvious to an outsider. But Sophie noticed he would become more lenient, more playful. He was less apt to remind her of the rules she was breaking and, when she did break them, she wasn't punished for her indiscretions.

Sophie found comfort in this routine. It was something she could rely on. It felt safe. She knew what to expect. She understood what to do, how and when to do it. The anxiety that was her constant companion at home was no longer present. As long as she fulfilled Adrien's expectations, she had nothing to worry about.

That was, until everything changed.

It started off the same as any other night. She had woken from a nightmare, brought to consciousness by the sound of her own scream. Before she was fully awake, before she had even stopped screaming, Adrien was there. He caressed her back, helped her out of bed. Silently, they made their way to the balcony off of his room and she indulged in the sweet savor of smoke that would allow her to sleep the rest of the night.

The familiarity of the high enveloped Sophie like an embrace from a friend. It made her heady and relaxed. On more than one occasion, it allowed her mind to pander to her curiosity, coercing her to voice her inquisitions like a child peering over a brick wall into a no-trespassing zone. Tonight, she wandered to a place her mind had never allowed her to wander before.

"Why did you choose me, Sir?" She exhaled another hit, passing the joint back to Adrien.

"Why do you ask?"

"I'm just curious, I guess."

"Because you were there, *Chevrette*. That's all. It was a matter of convenience."

Was he trying to make her feel better? His answer was so final. As if he had told her, *"It's not your fault, you couldn't have stopped it."* But could she have? Her mind drifted to Megan. Had she not asked him to spare her friend, would she be here instead of Sophie?

"What about my friend? Why didn't you choose her?"

"I thought that was obvious." He paused to place his lips on the joint. He inhaled, holding the smoke inside before letting the air *whoosh* from his lungs. "You asked me not to."

"What if I hadn't asked? What would you have done?" She

turned to him, as though studying him might give her his answer. He seemed to be doing the same, his eyes trained on her face. She could see the thoughts flitting across his eyes as he chewed his lower lip, sense his hesitation to answer. Finally,

"What is it that you really want to know, *Chevrette?* Are you wondering if I would have taken her instead of you? Or are you wondering if I would have let her go no matter what?"

"Yes."

"Yes?"

"Yes to both of those questions. I want the answers to both."

A pause. "No, I wouldn't have let her go. And no, I wouldn't have chosen her instead of you."

His answer was relieving, albeit confusing. Sophie had effectively gotten Megan out of a fate that, no matter what, Sophie herself would not have been spared from. It still left her with the sense that there was something she had done to be chosen. Something she could have done differently.

"So, why me then? What did I do to make you take me?"

At this, Adrien smirked. Despite the smile, his eyes held sadness. "You fascinate me."

Sophie was taken aback by his answer. *That was it?*

"And do you choose all of your trainees that way?" The question came out harsher than she had intended, but she didn't care. His method of selection seemed so arbitrary, it irritated her.

"No, *Chevrette*. Never." He sighed before correcting himself. "Until now, that is."

Those words did strange things to her. *You fascinate me.* He had said it with such reverence, like the very revelation was precious. Was she special to him? She wondered about his other trainees. Did they, too, get to see this side of Adrien? Something told her that this piece of him, the one she was lucky enough to witness during their late nights, was something very few got to experience. And *that* was fascinating.

"Come on, I'm hungry," he said, getting up from his chair. She recognized his avoidance tactics almost immediately.

No, she decided, *not many people get to see this side of him at all.*

She followed Adrien to the kitchen, pulling herself up to sit on the countertop as he opened the fridge. He took out several items, placing them on the counter near Sophie. She grabbed the carton of raspberries, opening it to pop one of the little morsels of fruit into her mouth.

"Open your mouth, Soph," Josh said, a raspberry in his hand. She opened wide, waiting for Josh to aim. He arced the raspberry through the air and Sophie caught it with ease. She smiled, lifting her arms in triumph. Josh laughed.

"Nice catch." He moved closer to her, this time taking a raspberry and putting it between his thumb and forefinger. He held it up to her mouth, just out of reach, teasing her. She leaned forward from her perch on the barstool in his apartment. She parted her lips, tongue darting out to capture the fruit, before encapsulating his forefinger in her mouth. Gently, she sucked the raspberry from his fingers into her mouth.

Her eyes met his. Mission accomplished, *Sophie thought triumphantly.*

"Fuck, baby," he moaned before closing the distance between them. Cradling her head in both hands, his lips landed on hers. Hungrily, he parted her lips, seeking her tongue with his. He broke the kiss abruptly, dragging her off the stool. "Come on, let's go." He pulled her toward the bedroom.

Registering her sudden loss of the raspberry carton as Adrien took it from her hand, she came back to reality. She blinked a few times before focusing on him. He was no longer at the fridge, but had placed himself between her legs, which were dangling off the counter. Due to the counter height, he no longer towered over her. His blue-gray eyes were perfectly level with her green and, despite the patience in his voice, she could see annoyance lurking in the deep-blue hue that ringed his irises.

"Welcome back, *Chevrette.*" And, as always, "Care to tell me where you just went?"

No. But he wouldn't tolerate her insolence, would he? Despite the night's reprieve, she'd learned her place. She had to answer. "Just a memory…about raspberries."

He looked amused. "What about them?"

Avoiding his eyes, in a meager attempt to hide her vulnerability, she provided context. "I, um…my boyfriend was feeding them to me." She glanced up, hoping her explanation would suffice.

His jaw set, the amusement in his eyes vanishing. It was replaced by something else. *Was it jealousy?*

"Is this the same boyfriend that called you fat?"

She was taken aback by his question. *He remembered that? And did that matter to him?* "Yes," she replied hesitantly. A flicker of anger and then…nothing. He blinked his mask into place, effectively shutting Sophie out.

"So, then what happened? In this memory of yours?"

"It um…it got intimate."

He laughed and she shifted uncomfortably, suddenly very aware of his nearness.

"I see…" It came out almost as a purr. He took one of the raspberries and placed it in his mouth, swirling it around before beginning to chew. His eyes darkened as they moved from Sophie's eyes to her mouth. "Tell me…in this memory, did he kiss you?" She squirmed under the scrutiny of his hooded stare, lust building in the tender spot below her waist. She nodded, unable to form words.

Involuntarily, she bit her lip, wondering what it would feel like if he nibbled it. He made a soft noise, something between a grunt and a moan, as his hand reached up to her mouth, freeing her lip from her teeth's grasp. The pad of his thumb lightly grazed her lips, taking pleasure in their softness. She imagined the same tenderness given to her clit, the pad of his thumb rubbing her toward ecstasy. She could feel wetness pooling in her panties, and she parted her lips to meet the tip of his thumb. She licked, ever so lightly.

Sophie heard the sharp intake of breath, the whispered word "fuck," and then his mouth was there, his lips feathering over hers. He hesitated, looked at her for permission, his dominance abruptly forgotten and, in that moment, she was given control. She closed the distance between their lips, bringing her hand to his hair, running her fingers through it, grasping the unruly strands, and pulling him closer.

His lips were soft at first, capturing her mouth gently. His tongue licked at the seam and she parted to allow him entrance. He didn't, though. Instead, he took the opportunity to nibble on her bottom lip, alternating between nips and licks, before finally allowing his tongue to join with hers. Even the way he kissed revealed the man she knew. Strong and passionate, dominant, yet simultaneously gentle. And this is what it had become. Passionate, heady. His hands grasped her waist. She could feel his need, his tongue no longer mingling, but seeking.

He pulled away from the kiss, breathing heavily. He hadn't pulled away from her, though, and he rested his forehead against hers, his eyes squeezed shut.

"You need to tell me to stop." He whispered the words, a demand that didn't command. Even she knew that it wasn't what he wanted. Ignoring himself, he began trailing kisses down her jaw, along her neck. As his mouth moved downward, his hand moved up from her waist finding the hem of her shirt and dipping underneath. He moved slowly, and she arched toward his touch as he cupped her breast. He brushed her nipple with his thumb, sending spiking currents of desire through her core. She moaned, tipping her head back, arching to give him even more. He took her invitation, pinching her nipple with just enough pressure to keep the pain from overshadowing the pleasure. She cried out, wanting more. At some point, she had wrapped her legs around his torso, and began pressing her hips against him, bringing him closer. She could feel his arousal through his jeans.

She needed him, wanted this. It had been so long since she had felt this way, and the feeling was intoxicating. Her words came out in a breathy voice, one she hardly recognized. "I want you. Adrien, please—"

The change in him was instantaneous. He pulled back, removing both hands from her body. Out of sheer astonishment, she dropped her legs from their perch around his waist. He stared at her with what she could only describe as furious panic.

"What did you just call me?"

Shit. Adrien. She hadn't realized what she said. She had known his name for weeks, but had kept it to herself. It was safer that way. She hadn't wanted to disobey the rules and call him anything but Sir or Master. And now, she was frozen in fear and horror at having done so.

"I'm so sorry, Sir. I'm so sorry. I let it slip—it won't happen again." She could hear her voice begging, pleading for mercy. *Was it so terrible that I used his name?* She knew by his reaction that it was, and that it warranted the groveling she was ready to partake in. She'd seen the same look in his eyes the night he had flogged her. She would do anything to avoid that again.

"Where did you hear that name?" His voice came out steady, offering false comfort. If she wasn't staring him in the face, Sophie might have thought he wasn't upset at all.

"It was that night—your brother—I overheard him say it." Her sentences were coming out in panicked gasps. "I'm so sorry." She looked at Adrien to see if her explanation had quelled his anger. He seemed to be thinking back to that night, wondering where the transgression had occurred. He shook his head, refocusing on Sophie.

"You've known for that long and haven't said anything about it until now?" His anger seemed to have dissipated. Sophie hoped, at least. She nodded.

"Are you going to punish me?" Her voice was barely a whisper. *Please say no, please say no.* The words tattooed an accelerating rhythm in her head that matched the beating of her heart.

His hands grasped her shoulders, pulling her from the counter. She now stood facing him in the kitchen, no longer eye-to-eye. He towered over her once again, and Sophie didn't have to wonder if this was on purpose. He was, once again, her dominant master.

"I'm not going to punish you right now. You haven't done anything wrong. Yet. But listen to me very carefully, *Chevrette.* This is very important." He shook her by her shoulders, ever so slightly, ensuring he had her full attention. It was an unnecessary gesture. Sophie couldn't focus on anything else at the moment. "If you ever—*ever*—speak that name again, if you ever even *whisper* that name, you will regret it. Do you understand me?"

"What will you do to me?" She couldn't help it. The morbid curiosity that crept into a person's psyche when they were already on the thinnest of ice. But she needed to know what she was getting herself into, needed the motivation to never speak his name aloud again. Now that she'd said it once, savoring the sound it made on her tongue, she wanted to say it over and over again.

He inhaled, setting his jaw. He thought for a moment before responding. "It's not what I'll do to *you*. It's what I'll do to your friend—what's her name? Megan? Megan McDonald?"

Sophie's jaw dropped open, her head snapping back with surprise. *She hadn't told him Megan's name, had she?* She racked her memory, certain that she hadn't. *How does he know?* A feeling of unease crept up her spine, wrapping its bony fingers around her heart and lungs. She took a deep breath to fight the impending panic.

"You wouldn't," she whispered. It wasn't a challenge. It was a question.

"Do you want to find out?" *That* was a challenge.

The tears started then, pooling in her eyes before spilling over the ridges, slowed momentarily by her long lashes, before cascading down her cheeks. Stupidly, she wept in front of him, overcome by a feeling of loss. The loss of herself, of her life, of her friend, of her family, of Josh, and now—this was another loss. Whatever *this* had been. Comradery maybe? Lust? Friendship? Something else? But in that moment, it was lost.

"I hate you," she blurted out through her tears.

"Good." He nodded. "That will make all of this easier for you."

Guilt was not something Adrien was used to. It was not something he generally felt. Didn't let himself feel. Guilt was a weakness, and he was not weak. But somehow, it had managed to wriggle its way in. Guilt was not subtle. It was a punch to the gut, a sudden doubling-over of pain that you didn't see coming. It had a funny way of making him feel bad and had conned him into putting another's feelings before his own. And that was something to which Adrien was not accustomed.

He felt guilty immediately upon threatening Sophie—*Chevrette*—with her friend. First, it was guilt for lying. If there was one thing he prided himself on all of these years, it was that he always followed through with the things he said. And in truth, he had no intention of hunting Megan down and harming her. Not that he *couldn't.* It just wasn't worth his time or effort. She had almost called him out on it, but his response was effective in dodging that line of questioning.

But the second reason for his guilt was what bothered him most. It was the look on Sophie's face, the look of utter betrayal. He had hurt her and broken her trust, and seeing it there in plain sight had done something to him. It—the betrayal— made him realize that he meant something to her. And it—the guilt—made him realize that she meant something to him. It was for that reason that he had told the lie. To protect her.

Knowing Adrien's name was dangerous. It was dangerous for him, and it was dangerous for her. One doesn't get into the business of selling pleasure slaves without making enemies. And Adrien had plenty of enemies. But his family had always been smart about it, never using their real names when dealing with customers to avoid being traced and found by the dissatisfied ones. And Adrien had many disgruntled customers. Many of them were men he refused to do further business with. Adrien was picky about whom he sold to. He had heard too many stories of women dying unnecessarily at the hands of their masters. He would take no part in that. But the men he refused to sell to were dangerous men, and Adrien had to be very careful. He had no doubt that his enemies would go to great lengths to obtain information about him. He and his family had taken great measures to protect their identities. Until, that is, Etienne let Adrien's name slip.

Fucking idiot. He would deal with Etienne later.

*But now…*Adrien sighed. Now, he had to deal with himself.

Adrien undid the button of his jeans and pulled the zipper down. He tugged the pants down, stepping out of them, and folding them neatly. He placed them methodically on the cold concrete near the door. Next, he tugged at the fabric of his t-shirt, pulling it from the shoulders to bring it over his head. The soft cotton rubbed against his scars as he removed the shirt from his back. This, too, he folded with delicacy. Finally, he slipped his thumbs under the elastic of his boxer briefs and removed them, folding and adding them to the pile of clothing.

He walked over to the wall where his tools hung, waiting for him. He grabbed the cat o' nine tails after quick deliberation. It was either that or the flogger—they were the most effective and easiest to use on himself. But the flogger was now marred by memories of *her.* And she was the reason for all of this.

He knew it needed to hurt. *Really* hurt. He walked over to the wooden chest that sat near the tools, opening the lid to rummage through its contents. He found the small box he was looking for containing the jagged pieces of metal. He clipped the extensions onto the ends of the weapon. He had bought this contraption early on in his self-flagellation, enjoying its versatility in doling out varying degrees of punishment. Tonight, he would show himself no mercy with the highest degree of punishment.

Adrien walked to the center of the room, distancing himself from anything that may catch on the braided tresses, anything that could prevent him from striking himself with full force.

He closed his eyes as he felt his heart rate increase. The familiar sickening feeling filled his stomach, but he denied the desire to retch. It was a conditioned response. Even knowing he could stop at any time, knowing that he had complete control over this, didn't help him push away the knot of fear that he associated with the beatings. He had his father to thank for that.

Despite his nerves, he knew he needed this. Needed to be reminded of his place. Needed to be reminded that Sophie was merely a commodity. And he needed to be reminded not to lose control with her again.

Sophie. He sanctioned the thought of her, causing his cock to stir with lust, all while knowing the pain that was about to ensue. Physically, certainly. *Emotionally?* Maybe.

God, he had wanted her. Maybe more than anything he had ever wanted before. He loved the way she moaned into his mouth. He loved the taste of raspberries on her lips as his tongue swept over hers. Loved the arch of her back as he tweaked her hard little nipples. He could feel the heat of her pussy against him as she had moved her hips into him. He knew he would have taken her right there on the kitchen counter, given the chance. He had asked her to stop him and she didn't. She wanted it. Wanted him. *Fuck, he wanted her.*

His dick was hard now, unabashedly throbbing with every detail of the night. He fisted his shaft, wishing his hand were her tight pussy clenching around him.

Thwack!

The first blow was always the hardest. The anticipation of whether or not to actually go through with it. Adrien was surprised every time he did it. He exhaled, only then realizing that he had been holding his breath. He readied himself for the second blow.

He thought about what it would be like to lick her cunt, savoring her silkiness, lapping at the wetness between her folds.

Thwack!

Adrien grunted from the pain and exertion, his teeth clenched together. His breathing had become uneven. From thoughts of her or from the pain? He couldn't tell. It didn't matter. He continued.

He wanted to know what she sounded like when she came. Did she whimper and moan? Or did she scream and cry out? He fantasized about the sound of his name on her lips, like a mantra, as he fucked her.

Thwack!

Adrien cried out this time, feeling the blood trickle down his back. Still, his cock ached, painfully erect.

Thwack! Thwack! Thwack!

Three in succession. This was going much too slow for Adrien's liking, the re-conditioning not having the desired effect.

Thwack!

He continued like this, varying between fantasies of Sophie and blows to his back. In the end, the castigation was thorough, only ending on the brink of pure exhaustion. Adrien's cock, however, remained unfortunately stiff at the thoughts of Sophie.

———

13

Sophie had always considered 'hate' to be a strong word. She never could treat it arbitrarily the way some people did, using it as a euphemism rather than a truth. So, when she said it to Adrien, the word held a certain weight.

As the sun came up, she reviewed the previous night's events in her mind over and over again. She couldn't sleep thinking about it. In a way, she should have expected it. Mercurial, after all, was a perfect word to describe Adrien. He was a paradox, an odd mixture of contradictions. Dominant and gentle, cold and caring, dangerous and trustworthy. She was beginning to realize that he was neither a wolf in sheep's clothing, nor a sheep masquerading as a wolf. He was both of these things, a hybrid. Life wasn't so black and white, as it turned out. And neither were her feelings for him.

She was ready to accept that she did feel something toward him. She knew that, otherwise she wouldn't have been so hurt by his actions. In truth, she felt a gamut of emotions when it came to Adrien: affection, lust, fear, excitement, desire…hatred.

The reemergence of these emotions presented themselves on a color wheel inside her, varying shades of yellows, blues, and reds all mixing together to create a muddy brown.

Sophie heard the beep as Adrien unlocked the door. She glanced over at the clock. It was 8:30 already and she hadn't even realized it. She was still lying in bed, and didn't make an attempt to get into position as Adrien entered the room.

If he was irritated by her defiance, he didn't let on. He strode to the bedside table, placing the tray down next to her. Crossing his arms in front of him, he turned, staring down at her impassively. She glared back. Another act of defiance.

Adrien moved so fast, Sophie didn't have time to scoot out of the way of his hand, which shot out and latched tightly to the shell of her ear. He pulled her toward the edge of the bed, yanking so hard that she thought he would rip her skin. She cried out, with no choice but to follow his movement to minimize the pain. As he dragged her, he grabbed her roughly by the wrist with his free hand and swung her off the bed, practically dropping her on the floor. She landed with an ungraceful thud on her knees. Adrien bent over her, his hands firmly holding her in place.

"It seems I owe you an apology for letting you forget your place here, *Chevrette*. It won't happen again." He held her head down, preventing her from looking at him. She recognized the transformation. It was an act of dominance, like how one would train a puppy to know who its master was. It was a fitting analogy, she supposed. And maybe she would have submitted a week ago, a day ago, even. But not now.

He was the one to rip her from her cocoon. He was the one that made her feel all these overwhelming emotions at once. She wanted to show him what he had done to her. Show him how angry she was. She wanted him to feel how much she hated him in that moment.

Adrien still gripped her head as he grabbed the bowl of oatmeal from the tray. He placed it on the floor next to him, crouching to meet her at eye level before taking a spoonful of the cereal, pulling Sophie's head back, and shoving it into her mouth. She opened her mouth willingly, swirling the warm cinnamon-flavored mush in her mouth before taking her opportunity. Rearing her head back, the motion slightly hindered by Adrien's hold, she spat the food back in his face.

It landed with a wet smacking sound on his cheek and the soft dip below his eye. He reflexively blinked, but kept his lids closed, letting her behavior sink in. He released his grip on her hair. He seemed to be moving in slow motion as he reached for a napkin from the tray to wipe the food and spit from his face. Sophie could see the way the napkin trembled in his hands, as though even the napkin feared for its life in Adrien's grasp. When he finally opened his eyes, the emotionless depth of his gray-blue irises frightened her more than if she had seen rage there. He took a deep breath before speaking. His voice came out low and controlled.

"You're going to wish you hadn't done that."

Immediately, Sophie's fight or flight instinct kicked in. And she did both. She attempted to scramble away, but Adrien's hands grabbed her waist before she could get out of reach. She screamed, kicking out at him. She managed to land a blow to his stomach, but it didn't do much to stop him. He lurched to his feet, his palms and fingers still firmly around her waist, bringing her with him. Sophie was suddenly all limbs—elbows and knees flailing at all angles in a frantic attempt to get away from him. She heard her own voice before she even realized she was screaming.

"Don't touch me! Get your hands off of me!" She struggled

in his grip as he managed to capture both arms behind her back, pushing her forward so she was pinned face first on the bed.

"Tsk tsk, *Chevrette.* That's not what you were saying last night."

She wriggled under his weight, which was effectively holding her down against the mattress, her knees hitting the box spring, walled in by the pressure of Adrien's legs against hers. "Fuck you!" she spat.

He leaned into her, bringing his mouth down to whisper in her ear. "I was rather looking forward to fucking *you*, actually. But seeing as how you're misbehaving, I'm thinking a spanking is really what you need." He straightened, pushing his hips into her ass. She could feel his erection through the rough denim of his jeans.

The fucking bastard is turned on! Her stomach lurched. *What the fuck is wrong with him?*

Adrien moved swiftly, maintaining control of Sophie's arms behind her back. He picked her up like a rag doll as he sat on the bed, laying her on her stomach over his knees. With a quick motion, he yanked her shorts and panties down, exposing her ass. She wriggled in his grasp as a last ditch effort to escape.

"Stop fucking moving or I'll make this hurt more," he said through gritted teeth. "Tell me why I'm doing this, *Chevrette.*" He began rubbing her ass cheek, preparing it for the stinging pain she knew was coming.

She saw his hand raised above his head, saw him flinch slightly, before he landed the first slap. She cried out, stunned by how much it hurt.

"What was that for, *Chevrette?*"

"I—because I wasn't kneeling when you came in."

Slap! Another burst of incredible stinging. It brought tears to her eyes and she squeezed them shut to keep the flood at bay.

"What else?" He rubbed the spot he had just hit, alleviating some of the pain. She wondered why he bothered.

"Because I spat at you."

Slap! The sting of pain was equally harsh as the sting of humiliation. Sophie hadn't been spanked in—ever. Never in her life, not even by her parents.

"Is that respectful behavior?" More rubbing. In a way, she was grateful for the gesture.

"No."

Slap! It fucking hurt. She wondered if the skin would rise like a welt. She wondered how long his red handprint would remain on her white skin, even as he rubbed it away.

"No, what?"

She couldn't help the tears from spilling over now. "No, Master."

Slap!

"Have you learned your lesson?"

"Yes." She mumbled it, defeated.

"Good." He let go of her hands, helping her sit up. He faced her as he said, "I don't like doing that. Don't make me do it again."

In one minor act of defiance, she raised an eyebrow. "Really? It seemed like you enjoyed it just fine." She glanced down at his crotch, the evidence of his arousal still apparent.

She was met by what Sophie could only describe as a wicked grin. He grabbed her chin roughly and said, "I didn't realize you had such a smart mouth, *Chevrette.* I quite like this side of you." He got up and moved toward the door. He paused for a moment, turning back to her. "It's good to see you have some life in you. It's nice to finally meet you, Sophie Kingston."

She reeled at the sound of her name.

He didn't come back for her that day. Not even to give her dinner.

Adrien's wounds had wept from the strain of punishing *Chevrette.* The tightness of his skin had made it difficult to restrain her, and even more difficult to raise his hand to spank her repeatedly. He hoped his own pain wasn't evident, hoped he had hidden it well enough behind the punishment he inflicted on her. Adrien stood in the shower, letting the cold spray wash away the blood from his lashes. Having no real ability to dress and care for the wounds had always been the worst part of his castigations.

Her defiance had certainly surprised him. He hadn't realized she had it in her. Up until then, she had been the perfect submissive, aside from the lackluster impression of life that she seemed to carry. But something had changed in her, something ignited. He had been noticing her transformation over the past few weeks, a kindling for life. Apparently the spark she needed was a threat to her friend's safety. Had he known, he would have done it much earlier. And now, she was alight.

It's what he had wanted. It's what he had been working toward. So, why did he feel like he had done something wrong?

She hates you. He didn't want to think about it. The idea did odd things to him, made him feel like he cared. He didn't care. He couldn't. He had learned his lesson once, through Etienne.

Frederic had called him earlier that day instructing Adrien to meet him at Etienne's. It was important, whatever his father wanted to talk with him about. Adrien had tried to get Frederic to explain in more detail over the phone, but the line went dead before he could finish asking the question.

The request was out of character for his father. Pure curiosity had him following Frederic's directions and, at 6:00 p.m. that night, Adrien showed up on Etienne's doorstep. Etienne answered the door, shirtless, a look of confusion plastering his face.

"What are you doing here?" he asked.

Adrien, mirroring his brother's confusion, simply said, "Father told me to come."

The two looked at each other for a moment, neither quite grasping the gravity of the situation. Slowly, Etienne opened the door. Adrien entered, feeling like a stranger in his brother's home. Etienne's latest trainee was standing in the foyer, a look of pure shock and humiliation on her face as she feebly attempted modesty by hiding behind her hands.

"Get dressed, quickly," Etienne told her. Adrien noted the kindness in his tone. He marveled at the sound. It wasn't something he was used to hearing, his brother having been long hardened by the events that illustrated the storyline of his life. Turning to Adrien, Etienne asked, "So, what is this about?"

Adrien shrugged his response.

The sound of footsteps brought their attention to Frederic, waltzing in through the front door without knocking. He always had a tendency to act like an owner, even when he wasn't one.

"Father," Etienne said, a hint of surprise and confusion in the greeting.

"Where is the girl?" Frederic's eyes, so similar to Adrien's and Etienne's, glowered, searching the foyer for his target. In that moment, Adrien realized that's just what she was: a target. For what purpose, he wasn't sure.

"She's…in her room. Why?" Etienne asked. Adrien looked at his brother, finding the omission of her getting dressed intriguing.

"Bring her here."

Adrien could feel Etienne's unease mount as he turned to get his trainee. When he returned, he held her by her forearm, having hastily tied a robe around her to hide her nakedness. Etienne gently pushed her forward to stand in front of Frederic. Adrien could see her trembling from where he stood. He felt that perhaps he had reason to be trembling, too.

Frederic stepped forward, grabbing the girl's arms and spinning her to face Etienne, his arm wrapped across her chest, holding her against his own. A blinding flash caught Adrien's eye. Frederic had a knife.

"What is this, Etienne?" he spat.

Adrien's heart beat furiously in his chest. He had seen Frederic inflict violence on the girls before…but his blatant use of Etienne's name in front of a slave was something Frederic had always been cautious not to do. What the fuck was going on?

"Father! Don't!" Etienne cried. Adrien had never heard Etienne like this before, had never seen this level of fear and panic in his eyes. Adrien suddenly realized he was witnessing something very personal.

"Explain this to me, Etienne."

"Father, let her go. Please. I—I love her."

Adrien's gaze snapped between Etienne and the girl in Frederic's arms. Etienne had fallen in love with a trainee. Adrien had never even considered love to be a possibility—at least not since he was seventeen. And yet, there it was, in that very room with him. In a way, he felt cheated. He felt like its presence should have been overpowering—it should have held the authority, the command, to make itself obvious. But Adrien hadn't recognized it until the word was spoken aloud.

"Father…" Adrien's voice was low, his tone both calm and pleading. He wasn't sure what he was going to say, just that he knew Frederic wasn't likely to listen to Etienne at the moment.

"Shut up, Adrien. Your weakness does not become you. I would

have expected this out of you, but not from you, Etienne. Have you learned nothing from me?"

The girl yelped in his arms as Frederic pushed the knife against her throat, pricking her in the process. A trickle of blood leaked from the spot, falling down her neck, a trail of crimson in its wake.

"Let me make myself clear, to the both of you. This—whatever you feel with these women—is not real. They don't care for you. They don't love you and never will. The way they act toward you has nothing to do with affection. They just want you to let them go and they'll act like whores, try to seduce you until you give in. Do. Not. Give. In."

The blood was instantaneous. An outpouring. The slicing of flesh had barely made a sound, but it was the gurgling of the girl drowning in her own blood that had Adrien doubled over.

It wasn't the killing that had bothered Adrien so much. It wasn't the first time he had been in the presence of murder. It was the way it had affected Etienne. He was never the same after that. Adrien never saw him care for anyone again. All kindness was replaced with cruelty. In Adrien's mind, what Frederic had done was irreversible and unforgiveable.

After that night, both of them stopped referring to Frederic as 'Father.'

Phase Three

14

How did he know her name? It bothered her for some reason. She had known his name, unbeknownst to him, and yet, she felt it was somehow unfair that the opposite could be true as well. How long had he been holding onto it? Would he still call her *Chevrette*? Or was she Sophie to him now, even though she could never call him Adrien?

It wasn't her questions that kept her awake. It was the hunger pains. Sophie hadn't eaten much of the oatmeal after her outburst that morning, and Adrien hadn't come back to feed her that evening. She wondered if it was a new way of punishing her. She almost laughed at the thought, given how forcefully he had made her eat when she first arrived. It seemed preposterous that they had gotten to this point.

But a lot had changed since Sophie had been kidnapped. She wasn't sure how long she had been there exactly, but remembered Adrien telling her that the training would last six weeks. She guessed half that time had already lapsed. And yet, in just three weeks' time, Adrien had managed to do what

Sophie couldn't in thirteen months. Her appetite was back. Her energy had increased. Even her zoning spells seemed to be happening less frequently. He had been right when he said that she still had life in her.

And she would have been grateful for it if she were facing a different fate. But what was the point in feeling alive when you were destined to lose your freedom? She had wanted to feel normal for so long, wanted to feel anything and, now that she did, she wished she couldn't. The irony killed her.

Sophie got out of bed to position herself for Adrien's arrival with breakfast. She would be obedient today, if only for the food. She took her clothing off and knelt by the bed with her knees together and head bent toward the ground. And waited.

She registered the beeping of the keypad and the click of the door.

"Well, well. This is a big change since yesterday." Sophie heard the tray set down next to the bed, the clink of silverware as Adrien took the items from the tray. The decadent smell of eggs and bacon reached her nose. The hunger pangs jolted in her stomach at the aroma, her mouth beginning to salivate.

Adrien crouched on his haunches in front of her and waved a plate of scrambled eggs, bacon, and buttered toast in front of her face. Sophie practically swayed from the movement.

"Hungry?" he asked, taking a piece of bacon and lazily placing it in his mouth. Sophie couldn't help but watch as the precious morsel disappeared, leaving less for her.

"Yes, Master." She knew he wanted to hear those words, just as he knew she wanted the food.

"Good girl." He handed her the plate and a fork. She took it greedily, shoveling the food into her mouth. She heard him make some noise between a scoff and a snort.

"This is a far cry from the girl I had to force feed just a

few weeks ago. A lot has changed in you, *Chevrette*," Adrien commented as she continued eating. She didn't bother to look up, but noticed he had resumed using her pet name. Maybe he never really intended to call her by her real name. Maybe the rules applied both ways in the matter of monikers.

"The fire in you is a big change, too. Hating me seems to have done wonders to bring the life back into your eyes." He was staring at her now, his gray-blue eyes transfixed on her. She finished her food, setting the plate aside. "That's what it is, right? Hatred?"

Was that a rhetorical question? What's he fishing for? Sophie wondered. His eyes told her he genuinely wanted an explanation.

"You threatened the one person that means everything to me. I have no one else in this entire world. So, yes, I hate you for that." Her voice broke as she said it. She made an attempt to reign in her emotions, not wanting him to see her cry.

He nodded, as though taking in the information and accepting it for what it was. In that moment, he seemed almost sorry. And then, "She's safe. She made it back to Boston."

The words enveloped Sophie like a caress. She let them sink in and settle into her being. She reveled in the relief that swept through her as the tears began to fall.

She knew he didn't have to tell her that. It was for her benefit alone that he said it. And it eased the anxiety she had been holding about the unknown. About where her friend was and what had happened to her—the guilt of knowing she had sent Megan to whatever fate came upon her. But Megan was home. She was safe. And for that, Sophie was grateful to the man sitting before her.

"Thank you for telling me."

She did an odd thing then. An urge overcame her. She crawled into his lap, knocking him from his haunches so that he was sitting on the floor. With her legs wrapped around his waist and her arms around his neck, Sophie hugged him.

She buried her face into his neck and wept.

Gingerly, he placed a hand on her back. It was as though he were unsure of what to do. Unsure how to hug someone. Slowly, the other hand came up and found a spot lower on her back. He held them awkwardly in place, an air of uncertainty and hesitation lingering.

"I thought you'd be happy?" His voice was laced with confusion.

Sophie pulled away from the crook of his neck, far enough to respond, but not far enough to put any real space between them. "I am. I'm so relieved."

He rubbed circles on her back for a moment with his thumbs. "Then why are you crying?"

She pulled back farther, studying him. *Is he serious?* Yes, he was. *Maybe he really is just a normal guy with an ineptitude for women's emotions.* Sophie smiled at the thought.

"I'm crying because I'm happy."

It was Adrien's turn to do something odd. He reached his thumb to wipe a rogue tear that had begun to fall from Sophie's eye. He held it there, studying its wetness, weighing it as though trying to decide if it were somehow different from other tears shed. Sophie watched in fascination at the man before her, so entranced with her tears of joy. It made her wonder if perhaps he'd never seen them before. Perhaps he'd never experienced them himself. It made her sad, and she hugged him harder.

"That's enough, *Chevrette.*" His voice came out softly, almost regretfully. He made no move to untangle her. They remained there for a moment longer, Sophie's limbs wrapped tightly around Adrien, Adrien's hands tenderly on Sophie's back.

The moment eventually passed as they have the tendency to

do. But as is the outcome of all moments in this life, Sophie was changed by the events that passed in those few minutes. It reminded her that Adrien, despite his demons, had something very human inside him.

⁂

He led her to yet another unexplored portion of the house. The door had a coded lock on it, similar to those throughout the rest of the house, similar to the dungeon she had been taken to for her punishment. And when Adrien opened the door and stepped back for Sophie to enter, she was transported back to that dungeon.

Sophie gasped at the sight before her. A wrought-iron, four-poster bed was placed in the center of the room. In place of a typical canopy, the posts connected at the top with chains that crisscrossed until forming a mesh rectangle. Sophie looked at the far wall, adorned with shelves of what Sophie could only assume were sex toys. Some of the objects seemed harmless enough—feathers, silk strips of cloth, things Sophie didn't even recognize—but it was the instruments that drew Sophie's attention. The same instruments that she had seen in the dungeon.

Fear gripped her heart as the memory of pain and the ensuing ambush of other emotions that accompanied her punishment flashed before her. Her knees felt weak, panic squeezing her lungs. She needed to get out. She couldn't be here. What would he do to her?

She turned as though to run, but Adrien's body formed a barricade from which she could not escape.

"Please—don't. I don't want to be punished. Please don't hurt me," Sophie's voice trembled as she struggled to get around

181

Adrien. His strong arms enveloped her, the same arms that held her just moments before, turning her to face the center of the room.

"Stop. It's not what you think."

She continued, earnestly trying to escape from his arms.

"*Chevrette!*" His voice was stern and she gasped, the sharp pin of fear, a now familiar sensation, piercing her heart. Instantly, he softened his tone. "This room is about pleasure, not pain. You won't be punished here."

The words landed on Sophie's ears but didn't quite register. She stopped struggling, recognizing its futility against Adrien's strength. He loosened his grip but maintained a firm hold to make sure Sophie had regained the strength in her knees.

She felt the warmth of his breath against the nape of her neck as he leaned in. His lips touched the shell of her ear as he whispered the words "Trust me."

They acted as the flicking of a light switch in her dark room of confusion. She was no longer on the fence about trust. His command wasn't necessary. She already trusted him. She knew he wouldn't go against his word. He might hurt her again, but it wouldn't be in that room. The confusion about *how* she could have possibly placed her trust in a man who kidnapped her with the intent to sell her, remained in wait.

How did this happen? How did I get this fucked up? Sophie squeezed her eyes shut at the infiltrating feeling of stupidity.

Adrien stepped in front of her, his frame towering over her. Sophie opened her eyes to stare at the center of his chest. His finger lifted her chin as he looked at her expectantly. She nodded. *I trust you.* He smiled down at her.

"Come." He held her hand and walked her toward the bed. "Sit."

Sophie did as she was told, her nakedness taking meager

comfort in the silky, red sheets covering the bed. She sat with perfect posture, allowing her feet to dangle over the edge, her palms on her thighs just in case Adrien expected her to be in a submissive position. She kept her eyes lowered as he stood before her.

"Eyes to me, *Chevrette*. I want you listening carefully." She obeyed immediately. The softness that coated his voice just moments before was gone, replaced by a hard, business-like demeanor. Adrien continued, "You'll be spending a lot of time in this room, so become familiar with it. We have a little over three weeks left of your training. We will continue to do physical exercise in the morning, but it will be cut down significantly. The rest of your day will be spent in here.

"We'll begin slowly, but I will be honest with you, there are going to be things that you won't want to do. You will do them regardless of whether you want to or not. It's important that you know this. I will try to make things as pleasurable as possible, but it's up to you whether or not you allow yourself to enjoy it.

"The purpose of this training is to acquaint you with what my clients generally expect of their girls. Most of the activities my clients take pleasure in are not…conventional. I'll help you get used to it. Maybe you'll even grow to like it." Adrien smiled before continuing.

"There are two parts of this training. First, you'll learn how to give and receive pleasure based on my overall client base. Once I figure out who your new master is, I'll then train you on catering to their particular tastes. Understood?"

Sophie nodded slowly, letting it all sink in.

"Good. Any questions?"

Yes. A million. Sophie selected the most poignant. "Will any of it hurt?"

Adrien pursed his lips and, after a moment's pause, sighed,

"Yes. But that's why I'm taking the time to train you. If you let it, and it's done correctly, pain can feel immensely pleasurable."

"How do I do that? How do I let it?" It was a desperate question. She knew she wasn't a masochist and didn't want to feel pain for the rest of her life at the hands of a stranger.

Her concern triggered simultaneous waves of light and dark in Adrien's eyes as his mouth pulled into a full grin. "We'll get there eventually, *Chevrette.* For now, let's focus on the simpler pleasures," he said, moving to one of the shelves on the wall and contemplating its objects. Sophie couldn't see what he was looking for from her position on the bed, but Adrien swiftly selected something and returned to the room's center.

"Move back on the bed."

Sophie pulled herself to the head, lying slightly upright against the soft pillows. Adrien moved along one side of the bed to meet her there. She looked up at him, wondering what he had in mind for her first training. His smile was sly as he handed her the object that he had selected.

She reached out, recognizing it immediately. She smirked.

A vibrator. That's it? The shiny purple object seemed so anticlimactic given her expectations.

Adrien's laugh regained her focus. "What, *Chevrette?* Expecting something else?"

Smirking still, "Kind of..."

"I told you we would start slow. Or would you rather we start with the fucking machine?"

The what?!

"No!"

He raised an eyebrow, apparently unamused by her outburst.

"I mean, no, Master." She bowed her head, hoping her indiscretion wouldn't get her punished in some way.

"This first lesson is about getting to know yourself. You need to know exactly what you require to come. Most of my customers will expect you to be able to achieve orgasm…even if what they are doing to you isn't giving you the pleasure you need. You will be responsible for your own climax in those cases."

"Oh." What else was there to say?

Adrien's eyes darkened. "Make yourself come, *Chevrette.*"

He stood back while Sophie realized what he was telling her to do. Uneasily, she turned the end of the vibrator, bringing it to life. She delicately moved the hood of her clit back, exposing herself to the cold, inanimate plastic. She winced at the temperature, but soon felt the warming in her core. Her eyelids fluttered at the ambush of sensitivity and she lightened the pressure in response.

She let out a small sigh as she began moving the vibrator in circles around the small collection of nerves. She hadn't had an orgasm since before Josh's death and, even when he was alive, she was accustomed to using a vibrator to give her what he couldn't.

She allowed her mind to wander to help reach her climax. She thought about Josh, the way he touched her, dipping his fingers into her before sliding himself between her legs. Despite the erotic pictures moving through her mind, Sophie's stimulation strayed from pleasure to a strange numbness. She opened her eyes to see Adrien watching her curiously.

"I—I'm sorry. I don't think I can do this with you watching." She removed the vibrator, but didn't turn it off. She knew he wouldn't let her stop that easily.

He nodded, seeming to understand. "You have two options. Learn to make yourself come even when you're uncomfortable, or learn how to fake it so that it's believable. But know that if you try to fake it, and you don't pull it off, most masters will punish you. Your choice. I recommend the former."

Sophie took a deep breath, bringing the vibrator back to her mound. She used her other hand to separate her folds, moving the vibrator in a new rhythm against her sex. She closed her eyes to invoke her fantasies once again.

It was different this time. Josh's gentle touch didn't reappear in her erotic daydream. Instead, she imagined a tall, strong stranger with gray-blue eyes, thrusting into her as she stood bent over a kitchen counter. She bit her lip as the tugging in her lower belly intensified, sending tingling sensations from her core, through her limbs, to her toes and fingertips. She quickened the rhythm of the vibrator as the man in her fantasy fucked her harder. She could feel her climax begin, a slow roll that soon crested in a powerful crescendo. Sophie cried out, grinding her hips as the intensity of her orgasm overtook her entire body.

She eased the vibrator from her sensitive clit, her heart pounding as she came down from the euphoria that left her breathless. The strength of the orgasm amazed her and Sophie suddenly felt embarrassed that she had come so loudly in front of someone's prying eyes.

She glanced at Adrien, only to discover that he seemed similarly perplexed by the intense climax he had just witnessed. But there was something else about the way Adrien looked at her that left Sophie feeling peculiar. He looked like he wanted to devour her. Sophie suddenly found *Chevrette* to be a very fitting name.

Sophie watched Adrien visibly swallow, before ordering in a low, husky voice, "Again."

Sophie blinked in surprise. "What?"

"You heard me. Do it again."

Adrien permitted Sophie to stop after her sixth orgasm. He had watched her the entire time, his own arousal evident through his tented pants. Each time she looked at him, careful to keep her eyes squeezed tight to appear as though she had them closed. She couldn't help but watch him, moaning as she heard his shallow breaths and saw him clench his own jaw in restraint.

Her legs shaky and her body exhausted from the successive ebbing and peaking of her climaxes, Adrien helped her from the bed. Sophie looked back at the sheets, a wave of shame washing over her as her eyes landed on the damp spots. Her cheeks flushed as the past two hours registered. Humiliation surfaced at the thought of herself splayed on the bed of her captor, wanton and willing to come over and over again, before his very eyes.

"Don't." Adrien's voice cut through Sophie's thoughts, tearing her eyes from the spot on the bed to meet his own. "I can practically see the shame creeping in. Don't let it overbear the pleasure you just experienced." He took a step toward her but, instead of standing, he lowered himself to his knees, bringing his face level with her still throbbing clit.

Sophie's breath caught in her throat at the nearness of his mouth.

Adrien's hands landed on her hips, drawing her nearer still. "Has anyone ever told you how beautiful you are when you come?" Adrien practically whispered the words. Sophie shook her head. Her breathing shallowed as she felt his breath glide across her body. She placed her hands on his shoulders, steadying herself, bracing herself. She gasped as Adrien's tongue grazed her inner thigh, trailing up to meet the sensitive flesh at her center. Slowly, Adrien mirrored the action on the other side, stopping just before his tongue met the moisture between her legs. With utter care, he placed a soft kiss on her swollen clit before sweeping his tongue to gather the silkiness that had gathered there, licking and lapping as though it were honey. Sophie shuddered at the sensation of his tongue, softly crying out.

"Fuck…" Adrien whispered as he licked her again. There was finality in the action, and he drew away and stood before her. "Come here," he said, grabbing her hand. He pulled her across the room and through a doorway, which led to a bathroom. Adrien guided Sophie in front of the mirror, standing behind her. He wrapped an arm around her waist, pulling her so that her back was pressed against his front.

"Look at yourself in the mirror," he commanded. Sophie did as she was told, and Adrien took his free hand and placed it between her legs. Taking full advantage of the slickness that lingered there, Adrien began caressing slow circles around her still throbbing roll of nerves. Sophie cried out, throwing her head back against Adrien's shoulder, and closing her eyes from the rapidly building intensity.

"Open your eyes, *Chevrette*. I want you to watch yourself."

Sophie opened her eyes, bringing her head up, hardly recognizing the writhing woman staring back at her. Sophie's hips met Adrien's rhythm as she moved to meet the pressure of his thumb. She could feel the tightening in her core as Adrien's skilled fingers brought her toward ecstasy. Her eyelids begged to close as she came closer to her peak.

"Don't you dare look away, *Chevrette*." Adrien's voice was hoarse, once again betraying his self-restraint.

Sophie watched herself through hooded eyes as the tingling explosion overtook her, causing her to writhe, to pull away from Adrien's hand while simultaneously wanting more. As the sensation ripped through her, Sophie cried out and pressed herself into Adrien, becoming very aware of his erection. She allowed herself a glance at Adrien in the mirror to find his eyes darkened with lust, his arms clutching her for dear life, and his shallow breath matching her own. It was then that Sophie realized the effect that she had on him—the power she held in these moments.

Adrien's touch lightened as he eased her down and her heart rate returned to normal. Still somewhat breathless, Sophie looked at Adrien in the mirror.

"Now do you understand why you should never be ashamed of that?" he asked, desire still lingering on his face.

She wondered if he had intended to show her how powerful she actually was, given the fact that she was destined to be a slave. Regardless, she nodded.

"Yes."

Once again, she had taken him by surprise. The sheer willingness with which she engaged in her training was unprecedented. Most of his trainees fought this final phase of training. Some even begged to be spared as though their tears could somehow convince Adrien not to go through with it. But the way they sniveled and pled made things much easier for Adrien. He detested the behavior and it made it easier for him to maintain his distance and remain professional, despite the compromising position in which he put the girls. He'd never once entertained the idea of using Phase Three for his own sexual gratification. It had never turned him on.

That was before.

There was something about her. It had been there since the

beginning. Adrien couldn't get Sophie out of his head. And he had broken another one of his rules. Touching her would have been fine, he had to do that in this line of work. But he had tasted her and now he couldn't get her flavor off his tongue. Didn't want to.

It was going to be a long three weeks.

———————————

15

There was a familiar song playing on the radio, but Sophie couldn't quite place it. She knew she should know the words. Josh sang along in the front seat next to her, both hands placed neatly on the steering wheel. Sophie looked out the front windshield as the car twisted and turned with the road.

"Where are we going, Josh?" Sophie heard herself ask. Had she willed her mouth to move?

Josh stopped singing momentarily to answer. "To visit your parents!" He seemed so excited, and the effect was contagious. Sophie could feel the elation bubbling in her chest. It dawned on her that it had been so long since she had seen her parents. The thought of visiting them made her giddy.

"Don't believe him, Sophie," a new voice warned from the backseat. It was such a familiar voice and yet, it felt so out of place in the car with her and Josh. Sophie turned around to find a man with beautiful gray and blue eyes watching her. She knew him, but it was from a different life. He shouldn't be here.

"Sophie, listen to me. You need to get out of the car," he said,

his voice pleading. She heard the words, but they didn't make any sense. She was going to see her parents. Josh was here. Everything was fine.

"Sophie, who is this guy? Don't listen to him. You don't even know him. You know me. You trust me. Ignore him." Josh's anger was palpable. She hated it when he got angry. As though the man in the backseat could sense her apprehension, he leaned forward in a flash, wrapping his arm around Josh's throat.

"Adrien!" Right, that was his name. "Adrien! Stop!" Sophie begged, but Adrien ignored her, squeezing Josh's throat tighter. Josh let go of the steering wheel and began clawing at Adrien's hands.

"Stop! Please!" Sophie screamed, but the two continued to struggle. Sophie could feel the car jerk, could feel the falling sensation as they careened over the cliff. "Stop! Stop it!" Desperately, helplessly, Sophie's voice pierced the night air.

"Sophie!" Adrien's voice reached her ears…it sounded so close.

"Sophie!"

Sophie jolted upright in bed, colliding with strong hands that held her firmly in place as she fully awoke, a cold sweat coating her body. Her body shook from the adrenaline still coursing through her from the dream, lungs gasping for air as her heartbeat raced out of control.

"Hey…" Adrien's voice averred concern as his hands gently rubbed her upper arms, sweeping up to move the hair from her face. Sophie's eyes adjusted to the room around her, brightened by the light that he had apparently turned on, as the remnants of the dream began to fade. She closed her eyes, returning to the comfort of darkness and taking a few deep breaths before looking at Adrien.

He had clearly been sleeping. His hair was messier than usual and he wore only a pair of long shorts. His chest was bare, revealing defined muscles that gave hint to hours spent in the gym. His torso tapered from his broad chest to his lean waist, and her eyes followed the line of his muscular abs to his hips and down. Sophie noted that this was the first time she had seen him without a shirt on, and the sight evoked nostalgia for her long-ignored passion for art. His body was perfection, and she felt the urge to capture it on paper with sweeping gray lines of charcoal. But her thoughts were quickly replaced by the realization that this was the first time, in all of the days that he had come to rescue her from her nightmares, that she had actually woken him up. And she suddenly felt very guilty for taking the precious gift of sleep away from him.

"I woke you up. I'm so sorry."

The confusion on his face was lightened by a hint of a smile as he ran his hand through his unruly hair. The motion made his arm flex in a way that had Sophie's stomach doing flips. It was unnerving, her attraction to a man who had just tried to choke her dead boyfriend.

"It's fine…are you okay?"

She nodded, playing with her hands in her lap, a measly distraction from ogling his undressed chest.

"Do you want to smoke?" he offered.

Yes. "No, that's okay. You should go back to sleep. I'll be fine."

He sighed, taking a step forward and leaning his hip against the bed. "We need to figure this out, *Chevrette*. I don't mind the late nights, but I can't say your new master will tolerate them. Being woken up every other night might…" he sighed again before continuing, "I can't guarantee you won't be punished for it."

The information hit Sophie hard. She didn't want to be sold to someone who couldn't understand that she wasn't in control of her nightmares. It scared her to think her next master wouldn't be like Adrien—patient, concerned…gentle. The anxiety of the unknown began to creep under her skin. What would her new master be like? Would he be cruel? Would he punish her for no reason? The questions swirled in Sophie's mind, and for the first time since arriving in this living nightmare, she felt pity for herself. For the first time, she wondered if Adrien might have it in him to let her go free. Could she say something? Would he listen?

Sophie wiped away the first of the tears, but they began to fall so quickly she couldn't keep up. She had yet to vocalize her feelings about her kidnapping, hadn't fought or even questioned the inevitability of her fate. Even her tears fell in silence.

Adrien reached out to brush a tear from where it dangled on Sophie's chin. Even they couldn't escape a fate controlled by Adrien.

"I don't think I can do it." She whispered the words, gathering courage as she spoke. "I don't think I'm strong enough." She looked at Adrien, hoping the care and concern that had accompanied him into the room would remain in this moment. Sophie imagined what it would be like to hear him tell her what she wanted to hear. She could picture how softly and sincerely the words would sound as he told her that he couldn't sell her, that she could go home. Or that she could stay with him. *Do I want that?*

But it was a fleeting fantasy as Sophie registered the impassive look on Adrien's face. He seemed irritated, almost bored. It reminded Sophie of a parent waiting out their child's temper tantrum.

Of course. He doesn't want to hear your whining, Sophie chastised herself. He had probably heard it from however many other girls he had trained. And Sophie assumed the only way those girls made it out of this house was through the exchange of money for sex. Sophie wiped the last of her tears, once again resigned to her fate.

"Are you finished with your pity party?" His voice sounded cold. Detached, even. So different from the Adrien just a few minutes ago. Sophie was baffled by how he could do that—compartmentalize and change so quickly. Maybe he could teach her *that* during her training.

It was meant to be insulting, but she was afraid not to answer, so she nodded.

"Good." He paused. "Do you want anything to help you sleep?"

She pondered the offer before asking, "Do you have tea?" She knew the caffeine wouldn't help her sleep, but something about a hot drink seemed so appealing. Adrien nodded and turned toward the door, motioning for her to follow. In turning, Sophie caught sight of his bare back.

She held in a gasp, but only by covering her mouth with her hand, her eyes transfixed on the marks covering his back. Long scores of faded white and pink hues crisscrossed in a chaotic scribbling. It was evident that some of the slashes were recent by the way they glared a deeper pink, not yet fully healed. Other marks were barely noticeable among the array of scar tissue. But it was the sheer number of them that had Sophie's stomach churning and her heart panging for this man. *What had he been through to get those scars?* She couldn't even imagine.

Adrien had opened the door and was waiting for her. He turned to find her frozen in place, her hand still over her mouth, her eyes perfect circles of terror. Confusion lingered on Adrien's face for a moment until he registered what she had seen. Irritation replaced his confusion.

"Let's go. I don't have all night," he snapped.

His abruptness left her feeling mortified for staring, and

she quickly regained her composure, walking out the door with her eyes on the floor. It was the first time Adrien allowed her to lead him through the house, and the gesture wasn't lost on her. He didn't want her looking at his back anymore. Her embarrassment lingered as she walked down the now familiar halls toward the kitchen. She had been appalled at the sight of it, but that certainly didn't give her the right to stare like he was some zoo animal. She felt the need to apologize.

They entered the kitchen and Adrien began searching through cupboards for a cup and tea bags. Sophie noticed that he carefully kept himself angled so that his back never faced her. Heaviness settled in her chest at the thought of his shame, that he felt the need to hide himself from her, from the world. Her empathy cleared a path for an old self from a different life to re-emerge: the Sophie that spent hours counseling and helping others more broken than herself.

"I'm sorry I reacted that way," she broke the silence, hoping it was enough to also break the ice. But if Adrien had heard her, he didn't let on. He had found a mug and was now looking for tea bags, Sophie assumed. She tried again.

"I was surprised, and it caught me off guard. But I had no right to stare at you the way I did. I'm sorry."

He located a box of tea and was looking at the label. "Is green tea okay?"

"Yes. Thank you." She nodded, inferring that Adrien was not open to discuss what had transpired. She watched as he poured water in the mug and brought it over to the microwave. He set the time and leaned back on the counter, avoiding Sophie's eyes.

After a few seconds, he spoke. "I know it's not pretty to look at."

She shook her head. "It doesn't matter if it's pretty or not."

Sophie paused before continuing, carefully preparing for what she was about to say next. "After I first cut myself, I tried to hide it," she began. She wasn't sure if it was welcomed information, but wanted him to know. "I used to wear these really gaudy, thick bracelets to cover the scars. Then, when they started to heal, I would put makeup over them."

She noticed him glance in her direction, although briefly, and it gave her the courage to continue. "After a while, I just didn't have the energy to hide it. I stopped caring. I had stopped caring about most things at that point. It was too painful, and it was nice to care less about what people thought when they'd see my scars. It kind of became a way to show people who I am. The scars are a part of me, you know?"

The microwave beeped and Adrien turned, again angling himself away from Sophie, to remove the steaming mug and dip the tea bag into the hot water.

"I guess what I'm trying to say is, you don't have to hide your scars from me. And I'm sorry if I made you think that you do. They're a part of you. They're a part of your story, whatever that may be."

He responded by handing her the steaming cup, which immediately warmed her hands as she stood holding it. Her eyes never left Adrien. She was trying to read him, see if anything she said had connected with him. His jaw remained set, his mask of impassivity still in place, but he was staring at her wrists, searching for her scars. She sipped her tea, scrutinizing him the entire time, wondering what was going through his mind. In all the time she had spent with him, he never really opened up to her. It made sense; he probably never opened up to anybody. Not to mention, she was, after all, his job. But maybe that was what he needed. If, perhaps, he could talk about the things he had been through—*What?*

Then he could change? No. That's not what she expected. But it might help in some small way.

This was the reason behind Sophie's work as a counselor. And this was no different. *Was it?*

"How did you get your scars?" It was a bold first question, but she knew he wouldn't give her the chance to ask many.

Adrien's eyes snapped up, incredulous. Sophie was certain he wouldn't grant her the satisfaction of an answer. But then, "The same way you got yours."

Sophie took a sip from her tea to hide her confusion. *I cut myself, isn't that obvious?* Then, it clicked.

"You did that to yourself?" She was careful to make sure her voice did not betray the shock she felt, knowing she must remain unassuming if he was going to open up to her.

"Some of it, yes." He crossed his arms in front of his chest, still leaning on the edge of the counter.

Sophie pondered this for a moment. She had a million questions, but she wanted to choose carefully. She thought about asking why he would do that to himself, but, having been through her own emotional turmoil, she understood the darkness that led to self-harm. In her mind, it was a waste of breath.

"Some of it you did yourself…and the scars that aren't your doing? Who gave you those?"

Sophie noticed the change in Adrien almost immediately. It was slight, but she was watching for it. His back stiffened, his muscles tensed. His jaw, already set, was now clenched. By his reaction alone, she could tell it was painful for him to even think about. She was on the verge of telling him that he didn't have to answer her when he replied, "My father."

He said it so matter-of-factly, as though she'd just asked who was at the door, as though it had no consequence on anything.

But Sophie knew better, and it broke her heart to imagine Adrien whipped by his own father. She wanted to say so much to him in that moment, but all that came out was, "I know I don't know you and I don't know what you've been through… but I do know that never should have happened. No one should ever have to go through that." Tears stung her eyes as she said it, sincerity overtaking her emotions.

Adrien shifted, looking almost uncomfortable. His face softened, along with his posture, but his tone remained harsh. "Are you finished?"

Did he mean with the tea? Or with the questions? Truthfully, Sophie was finished with neither, but she could tell that Adrien was. She nodded and walked her cup over to the sink to rinse it out.

At least he allowed Sophie to follow him back to her room.

Sophie tossed and turned the rest of the night, unable to fall asleep. It had nothing to do with the caffeine from the tea and everything to do with the images of Adrien subjected to the tools she had seen in the dungeon. She wondered if his father had used whips and floggers, or maybe the cat o' nine tails and paddles, to scar Adrien so badly. She wondered how Adrien reacted when it was all over. Did he cry? Or did he keep his mask in place, his emotions cocooned within him? Perhaps his father's house was where he learned how to do that in the first place.

Adrien had remained closed-off during their conversation but had given her more information about himself than he had in three weeks. His give and take reminded Sophie of the adolescents she had counseled—not trusting anyone with their vulnerabilities but wanting to more than anything in the world. She reminded herself that he wasn't a client. With clients, she would never engage in a relationship deeper than what was necessary for therapeutic work to occur. Here, though, in her current situation, she had come to rely on Adrien. He fed her, gave her basic necessities; he even went beyond this on nights when she woke from her nightmares. He, in a sense, had given her life back. Forced it upon her, really. She was attached to him, grateful to him. Even in his crueler moments his actions were ultimately for her own good. In some sick sense, it was like he was protecting her from her future master, despite the fact that he was her deliverer. And there was something more. She cared for him. *Loved him?*

She didn't want to think about it.

Adrien took a long drag off the joint, leaning his forearms against the balcony. He was in for another sleepless night, but that wasn't what bothered him. Exhaling through his nose, he focused on the tingling sensations of the scars on his back. They had always had a life of their own, akin to what he imagined a phantom limb might feel like. As soon as her eyes landed on the crossroads of slashes etched into his back, he could feel them burning under her scrutiny.

It was a mistake. He heard her screaming and hadn't even thought to put a shirt on before running to her. He stubbed the joint out on the balcony railing, frustrated with himself. He had left himself vulnerable to her probing questions—the kind that no one bothered asking—and he hadn't quite figured out how to avoid answering. He wasn't sure what to make of her response, either.

Odd, he thought. *Is this what compassion feels like?*

He was being soft with her. He knew this. But he also knew that she was fragile. She required these moments of tenderness. But he couldn't be too soft with her, either. If he were too soft, she might begin to see him as weak. She needed the hard moments, as well. Otherwise, he would never be able to train her properly. That was the end goal, after all.

Fix her. Train her. Sell her, he staunchly reminded himself.

16

Sophie was ready and waiting for Adrien in the morning. She dutifully ate her breakfast, dressed in her workout clothes, and followed Adrien to the gym. Adrien was silent throughout the morning, and Sophie resumed her position as the submissive trainee. She asked no more questions, and followed the routine that was expected of her. She was surprised when Adrien turned on a treadmill next to her, and the two jogged their separate workouts together. When Adrien indicated that their runs were complete, Sophie stepped off the machine, waiting for him to do the same, with her eyes downcast and hands in position on her thighs.

He led her from the gym and brought her back upstairs, stopping along the way to get something out of a closet in one of the bathrooms.

"I want you to go back to your room and get ready for training. Go to the bathroom and empty yourself completely. Do I need to explain further?"

"Um…no." She knew what he meant, she just wasn't sure

why he was asking her to do it.

"Take a shower. Use this to clean yourself. Do you know what this is for?" He reached into his pocket and handed her an empty tube with a balloon-shaped receptacle at the end. Sophie recognized it. An enema. She took the object, staring at it a second before nodding. Yes. She knew what this was for.

"Good," he said, and continued the walk to her room. He keyed in the code and held the door open for her. "I'll be back in a little while."

⸙

The room seemed more ominous today, but that was because Sophie now knew what to expect. She felt uneasy as she stepped, already naked, into the room. Her stomach was tied in knots as she tried to push the thoughts—the memories—from her mind.

She waited on the bed as Adrien picked out whatever objects he planned on using today from a shelf on the far wall. She toyed with the silky sheets on the bed, cleaned from yesterday, running the material through her fingers. Her thoughts wandered to Adrien being so domestic as to do laundry. Perhaps he had a housekeeper that she was unaware of.

Adrien approached the bed, holding something in each hand. Sophie recognized the bottle of lubricant in his right hand, but couldn't place the cone-shaped object in his left.

"Turn around and get on your knees," he commanded, looking down at her with intent. She did as she was told, turning so that her ass was facing him. She felt the bed shift as he placed one knee beside her, leaning over her to adjust her arms so that she was arched down with her forearms flat on the bed. The mattress shifted again as he brought himself upright behind her. She heard him open the bottle of lube and squeeze some out.

Anxiety overtook her, and she couldn't help but blurt out a frantic, "What are you going to do?"

"It's just a butt plug, *Chevrette*."

The memories she was trying so hard to eradicate came crashing down around her.

"It's just anal, Sophie. People do it all the time," Josh pushed her, practically begging.

"I know, I just…I don't know. I'm not comfortable with it. What if it hurts?"

"People wouldn't keep doing it if it hurt," he argued.

In the end, Sophie had given in. She always gave in to what Josh wanted. And in the end, it did hurt. The pain was a muddled mixture of pressure and aching that intensified with every thrust. She asked him to stop, but it came out muffled against the pillow into which her face was pressed repeatedly. Josh continued plunging into her, oblivious to her pleas as he came inside her.

Sophie came out of her zoning spell fighting and screaming. She kicked at Adrien in an attempt to scramble off the side of the bed, but his arms were already firmly around her, his legs pressing against hers to hold her in place. She was effectively pinned.

"No! Don't! It's going to hurt!" She repeated it again and again, like a mantra, as she attempted to squirm from his grasp. He didn't say anything, didn't tell her to stop like he had the previous day. He just let her scream and fight until she was too winded to continue. When she had finished, he eased his grip, but remained wrapped around her.

Still on her knees, she pressed her face into the bed, allowing silent tears to slip down her face. She felt his warm hand on her back as he rubbed the length of her spine. It was meant to be soothing, but it just made her feel foolish.

After a few minutes, Adrien shifted away from Sophie, taking her across the shoulders and under her knees to hoist her onto his lap. She took comfort in his arms, burying her head in his chest, savoring the ginger and lemongrass scent that she had come to know as his.

After a period of silence, Adrien asked, "What was the memory about, Sophie?"

Her eyes shot to his at the sound of her name. This was only the second time he had used it, the first being when she hadn't even known he knew it. It was oddly comforting this time, to hear her name in his voice. He was asking her a question, but he was also making a statement. In that moment, she wasn't just his trainee, wasn't just *Chevrette*. In that moment, she was a fellow human being. A human being that maybe he even cared for. She relished the thought.

"It was about my boyfriend…he um…wanted to try things. Made me do things," she began.

"Is this the same one that called you fat?"

She almost smiled at his insistent recalling of that fact. "Yeah. He, um—it hurt. I wanted him to stop, but…I don't know. I guess he didn't hear me say it or something."

She felt Adrien's muscles tense around her. She had been staring into his chest as she spoke, but now she looked up to his clenched jaw as he stared across the room.

"He didn't mean to." She suddenly felt the need to preserve Josh's character, to defend him in front of Adrien. The image of Adrien's hands wrapped around Josh's throat popped into her head.

Adrien moved swiftly, lifting Sophie and placing her back down on his lap so that she straddled him, his hands planted firmly on her waist. They faced each other, their noses practically touching. He lifted one hand from her waist to cup her face before he very firmly spoke.

"Listen to me. That's not how it's going to go this time. It's not going to hurt—I won't let it. But I need you to relax and trust me; otherwise, it might still be uncomfortable. And if you need me to stop, say it and I *will*. We'll take this slow."

Sophie nodded. "Okay."

Adrien lifted her again, placing her back on her feet. She sat on the edge of the bed, unsure what to do next.

"It'll help if you're already turned on," Adrien said, returning to the shelves. He came back with a familiar toy this time—the vibrator from yesterday—and handed it to her. Sophie took it, turning it on as she leaned back on the bed, her legs still dangling over the side. She proceeded in a similar routine as the previous day, moving the vibrator over her clit with Adrien watching.

After a few minutes like this, Sophie felt Adrien kneel in front of her. She maintained her rhythm, though now distracted by what Adrien was doing. She gasped when he touched her, trailing a finger along her wet seam. She could hear his groan over the whirring of the vibrator. The sound made her clit tingle as she neared orgasm. Her breath quickened as she felt Adrien's finger dip into her, caressing her for a moment. She cried out, moving her hips to welcome the sensation, begging for more. Instead, he removed his finger, trailing it down to her other opening. Instantly, she tensed.

"Relax, *Chevrette*," he whispered, trailing his finger over her puckered entrance. She took a deep breath, trying to relax. She hadn't realized she had stopped using the vibrator until Adrien took it from her hand and placed it on the bed beside her. He didn't bother turning it off, and she felt the sheets moving in protest, their space disturbed by the foreign object.

Adrien continued to move his finger, gently rubbing but not yet probing. Sophie began to relax, acclimating to the foreign feeling. But then, a new sensation. Adrien's tongue licked at her seam, moving up toward her clit. It was something she wasn't used to, not only because she hadn't been intimate with anyone in over a year, but also because even when she was with past boyfriends, they never bothered pleasuring her with their mouths.

Sophie gasped as Adrien reached her bundle of nerves, sucking her hood into his mouth while simultaneously moving his tongue against her. It was instinct that brought her hands to his head, running his hair through her fingers, grasping at the unruly tufts. The abrupt loss of that wonderful stimulus served as an admonishment.

"Hands to yourself, *Chevrette*," he warned. She immediately obeyed, willing to do anything to bring back the gentle firmness of his tongue.

He resumed sucking, and Sophie felt something else. She barely noticed that he had deftly slipped his finger inside her. Now, as he moved his tongue in rhythm with his finger, she felt her orgasm begin to build. This sensation in her rear was new but not unpleasant, and certainly not painful. She finally understood how some people might actually enjoy it.

Adrien moved away from her, and she raised her head to look at him inquisitively.

"Get back on your knees, further up on the bed." He removed his finger and waited for her to follow instructions. She did as she was told, getting back into the same position as before, with her ass toward him and her head resting on the mattress.

"Good girl." Adrien's voice was laced with need as he kneeled behind her. Sophie allowed herself to picture what it would be like to have him naked behind her. She bit her lip to keep from moaning at the thought.

She heard the squirt of the lube as it shot from its tube into his hand. This time, she didn't flinch or fight. Adrien's arm wrapped around Sophie's waist, using his thumb to resume the work his tongue had started. Sophie cried out as her body readjusted to the pleasure. Adrien used the perfect amount of force as he continued to rub against Sophie's wet, pulsing clit. She barely registered the slight pressure as Adrien placed the tip of the plug into her anus.

"Take a deep breath," he said as he leaned against her. She inhaled and felt him place a soft kiss on her back as he pushed the object slightly farther, causing her to feel increasingly full. Adrien continued his motion against Sophie's throbbing pussy, pressing the plug farther inside and eliciting another deep breath from Sophie as she approached the brink of complete fullness.

And then, Adrien pushed it in the rest of the way.

She felt full, but, other than that, she simply felt foolish for making such a big deal over nothing. Adrien had been right. It didn't hurt. She was relieved, but also upset that Josh had given her such a bad experience to begin with. These thoughts were fleeting as Adrien flipped Sophie onto her back, bringing her back to the present, trapping her between his glorious arms, his body hovering over hers.

"See? Not so bad, right?" He smiled mischievously down at her. She returned his smile, reveling in his radiance in that moment. She liked seeing him like this—not so serious. She bit her lip in embarrassment, shaking her head.

"Stay here," he commanded, leaving her body cold in the wake of his warmth.

He came back a moment later with silky-looking straps.

She watched as he tied one end to the wrought-iron bedpost, securing it before taking her wrists in one hand. It took her a second to realize he was restraining her. As he methodically slipped the silk around one wrist and then the other, he looked at her scars, gently bringing them each to his lips before securing the restraint.

Sophie, now splayed on her back, arms spread upward in a long V, watched Adrien as he stood over her, thumb perched on his lip, contemplating his next move. He gave a slight nod as though confirming his decision. She watched him stalk back toward the wall that housed the shelves of objects, grab something, and return. The sound of him reopening the bottle of lubricant, squirting some onto the object. As if seeing the question in her eyes, he lifted it to her line of sight.

Just a dildo.

The biggest dildo Sophie had ever seen.

He wants to put that thing inside me? Sophie's anxiety peaked at the thought, her teeth capturing her lower lip for comfort.

Adrien's brow rose in question at the look on her face. "You just took a plug in your ass and you're worried about a dildo?"

Her teeth scraped across her lip as she answered, "It's huge!"

Adrien laughed, shaking his head. He muttered something in a language Sophie couldn't understand, then switched back to English. "Well, you'd better get used to it. My guess is, you're going to like it." He smirked, holding the dildo at her entrance.

Sophie's body heaved at the sensation as Adrien plunged the dildo into her pussy, still wet from the previous foreplay. With the dildo alone, she would have felt at capacity, but with the addition of the plug pressing against her, it felt almost unbearable. She cried out, begging Adrien to stop.

"Oh my God. Please—I don't—I can't handle it. It's too much," she implored, strained desperation in her voice.

He shot her a dirty look. "You're fine, trust me. Push through it." Despite his harsh tone, he eased the dildo out slightly, permitting Sophie to adjust to the feeling before slowly moving it back in. A moan escaped her lips from the accompanying feeling of fullness. Again, Adrien rested there so she could adjust. She felt him let go of the dildo and watched as he walked away. He grabbed another of the silk straps before returning to her side.

"Open."

Sophie's eyes pleaded with him. *Why?* "I promise I'll be quiet. I don't need it."

Adrien rested his free hand on Sophie's neck, his thumb lightly pressing against her throat. She could feel the power behind it, threatening her windpipe, her precious lifeline that lay just below the surface. Adrien leaned down, bringing his lips to her ear.

"Haven't you learned yet, *Chevrette*? You don't get to decide what you need anymore."

In the end, she was thankful he had gagged her. Thankful to have the soft cloth absorb her piercing screams of ecstasy as she came over and over again to the synergy of two inanimate objects touching just the right spots deep inside her.

Sophie had showered, eaten her dinner, and was indulging in her usual routine of reading before bed amongst a plethora of pillows, when she heard the familiar beeping of the keypad and click of the door unlocking. Stopping mid-turn of the page, she looked up from her book.

He was there, leaning against the doorframe, his gray t-shirt taut against that muscled chest.

"We're going to try something new tonight. Come on." He stepped back from the door, holding it open for Sophie. Sophie dog-eared the page she was on and set it aside, planting her bare feet on the floor. Curiosity was eating at her, but not enough to ask the question, so she exited the room silently. Adrien walked in front of her, leading her to his room, a familiar place. He opened the door, indicating she was welcome inside. The door to the balcony was already open, so she walked out into the night air. Adrien followed close behind her.

She noted the joint and the ashtray on the little table between the two chairs, and looked at Adrien quizzically.

In response, "I figured, rather than wait for the nightmares to come, let's be proactive and see if we can give you a good night's sleep." He shrugged and she smiled at the gesture. Sophie moved to sit in her chair, Adrien in his. He picked up the joint, pulling the Zippo lighter from his pocket.

She watched as he placed the lighter's flame at the tip of the joint, allowing the bud to ignite before clicking the Zippo shut. Sophie smacked a mosquito that landed on her bare leg before teasing, "You know, if my new master doesn't smoke, I'm kind of screwed." A smile ghosted her lips as she acknowledged the macabre humor of her situation. *Sick.* But what else could she do?

"Maybe I'll send you off with a parting gift," he teased her back, inhaling the smoke and passing Sophie the joint. She smirked as she pinched the roll with her fingers.

"I don't even know how to roll a joint," she admitted, taking the sweet, heavy smoke into her lungs. She welcomed the burning sensation that she now associated with a dreamless sleep. She sighed, handing the cigarette back to Adrien who was preoccupied with waving away mosquitos before they could make a feast of them.

Adrien took the joint and flicked the ash before taking his next hit. "You're right, though. We need to come up with a different solution."

Sophie nodded. Her motive was different, however. It wasn't that she wanted the nightmares gone so she could remain in the good graces of her next master. Really, it was just that she wanted them gone. Period.

"What are your nightmares about?" Adrien asked, his voice now serious. Sophie wasn't surprised by the question. Adrien had been probing her about her zoning spells for the past few weeks, why wouldn't he ask her about her dreams? She remembered wondering why he was asking about her zoning at the time, but felt it best not to argue. Fear of what might happen if she didn't answer had her spilling her memories to him. And it had been helping. Whether it was just sharing them with someone, or the fact that Adrien always seemed to take her mind off her thoughts afterwards, Sophie noticed fewer and fewer memories surfacing.

Now, as he sat in front of her asking about her nightmares, she wanted to confide in him.

"They kind of all follow the same theme. Sometimes they're different, but they're always comprised of the same elements," Sophie began. "My parents died when I was nineteen. They were driving when their car hit an icy patch and slid off the road. They were in a pretty rural area and there weren't any guardrails to stop the car, so it fell down this...ravine, I guess. It took hours for anyone to even realize they were missing and, by then, they had both died."

She looked at him, expecting the usual pitying glance. She hated the pity. But it wasn't there in his gaze and she was grateful for its absence. Adrien nodded his head, urging her to continue.

"So, mostly my dreams are about driving with them. And at

first, it's awesome. It's so good to see them. But…then usually my boyfriend kind of appears. You know how that happens in dreams? Where one minute someone's not there, and then they are, and it just seems to make sense?" She looked at Adrien for confirmation. His lips quirked into a half smile as he nodded, remaining silent.

"Well, he's suddenly there. And that's great, too. It's so good to see him. Because…" Sophie took a deep breath, "he died, too. A little over a year ago." Tears stung Sophie's eyes as she forced herself to go on. "So, Josh is there and…then things start to feel unsettling. And it's like I know what's going to happen, but I don't want to stop it. Most of the time the dreams end with us crashing or falling. Sometimes something else happens. But in the end, I always end up knowing I'm going to lose them again." Sophie sniffled and wiped a tear as it slid down her cheek. She glanced up to see Adrien studying her.

He cleared his throat before speaking. "How did he die?"

Sophie wiped away another tear that threatened to fall. "He overdosed. On cocaine." She stared at the sun setting low in the sky. "The worst part is, I had no clue he was using. And the thing is, he had been using my money for it. The inheritance from my parents. And I didn't even notice. I never really had a reason to look at my bank statements before, so I had no idea how much he was withdrawing. I felt so stupid—I *feel* so stupid. I could have prevented it if I'd just known." Sophie couldn't help the tears from falling now.

She was brought from her thoughts by the sound of foreign words, laced with anger, as they poured from Adrien's mouth. She looked at him questioningly, confused by his reaction, wishing she could speak French.

He glared at her, flicking the ash from the joint. "Hoping for a translation, *Chevrette*?"

Slowly, she nodded, unsure whether or not she wanted to know what was going on in his mind. He was angry, that much was clear.

"I said I'm glad he's dead."

The words smacked her in the face, eliciting her own angry and indignant reaction. Before she could respond, Adrien leaned forward in his chair and trained his eyes on Sophie's.

"What did you expect from me, *Chevrette*? Did you want sympathy? Empathy? I don't have it. And I definitely don't have it for that prick. He treated you like shit."

Her mouth dropped open. "You think he treated me like shit? Seriously? You have no idea how he treated me," she snapped. She acknowledged that her statement wasn't exactly true, that through sharing her past with him, he sort of *did* know how Josh treated her. She brushed the thought away, continuing, "And you treat me any better?!" Her voice was shrill, her anger and disbelief muting the tiny voice reminding her to tread carefully and avoid punishment.

Adrien straightened in his chair. Sophie watched his jaw clenching and ticking as he seemingly took a moment to compose himself. *Always so self-controlled,* she thought. He took in a slow breath. The mixture of fury and tranquility had her heart pounding in her chest. She wasn't sure what to expect. Would he stay calm and rational? Or would his anger win out? She swallowed uneasily in anticipation.

When he finally spoke, his voice came out so softly that Sophie had to lean in to hear him. "You seem to forget the nature of our relationship, *Chevrette*. This," he pointed back and forth between himself and Sophie, "is not a relationship founded on mutuality. You may think I'm a monster, but I'm not the one who entered a *consensual* relationship under the guise of love and trust when, in reality, he lied to you, fucked up your life, and left you shattered. What kind of a person does that? I hardly know you and I can see that he's completely broken you. I'm not an idiot. I've noticed all of your flashbacks are about *him*. He fucked you over and he's continuing to do so. He's an asshole and he deserves what he got." Adrien stubbed out the joint in the ashtray. "Talk sessions are over. Get in your room."

Adrien stood, towering over Sophie, still sitting in her chair. He rubbed a hand over his face as if to dispel the past few minutes. It took him a moment to realize that Sophie hadn't budged. "Well?" he snapped at her.

She looked up at him, chin trembling from the encompassing pain over the past few minutes. And yet, despite everything he had just said, she couldn't help but add, "I never said you were a monster. I don't think that."

Adrien seemed taken aback. But if he was surprised by her words, he quickly recovered. "You don't know me very well, then, do you? Get. In. Your. Room. Now."

For once, the marijuana didn't deliver a dreamless sleep. Sophie tossed and turned as scenes of monsters battling one another invaded her subconscious. In the dream, her heart had been ripped from her chest and laid like a trophy on a pedestal, still beating, as it awaited its winner.

Adrien paced barefoot along the concrete floor, contemplating his punishment. The whips and paddles taunted him from their perch along the wall as he determined the best course of action.

Adrien hated gray areas. And Sophie was definitely a gray area, one that was quickly mixing Adrien's black and white world into its own static mess of in-betweens. He hated her for it. Or did he hate himself? Perhaps, he hated them both. Yet another gray area.

In a black and white world, Adrien was a trainer and Sophie was his trainee. Her previous life didn't matter. What mattered was that Sophie learned the rules of her new life and that she obeyed them. Nothing more, nothing less. There was nothing personal about it. There was no room for feelings. But in this new, gray world? Their latest conversation left him furious at the feelings it had evoked.

Jealousy. Adrien felt jealous that Sophie loved a man who lied to and hurt her. And despite the things that her boyfriend did, Sophie still wanted him. Adrien was never one for self-pity. In that moment, however, he wondered why, despite his faults, no one could ever love him. But, of course, he knew the answer: because he was a monster. And people don't love monsters.

He chose the flogger, craving its sharp sting against his skin. Three blows, he decided.

One, for being jealous of a dead man.

Two, for hoping that someone could love him.

Three, to remind him of what he truly was.

17

It now occurred to Sophie that her grief had morphed her relationship with Josh into something it wasn't. Somehow, his imperfections had been wiped clean when he left this world, leaving her with a skewed version of his image. She cringed at her own naivety. Adrien's words had struck a chord within her, the sound reverberating so loudly that it reawakened Sophie to the knowledge that Josh had been playing her all along. But what would it mean if Josh really hadn't treated her well? What would it mean if Adrien really were the trustworthy one between the two? As she sat, locked in a room, awaiting a man who planned to train her and sell her as a personal sex slave, Sophie finally opened her eyes.

And quickly slammed them shut again. Because what would it mean if Sophie were ready to move on from Josh? What would it mean if she were actually falling in love with Adrien? Even her naivety wouldn't permit her to believe that it was a good idea. *Stockholm Syndrome,* she reminded herself. *That's all this is. It's normal in these circumstances.* The explanation made sense in her mind, but fell flat as her heart skipped in anticipation at the sound of the door opening.

Adrien's lean, muscular frame entered the room. He was dressed in his usual—jeans and a plain t-shirt, this one a deep blue, bringing out the rings of blue in his eyes. Sophie had difficulty keeping her gaze downcast as she appreciated his masculinity. A familiar pull tugged below her naval as a spike of heat flashed between her legs.

Maybe it wasn't love. Maybe it was just lust. *Maybe I just need to get laid.* Sophie suppressed a laugh.

"Something funny?" Adrien asked, his voice lined with irritation rather than curiosity as he handed her a plate with a bagel and cream cheese on it.

She took the plate, contemplating whether or not to share her thoughts with him. He didn't seem like he was in the mood for jest. In fact, his sour mood from the previous night seemed to still linger. Sophie shook her head as she took a bite of her breakfast.

She watched him as she ate, overtaken with curiosity. After the things he had said to her, she was the one who had every right to be in a sour mood, not him. So, what was his problem? Perhaps he thought she equated him with a monster? But she had assured him that he was mistaken.

He doesn't believe you. Of course, he wouldn't. He's probably been treated like a monster his whole life. Remember what his back looks like? He hasn't been treated like a human being by anyone. The thoughts made her feel sick. Sick for the boy Adrien had been, and sick for the man he was now. She wondered if anyone had ever loved him.

And suddenly, she didn't want to fight it anymore. She wanted to allow herself the feelings she had for him—whether it was just lust or something more. Because he deserved that much, this she knew. He had saved her from herself. He had shown her how to feel again, and that even when the emotions were hard to handle, they were better than not feeling anything at all. He had given her life again. She was ready to move on from Josh. She needed to.

❧

Sophie and Megan had always laughed at the euphemism 'fucking machine.' They used the term together often. Megan described many of her one-night stands as such.

"He was a bona-fide *fucking machine*," she would giggle over a glass of chardonnay as the two sat at the island bar in their apartment. Sophie loved those stories, even when Megan would inevitably go into *way* too much detail.

So, when Adrien used the words 'fucking machine' after he tied Sophie's hands to the bedposts, Sophie was confused. As it turned out, Adrien was not referring to a euphemism. He was talking about an actuality. A fucking machine.

Sophie lay, surrounded by silk, even bound by silk, on the bed. Adrien had positioned her so that she was lying on her back, her ass close to the edge, and feet dangling over. He stepped back, assessing his handy work, before quietly disappeared from her line of sight. He re-emerged a moment later with what appeared to be a bar with two cuffs on either end. He disappeared again as he crouched at her feet.

"What are you doing?" she asked, her voice hinting at unease.

"Spreader-bar," he replied, and she felt his strong hands strap her ankles into the cuffs. She tried to move her feet. She couldn't. Spread open, she realized there was no way she could close her legs, much less move. It was an aptly named tool.

221

Her unease mounted.

Adrien popped into her line of sight again, his eyes scanning her body before a smile crept across his face.

"Stay there." He chuckled at his own joke as he walked away. She could hear him rolling something in her direction. Its wheels squealed and squeaked with each rotation. It vaguely reminded Sophie of a shopping cart—she always seemed to get stuck with the one that made the worst noises. It was such a mundane thought. *Shopping.* Would she ever go shopping again? It seemed like such a different reality. Funny, Sophie realized she didn't care. She hated shopping anyway.

It was thoughts like these that drove her crazy while cementing her sanity at the same time.

The squeaking stopped and Sophie lifted her head, curious. Her eyes widened at the sight of the machine. Its bulk was made of metal, with a wheel that Sophie assumed motorized the rotation of the shaft. At the end of the shaft was a dildo. Sophie's trepidation grew at the idea of a machine pistoning into her. Adrien adjusted the height of the mechanical arm that would thrust forward, and tinkered with a few other settings, as well. Without looking up from what he was doing, Adrien asked, "How do you want it?"

Sophie blinked. "Excuse me?"

He stopped his tinkering, a predatory smile slowly spreading across his face. He moved between her legs, still dangling off the edge of the bed, and placed both his arms on either side of her body. He leaned forward, bringing his face down to hers. His eyes swept over her mouth and back to her eyes as he answered, "How do you want to get fucked?"

The words caused her stomach to do a somersault. Her heart pounded in her chest at the nearness of him, desire sweeping over her. For the first time in a long time, Sophie allowed it to happen. She let lust drive her as she answered Adrien's question.

"I want *you* to fuck me, not *that.*" She nodded toward the machine.

He was still hovering over her, so close that if she breathed deep enough, her breasts would graze against his chest. She took the opportunity, her peaked nipples hitting their mark as a spike of pleasure shot to her core. Adrien's eyes lowered to her breasts for a brief second before flitting back to her face. She had hoped for more of a response from him, but his expression remained impassive.

"Please," she whispered. "I know you want to. I can see the way you look at me. Why not just do us both the favor?" She was begging, she knew it. But she didn't care.

Adrien's eyes darkened at her words as he let his body press lightly against hers. His lips brushed against her ear, coaxing a gasp from her as they trailed down her neck. "You want me to fuck you, *Chevrette*?"

She nodded as his lips continued to trail along her collarbone.

"Tell me what you want me to do to you."

His words sent a new jolt of sensation between Sophie's legs and, growing wet, a frenzy of images played through her mind. She had never been a dirty talker before. The idea of voicing her fantasies always made her blush. But there was something in the strained command of Adrien's voice that broke down her inhibitions, pushing aside hesitation.

He moved his lips, alternating between sucking and nibbling kisses along her neck and across her collarbone. She moaned as goose bumps rose on her arms. Arching her back, she pressed her breasts against him.

"I want you to suck on my nipples." She couldn't believe

she had said the words aloud. Briefly, she marveled at the person she had become in such a short time, but the thoughts abruptly ceased as Adrien's mouth captured a peaked nipple, his tongue swirling and sucking. Sophie cried out as Adrien brought his hand to her other breast, pinching and twirling the hard nipple between his fingers. It was a perfect blend of pain and pleasure. Sophie arched into his touch, rocking her hips upward in an involuntary plea.

"What else, *Chevrette?*" Adrien asked, capturing her other breast in his mouth and mirroring his actions on the other side.

She could barely concentrate as Adrien continued his assault. She bit her lip, trying to think of an answer between moans and gasps. "I want you to touch me. Finger me."

Without hesitation, his hand left her breast, sliding down the side of her torso to her hips. His hand briefly left her body, making its way to the inside of her thigh. Her hips bucked as he lightly moved up and over her silky folds, parting her to dip a finger inside. He groaned against her breast as he inserted another finger.

"God, you're wet."

The pad of his thumb slowly grazed circles around her clit as his fingers moved in a rhythm of their own, bringing Sophie closer to orgasm. Her breathing was uneven as she arched and writhed beneath Adrien, her pleasure building as he worked like a potter at his wheel.

"I'm going to come," she gasped, "and then I want you to fuck me."

"How do you like to get fucked, *Chevrette?* Tell me."

"From behind." His rhythm faltered, his own breath now uneven. She knew he was turned on. She loved the effect she had on him. It spurred her forward. "I want you to start slow, but then I want it fast. I want you to fuck me hard."

"Fuck," Adrien muttered as he pressed his fingers farther into Sophie, rubbing his thumb harder, coaxing her climax. She cried out when he brought her over the edge, waves of pleasure rippling through her, hips gyrating while her pussy clenched around Adrien's fingers. He slowly withdrew as the orgasm faded, grabbing her by the hips to flip her onto her stomach, her arms crossing in front of her from her silk shackles. She was now standing at the edge of the bed, feet flat on the floor with her legs spread from the bar at her ankles, body bent over the mattress with her torso resting on the bed. Sophie bit her lip in anticipation, wanting the feel of his cock inside her.

But instead, the harsh squeak of wheels accosted her ears. Her head shot up in alarm, looking back at Adrien.

"What are you doing?" She couldn't mask the panic in her voice. He looked at her a brief second before his eyes darted from hers. In a swift movement, she felt the tip of the dildo nudge at her entrance.

"I don't do *favors, Chevrette*," Adrien answered. He met her incredulous stare before adding, "But I'll be sure to let your new master know your…preferences." With that, he turned on the machine.

It took Sophie a moment to realize he hadn't actually slapped her.

Sophie certainly hadn't wanted to get fucked by a machine, but that didn't stop the moans that now escaped her lips. They began almost immediately, reaching Adrien's ears over the hum of the motor. He had set the machine to begin at a slow, pulsing rate and steadily increase to a hard pounding, like she had asked. It was the least he could do, he figured. He made his way across the room, his dick rock hard and balls aching for their own release from the events that had just transpired. He paused by the door, stretching one arm out to prop himself against the wall. He hesitated to leave.

Over the years, Adrien had acquired an appreciation for torture. It was a test of strength by its very nature. One either broke under the pressure—giving into their weaknesses—or they didn't. There was never an in-between when it came to torture. Adrien's torture began at the hands of his father, later turning into self-torture as Adrien sought to eradicate his weakness. It had become a game. *How much could he take before he broke?* It was a game that Adrien always won. He never, under any circumstances, gave into weakness.

He thought he had won this round, as well. To be able to touch Sophie, to have her writhing on his hand while her pussy milked his fingers, to be able to walk away from that—it was a new kind of torture. She was a new kind of weakness.

In testing himself, embellishing the technique, he had inadvertently fueled the erotic images that he was trying so hard to push from his mind. Scenes of Sophie bent over while he fucked her from behind filled his head. And now he knew exactly how she liked it. It made his cock twitch.

Adrien was at a crossroads. He knew he should just walk out of the room. Maybe take a cold shower. But as the machine picked up its pace and Sophie's moans turned to screams, Adrien felt himself breaking under the pressure. He had managed to walk away from the temptation of her bent over the bed, begging him to bury himself inside her. All he had to do was open the door and step out. But he couldn't bring himself to do it, to get away from the erotic sounds that chipped away at his strength.

He glanced back toward the bed. He knew she couldn't see what he was about to do. She wouldn't even be able to hear him over the sound of the machine and her own cries. He made his decision.

Unzipping his pants, he took the hard flesh in his hand, stroking himself in time to the rhythm of the machine. He faced the wall, one arm stretched out to support his weight while his other hand moved up and down his shaft.

"Fuck, yes," he hissed, allowing himself this concession. Pre-cum glistened at his tip, his pace quickening at the sound of Sophie climaxing once again. He leaned his forehead against the crook of his arm, breathing heavily, nearing his orgasm. His breathing became shallower and he let out a low moan at the thought of sinking into Sophie's tight pussy, bringing him beyond his threshold. White ribbons of cum splashed against the wall as Adrien pumped himself again and again.

Catching his breath, he stopped stroking as shame overtook him. No longer made of stone, he had broken under pressure. He had lost in the game of torture. She had gotten under his skin, and he betrayed himself because of it. And now he would have to clean the wall.

The wall. The evidence of his weakness.

There was a point at which the fucking machine wasn't just doing a number on her body, but began to fuck with Sophie's mind, as well. That point occurred every time the machine slowed and her orgasm ebbed, when her mind morphed from a strikingly blank canvas at the peak of climax, to a vessel filled with unrelentingly invasive thoughts. And the worst was the realization that this was the best fuck she had ever had. *Pathetic.*

That thought occurred after her third orgasm.

After the fourth, she asked herself, *How did I go so long without sex?* Thirteen months without so much as a hint of sexual gratification from another human being. *Pathetic.*

And then there were the thoughts of Adrien. Or, rather, the fantasies. Somehow, her mind—or was it the fucking machine?—convinced her that she heard him for a split second. It was an erotic sound, as if he were on the verge of coming. This fantasy aroused a fifth orgasm, despite the slowed tempo of the mechanical arm. *Pathetic.*

After a few more orgasms, Sophie began to crave something besides the mechanical touch of the machine. She had always liked affection, was someone who sought human contact—a hug, a kiss, a cuddle, an involuntary touch. She hated sleeping alone. She wasn't sure how that had changed so drastically after Josh's death, now feeling the full weight of loneliness from the past thirteen months. And if the purpose of the incessant waves of venery from an inanimate object was to somehow satisfy her, it had done the opposite. Sophie was in no way satiated by the time Adrien approached and turned off the machine. If anything, her desires to touch and be touched had multiplied since her previous attempt at seduction. It wasn't that she needed sex. She just needed humanness. Some form of contact that would remind her of the warmth that existed between one person and another.

Adrien crouched by the bed to unlock the spreader bar, rubbing each ankle as he did so. The blood flowed more easily without the weight of the shackles, causing a slight tingling despite Adrien's massaging. When he was satisfied, he stood between Sophie's legs and grabbed her by the waist to flip her onto her back, simultaneously moving her away from the edge of the bed. The pain from the restraints at her wrists and the tugging in her arms ceased, and she sighed in relief, not realizing until that moment how uncomfortable she had been.

Adrien leaned over her to undo the silk ties, massaging each wrist before gently pulling Sophie upright. Not daring a look at him, but emboldened by her need for touch, Sophie used the forward motion to wrap her arms around his neck and press her body against his before placing her lips to Adrien's.

She felt him freeze, stiffening as soon as she wrapped her arms around him. His arms remained at his side, not reciprocating the embrace she so desperately craved. And yet, he didn't stop her, didn't pull away. Hungrily, she pulled him closer, parting her lips to sweep her tongue over his lips, enticing him to open his mouth. And, for a fleeting moment, he did. He allowed their tongues to mingle.

But as soon as the kiss began to deepen, Adrien's hands gently pried Sophie's from the back of his neck, holding her wrists firmly. He pushed her back down onto the bed, taking a step back.

"No more," he scolded. She still couldn't look at him. The fear of disobedience wasn't preventing her—this time, it was humiliation. He had denied her again—twice in the same day. *Pathetic.* It broke her. She looked down at her hands and began to cry. Her tears fell silently at first, but turned into a torrent of sobs as the day's events and emotions began to reemerge, tumbling through her mind.

She felt herself being scooped up, Adrien's arms cradling her, carrying her like a child as she continued to cry. Burying her face into his chest, she inhaled his scent and wept the entire way back to her room. *Pathetic.*

Twice in the same day she had tried to seduce him. Perhaps he really *had* been too soft with her. Perhaps she could see his weakness. *Pathetic.*

Either way, it couldn't keep happening. He would have to teach her another lesson.

18

Sophie's dreams melded into erotic scenes of Adrien between her legs, thrusting in a steady rhythm, but when she awoke, the only rhythm she felt was the pounding of a headache. She was wet from the remnants of the dream and sore from the remnants of yesterday's machine.

She rolled over to check the time. *7:09 a.m.* Adrien would be there soon, and hopefully he could bring her a pain reliever for both the headache and the tenderness between her legs. She had fallen asleep almost as soon as Adrien had tucked her into bed, skipping both dinner and the shower that she probably desperately needed. It didn't surprise her that she now had a headache. But she had slept relatively well—no nightmares, at least. And, not counting the sex dreams, she hadn't woken up at all during the night. She wondered how long she had slept. *Twelve hours?* At the least.

Maybe I really did just need a good fuck, after all, she thought as she pulled the covers from her body and swung her legs over the side of the bed. Somehow, the thought was less amusing now. She made her way to the shower, hoping the steam and hot water might alleviate some of the aches and pains.

When she emerged from the shower, headache still firmly intact, the first thing she noticed was the tray at her bedside table. The second thing she noticed was the time. *7:30 a.m.* Adrien had come early and, what was more, he had dropped off her breakfast and left. He had never done either of those things before.

Odd, Sophie thought, making her way to the tray. She took the toast, already buttered, and sat in bed with her back against the headboard, nibbling absentmindedly at the bread. She wondered if maybe he was avoiding her. Maybe she had done something wrong to cause this new morning routine. *Or maybe you finally did something right and he doesn't need to watch your every move anymore.* The thought left her feeling strangely unnerved. Finishing the toast, she drank the glass of juice that was on the tray and decided to lie down again until she needed to get into kneeling position for Adrien's return. Assuming he would be back around 8:30, his usual time, she would give herself until 8:25. Just a few more minutes of sleep to help ease the headache…

"What the fuck is this? Get up!" Adrien's voice boomed across the room, jolting Sophie from sleep. She shot up in bed, searching for the time. *8:35 a.m.* She had overslept and, by the sound of the anger in Adrien's voice, he was in no mood to deal with Sophie's shortcomings this morning. Before he could reach her side of the bed, she scrambled up and onto the floor, kneeling as he approached her. He towered over her as he spoke. "Have you forgotten the rules already, *Chevrette*?

What do I expect from you when I enter a room?"

Keeping her eyes cast to the ground, she answered, "You want me to be kneeling, Sir." *Sir. Maybe that would placate him.* She hadn't called him Sir since having addressed him by his real name, finding it easier to just forgo names.

"Clearly you haven't forgotten. Which tells me you were just blatantly disregarding my expectations. Am I going to have to teach you a lesson for that, too?" *Too?* Alarm bells rang in Sophie's head. What else had she done to deserve punishment? *Has he gone insane? Was he ever sane to begin with?* She shivered at the thought. But maybe if she explained why she was asleep, he would understand, and waive the punishment for her digression. Regarding the other lesson he referred to, she felt explanations wouldn't suffice. She had no idea what he was even talking about.

"I'm sorry, Sir," she began, "I had a headache and I was trying to rest before you got back. I didn't mean to oversleep. I intended to get up by 8:25, but…" She wasn't sure what her excuse was, really. *Why hadn't she just set the alarm?* "I'm sorry."

He didn't reply immediately, and Sophie held onto the hope that he would be reasonable. "I see. And do you still have a headache?"

"Yes, Sir," she nodded. She figured it was a bad time to ask for the pain reliever.

He didn't respond and Sophie had to fight the urge to look at him. *What goes through his mind at times like this?* Finally, his voice reached her ears. "You need to learn to push through the pain and still be able to do what is expected of you." *There goes asking for painkillers.* Sophie pressed her lips together, fighting the desire to ask anyway. Instead, she nodded, squeezing her eyes shut. Even that small motion alleviated the pain in her temples.

"Get up. It's time for you to learn your other lesson." She stood immediately to avoid any further punishment while her mind frenzied trying to figure out what she had done wrong. Her heart pounded in time with her headache at the thought of the whips and paddles in the floors below. *Would he bring her back there? Or would he spank her again?* She wished she could pick. She would choose the spanking any day.

"Sir?" she tried. When she heard no objection from him, she continued, "May I ask what I'm being punished for?"

He stepped toward her, lifting her chin with the crook of his index finger. His eyes sparkled as he answered, "This isn't punishment, *Chevrette*. You haven't broken any rules…aside from that one transgression this morning, but I believe you're paying for that already." Playfully, he tapped her temple with his forefinger, causing her to wince at the reminder. "You haven't done anything to deserve *punishment*, per se. This is just a lesson that you need to learn. One that you need to remember." Adrien stepped back, putting space between the two of them as he held out his hand for her to take. "Now, let's go."

⸎

Like water being poured into a tall glass, apprehension filled her with each step she took. By the time they reached their destination, Sophie felt like she was drowning in it, unable to breathe for fear of water seeping into her lungs. Her chest burned at the notion. It seemed so paradoxical—water that felt like fire.

They had arrived at the training room. Perhaps it should have eased her mind; nothing bad had ever happened to her in that room, after all. In fact, she felt quite the opposite about what had occurred—what was occurring—among the silk sheets and bondage tools. She had yet to feel violated or hurt in any physical sense, and had experienced more pleasure there in the past several days than she had in most of her adult life. What Adrien said rang true. When she allowed it, everything that transpired in that room had been pleasurable. As she approached the bed, her heart continued to thud in her chest. From apprehension or anticipation, she wasn't quite sure.

"Sit," Adrien commanded, pointing toward the bed. She walked toward it, noticing the sheets had been freshened once again. She sat at the edge as she watched Adrien stride toward her with leather cuffs in hand. He secured the cuffs to the bedposts, clasping them to the wrought-iron curve of the metal rungs. When he was satisfied with his preparations, he indicated for Sophie to lie back. She obeyed, stretching her arms out on either side of her head as Adrien placed her hands in the cuffs and tightened them. The cool leather felt soft against her skin despite the tightness of the restraints. Remaining still, he cuffed her feet, once again using the spreader-bar to create a perfect X out of Sophie's limbs. Unlike yesterday, her body lay completely flat on the bed, allowing for some comfort in the position. She wasn't able to move her limbs, but at least she could sink her weight into the welcoming silk sheets.

Her eyes followed Adrien as he made his way toward the shelves, grabbing a black cloth before turning back to the bed. She recognized the shape. A blindfold. Nerves fluttered in her stomach at the idea of not being able to witness what was going to happen. Adrien had always let her see what was coming, had even explained it to her. Now, she wondered what it was that he didn't want her to see.

"Do you have to put the blindfold on me?" she implored as Adrien propped his leg on the bed to lean over her. He didn't answer her. Or rather, not with words. He deftly placed the blindfold over her eyes, rendering her world dark.

She felt the shift almost immediately as her other senses heightened. She was reminded of the warehouse in which she was gagged, blindfolded, and bound only a few weeks ago. She felt the beating in her chest, heard her breaths become more frequent, felt the knot in her stomach grow. The haze intensified with a slow shift of the sheets in response to his movement, his hand as it sank into the mattress beside her shoulder. The scent of lemongrass and ginger invaded the air around her, the atmosphere turning warmer, intoxicating.

And then, the unmistakable feel of Adrien. He wasn't touching her, but she could feel him hovering above her. Looking down at her. Hesitating? She could picture his look of contemplation, unsure of what to do with her. She speculated the options he could be considering.

The mattress shifted again as Sophie sensed the gap in their proximity beginning to close. She took a deep breath, just to see. And she was right. Her chest rose to graze against his. The connection made her heart rate quicken. She felt the roughness of his thumb against her jawline, causing a breakout of goose bumps along her arms. Ever so lightly, his lips met hers. She felt him pause, as though questioning, and she parted her lips to invite him in. The hesitation melted, gone in an instant. Adrien kissed her, his tongue hungrily seeking hers. It felt passionate—desperate, even.

She wanted to hold onto him, cling to him, bring him closer, press her body against his. She burned for his touch, but the restraints prevented it. She moaned into his mouth in frustration, her own desperation surfacing.

He pulled back, his breath ragged and heavy. "See that? That right there is the problem, *Chevrette*." He sounded irritated.

What did I do wrong? He was the one who kissed me! She lay there in silent disbelief, hoping he would fill in the blanks for her.

"You take what isn't being given to you, *Chevrette*." He must have sensed her confusion. "You need to learn to take only what is being offered." His words sank in as she lay staring into the blackness of the blindfold. *So this was about yesterday? About trying to get him to have sex with me? To kiss me?*

"But…you said I'm responsible for my own pleasure. I was just taking responsibility. I wasn't doing anything wrong." She heard his sharp intake of breath. She saw him considering her words in her mind's eye, imagined his hand cupping his chin while his gray and blue eyes squinted in thought. She awaited his deliberation.

"You're right. I said that. But let me clarify. You are responsible for your own pleasure *when it is being offered.* If it is not offered, you are not to take it. Your master is to be in complete control at all times. If your master tells you to come, do it. If they tell you not to, then don't. You are not to undermine that, and it won't be good for you if you do. I'm teaching you a lesson, but if you don't learn it here, you will be punished. So, I suggest you pay attention." Sophie felt the bed shift again as Adrien withdrew. His footsteps fell lightly on the floor as he moved away from the bed toward the back of the room. Sophie heard some shuffling of items before the *tap tap* of his footsteps announced his return.

She felt Adrien's fingers on her nipples then, twirling them mechanically until they stiffened under his touch. She didn't get the feeling he was being sensual, just that it was something that needed to be done. He stopped and she felt the cold metal on first her right nipple, then her left. She heard him begin to twist something as if screwing it in, and she felt the pressure on her nipple tighten as though it were being squeezed by a clamp.

Just before it got unbearable, he stopped, moving to the other side.

"There," he said satisfied, and she felt a tug on both clamps as though the clips pinching her nipples were joined together by some sort of chain. The tugging motion caused a sharp piercing sensation and she gasped at the discomfort. He laughed in response. "That's nothing yet, *Chevrette*. Don't move too much or it will get worse."

She felt him move lower, heard him pick up a new object. She felt a sudden cool sensation as he rubbed the slick lubricant onto and around her body, baffled as to why he was applying it around her vagina and not on the typical areas. Her nerves fluttered again as she felt something plastic cup her sex. *What the fuck is that?*

"Have you ever used a pussy pump before?" His voiced was tinged with amusement. Was he mocking her? Or was he simply asking the question only to answer hers? Her thoughts were cut short as she felt a sudden suck of air surrounding her mound. Then, a tugging at her breasts followed by the sound of a click as the chain served to connect the two devices; one pinching the buds of her nipples and the other cupping her sensitive flesh. It was uncomfortable, especially the sharp pull and aching squeeze at her nipples. Sophie wanted to move. If only she could adjust, it might be more comfortable. She raised her hips in a meager attempt, but was met by a sudden and excruciating pain from the chain.

She cried out. Adrien *tsked*, as if admonishing a disobedient child. "I told you not to move, didn't I? Haven't you learned to trust me by now? Have I ever lied to you, *Chevrette*?" She felt trapped, contained by the sensations as though being held hostage. *Fitting.*

"What are you going to do to me?" The apprehension was

back. He had yet to hurt her, but he had warned her on her first day of training that some things would hurt. She felt the growing presumption that pain would be involved.

"I already told you. I'm teaching you to take what is being given to you."

"I know, but…how?" She could hear the anxiety in her own voice. It sounded weak. Childish.

"I'll give you a hint." He pumped the device a second time, the sensation like a vacuum while pressure built inside the cup. It wasn't an unpleasant feeling. In fact, her sensitivity was already heightened. She flexed her hips instinctively, wanting more, momentarily forgetting about the chain that held her captive. She cried out again as another shot of pain bolted from her nipples to her core.

She only needed one hint to understand what he meant. She would lie there and take what he gave her. She would ask for no more or no less than what he was offering, otherwise the consequence would be painful.

She squeezed her eyes shut under the blindfold, bracing herself for more. Another pump came, but she didn't flinch this time. Without the sharp pain from the nipple clamps, Sophie actually liked the feeling of the pump. Adrien pumped once more and, again, Sophie took it without moving.

"See that, *Chevrette*? If you can just accept what your master is offering, it will always be much better for you." Sophie bit down on her lip as Adrien pumped again.

"Yes, Sir," she whispered, afraid that even nodding her head would cause the nipple clamps to tug.

"Good. I'm glad you understand." Sophie felt Adrien's weight shift on the bed. She half expected that to be it. She had learned the lesson. The blindfold would come off, the pussy pump removed.

Instead, she heard the unmistakable whir of the vibrator.

"What's the other lesson you are learning today, *Chevrette?*" Adrien asked.

"Um…" Sophie barely registered the question over the humming vibrations, distracted by the suction around her clit.

"Have you forgotten already?" he asked, flicking the cup. Her sensitivity already heightened by the pump, Sophie gasped as the feeling of pleasure intensified. She couldn't help but move in the process, causing a simultaneous sting of pain to jolt through her. Both the pleasure and pain took a similar path, meeting at her core. It was a conflicting sensation.

It was her reminder. "I'm supposed to push through the pain." She said it through gritted teeth, coming down from the intensity. As she said the words, she realized his intentions with the vibrator. Her mind whirred in tandem with the sound, her thoughts creating their own vibrations. She would have to move. It was inevitable. There was no way her body could lay still with the onslaught of a vibrator.

How much will it hurt?

How much will I enjoy it?

"Good girl." Adrien's voice brought her back to the moment. She felt his hand softly on her hip, caressing her. "Relax, *Chevrette*. Let yourself enjoy what you can." His voice was soothing, like his caress. It made her *want* to push through it, experience the ecstasy. "Are you ready?"

She nodded, took a deep breath, and let it out in a low moan as he placed the vibrator over the cup. As an explosion of intensity swept over Sophie, she arched to meet it, concurrently pulling at the clips on her nipples. Her moan turned into a cry of pain, and the vibrator retreated a fraction of a second later. As her body readjusted to the sudden loss of pleasure, her mind acclimated to the discomfort. It wasn't as strong as the feeling of ecstasy accompanying it. She missed it, wanted more.

She felt Adrien shift on the bed again. For a brief moment, she panicked at the thought that he might stop. Instead, she felt the mattress sink from his weight, creating a divot as he moved closer. His scent filled the air around her again, hovering.

"Again?" She could hear the question mark in his voice, but the way he said it sounded more like a statement. An inevitability. Inevitably, she nodded. As her body was again presented with the strong mixture of agony and desire, Adrien's mouth captured her cries, his tongue seeking, taking from her. His kiss flared with desperation, deepening with Sophie's building climax. He held the vibrator over the pump, the suction contributing to the overwhelming sensation consuming Sophie's body. It was too much and not enough. She returned Adrien's kiss, arching against the pain of the nipple clips, now welcoming the pulling and tugging they offered. She couldn't stop it and, in that moment, she didn't want to. As she began to feel her body climb to the edge of orgasm, Adrien broke away from her body.

In an instant, the suctioning disappeared and the tugging chain went slack. For a brief second, her climax waned, but was quickly reignited as Adrien placed the vibrator directly on her swollen clit. Her orgasm hit, crashing around her as wave after wave swept through her body. Sophie's hips bucked involuntarily. She was electric, a live wire jumping from the energy coursing through it.

Adrien eased the vibrator, allowing Sophie to come down. She panted heavily as her heart rate sought to slow itself. After a moment, Adrien removed the blindfold. Sophie squinted to allow her eyes to readapt to the brightness of the room. Next,

Adrien worked to unbuckle the restraints, taking care to rub each of her wrists where the band had pulled tight against her skin. She lay there, exhausted by the intensity of her orgasm, her mind and body absolutely wiped.

Adrien looked down at her, a slight smile shadowing his lips. "What did you learn today, *Chevrette*?"

She looked him in the eye as she said, "To take what my master gives me, no more, no less, and to push through the pain. It's better that way."

Adrien stared into the steaming water as it flowed from the spout and splashed into the large tub below. Water itself had never been a problem for Adrien; it was bathtubs that made him nervous. Ever since his mother, he had never stepped foot inside a bathtub. But his mind was elsewhere as the tub filled.

There comes a point in every training—that moment right after Adrien broke them—when the girls hover, held hostage between who they once were and who they were about to become. Often, Adrien wondered what he would create, *whom* he would create, really, if he could just hold them there long enough. A psyche, suspended in time.

A noise from the bedroom brought Adrien from his thoughts. He looked out at Sophie—*at Chevrette*, he reminded himself— where she waited on the bed. When had he started thinking of her as Sophie rather than *Chevrette*? He hadn't noticed.

His eyes swept over her. She sat upright, still naked, with her head held in her hands. *Her headache must still be bothering her,* Adrien noted. He would get her the Ibuprofen when she was finished bathing. He glanced back to the tub. *Almost done.*

It's too late for her, anyway, he thought. In just another week, he would bring her to the pre-auction event to find her buyer. She was too close to becoming what he had always created in the girls: a sex slave. Nothing more, nothing less. The holding point had almost passed for Sophie.

His stomach knotted at the thought. Or maybe it was just the bathtub. It was full.

19

The car was falling. It always fell. Adrien had been there a moment before. He always seemed to be around now. But she didn't listen to him when he told her not to get into the car. And now she was falling, trapped inside the machine, bouncing down the ravine. With every tumble, her head smacked against the window.

Thud.

Thud.

Thud.

It was the pounding of her head that finally woke Sophie. The headache hadn't gotten better despite the pain reliever Adrien had given her. If anything, her head was worse, accented by a dull pain in her eyes. The cold sweat was secondary. She shivered, pulling the duvet cover over her. Her skin felt hot and clammy, her stomach churning. She tried to ignore it, instead, concentrating on the exhaustion as she drifted back into a restless sleep.

She awoke several times, vaguely registering the pain and

nausea, knowing that Adrien would walk in and she wouldn't be kneeling. He wouldn't be happy. Two days in a row she would still be in bed when he arrived. But she couldn't push through this pain. It felt impossible, overwhelming. Fevered thoughts lingered on her potential punishment for disobeying. She was supposed to have learned her lesson yesterday. She would have to make him understand, listen, and see reason. She knew what she would have to do, knew how dangerous it could be. But as her fever climbed higher and higher with each toss and turn, she became convinced it was the only way he would understand how serious this was. She just hoped it wouldn't backfire.

The beeping of a keypad. The click of a door. Then again, she thought she had heard the click of the door several times in the past few hours. Too exhausted to roll over and see if he was actually there. Again and again she had called out to him, hoping he would hear her, come to her side, understand. But he never responded. Because it wasn't really the click of the door she heard. Just her imagination running away with her fever.

This time was different, though. This time, she knew he was really there. She could feel his presence, even before she heard his muttered irritation. "What the fuck is this?" More to himself than to her. Or maybe she just couldn't hear him that well over the pounding in her head.

"Adrien?" *There. She said it. Would he be mad? Would he hurt Megan like he said he would? Or would he understand how serious this was—a pain she couldn't push through?* He had paused at the sound of his name; she heard his footsteps coming toward her when he entered the room and their falter when she spoke. She took a deep breath. "Adrien, I don't feel right."

He was there, at her side. Had she fallen asleep? Or had he moved so quickly that she didn't register the sound of his strides? She couldn't tell. She was exhausted and aching. The pain was no longer just in her head. It had spread like a cancer, seeping into her bones.

"What's wrong, *Chevrette*?" His voice sounded so distant. She just wanted to sleep. And cry. She wanted to cry because of the pain. Had he asked her something? She couldn't remember. She felt his hand on her forehead, heard him swear in French. At least, she assumed it was a curse; it had the same cadence. His voice came again, this time in Spanish. He was talking to someone, but not to her.

"I need you here. Now," he demanded, still in Spanish. Was someone in the room with them? No, it was definitely a one-sided conversation. He paused, apparently listening to the person's response. Then, "I don't care what time your shift ends. I need you *here.*" Another pause. She wondered who was on the other end. "If I'm not mistaken, your son—what's his name? Eduardo?—he really enjoys that private school you send him to. I've watched him on the soccer field. He's got quite a talent. I wouldn't want to have to stop those payments…" A brief pause. "Do you really want to find out? …That's better. Yes, that's fine. Call me when you're here, I'll let you in."

Did he just threaten someone? Sophie bristled at the notion. If he could threaten someone over the phone like that, what would he do to Megan? She had broken his rule and used his name. Entirely aware of the consequence and yet, she had said it anyway. *Adrien.*

"Please, don't hurt her." She said aloud, meaning for it to come out strong and convincing, but even she could barely hear herself. There was no response.

Where is he? Sophie realized he was no longer at her side. She heard the faucet in the bathroom running. After a moment, the faucet turned off and Adrien's footsteps fell once more against the floors. He'd returned to her side, smoothing the hair from her face, the sweat acting like glue. A cold cloth met the heat of Sophie's forehead.

"Please," she tried again, this time forcing strength into her voice. "Please don't hurt her."

"Shhh, *Chevrette*. No one is getting hurt," Adrien hushed her as he readjusted the cloth so the cooler parts absorbed the fever's heat. His response didn't make sense to her. Perhaps he hadn't understood what she meant. Perhaps he thought she was fevered, not making any sense. She needed to explain.

"Don't hurt Megan. I said your name, but I just needed you to listen. Please, don't hurt her. Please…" Her voice trailed off, her energy completely spent.

He sighed a weary sigh. "I'm not going to hurt her, Sophie. You don't need to worry about that right now." It was tit for tat. She had used his name, hoping he would listen. He had used hers, indicating she should do the same. She trusted him. What choice did she have?

His thumb grazed her cheek. She leaned into his touch, wanting to thank him but lacking the energy.

Within minutes, Sophie was asleep.

She awoke at the touch of a hand on her shoulder, gently shaking. The pain behind her eyes was excruciating. She didn't want to open them. Whoever it was could go away. They could wait until the pain subsided, until she could move again.

"Sophie, I need you to wake up. The doctor is here to see you," Adrien's voice whispered next to her ear. She rolled toward it, grateful that he had brought someone to help her. That must have been to whom he was talking earlier. It seemed so long ago. "Come on, try to sit up." Adrien's hand helped lift Sophie into a sitting position. Her eyes remained closed, the pounding and aching in her body increasing with each movement. She opened her eyes, ever so slightly, before quickly slamming them shut again. Even the light hurt.

She heard the doctor's voice. Familiar. It was the same woman who examined her earlier in training. The doctor spoke in English to Sophie. "Can you tell me your symptoms, Miss?"

"It hurts. Everywhere. It was just a headache at first, but now it's everywhere. My eyes. My bones. It feels like my bones are being split apart." Sophie said this while the doctor took her blood pressure and checked her temperature. The pressure from the cuff was agonizing.

"Have you been drinking any of the tap water here?"

Sophie shrugged. She really wasn't sure where the water Adrien gave her came from. She heard him offer a response. "No. Only bottled water. No ice cubes."

The thermometer beeped. "You have a pretty high fever. Have you been outside at all? Have you gotten bitten by any mosquitoes?"

She tried to think. She had been outside plenty of times with Adrien but could only recall the mosquitoes bothering her once a few days prior. It had been earlier in the evening than usual, just about dusk when they had gone outside to smoke. She had swatted a few mosquitoes away but couldn't remember getting bitten.

The world tilted like it wanted to shake Sophie off its surface. The shift came so suddenly, Sophie grasped at the bed sheets, holding on for dear life. *Strange*, she thought, recalling how she had contemplated letting go of life just a few weeks ago.

"Miss?"

"What the fuck just happened? Is she okay?" Sophie registered the concern in Adrien's voice before everything went black.

"The symptoms indicate dengue fever, but I'm going to need to take a blood sample," Dr. Martes stated.

"Fine. Do what you need to do," Adrien replied, distracted by the fact that Sophie had just passed out mid-exam. He kept his eyes trained on Sophie as the doctor walked to her bag.

"Have you been using bug spray when you're outside?" the doctor asked as she rifled through her things. Adrien was irritated by the question. Or, rather, irritated by its answer.

"No," he muttered. Dr. Martes shot him a dirty look from across the room. That irritated him, too. But she was the best doctor in the area, so he put up with it.

"She needs rest and fluids. And plenty of them. I don't know exactly what you do here, but I suggest you take a break from whatever it is. If you push her too hard, she could develop hemorrhagic fever, she could go into shock, her organs could start shutting down…shall I keep going?" Her tone was biting. *God, she could be a real cunt sometimes.*

It was Adrien's turn to glare. "I won't push her. How long will it take for her to recover?"

"It could be weeks, depending. The fever is in the early stages, so you need to monitor her closely. She's going to need to stay hydrated. If a rash develops or you notice any bruising, call me immediately. She may need an IV. I can bring one from the hospital."

"Calling you won't be necessary. You'll be staying here until she's better."

"Excuse me?" Dr. Martes looked bewildered.

"You heard me."

"You know I can't do that. I have to take care of my son."

"I'll see to it that he's taken care of. You can stay in this room, I'll move her to a different one."

The doctor began to argue, but Adrien was ready to move on from the conversation. "Take the blood sample, Dr. Martes," he demanded with finality. Her mouth seemed to have stopped working. It just hung open as though it wasn't sure what to do when words weren't coming out. Slowly, she deflated. She knew she couldn't win. Adrien had too much power. She took the blood sample.

"I'll need to send it to the lab," she said quietly.

"I'll see to it," Adrien replied, walking over to where Sophie lay and hoisting her into his arms.

⸎

She vaguely recalled an argument, two familiar voices whispering an angry staccato of words. She was too exhausted to try to decipher the conversation, but she knew they were talking about her, arguing about her. And then, a needle's pinprick, hardly noticeable above the calamity of pain in the rest of her body. She wished nothing more than to drown out its noise.

And then, her world was tilting again, but this time she was wrapped in lemongrass and ginger and warmth. She floated there, swaying for a moment before being righted again, her body coming back to earth, gravity restored, back from its fleeting hiatus. She was somewhere new and soft—a bed?—encompassed by the scent that was distinctly *him*, as though the very bed itself exuded the fragrance.

"Sit up, Sophie." Adrien's voice was soft and soothing in her ear as he lifted her into a sitting position. "You need to drink." She obeyed him, and probably always would. She took a sip from the glass he held to her lips, her own hands too weak to hold it herself. He tilted it, slowly pouring the liquid into her mouth before patiently moving the cup away, waiting for her to swallow. The water felt like daggers going down. They repeated this routine until Adrien was apparently satisfied that she'd had enough to drink. He gently laid her back down.

"Please don't leave me." Where had she found the strength to say it? She didn't want to be alone through this. She felt like she was dying and it scared her. It didn't elude her that only a few weeks ago she would have embraced this. But now, she feared it.

Tugging the sheets over her and smoothing her hair he murmured, "Go to sleep."

As always, she obeyed.

It was his fault. He had pushed her too hard. He should have listened to her when she said she had a headache. He should have given her something for the pain instead of trying to teach her a lesson. Maybe then things wouldn't have gotten this bad.

Why do I care? The thought nagged at him. He couldn't come up with the answer, or maybe he didn't want to. Either way, the guilt festered.

He had whispered apologies to her while she slept. The words sounded unfamiliar in his ears. Apologize was something Adrien never did—he couldn't even remember the last time he said the words 'I'm sorry' to anyone. Most likely, he had been made to apologize to Etienne for some reason or another as kids. He doubted he ever actually meant it. So he was surprised by the sincerity he felt when the words tumbled from him as Sophie slept. His pounding heart and his pleading whisper sliced through the silence between them. He was glad she wasn't awake; it comforted him to know she couldn't actually hear him.

The rash appeared overnight. Little spots emerged on her hands, as though the blood vessels were too full to remain intact, relieving the pressure by bursting open beneath her skin. She hadn't woken up for two days, except when he forced her to drink water. Even then, she was barely cognizant, accepting the water but unable to accept any other form of external stimulus. He stayed by her side, sleeping in an armchair while she lay in his bed. She slept fitfully, thrashing about and murmuring in her sleep. Whenever she began a new fit, he would reach out to her. Sometimes he found himself tracing the curve of her jaw, other times just a touch of her shoulder, or fingers through her hair. The result was always the same. She stopped, settled. *Comforted?* The power made him feel heady, which, in turn, made his stomach feel as though the room were full of bathtubs.

⸙

Sophie was running along the beach, sprinting as fast as she could. Her lungs greedily gulped in the air around her as she pumped her arms and legs, willing her body to move. She couldn't remember if she was running from something or toward something, but whichever it was, it held importance. She had to run or something bad would happen.

The sound of a branch snapping under foot slowed her pace. Trees loomed around her, the forest so dense and thick she could no longer see where she was going. Odd, *she thought,* wasn't I just on the beach? *She couldn't recall how she had gotten here. She must have been running faster than she realized.*

Another twig snapped, indicating she wasn't alone in the woods. "Sophie?" *A voice called out. She recognized it. It was Josh's. Her heart hammered in her chest, but not from her sprint. From something else. Fear? Yes, fear. She could feel it creeping in like a fog. She was afraid of Josh. She began sprinting again, trying to escape, not wanting him to find her.*

She was running from him. But then she remembered she was running toward something, too. Toward Adrien. He was here somewhere. Back on the beach? *She turned, looking for the sand and ocean in the moonlight, but the trees were too thick to see out. She screamed in desperation, calling his name.*

"Adrien!" Another twig snapped nearby. Panicking, she quickened her pace, running away from Josh, hopefully toward Adrien. "Adrien! Where are you?" She continued to scream his name, knowing she was giving away her whereabouts to Josh. If she could just get to Adrien, though, she would be fine. She would be safe. And she had something important she needed to tell him.

She felt someone grab her hair. She was being tugged backward. Josh's hot breath was on her neck as he snarled into her ear, "I barely even recognize you anymore, Sophie. I miss the way you were before." He was pulling her away from where she knew Adrien was waiting. And the screams ripped through her...

Adrien had been pulled out of an uncomfortable night's sleep in the armchair by the sound of his name on her lips. At first, he thought she was finally awake, but soon realized she was dreaming. *Of him.* He froze at the realization, unmoving, not daring to reach out to her. It was selfish of him, he acknowledged this, but he wanted to know—was he the subject of her nightmares? Or was she dreaming about him?

"Adrien, where are you?" It came out as a whimper. His chest constricted. Was she looking for him? This didn't sound like a nightmare.

The scream ripped through the air, jolting Adrien back in his chair. He hadn't noticed he was leaning forward, on the edge of his seat like he had been watching some sort of blockbuster movie. Sophie's scream subsided without waking her. But it had jarred Adrien from his daydream. How foolish to think that she had been dreaming of him. Of course it had been a nightmare.

For the first time in days, Adrien got up from the chair and left the room.

Sophie's eyes took in the room around her as she woke, taking a moment to register why it seemed familiar. For some reason, she was in Adrien's room. In Adrien's bed, rather than her own. The bright windows illuminated the artwork on the walls— Degas's ballerinas, similar to those on the other end of the house. She looked around, noticing the armchair next to the bed, adorned with a bunched-up throw blanket hanging over the side. He had clearly been spending time there but wasn't currently in the room. She looked toward the glass sliding door and out onto the balcony.

Adrien sat in one of the chairs, his bare feet resting on the balcony railing. His long legs were covered by his sweatpants, but he was shirtless, his tanned skin soaking in the rays of the sun. His elbow was propped on the chair's arm, his hand acting as a pedestal for his chin. He sat like that, with his head cradled in his hand, staring out at the bright morning sky. She watched him, saw the sadness in his gaze, as though he were grappling with the fact that he would never see the way the stars shine during the day. She had the sudden urge to interrupt the sun.

He shifted in his seat then, snapping out of his trance. He took his legs off the balcony and rose, sliding the door open and entering the bedroom. He looked toward the bed as he shut the door, a look of surprise appearing on his face. If Sophie weren't mistaken, she may have even seen a sense of relief pass over his features.

"You're awake," he said as he walked toward the bed. She smiled and nodded in response. "How are you feeling?"

She hadn't even acknowledged how much better she felt upon waking. Her fever had broken and the pain had certainly subsided. She was still exhausted but, overall, felt much better. She reassured him she was feeling better before asking, "How long have I been out of it for?"

"Five days," he replied, his voice etched with concern. Her mouth dropped open. *Five days?* She hadn't even realized how long it had been. *Two days maybe, but five?* "I'll have Dr. Martes take another look at you just to make sure everything is fine," he added. Sophie nodded her consent.

"Can I take a shower first?" *Five days feverishly sweating without a shower?* She cringed at the thought.

"Of course." Adrien got up and motioned toward the bathroom. "I'll grab you some clean clothes."

She headed to the bathroom, not bothering to close the door. Privacy wasn't something she even considered anymore. The bathroom was beautiful, even more so than the one in her room. The shower itself was huge, boasting a double showerhead on either side of its square shape, with a rain showerhead hanging from the center of the ceiling. Sophie peeled off the grimy t-shirt and shorts and turned on the shower faucet. Water fell from the showerheads in large droplets, reminding her of the rainstorms so frequent in Costa Rica. Once the water was warm, she stepped in, allowing it to cascade around her and down her body. She stood there for a few minutes, reveling in the storm, letting the water completely consume her. She lifted her face to the spray and squeezed her eyes shut.

The movement caused an unexpected wave of nausea and dizziness. She took a deep breath, realizing she needed to sit. She lowered herself to the floor of the shower, kneeling on the cool tile to regain her balance. Dark spots danced before her eyes as unconsciousness threatened to take her.

"Sophie?" Adrien's voice hesitated at the door of the bathroom.

"Adrien?" she called out. When had he started calling her by her name? When had she started calling him by his?

"*Fuck.* Sophie, what happened?" She felt his presence at the glass shower door. He opened it, stepping into the cascading water, his sweatpants beginning to drench. He crouched down beside her, his knee inadvertently brushing against hers on its way to the floor. So many times she had knelt before him. It felt odd to have him kneeling with her. Even then, though, he didn't kneel completely. She wondered if he did that on purpose, to maintain some semblance of hierarchy.

"I just got dizzy. I think I'll be fine in a second," Sophie reassured him, not truly convinced herself. She waited as the spell passed, replaced by an intense fatigue that seeped to her core. She shook her head, frustrated with herself, with her body. "I'm too tired." She whispered it, embarrassed that she couldn't even take a shower.

She felt his hands gently beneath her arms. She followed his guidance as he helped lift her to her feet. "Lean on me." It was a command, but it was gentle. She wrapped her arms around his torso, placing her forehead against his chest. To an outsider, it may have looked like they were embracing. To Sophie, she knew this was the closest they'd ever come to an embrace.

He began washing her with the bar of soap, carefully gliding it along her skin. She worked with him, moving and readjusting as he lathered. She could feel him stiffening as her body glided against his. Had she not been so exhausted, she would have considered the scene erotic. She would have wanted to do something about the way his erection pressed against her.

He began lathering her hair with shampoo. It was different than the shampoo in her shower. This was *his.* Distinctly lemongrass. She inhaled, smiling at the thought. "It smells like you."

His fingers paused in her hair for just a moment, a barely noticeable arrhythmia of the heart. "I didn't realize I had a smell."

"Everyone has a smell."

"Do they?" He seemed amused. "Tell me more." He continued her head massage.

"It's like…a mix of people's shampoo and something else that makes it distinctly their own. The scent of their shampoo and their soul." She was mumbling into his chest, enjoying the feeling of his hands in her hair. He began to rinse the suds, maneuvering them both back under the spray of water.

He considered her words for a moment as he smoothed his hands through her hair. Then, so quietly, "I think you're mistaken, *Chevrette.* I don't have a soul."

She moved her head from his chest, arms still wrapped around his waist as she peered up at him. "You do, though. It smells like ginger."

Sophie climbed back into Adrien's bed. Her wet hair made a damp spot on the pillow as she settled back into its warmth and softness. Adrien ducked into his closet, emerging a moment later in a dry pair of jeans and a t-shirt. His wet hair fell in a limp mess over his forehead. She watched him as she lay there, willing her eyes to roam across his body. He walked over to the armchair beside the bed and sat down, watching her watching him.

"Do you want to rest a little while before I bring Dr. Martes back in?" he asked. She nodded in response, still not taking her eyes from him. He leaned back into the chair, seemingly getting ready to just sit. She smiled.

"When I was little, my mom used to sit by my side whenever I was sick. Like, *whenever* I was sick—even if it was just a cold. She would be there when I fell asleep and she'd be there when I woke up hours later. It was kind of ridiculous now that I think about it." Sophie yawned, letting her eyes close. She wasn't quite sure why she shared that with him. Maybe the fever had done something to her brain. Verbal diarrhea induced by dengue. She would have to look it up.

"Mine used to, too." Adrien's voice pulled her eyelids open. "She'd pull up a chair and just sit." That sad gaze was back—the one without the daytime stars.

"What is she like?" Sophie turned toward him, shifting her body to lie on her side.

He paused. "Was." It was a correction. *What was she like?*

She knew what it was like to tell people about loss. It evoked pity. Pity was the worst. "What was she like?" She asked again, careful to acknowledge without pitying.

He looked at her. *Really* looked at her. She could practically see the wheels spinning in his head trying to figure out if he should answer her, how he should answer her. She wondered what he'd say if he could just say anything. She hated the fact that she would have to settle.

"She was a dancer. Loved the ballet." He was looking at her but wasn't seeing her. His eyes were somewhere else. He was somewhere else, in the recesses of his memories. She suddenly felt intrusive, like she was spying on him.

"Is that why you have so many Degas paintings?" Sophie wondered aloud, breaking his trance.

He smiled, returning to the room from his mind's brief hiatus. "You're familiar?"

She nodded. "I studied fine arts in undergrad." He stared at her blankly for a moment before shifting in his chair. He looked away as though suddenly uncomfortable with meeting her gaze. She wondered about his sudden shift in demeanor. She wished it away, wanted the ease with which they had just been talking to return. She tried to salvage the moment. "Do you have a favorite Degas?"

He stared at her again. "L'etoile," he began, slowly, as though he wasn't quite sure if he wanted to continue. "Do you know it?" She nodded. She remembered it well—*The Star*. It depicted a dancer, her arms outstretched in mid-leap. "It reminds me of her, when she would dance. Like there was nothing else in the world that mattered. Sometimes I wonder if it was the only time she was ever unburdened." He fell silent. Sophie got the distinct impression that Adrien felt that he'd said too much. But he hadn't. In fact, she felt the opposite. He hadn't said enough.

"What happened to her?" She watched the emotions play across his features—sadness, anger, hurt, despair—before he seemingly shut a door. Adrien shook his head. She already knew that he wouldn't answer her. She marveled at the way he could hide inside himself so easily.

"You should rest, *Chevrette*." The hierarchy was reinstated. She missed the sound of her name already, the way its syllables floated off his tongue, cradled by the baritone in his voice. "You're going to have a busy week next week and you need to get your strength back up."

She suddenly didn't feel tired anymore, her curiosity piqued. *What was he planning?* "What do you mean?" Sophie asked.

"We're going on a field trip."

20

When Sophie was young, she used to love going on field trips. There was always something so exciting about them: the promise of no homework, the thrill of exploring a new place, the experience of buying overpriced trinkets from souvenir shops. The night before a field trip, Sophie always had trouble sleeping. It was the anticipation that kept her awake. But this was a different kind of anticipation. A different kind of field trip. Excitement was not what kept her awake. *Field trip.* Adrien had said those two words like it was any other field trip. Like it stood right beside all of the museums, aquariums, and pumpkin patches of her childhood.

He wouldn't tell her where he was bringing her. She had asked several times only to be met with silence. She stopped asking after a cold stare began accompanying his silence.

Anxiety gnawed at her as she watched Adrien pack a bag for her. He stood in her closet, picking through the outfits before selecting a few, like they were going on vacation. She deduced they would be staying overnight. Or, perhaps this was it. This was the end of her training and he would be dropping her off somewhere, indefinitely. How had she not thought of the possibility sooner?

"Ready?" Adrien emerged from the closet. *Am I allowed to say no?* She opted for silence, giving him a taste of his own medicine (sans cold glare, although she would have liked to). He didn't seem to notice. Adrien headed for the door, putting in the code, pressing his thumb to the pad, and stepping aside for Sophie to pass through. She moved forward, feeling the need to pause and take a deep breath before stepping across the threshold. As though she were resigned to her fate, stepping through to *'The Rest of My Life.'*

"You'll be fine, *Chevrette,*" Adrien reassured. He had reverted to calling her *Chevrette* when the doctor had officially cleared her as "healthy enough to finish training." It was compartmentalization at its finest. She missed being Sophie to him. Sophie had connected with Adrien. *Chevrette* was just another commodity, a trainee to her master.

"Why can't you tell me where we're going?" she asked. One last attempt. Hearing her voice crack, she tried to push away the tears that threatened.

Silence.

He led her through the house, past the kitchen before pausing at a door she had never noticed. This one held the familiar number pad, but had a large, smooth pad for...large thumbs? Sophie watched as Adrien entered the code and placed his entire palm against the pad. The door beeped open and Sophie realized why the added security measure.

It was a garage. With cars. Three of them to be exact, and a motorcycle. Four ways of escaping. Her eyes swept over the Jeep and landed on the sports cars. She had never much cared about what types of cars people drove, but she knew enough to know that these cars were expensive. *Really expensive.* Adrien led her to the beat-up Jeep, opening the passenger door and throwing her bag into the back. His, it appeared, was already in there. *At least wherever we're staying, he's planning on staying, too.* She took comfort in this thought as she climbed into the car.

"Put your seatbelt on," he instructed as he stood outside her door. After she'd clicked it into place, Adrien took a silk tie from his back pocket, the kind he used to blindfold her during training. "Put your head forward." She closed her eyes in defeat and obeyed. As he tied the blindfold around her eyes, his voice met her ears. "I trust I won't need to tie your hands."

She wanted to scream. *Why? Is it because you called me Sophie? Is it because you let me call you Adrien?* Instead, silence.

The car started and, a moment later, she felt it begin to move. She felt the warmth of the sun filtering through the front windshield as they drove out of the garage. She felt them bump down a rocky dirt road before turning onto smoother ground and picking up speed. She tried to memorize the Jeep's movements and turns, wondering if she could ever find her way back there. *For what?* she wondered. *Escape.* She hadn't thought about it in weeks, but suddenly, it felt plausible. Maybe she could jump out of the moving car, roll to safety, and then lead officials back to the house where she had been imprisoned. She pictured the headline—*International Heroine Leads Officials to Save Hundreds of Future Victims!* She imagined them leading Adrien out in handcuffs and quickly discarded the image, replacing it with a storyline in which Adrien was never found—*Disappeared Into Thin Air!* it read, with a tagline *A Victim Himself.* Somehow, that was a more satisfying story.

"There are a few things we need to talk about." His voice cut through her daydreams. She turned toward his voice, as though talking with a blindfold on was a normal occurrence.

She heard him clear his throat, the way people do when they're about to declare some difficult truth, or ask for a really big favor. "I need you to promise me something." He paused. Odd, it didn't feel like a command. It felt like an asking. She waited for him to continue, although she was beginning to really like silence for an answer. "Where we're going, under no circumstances can you say my name. Is that clear?"

"I thought that was already clear." She decided to clarify. "The only reason I said your name before was because I needed you to listen. I'm not risking you hurting Megan—it won't happen again." She heard him sigh. He didn't believe her, she could tell.

"You haven't just said my name to get me to listen, though. You say it in your sleep." Mortification hit her. "Which tells me you don't think of me as your master. You think of me as Adrien. And I can't have that. Not where we're going."

She tried to keep her face from glowing red. *What do I say in my sleep?* Her thoughts began to run rampant with all of the embarrassing things her dreams could have revealed. She felt the car slow down, a distinct bumpiness indicating that they were pulling over. A sudden brightness. She squinted into the sunlight. He had removed the blindfold. Her eyes adjusted to the onslaught of light as Adrien's hand cupped her chin, guiding her face in line with his.

"It would help if you told me where you're taking me." It should have been a bold statement, but it came out more like a plea. His eyes searched hers for a moment before answering.

"It's called a pre-auction." He let the words settle in the air for a moment. "We're finding you a buyer."

Sophie felt like she'd been punched in the stomach, the wind knocked from her lungs as tears stung her eyes. She doubled over in her seat, bringing her head to hang between her knees. She felt like she was going to pass out. *So, this was it.* She was being sold.

"Are you okay?" Adrien asked.

Anger coiled inside her. *How dare he ask if I'm okay? Of course, I'm not okay!* "Why the fuck do you care?" she snapped, not bothering to lift her head. His hand on the nape of her neck grasped her hair, pulling her from her lament and forcing her to look at him.

"Watch your language, *Chevrette*. You know what I think your problem is? You forget who I am and what I'm capable of. Do. *Not.* Make me remind you," he snarled, letting her head go with a snap. The sudden release almost caused her face to smack against her knees. The car rumbled as Adrien put it into gear and resumed the drive down the dirt road. They drove in silence for the rest of the way.

He didn't bother to replace the blindfold.

Sophie had always found it funny how the days that change your life forever start off feeling like any other day. They hide behind the normal mundanity of life, just waiting to reveal their terrible surprises. The day her parents died, Sophie went to class, laughed at lunchtime, and fretted over her upcoming assignments. She had a drink before going to bed, all while having no idea that her parents' car had lost control and tipped over a ravine. No idea that they had waited in pain for hours. No idea that the point at which her parents realized help wasn't coming had come and gone. As Sophie slept dreamlessly, there was no indication that her parents had taken their last breaths. Sophie always felt like those life-altering days should be accompanied by a feeling of foreboding, at the least. After the fact, she searched her memory for some sign the universe had given her to indicate that her world was actually falling apart. There was nothing.

Hours of silence ticked by as they drove. Sophie stared out the window and watched as the world sped by without her. She saw signs for San Jose, and wondered if they might be headed toward the capital. She wondered if she could get out, get lost in the city, find help. At one point during the ride, she moved her hand to the door handle, only to be met by Adrien's biting tone. "You don't think I disabled the handle?" Like she had outwardly called him stupid. She supposed she had though, in a sense. She implied he wouldn't think to ensure her captivity. It really would have been stupid on his part. Eventually, they pulled up to a gate. Adrien rolled his window down to speak into an intercom. They were greeted by a tinny voice on the other side (wherever that was) asking for their names.

"Master Degas," Adrien replied, and immediately the gate clicked open, revealing a winding, gravel driveway. Sophie looked at him, pondering the name. *Had he chosen it in remembrance of his mother? Or was that actually his name?* She decided on the former, since he seemed so bent on people not knowing his real name.

They pulled up to what Sophie could only describe as a mansion. It reminded her of an old Spanish villa with its stucco exterior and clay-colored roof tiles. Gardens filled with color lent by exotic flowers splashed the grounds surrounding the house. By the mountains in the backdrop, Sophie guessed they were far from the coast of Tamarindo from where they had come. It was idyllic. *But it's always what's on the inside that counts*, Sophie reminded herself.

Adrien pulled the car into the circular turn-around near the front of the house. He turned the car off and leaned over Sophie to open the glove box. Sophie saw him pull a handgun from the box and quickly secure it behind his back in the waistband of his jeans. Her heart raced at the sight.

"What is that for?" she asked.

"Just in case." His answer was crisp as he turned around to grab their overnight bags from the back seat.

It wasn't that she had never seen a gun before. Having worked as a mental health counselor in some of Boston's most crime-ridden neighborhoods, she had certainly seen her fair share of them. It was the idea that Adrien felt he needed a gun for protection. "So, you mean to tell me that you need a gun, *here*, for protection from *these people*," Sophie asked, waving her arm toward the mansion, "from the *same people* that you plan to sell me to?" Now she really was talking to him like he was stupid. She couldn't control the tone of her voice. In that moment, to her, he really was an idiot.

She watched as he gritted his teeth. He didn't look at her. He refused to look at her, despite her glare daring him to. Instead, he opened the door, taking their bags with him, and got out. *She had challenged him. Why didn't he react?* Her eyes didn't leave him as he walked around to her side of the car and opened the door. "Let's go, get out." She knew he meant for it to sound dominant. It came out sounding tired. He held the car door for her as she stepped into the hot mid-afternoon sun.

"May I assist you, sir?" A voice behind Adrien cut in. Sophie looked up at Adrien, whose eyes were trained on her. She hadn't realized he was staring at her. Without turning to the man, Adrien responded.

"The keys are still in the ignition."

The man gave a slight nod of his head. "Yes, sir." He walked around the car to the driver's side and got in as Adrien headed toward the mansion.

"Come on." His voice had softened, like he understood that Sophie didn't want to go. More than that, that he understood *why* she didn't want to go. But he said it as though they were both resigned to some irrefutable fate and didn't have a choice. Maybe they really didn't. She decided to pretend that was the case. She followed, allowing him to lead the way up the massive marble staircase to the wide, wooden double-doors. Before knocking, the doors opened and another man dressed in khaki pants and a white linen shirt greeted them and took their bags.

"Master Lucas will check you in," he informed them, indicating a concierge-like desk. Sophie took in her surroundings, realizing that the mansion served as a bed and breakfast-style hotel. The large foyer gave way to a bar area with seating and a piano. She guessed the upstairs had plenty of rooms for guests, and she could just make out a large dining area to the left. Adrien approached the concierge desk, nodding curtly to who Sophie assumed to be Master Lucas.

"Good afternoon, Master Degas," the man said politely in English. Sophie guessed Adrien to be a regular here considering everyone knew him by name. Or, by alias. "I have your key right here, sir." He shuffled through some things in the desk, emerging with a single key. "Unfortunately, there was a mix-up with the room scheduling and we don't have any adjoining rooms left, as you typically request." Sophie noticed that this bit of information got Adrien's attention. His eyes snapped to the concierge, jaw set.

"What do you mean?"

Instantly, the man became nervous. Sophie tried to hide a smile as the man fumbled with his words. Apparently, even non-trainees didn't want to get on Adrien's bad side. She thought about Adrien's interactions with others—how quickly he had grabbed his brother by the throat that night, and the way he had threatened the doctor. Perhaps he was more unstable than she was acknowledging.

"Well, uh, there was a mix-up, but there is a daybed in the room you're in. It should work well for the slave." Master Lucas, for the first time, acknowledged Sophie's presence. She watched as his eyes roamed over her, slowly appraising and taking her in. It was something she had seen Adrien do over the past few weeks. This, though, was different. This made her feel dirty.

Adrien cleared his throat, obviously irritated by Lucas's blatant staring. Lucas snapped out of his trance, nervously directing his attention back to Adrien. Sophie recognized the anger in Adrien's eyes. "Fine, it will do."

"Very well, sir. Here is your key." Lucas shuffled his feet nervously. "And I assume she will be taking part in the festivities?" Lucas asked, digging around in another drawer of the desk.

Sophie looked at Adrien. *Festivities?* He hadn't told her anything about what was going to be happening. Anxiety simmered in her stomach causing her to feel hot, making it hard to breathe. She watched as he worried his bottom lip between his teeth, glancing in her direction. Their eyes met for a barely perceptible second before he quickly returned his gaze to Lucas.

"Actually, she won't be."

Sophie blinked, hoping she hadn't heard wrong. Lucas seemed as surprised as she as he attempted to, once again, right himself in front of 'Master Degas.' Lucas continued his nervous shuffling, eyes trained to the drawer while he concentrated on his search. Finally, he smiled and his hand emerged grasping a necklace.

"You'll be needing this one then, Master Degas." It was a dainty, choker-style necklace with a clear, sparkling, diamond droplet hanging from its center. "The official language is

English for the weekend, so please conduct all business in that language. You know your way around? Or would you like a refresher tour?"

Adrien grabbed the necklace and the key from Lucas. "No. I know my way." Adrien's hand met the small of Sophie's back as he steered her toward the winding staircase. "Idiot," he mumbled as they moved out of earshot. Despite her anxiety, Sophie giggled at his comment. It sounded so…*normal* in such an abnormal situation. She dared a glance up at Adrien who was unsuccessfully attempting to hide a smile.

She wished she could have held on to that moment. That one second where fear and anxiety had melted away, and she and Adrien were just two people. But reality seeped back in as he led her toward the large, winding stairwell. Her eyes wandered to the open space surrounding them as they walked through the large lounge, past the piano and bar. It would have looked like any other hotel bar, with wealthy men and women drinking and conversing with one another. But there were other women present, clearly differentiated from the status of the other patrons. These were slaves. Or soon-to-be slaves like Sophie. She could see each of them wearing a similar choker-style necklace to the one Adrien now held, and most wearing little else. Some had chains that clipped at their breasts, the other end held by one of the patrons. Others knelt, while some even acted as a footrest or table to those enjoying their drinks.

"Keep moving. Don't stare," Adrien harshly whispered in her ear, giving her a gentle push. She hadn't even noticed that she had stopped moving. Adrien continued walking toward the staircase, Sophie hurrying to catch up. She didn't want to be left without him. Despite his intentions to sell her, she still trusted that he would protect her. She knew the notion was filled with stupidity.

"Master?" A meek whisper drew Sophie from her thoughts. She bumped into Adrien from behind, not realizing he had stopped walking. Sophie looked to see who had stopped Adrien in his tracks. A petite girl stood in the corridor, her long, blonde hair covering her naked breasts. She wore only a thong and a choker with a blue sapphire sparkling in the center. Sophie guessed she would have still been in college if she weren't standing before them in the hallway.

Sophie watched as a sad smile tugged at Adrien's mouth. "How are you, *Doll*?" The words were gentle, as though they had the power to shatter her if hurled toward her too forcefully. *Doll.* Sophie studied the girl in front of her. She did, in fact, resemble a porcelain doll, with that perfect powder skin, the type that Sophie had always been jealous of.

"Good, thank you, Master." The girl bowed her head, blushing at Adrien's words. Sophie was mesmerized by the reverence in her voice. She positioned herself in front of Adrien as he had taught Sophie to do in the presence of her master. This girl exuded submissiveness.

"I trust you're being treated well?" Adrien asked her. *Doll* parted her lips to answer, not letting her eyes leave the ground.

"Master Degas! To what do we owe this pleasure?" A man's voice cut their conversation short. The man's harsh accent contributed to a discernible tone of spite. Sophie recognized the accent as Russian. She watched the man step from one of the rooms, locking it behind him. He was tall and thickly built, his dirty-blond hair combed neatly to one side. His face was clean-shaven, giving him the appearance of youth, although Sophie guessed he must have been in his forties. He turned to them, not waiting for Adrien's answer before he continued. "You know I don't like my girls having conversations with anyone without my permission."

"And you know I reserve the right to check on my girls as I see fit, Mikhail," Adrien retorted, his voice matching the malice in the Russian's. It occurred to her that the stranger had addressed Adrien as Master, and Adrien hadn't bothered to do the same. She assumed Adrien had meant it as an insult. It appeared effective. Sophie watched the men stare at one another, the tension building in invisible waves around them. "What were you about to say, my dear?" Adrien addressed *Doll* without taking his eyes from Mikhail.

"He's treating me very nicely, Sir." *Doll's* reply came out meek, barely a whisper. She didn't dare look anywhere but her feet. Sophie's heart lurched for her. She wondered what it must be like living with Mikhail as a master.

"Good, I'm glad to hear that." Adrien broke the staring contest, turning to look at *Doll*. "You let me know if that changes." Adrien stepped past the girl, brushing Mikhail on his way. He continued down the hall toward their hotel room. "Let's go, *Chevrette*," he called back to Sophie. She had somehow become stuck to the floor, afraid to move past Mikhail. No longer having Adrien to glare at, the Russian's eyes were now trained on her. If it were possible to emit hatred and lust simultaneously, this man was doing it. The feeling sent a shiver down her spine as she mustered the courage to walk by him. Her stomach dropped when Mikhail licked his lips as she passed.

Her eyes swam in tears as she approached Adrien. He held the door for her and she quickly sped past him and into the relative safety of the room. When she heard the door click shut, she spun toward him. "Please don't sell me to him. He scares me."

Adrien sighed. "I'm not going to sell you to him." He walked toward the bed where nightstands sat on either side. He reached beneath his shirt to remove the gun that had been hidden in the waistband of his jeans. He placed it carefully in the drawer of one of the nightstands.

"Are they all like him?" Sophie asked, crossing her arms in front of her chest as though she could somehow protect herself that way. Adrien looked at her from across the room, fatigue having returned at this point.

"No, *Chevrette*, not all of them."

She squeezed herself, a weak attempt at a hug, hoping to console her apprehensively beating heart. "Please tell me what to expect. Tell me what's going on. I need to know. It will be easier for me if I know." She sounded desperate.

Adrien nodded. "I'll show you."

"Come here." Adrien beckoned to Sophie. He smiled as she immediately obeyed. It was clear to him that she didn't even have to think about it anymore—she did as she was told. She had turned out to be a natural.

He took the necklace from his pocket, holding it up for her to see. He watched her as she studied the diamond. Her eyes sparkled its reflection. He hated that he noticed. "Every slave here wears one of these. It's called a collar." He motioned for her to turn around so that he could fasten it around her neck. He moved her hair over her shoulders and clasped the choker. "The different color stones indicate status among the slaves. Sapphire indicates that they already have a master and aren't for sale. Did you notice the one *Doll* was wearing?" Adrien placed his hands on Sophie's shoulders, turning her to face him. She nodded. "Good. Amethyst indicates that they are part of the auction and are taking bidders. Ruby and black diamonds each indicate a specific type of slave for sale. Those girls with rubies have been trained specifically for masochism. Black diamonds denote girls specifically trained for sadism."

Adrien watched as Sophie cocked her head, digesting the information, and furrowing her brow in confusion. "What about mine? What's the difference between a diamond and an amethyst stone?"

"The slaves with amethyst are partaking in all of the pre-auction events." He waited, knowing she would have questions.

"What events?"

Adrien thought for a moment about how much to disclose. She wouldn't be partaking anyway, so why bother going into the details? "Think of it as a try-it-before-you-buy-it type of event."

He practically laughed as her mouth dropped. He wasn't entirely sure why shocking her was so amusing. Maybe it was the way she responded, her innocence about the world apparent in her mannerisms. He stepped closer to her, pressing his finger under her chin, effectively closing her mouth. "Don't worry, *Chevrette*. Your necklace—diamond—indicates that you're for sale, but you aren't to be touched unless expressly permitted by me. You'll be for display only."

Her green eyes blinked, then squinted to convey her suspicion. "Don't get me wrong. I'm so grateful that you're not making me do…that. But I just have to know. Why?"

He knew what the answer was supposed to be. *Because you're still recovering. No one will buy you if you're sick. I need to get rid of you and I can't have any more setbacks.* It was as simple as that.

And yet, for some reason, he couldn't look at her when he gave her an answer.

21

She was to be gotten rid of. Like an object in a cheap antique shop. He needed to make sure prospective buyers didn't realize she was broken, and so he had placed a 'Do Not Touch Without Assistance' sign around her neck. She scolded herself for wanting to hear from him that she was precious. That she was a priceless antique. One that came with a sign that simply read 'Do Not Touch.'

"You should rest before we go down for dinner," Adrien said as he began unpacking his clothing and placing them, neatly folded, into the drawers of the bureau.

"I don't think I can sleep. I'm not tired," she mumbled, her mind still preoccupied with being sold.

"Try," he demanded. She looked at him, his gray-blue eyes boring into hers. She felt a jolt of electricity ignited by the feel of his eyes on her, and quickly reminded herself that caring for and wanting him was useless now. In a few hours, he would be parading her around like a show dog for her prospective buyers' viewing pleasure. She had thought he might care for her, but she had been wrong. People that care for one another simply don't do what Adrien was so willing to do to her. Yes, he had cared *for* her, but that was very different than caring *about* her. Sophie knew she couldn't lose sight of that. Couldn't get her hopes up. She needed to save herself.

"I need you to try, *Chevrette*. I need you to be rested for tonight. You won't have to do any of the pre-auction events, but it isn't going to be easy. If you want to avoid gaining attention from people like Mikhail, then you'll need to be completely submissive. The buyers that you want to attract want pure obedience. Buyers like Mikhail enjoy the thrill of taming women. Don't give them any reason to be interested."

"Why do you care who I'm sold to? As long as you get rid of me, what does it even matter to you?" She couldn't hide the hurt in her voice as it cracked. She looked away, not wanting him to see the betrayal etched on her face. It was one thing for him to hear it, but it was another type of vulnerability altogether to let it be seen.

"I just do, *Chevrette*."

"And why didn't you care when you sold *Doll* to him?" She was being spiteful now, but her curiosity had gotten the best of her. *What was it about* Doll *that had landed her in Mikhail's possession?* She looked at Adrien, betrayal now replaced with an indignant glare.

"Things in this world are much more complicated than you can even imagine, *Chevrette*." His tone was harsh, edging on angry. "That's enough. I'm done answering your questions." He practically threw the last of his clothing into the drawer, slamming it shut. He looked up at her, his hand rubbing the back of his neck. His voice softened, his eyes pleading with her. "Take my advice or leave it. Do whatever you want."

She decided to rest before dinner.

Adrien locked the door to the room and pocketed the key in his Armani suit. Sophie cringed at the way her heartbeat quickened when he emerged from the bathroom wearing the tailored gray slacks and white button-up. He didn't bother with a tie, leaving the top button undone. He wore the suit jacket, though, a look Sophie would have expected from a top executive in New York City.

His eyes locked on hers as he reached out and brushed a lock of Sophie's long hair behind her ear. "Remember what I said. Eyes down at all times. Follow my lead." She nodded, bringing her eyes to the floor. She followed, her bare feet making no sound as they padded along the floor.

Sophie's black lace corset restricted her breathing as she and Adrien made their way down the winding staircase toward the bar. Clad in only that and a matching lace miniskirt that was more see-through than it was anything else, Sophie normally would have felt self-conscious. But normal was nowhere in sight. And strangely, she seemed overdressed compared to the other slaves that she spotted out of the corner of her eye. Most wore only a thong; others were completely nude with the exception of their telltale necklaces. Sophie worried her diamond between her fingers as she followed Adrien toward the busy lounge.

Sapphire-necklaced women brought around trays of hors d'oeuvres and drinks. Adrien stopped one, grabbing a flute of champagne before dismissing her with a curt nod and smile. He sipped the drink before handing it to Sophie.

"Here, it will help make this easier. Drink, quickly. Be discreet." He looked around, watching for anyone who might notice them. She did as she was told, gulping the cool, bubbly liquid. She handed the glass back to him, wiping the corners of her mouth. Her eyes stung with tears from the assault of carbonation. Adrien swigged the rest of the champagne, his body blocking Sophie's from the entrance to the lounge. He towered over her, his warmth shielding her from the prying eyes that she knew lay just beyond the threshold. "Ready, *Chevrette?*" he asked as he placed the empty flute on a side table.

No. Never. She nodded.

He turned and continued his path into the crowd. Almost immediately, Sophie could feel the focus of the room shift to them. Though her eyes were downcast, she could sense the interested stares. She could hear the hum of approval warm the air like a bass chord. In her periphery, she could see a multitude of well-dressed men hang in anticipation for a chance to speak with Adrien.

"Master Degas!" The first to call out was a husky man with an American accent. Instantly, Sophie felt betrayed by the man approaching. With wrinkles around his eyes and mouth, and a dusting of gray in his hair, the man looked old enough to be her father. *How could someone from my own country partake in this?* Her heart sank from the notion that no one was immune to this world. She kept her eyes cast to the floor, the weight of the realization compressing against her spine.

"Master Anthony, how are you?" Adrien smiled curtly as he shook the man's hand.

"Very good, sir, very good. What peach did you bring us this time?" The man, Anthony, turned his attention to Sophie. His eyes swept over her, lingering at her breasts, pushed up by the taut corset. "Very nice, I must say. A real looker! She's the one from Boston, right? Been all over the news up in the States. Will she be partaking in tonight's events?" Anthony's voice was jovial, hinting with amusement. Sophie glanced up for a quick second, instantly sickened by the lust-laden sparkle in the man's eyes.

Adrien cleared his throat, garnering the man's attention. "Seeing as how you're an American and it would be impossible for you to buy her and bring her into the U.S. without the Feds jumping all over you, I'm not sure why you're bothering to ask. You know I only entertain serious buyers, Master Anthony. So, with all due respect, even if she were partaking in the events—which she isn't—you would not be a top contender on the list to sample her services. Now, if you'll excuse us…" Adrien placed a hand on the small of Sophie's back, guiding them both around a speechless Master Anthony. Likewise, Sophie was reeling from Adrien's words. Like a flash of light, it dawned on her. Adrien would not sell her to anyone residing in the U.S. She was never going home.

"*Chevrette*? Are you all right?" Adrien whispered to Sophie. She glanced up, quickly remembering herself before looking down again.

"No…I don't think I am, actually," she admitted, so softly she could barely hear herself. She felt his thumb rubbing small circles where his hand still rested. He had heard her, and was intending to provide comfort. *Why bother?* she wondered.

They were approached by a succession of men as the night progressed. She didn't pay much attention to the interactions, though, her mind continuing on the perturbed path it had started down. *What would happen? Who would she be sold to?*

"*Chevrette*." Adrien's stern voice pulled her from the frenzy of questions running through her mind. She looked up, wide-eyed at having been caught not paying attention. *What would that mistake cost her?* He had told her to be obedient. Was she now being perceived as disobedient? The idea made her stomach turn.

"Look at me, *Chevrette*." Another voice, familiar to her. She looked at its owner and was met by the unmistakable eyes of

Adrien's brother. She shivered from the memory of their first encounter, at the feel of his hands callously groping her. Her heartbeat quickened—an instinctual reaction to being in his presence again. Though his eyes were Adrien's twin, looking in them brought no comfort and, instead, a wave of panic began to swell in her core. As if sensing her discomfort, Adrien's brother stepped toward her, bringing his body within centimeters of her own. Sophie let out a startled gasp, looking at Adrien to see his reaction.

"I didn't tell you to look away, did I, *Chevrette?*" His brother's voice held a hint of warning, and she immediately redirected her focus on him. He smiled at her quick reaction. "Still as obedient as ever." He took a step back. "And she looks much better than before. Well done, Brother." He clapped a hand to Adrien's shoulder, giving him a slight smirk. Adrien didn't return the expression. "Anyone on the list for giving her a try?"

"She's not partaking in the events." Adrien sounded annoyed. She watched as his brother's eyes clouded with confusion as he cast a glance at Sophie's necklace.

"I see…" he responded, clearly unsure what to say next.

"She was sick. Dengue. She needs to rest or I'll never get her off my hands." Adrien said this hastily, his eyes scanning the room. Sophie thought it interesting how he avoided his brother's eyes the same way he'd avoided hers when he said it earlier.

His brother burst into laughter, the sound ricocheting off the patrons, the furniture, the walls. It sounded harsh to Sophie. "She's keeping you busy, that's for sure." No longer being held hostage by his stare, Sophie retreated behind Adrien in an attempt to distance herself from his laughter. "What's this? Is she afraid of me?" His voice hinted with incredulity and amusement. Adrien said something in rapid French. Though Sophie couldn't understand the words, she understood his reprimanding tone.

"Oh come on. It was all in good fun. No harm done, right, *Chevrette?*" Adrien's brother teased her. She kept her eyes to the floor, not bothering with a response. She knew it was unnecessary. He wasn't really apologizing, anyway. Still, Sophie felt she couldn't get close enough to Adrien. Yet again, despite his intentions, she felt protected in his presence. She stayed behind him, playing with the hem of his suit jacket between her fingers. If he noticed the action, Adrien didn't let on, and carried on the conversation.

"Is Henry coming?"

"No, he was helping Uncle with one of the shipments back home. Couldn't make it out in time."

"So, what about the buyers?"

"I guess you get to choose. I'm sure he'll still take care of the negotiations as usual."

Sophie felt Adrien relax, his shoulders become less rigid. It sparked her curiosity. He was clearly unnerved about the idea of this 'Henry' being present. She wondered about his role in all of this. It sounded like he certainly played a large part, dealing with buyer negotiations. *Was he the one responsible for bringing Adrien into this world?* If she had to bet on it, she would guess that was exactly the case.

"And yours? Where is she?" Adrien asked.

"I don't have one this time. I was supposed to get one in but they weren't able to secure one for me. Actually, now that you mention it, when I asked them about it, they said *you* told them to let one go."

Sophie tried to steady her breathing, hoping Adrien's brother hadn't heard her falter. *He knew about Megan?*

"Does that sound like something I would do?" Adrien's voice came out steady, even, hinting at the absurdity of the suggestion.

"Yeah, I figured they weren't telling the truth. Probably thought they could get a pretty penny by going for ransom instead. I'll have to talk to Master Henry about dealing with them. All right, I'll let you get back to it." Adrien's brother clapped his hand on Adrien's shoulder one more time before throwing a wink in Sophie's direction. "Enjoy the weekend, *Chevrette.*"

She barely registered his words. Her thoughts were with Megan and what had just taken place. Adrien had outwardly deceived his brother to protect her friend. *Or just to protect himself?*

"Fuck, I need a drink," Adrien murmured to himself. Then, to Sophie, "Come on, let's go." She followed him to a quiet corner of the room where a server stood with a tray of wine glasses. Adrien took one, throwing a half-hearted "thank you" at the woman before stepping away and taking a long sip of the liquid.

"Thank you," she whispered, hoping he could hear. She glanced up and, though his eyes weren't meeting hers, he lifted an eyebrow in question. "You lied to your brother." She kept her voice low, barely moving her lips for fear that others might be watching, listening.

"I didn't, actually," he responded. She thought back for a moment, replaying the scene in her head. Sophie was amazed by how easily Adrien had manipulated the situation. He hadn't lied. He had merely asked a question in response, effectively steering his brother away from the truth.

He finished the drink, placing the empty glass on the tray and grabbing another. He took a small sip while guiding

Sophie by the elbow away from the servant. Blocking her body from view, he offered her the drink. "Do you want more?"

She thought about it for a moment, then shook her head. "I'm having enough trouble remembering what to do as it is. I don't want the alcohol to cause me to slip up." She looked up at him, his eyes intently staring down at her. Slowly, he nodded.

"You're right. Good thinking." He paused, his gaze still lingering on her, as though the conversation weren't quite over yet. He seemed to suddenly realize they were no longer talking and broke eye contact, taking a sip of the wine. After what seemed like minutes of silence ticked by, Adrien finished his glass and said, "There are a few others you should meet." His delivery sounded almost regretful. Sophie nodded her assent. It was time to save herself she decided.

She had thought about it a lot while she lay on the daybed before dinner. It occurred to her that she might be able to gain some control in the situation. If her actions could attract or repel certain buyers, perhaps she had a small part in choosing where she would end up. She had always been good at reading and responding to people's subtle body language—she had to in her line of work—and she might be able to put those skills to use with prospective buyers. She had just never done it in a sexual way before. She shrugged off her inexperience, likening it to flirting with a random guy at a bar. Not something she was used to, but certainly something she could do, and had done, if need be.

She took a deep breath, readying herself to play the role of a submissive slave. Or, had she already become one? *No.* She was suspended somewhere between her old self and a new one. One that had yet to be defined.

"Master Ahmed, may I introduce you to my newest trainee?" Adrien had guided her to a group of men where he addressed a man with dark rum-colored eyes that matched his deep complexion. Sophie stepped forward, guided by Adrien's hand at the dip of her lower back. She kept her eyes down, allowing her long waves to fall over her shoulders, spilling in cascades down and over her breasts. She held a submissive pose as Adrien had taught her, but inhaled deeply to emphasize what the corset was already accentuating. It had the desired effect.

"My, my, Master Degas. She's lovely." He stepped forward, taking Sophie's hand in his. She allowed it without hesitation, but, for effect, she looked at Adrien with hesitation. Perhaps if it appeared to Master Ahmed that she was seeking permission from her current master, he would see her as obedient. Sophie noticed a slight smile grace the man's lips as she did this, indicating that she had indeed guessed correctly.

Adrien nodded, giving his assent. She turned back toward Master Ahmed, keeping her eyes lowered but offering a tentative smile. He raised her hand to his lips, feathering a soft kiss onto her knuckles. "It's a pleasure to meet you…"

"*Chevrette.*" Adrien interjected.

"*Chevrette.* Ah, what a unique moniker. Lovely. Let me see those beautiful eyes of yours, *Chevrette.*"

Keeping her head bowed, Sophie looked up through her thick lashes, batting them subtly for further effect. She saw Ahmed's eyes darken as he took a sharp breath. She blinked several times, looking back toward the floor, as though too modest to keep looking at him.

"My God, she's beautiful," he said as he let go of her hand. "Will I have the chance to sample her tonight?"

"Unfortunately, she's recovering from a bout of dengue so she won't be partaking in any of the events this evening. But I assure you she is one of the best I've ever trained."

"Very good. Well then, keep me in mind, will you?" Master

Ahmed reached out to stroke Sophie's cheek as he spoke. She smiled, leaning into his touch.

"I will," Adrien assured him as he placed his hand on Sophie's waist to guide her away. She could feel Ahmed's eyes on her as they began walking through the crowd.

It felt powerful. She had done it—completely won him over without saying a word. She gave herself a mental pat on the back, trying to hide the proud grin that threatened to plaster itself across her face. She bit her lip to fight it off, glancing at Adrien. Likewise, he was gazing at her, a look of bewilderment brightening his features. If she could read his mind, she guessed his thoughts would simply say, *what the fuck was that?* She shrugged in response to the unasked question.

Adrien introduced her to several other men. Each time, Sophie emitted subtle flirtations to ornament her submissive stance. Each time, they were met with a slightly bewildered and irritated look from Adrien. After the third encounter with a prospective buyer, Adrien's irritation bordered irrational anger.

As the man, introduced to Sophie as Master Tom, lightly caressed Sophie's arm, she let out a delicate sigh, fluttering her eyelids closed at his touch. Eyes still closed, she heard Adrien's snap at Tom.

"Seeing as how you're apparently interested, I'll be in touch." With that, Sophie was dragged out of Master Tom's reach by her wrist and pulled in the direction of the bar. She became acutely aware of the emotions warring behind Adrien's eyes. It was something she had often seen in Josh whenever she offered a smile to another man. *Jealousy.* Adrien was jealous.

The realization rocked her, tilting her world once again. What did it mean that Adrien was jealous of her interactions with other men? *Would he change his mind? Could he stop this?*

Hope swirled within her. She tried to dampen it, tried not to let it escape and dissipate into the air.

She considered her options as she watched Adrien order from the bar.

"Whiskey, neat. Make it a double," Adrien barked at the bartender. He looked back at Sophie, who was studying him with the same intensity that he often studied her. Their eyes connected for a moment before he turned back toward the bar. "Make that two."

Shit. He knew she didn't want any more to drink. Was he trying to sabotage her?

The bartender set the two drinks side by side. Adrien handed Sophie hers while bringing his own to hover near his lips. She took hers, tentatively grasping the glass, looking into the amber liquid, swirling it around in the tumbler before looking back up at Adrien.

"Drink, *Chevrette.*"

"I don't want it," she whispered.

He raised a brow as he took a sip. "You've been so submissive all night. Why stop now?" He took a deep swig, emptying his glass. It made a loud knock as he forcefully placed the tumbler on the bar. "Drink."

She took a shot of the burning liquor. A second, then a third, and it was gone. She handed the glass back to Adrien, suppressing the urge to cough it up. She hadn't had any alcohol since she was at the resort with Megan. That five weeks felt like a lifetime ago. Still, it was a long enough hiatus to render her slightly tipsy after a glass of champagne and a double whiskey.

Adrien took the glass from her, placing this one lightly on the bar. Motioning to the bartender, he barked out, "Another round." The girl nodded, quickly making their next drink. Adrien bent over, touching his lips to the shell of Sophie's ear.

"You might want to know whose rules you're playing by *before* you decide to jump into the game."

He got her drunk. Not so drunk that it was obvious to others, but enough so that she required steadying by his hand. He wasn't going for sloshed. Just…impaired. He was careful not to cross that line.

He had recognized what she was doing almost immediately. The way she had seemingly gone from dejected to determined in a matter of minutes had caught him off guard at first. It was impressive, to say the least, to watch her work. She played a good game. The way the men responded to her reminded Adrien of a group of teenage boys getting into a stash of their father's porn for the first time. It was repulsive.

But the way she reciprocated their interest—*that* was what had him perplexed. The way she blushed while she bit her lip. How her breasts moved as she breathed. The sound of her sigh. It dawned on him that he trained his slaves in such a way that they craved sexual contact. It wasn't so far-fetched that she *wasn't* actually playing a game. And that idea fucked with his head. *Really* fucked with his head.

He was jealous. He had never been jealous before, at least not regarding the attention of a woman, and this was now the second time he was feeling this emotion in regards to Sophie. Sure, when he was younger he was jealous of Etienne. How he always managed to be the one to avoid the beatings. It was a different kind of jealousy, though, one that somehow stung less than this new type. Adrien realized it for what it was when he found himself wishing he was the recipient of Sophie's shy smile, when he found himself clenching his fists and fighting the urge to punch his own clients. And suddenly, all he wanted to do was to get her the fuck out of there, away from their prying eyes. That's where the alcohol helped.

As the crowd shuffled into the dining room for dinner, Sophie grabbed Adrien's hand, stumbling in the process. He allowed her to cling to him, for just a moment, to steady herself before removing himself from her grip. He did a cursory scan of the room for anyone who may have noticed her stumble. He couldn't let on that he was feeding her drinks. Too many questions about his intentions might be raised. And no one would buy a slave whose trainer had ulterior motives, especially motives fueled by jealousy. He had seen it before, a slave whose trainer couldn't get rid of her because of complications regarding emotional attachment. Even if this attachment was only perceived by the buyer and not, in fact, a reality, it was near impossible to receive asking price. And those that would risk the purchase were often not the men Adrien preferred to do business with. They were the type that would get off on torturing the girls just to see the trainer squirm. Never mind what they would do to a newly acquired slave if she were suspected of feeling something for her trainer.

Adrien glanced at Sophie, wondering if that were a possibility. He hoped not, for her sake. She looked up to him, catching his eye and giving a shy smile. "I don't feel very good. I think I need to go lie down, Sir," she whispered. Adrien tried to ignore the pang of guilt that bolted through his chest. Technically, she was supposed to be taking it easy, per the doctor's orders.

"I'll take you up after you have something to eat." The food would help sober her. The last thing she needed was to go to bed on an empty stomach. He led them toward one of the round tables that dotted the room. It had been set up to seat six, with small cushions on the floor beside the chairs for the slaves and trainees to kneel beside their masters. Adrien sat at a table with several buyers that he was familiar with, none of whom were currently accompanied by slaves. He sat in the chair, while Sophie unsteadily got to her knees next to him.

"Master Degas! We were just talking about you and your lovely trainee." Master Ahmed sat across the table. He beamed, looking down at Sophie. She didn't return the smile. Perplexed, Ahmed returned his attention to Adrien. "We noticed Master Henry isn't here this weekend."

Adrien stiffened at the mention of his father. It was a fitting alias; Frederic had chosen the same name as the English king who beheaded more than 50,000 of his subjects. Ruthless cruelty at its finest. He wasn't sure if Frederic had realized this when he chose the pseudonym or not. Adrien had never asked. Still, it colored the way he saw Frederic.

"No, he won't be joining us. I'll be dealing with all negotiations this weekend." He saw a few of the men nod, but his attention was drawn to his lap where Sophie had begun resting her head on his thigh. He pushed her off. She attempted to readjust herself, leaning her body against his leg. He moved his leg away, placing his hand on her shoulder, a silent instruction to stop. He made a point not to look at her as he did it. He didn't want to see the confusion in her eyes, didn't want anyone to witness his softness toward her.

He glanced around, confirming that no one's attention was on him and Sophie. The men had their eyes trained on the servant who had approached their table. Like all of the other servants there that night, this one wore the telltale sapphire necklace with matching nipple clips and sapphire-colored thong. She moved silently, placing a basket of bread on the table and then moving to fill each of their glasses with water. The servants were held to the same standard as all of the slaves, not allowed to speak unless spoken to. The men's eyes followed her movements, her breasts grazing their shoulders as she leaned over each of them to pour their water. *Weak. All of them.* Adrien could practically see the men drooling. The way they gawked at her. Fighting the urge to roll his eyes, Adrien took the opportunity to give Sophie a piece of bread, offering it to her inconspicuously under the table. She looked up at him in question. He nodded once and she took it from him eagerly. Gently, Adrien ran his hand over the soft silk of her hair. He allowed himself that one concession. *Enough,* he told himself. He was playing with fire at a table piled with dynamite.

Adrien managed his way through the rest of dinner. He conversed when he needed to, answering questions about Sophie—*Chevrette*—when asked. He gave her most of his dinner without notice from anyone. When the opportunity arose, he excused them both.

"No dessert?" one of the men asked, while his dark eyes mentally undressed Sophie. He wasn't talking about dessert in the literal sense. Adrien knew that the 'dessert' on the menu would be a tasting of sorts for the prospective buyers. Adrien clenched his jaw to hold his temper, something he did to rein in his urge to fight.

"Sorry, gentlemen," Adrien began, "but *Chevrette* won't be partaking in *dessert* tonight. It was our pleasure to have dinner with you. Enjoy the rest of the evening." He stood, motioning for Sophie to follow. A few of the men murmured to one another at the table, no doubt disappointed by the abrupt departure.

"Will she be taking part in tomorrow's showing?" Ahmed's voice carried over the dinner table.

Adrien paused, his jaw clenching further. "Yes."

22

Sophie stared at the reflection of her bloodshot eyes. She was beginning to sober up, despite the lingering tipsiness causing her to sway slightly in the mirror. Or maybe she wasn't swaying at all. Maybe she was just drunk and the world was spinning around her. It felt like a viable option.

She couldn't reach the back of her corset to untie her laces. Clumsily, she reached back again and again before finally deciding to ask for Adrien's help.

"Hey!" she whispered to him from behind the closed bathroom door. She wasn't quite sure why she was whispering. *Drunk*, she decided. Clearing her throat she called again, this time louder, "Hey!"

She heard his movements pause. And then, "Did you just 'hey' me?" He didn't sound mad, just…incredulous.

She giggled as she opened the door a crack, peeking out at him. He was looking directly at her as if he had anticipated that she would come seeking him. She spoke through the cracked door, "I can't get the corset off. Can you help?"

She opened the door further, her eyes taking him in. Still wearing his suit slacks and white, collared dress shirt, he had discarded the jacket on the armchair by the window. He had apparently been unbuttoning his shirt when she interrupted him. She drank him in, the muscled tone of his body apparent through the tailored clothing.

She watched him hesitate at her request before acquiescing and walking toward the bathroom where she stood. She retreated, turning toward the mirror to give him access to the ties at the back of the corset. She felt a slight tug as he began working at the laces. Her eyes followed him in the mirror. She watched him as he worked to free her from the corset, loosening it with care.

"Can I ask you something?" The alcohol was emboldening. Without looking up from what he was doing, Adrien replied,

"Sure."

"What's a showing?"

He still didn't look at her. "It's just what it sounds like, *Chevrette*. It's a showcase. A chance for buyers to see you up close. It's a little like a beauty pageant."

"Oh. I see." Sophie collected her thoughts before allowing the alcohol to free her inhibitions. "Why did you do that?"

He finally met her gaze in the mirror. "Do what?" But there was no hint of confusion or question in his eyes. He knew exactly what she was talking about.

"Why did you make me drink that much?" His smirk confirmed her suspicions.

"Because, my deer, you were playing a dangerous game."

"I was doing just fine until you interfered!" she interjected. His eyes, having returned to his task, now snapped to hers in the mirror.

"You have no idea who you were playing with."

"No, but if you were introducing me to them then I figured they were the type of buyers that would be…" She didn't want to finish the sentence with the word 'good' but she wasn't sure how else to put it. "Good for me."

"And so you figured you'd help ensure the sale?"

"Yeah, something like that."

He sighed. "I don't need your help finding you a buyer, *Chevrette*. As is, those men seemed like they would give up their empires for a chance to have you. Bidding wars are messy to deal with and negotiations can be sensitive matters. It's best if you just let me handle it. Trust me." He finished untying the corset, loosening it so that it would slip from her shoulders with ease. She shrugged out of it, freeing her breasts from the pressure of the corset. Gravity felt relieving. She began rubbing the blood flow back into her breasts and sides, where the corset had been most restrictive.

She saw his eyes flicker from hers to where she rubbed herself, flitting back up to land on her mouth before seemingly catching himself. He met her eyes again, his having darkened by whatever thoughts were going through his mind. Her heartbeat quickened at his carnal stare. It wasn't enough to see it through the mirror, as though reflections could somehow deceive. She broke her gaze to look at him directly.

The mirror hadn't lied.

She pressed against him as his hand tangled itself in the strands of her hair, pulling her mouth to his. His lips pressed against hers, his tongue parting them, seeking entrance. There was nothing gentle about the way he kissed her. She could feel the desperation, the jealousy surfacing in a kiss that claimed her. *She was his.*

His free hand gripped her waist, pulling her to him as though he couldn't get close enough. Sophie's hands grabbed the back of his neck, moving up to run through his hair, her own desperation a reflection of his.

She moved her hands down his back while his simultaneously moved up from her waist and along the curve of her torso. He took one nipple between his thumb and forefinger, tweaking it until it peaked. Sophie moaned into Adrien's mouth, the sound of her pleasure spurring his need. He continued ravishing her mouth as both hands gripped her waist to hoist her onto the bathroom countertop. She spread her legs, wrapping them around his waist to rejoin their bodies.

Her hands hungrily grabbed at the waistband of his suit, fumbling to unhook the belt. Feeling how hard he was through his slacks as she unbuttoned his pants, she lavishly ran her hand along his length through the clothing. Adrien pulled away from the kiss, pressing his forehead against hers as she freed his erection. His hands pulled at her hair, his lips grazing her cheekbones down her jaw as her hand wrapped around his thick cock. She stroked it, eliciting a sharp hiss of breath and a whispered curse from Adrien. It spurred her on, bringing her thumb to brush against his tip, where a bead of precum glistened. Her heart pounded in her chest, her desire pooling between her legs.

"Shit. You need to stop, *Chevrette*." His command came out as a rasp, a complete contradiction to what both of their bodies were telling them to do. She halted, confused. Had she misunderstood what was happening? Somehow misunderstood what he wanted? Had she misinterpreted the message behind his kiss? She was his, she was certain of that. So, why was he stopping this? She opened her eyes, searching for answers. His forehead had found hers again, his eyes remained closed as he steadied his breathing. She pushed him away, not forcefully, but enough to gain the distance she so suddenly needed from him.

His rejection hurt. Again.

"You're drunk, *Chevrette*," he offered weakly. Though there was hesitation in his voice, there was also clear finality for the moment.

Bullshit. "That's not my fault." Her response provoked a smile. It was hard not to do the same, to act as his mirror. His smiles—the real ones—occurred so seldom, it seemed only fair that the act be rewarded by a companion smile. She offered him a weak one before calling him on his bullshit. "So, if I weren't drunk, would this be different?"

"It's not that simple, *Chevrette*. It's never that simple." He shook his head, his eyes communicating regret.

"I think the answer you were looking for is no." She shoved herself off the countertop and walked out of the bathroom, leaving a speechless Adrien looking after her.

She heard the door close and the shower start a few moments later. *Good,* she thought. *At least he knows to give a woman some space when she's drunk and upset.*

She walked over to the dresser, where Adrien had unpacked both of their bags, folding their belongings neatly in the drawers. She chose a tank top and shorts to put on before flopping down on the daybed that was positioned at the end of the king-sized bed. Despite its small size, Sophie found it was actually quite comfortable. She lay there, looking up at the ceiling as she listened to the sound of the shower running through the wall.

She thought about Megan. *What would she think of me now?* There she was, finally ready to move on from Josh—something Megan had tried to get her to do countless times over the past year—and the one man she wanted was Adrien. She wondered, not for the first time, if maybe she had lost her mind. But she hadn't, and she knew it. Adrien had somehow done what she and even her closest support couldn't do over the past year.

Adrien had pulled Sophie from the wreckage and brought her back to life. She had been given another opportunity to live life again. Now, she just needed to figure out how to do it.

She heard her best friend's voice penetrate her thoughts. *Run.*

Sophie bolted upright on the daybed, the notion pulling at her like an animal with its kill. She would need to go out the front door. From what she could remember, the mansion was set away from any other houses. The driveway had been at least a mile long and was barricaded with a gate. She wondered if she could run into the woods. She doubted there would be a gate around the entire perimeter. She would have to move slowly to avoid detection. Besides, she didn't have any shoes. But that was fine.

The gun. Adrien had left it unlocked in the bedside table. The shower still hissed from the bathroom. Sophie got up from the bed and moved toward the nightstand. She reached into the drawer, picking up the handgun. It was heavier than she expected. She had never held a gun before. Would she even know how to use it if she needed to? She wrapped her finger around the trigger, searching for the safety lock. She smoothed her fingers over the surface of the gun, searching for the tab. Instead, she found a smooth square along the side of the gun. She brushed her thumb over it, tried pushing it like a button. Instantly, the edges of the pad lit red, making a short *beep* before going black again. Perplexed, she did it again. The sound was somehow familiar.

"What the fuck are you doing?" Adrien's voice caused Sophie's heart to jump to her throat. She spun around, not quite sure what to do with the gun in her hand. *Aim for him?* She knew she would never shoot him, but he didn't know that. Maybe she could bargain for her freedom.

She stared blankly at Adrien, his bare torso still wet from his shower. He must have jumped out of the water at the sound of the beep, wrapped a towel around himself, and came out to find her with the gun. Her eyes scanned his muscular shoulders down his taught stomach, her mind wandering back to their near miss earlier. *Drunk,* she reminded herself.

To her surprise, Adrien stepped forward, placing his hand on the barrel of the gun, yanking it from her grip. She suddenly realized she wasn't so sure that *he* wouldn't shoot *her.* She felt like shrinking, like hiding under the bed, disappearing completely.

Adrien held the gun out for Sophie to look at. "See that? It's a thumb scan. You couldn't have used it even if you wanted to." He placed the gun back into the drawer and closed it. "Same concept as the thumb scans on the doors at the house. My thumbprint is the only registered user. If someone else tries to use it, I'm immediately notified."

Oh.

"Now, tell me, *Chevrette.* What were you planning on doing with that?"

She didn't answer. She wondered if perhaps he would just believe she was drunk and didn't know what she was doing. She scanned the room. As though that might give her some answers.

"Dammit, *Chevrette!*" He grabbed her at the back of her neck, pulling her toward him. "Answer me. Were you going to hurt yourself?"

She blinked. *Was that what he thought?* "No. I haven't thought about that since…that first time you stopped me. I wouldn't do that." It was the truth. She wanted him to see it. Apparently, he needed to see it.

He seemed to be digesting the information. He loosened his grip. She watched him study her, watched as the thoughts churned in his eyes. "Then…*what?*"

"I—" she stopped, not sure what to disclose. She wanted to tell him the truth. "I thought maybe I could leave."

Adrien stepped back from her, releasing her neck. He shook his head as he spoke. "And you thought you could take the gun and just waltz out of here? Do you have any idea how stupid that is?"

When he put it that way…

"Do you honestly think that if someone saw you they would just let you walk out? I'm not the only one who brought a gun here! These men…" he seemed exasperated, "they don't give a shit about you. They see you as a slave. If they caught you they would kill you and wouldn't think twice about it." His eyes bore into hers, anger and irritation and *worry?* swirling together.

"I'm sorry. I wasn't thinking."

"Clearly you weren't." He began pacing the room, rubbing the back of his neck. He moved toward the dresser purposefully, as though looking for something. Sophie watched as his hand emerged from the drawer holding a restraint. Her eyes shot to his in question. He walked over to her, adjusting the straps as he moved. As though answering her unasked question, Adrien said, "And clearly I can't trust you like I thought I could." He grabbed her wrists, placing the restraint so her hands were bound together, then dragged her toward the daybed. He fastened the cuff around the bedpost of his bed, forcing her to sit on the daybed. He had given her enough slack to move around. She could lie down if she wanted to. But she wouldn't be getting out anytime soon. Or doing much else, for that matter.

"What if I have to use the bathroom?"

He smiled. Leaning down, he placed a swift kiss on her forehead before answering. "Just say the word and I'll be happy to accompany you."

She ran through the house, so familiar to her. It was home—where she had grown up, where her first memories had been made. And yet, there was something telling her to run. She knew she had to escape. She flew down the stairs, heading for the front door. Time seemed to slow as she neared the door. Her legs felt heavy, like running through the ocean in summertime, the water reaching just above her knees, preventing her from moving at full speed.

"Chevrette!" A voice called to her. It was Adrien. She wanted to follow his voice, but, for some reason, she was running away from it. He called her name again and she turned, met by a room full of people.

How had all of these people gotten into her home? She didn't recognize them, but they seemed to recognize her. They stared.

She stopped running. When had her legs stopped moving? She tried to head toward the door again, wanting to get away from all of the people. It was them she was running from. But she couldn't move. Her legs were frozen in place. She wanted to scream, needed to get out.

And that was when she noticed him. Mikhail. It had to be him, though she wasn't sure how she knew. Maybe it was the way he was looking at her. The hairs stood at the back of her neck. He was pointing something at her. She squinted, trying to figure out what it was.

It didn't register until the gunshot rang out. She flinched, expecting the pain, yet feeling nothing. She opened her eyes, noticing the crumpled form on the floor in front of her.

"Adrien! No!" she heard herself scream. She screamed and screamed and screamed…

"Jesus, *Chevrette*! It's okay. You're okay." Sophie felt a slight tug at her wrists as her hands were freed from the restraints. She opened her eyes, disoriented by her surroundings. Her heart pounded in her chest, the remnants of the dream still fresh in her mind. Her eyes focused, recognizing Adrien as he crouched in front of her, his body creating a shield around her. Relief swept over her at the sight of him. *He wasn't dead. It was just a dream.*

Swiftly, she moved off the daybed, lurching into his arms and knocking him off his haunches as she wrapped herself around him. She heard his mumbled "What the fuck?" as his arms embraced her, soothing her as they sat on the floor. She buried her head in his neck, fighting back tears.

"It was that bad, huh?" he asked her gently, stroking her hair. He smelled of smoke mixed with lemongrass and ginger and everything Adrien. She inhaled, wanting nothing more than to keep the smell of his soul inside her forever. "Do you want to talk about it?" he asked. She shook her head. What would she tell him? *I dreamt that you died and I was heartbroken? I think I love you?*

Adrien began to pull away from her, causing Sophie to hold on tighter. "Please don't let go yet." She whispered it, not sure if he would acquiesce. He resumed his embrace, rubbing small circles with his thumb on her back.

"You should try to sleep." He scooped her up and carried her away from the daybed and to the main bed. He pulled the duvet and sheets back before lightly placing her down on the mattress. She pulled the sheets over her, and it dawned on her that the bed was still made. She looked at Adrien as he smoothed the covers over her.

"You haven't slept at all?"

"No."

She glanced at the clock. Almost 2:30 a.m. and he hadn't slept. He always seemed to be awake late at night. She grabbed his hand, lightly tugging him as she moved over. He resisted her pull for a moment, ostensibly pausing to think about it before climbing into the bed next to her. She rested her head in the dip between his shoulder and chest, wrapping an arm around his stomach.

"*Chevrette…*" A warning.

"I just need this for a few minutes. Please?"

He sighed, "Fine, but then you need to stay on the other side of the bed."

"Why?" she yawned sleepily. Her eyelids were getting heavier as she succumbed to sleep. Her mind began to drift back into a place where thoughts were the beginnings of dreams.

"*Because I don't trust myself around you, Sophie.*"

She didn't know if she heard him say it, or if she had dreamt it.

<h1 style="text-align:center">23</h1>

The first time Sophie visited the zoo, she was seven years old. She remembered the day vividly. She was so excited to finally get to go. Her mom allowed her to pick out her outfit for the day—a white jean jumper with big, bright yellow flowers splashed randomly over the entire piece, with matching flower-shaped buttons to hold everything together. She wanted to wear her pink jellies, but her dad put his foot down about the shoes. She ended up wearing her princess sneakers that flashed like a neon pink strobe light with every step she took.

Later in life, Sophie couldn't recall which zoo they visited. Maybe they had driven all the way to New York State to the Bronx Zoo. Perhaps they'd stayed in Massachusetts to visit one of the smaller, lesser-known zoos. She had never been sure. She only remembered the drive taking *forever*. When they finally arrived, she jumped out of the vehicle and ran toward the ticket window.

Her parents followed her around that day, letting her choose which animals to see and which ones to bypass until later. Her goal had been to look at them all. She remembered wanting to visit the giraffes first, her dad picking her up and placing her on his shoulders so she could be tall like them. He was a giant to Sophie—taller and leaner than most of her friends' dads, he himself reminded Sophie of a giraffe. As they wove through the crowds of visitors, Sophie and her family kept passing by the gorilla habitat. Each time they passed, her dad would pause as if to go in, and look at Sophie.

"Not yet, Dad! That one's for last!" she would say each time, and continue moving along her decided course. Her parents would look at each other and shrug before continuing their trek, until Sophie was ready for the gorillas. Her dad stopped outside of the exhibit, expecting the same response from his daughter that he had received for hours prior. Only this time, Sophie grinned and walked past him and into the exhibit.

It was a circular building that offered an open roof with a large central space for the animals. In the center stood what Sophie could only imagine was the coolest jungle gym on earth. She walked around the exhibit, searching for its inhabitants through the glass windows. Her walk turned to a run as she searched desperately, stopping short when she caught sight of him.

The gorilla was huge, at least as tall as Sophie's dad and much, much wider. She slowly approached the glass, on the other side of which the gorilla was just sitting, gazing down at the ground. Her movement caught his attention and he looked up at her. She was mesmerized by his eyes, a chocolate-brown that reminded her of her favorite candy bar, with a darker ring around them to match the black, wrinkled skin of his face. Sophie wasn't sure how long she stood there staring into those pools of brown. She startled when the gorilla leaned forward toward her. Regaining her courage, Sophie took another step toward the glass. Without hesitation, the gorilla reached out, placing its hand on the barrier between them. Sophie looked at the hand, its dark skin pushing against the glass, as if reaching out to touch her.

That was when Sophie burst into tears. Her mom, behind her the entire time, scooped her into her arms and carried her out of the exhibit. Both of her parents figured the gorilla had spooked Sophie. Looking back, Sophie knew it wasn't the gorilla that had frightened her. It was its *humanness* that had scared her. And it was the idea that *humans* were responsible for this. That *humans* could and would do this to another animal, so like themselves. As her mother carried her away from the exhibit, the gorilla took its hand away from the glass, leaving the marks of its fingerprints behind.

On their drive home, Sophie asked her mother why zoos exist.

"Well, sweetie, because the animals are better off being there. Some of them don't have homes in the wild anymore, or some of them were sick and needed help. So, they went to live at the zoo."

"What about the ones that have homes? Or the ones that get better? Why can't they be let go?" She watched as her mother exchanged a look with her father. He cleared his throat, an obvious sign that he was trying to think of some answer that would satisfy the curiosity of a seven year old.

"They can't go back out into the wild because…because they don't want to," he offered. Her mom shot him a stern look, one that told him that his answer wasn't going to suffice. And it didn't.

"That one didn't want to be there anymore," Sophie pouted. She knew this, even at such a young age. There had been something unmistakably sad in his interaction with her.

"A lot of people don't like zoos for that same reason," her mother said, "but don't think of it like that, honey. Zoos are really meant to help the animals. Most can't go back into the wild because they get so used to relying on humans to take care of them that they wouldn't be able to take care of themselves if they went back to their homes."

Still, Sophie hated zoos after that.

❧

These men loved zoos, Sophie decided. They were the type who could minimize the emotion in the depths of dark chocolate eyes, could ignore the fingerprints on the glass. They could diminish the commonality of humanity.

They could buy women, hold them hostage, mistreat them, and still sleep soundly at night.

Sophie had acknowledged this the second she had walked into the mansion the previous day, but it didn't become so blatantly apparent to her until the showing. She knew that Adrien had only told her enough to appease her questioning. She had some idea what to expect, but, at the same time, had no idea. She only got an inkling when Adrien handed her the lace thong and demanded that she put it on.

"What should I wear over it?" she asked. Adrien's smirk was the only reply she needed. She wouldn't be wearing anything over it, that much was clear. He himself was lucky enough to be fully clad in another tailored suit, this one with black pants that he dressed down with a plain-gray dress shirt with the sleeves rolled up. She was irritated at his lack of exposed skin. Her annoyance getting the best of her, she didn't bother going to the bathroom to change out of the clothing she had slept in. If she was going to be exposed to the world anyway, what was the point? She stripped down in front of Adrien, throwing her tank top and shorts haughtily to the side before stepping into the barely-there wisp of material. She noticed his eyes sweep up and down her body, lingering on the curves of her breasts. She crossed her arms in defiance, instigating his eyes to meet hers.

"What?" The irritation in her voice was obvious, accented by a raised eyebrow.

He grinned, almost sheepishly at having been caught. "Just assessing the goods, that's all."

Sophie fought the urge to roll her eyes. She knew she was already pushing her luck, and apparently Adrien was in a good enough mood to find humor in the situation. Perhaps she should try to do the same.

He led her out of their room and down the stairs toward a back door. The late-morning sunshine heated her bare skin as they walked toward a large tent that had been constructed in the middle of the lush green yard. Surrounding it, Sophie could see pathways winding through and gardens dotting the property. She had noticed the flowers in the front of the house when they arrived yesterday, and took a moment to appreciate the beauty of the landscaping around the back of the house. She figured she might as well stop and smell the roses while she could, literally and figuratively. She passed an exotic-looking bunch of orchids, different and yet somehow familiar to the flowers she was used to, and brought a single bud to her nose to smell it. For an instant, she allowed herself to believe that her life consisted of that one moment, that one breath, the sweet scent of orchid traveling into her lungs and dissipating through her bloodstream. She was comforted by the idea that life was made up of those tiny moments and, if she could get through one, she could get through them all.

Adrien's warm hand wrapped around Sophie's fingers,

pulling her from her reverie, gently coaxing her to let go of the flower. She wasn't sure how long she had been standing there amid the orchids. The moment had stolen into another. Her eyes met his blue-rimmed irises, studying her with confusion, concern…reverence? She wasn't sure what she had seen twinkle across his eyes. The emotion behind his gaze was snuffed out the moment he released her hand. As if he suddenly remembered himself.

She wished they could just hide among the orchids, among all of those tiny moments.

"Let's get this over with." He turned and continued toward the tent. He had said it as though he didn't want to do it either. It provided some solace for Sophie's nerves as she entered the tent.

At least a dozen other girls were there, all naked except for their thongs and necklaces to indicate their status. Adrien guided her to the center of the tent where the other girls, and presumably their trainers, were standing. Sophie noticed a rod hanging from the tent's ceiling running perpendicular to the floor. The rod held chains down its length every few feet. Sophie studied it in question, only to realize its purpose when Adrien fished his leather cuffs from his pockets. She and the other girls would be chained up, on display for all to see.

The tears began to sting her eyes almost immediately. She swallowed, hoping they wouldn't surface, but knowing her efforts were futile. Adrien was turned away from her, fastening the cuffs to the chains. When he was finished, he turned back to her, but not before she looked away to wipe her tears. As usual, she didn't want him to see.

"*Chevrette*, listen to me." His voice was low, an audible whisper. She was forced to look at him, his hands cupping the sides of her face. "You *have* to do this. This is *nothing*. It's *nothing.* Do you understand me?" His strong hands shook her as he emphasized the words.

She understood. The showing was nothing compared to the other pre-auction events he had already saved her from. He wouldn't save her from this. *Couldn't.*

In a silent defeat, she raised her arms above her head. Adrien nodded and began to secure her wrists in the cuffs. They were high and Sophie had to stand on her tiptoes to prevent the cuffs from biting uncomfortably into her skin. Vaguely, she became aware of the other trainers doing the same to the girls around her. Adrien stepped back when he was finished, his eyes landing on her lips before roaming back to her eyes. He gave her a sad smile before stepping a few feet away from her, where some tables and chairs had been set up. He sat adjacent to her, within sight and within shouting distance. Other trainers wandered farther from their trainees. She wondered if that meant something. That maybe he cared.

"Ladies and gentlemen, thank you for joining us today," a Spanish-accented voice announced over a microphone. Sophie turned in the direction of the voice, noticing a man in a tux. She recognized him from the front desk the other day. *Master Lucas.* "As your Master of Ceremonies…" he paused, allowing for a few chuckles to resound through the air. "I'm glad you could all make it to our pre-auction showing. If buyers could please line up starting on the left-hand side of the queue of slaves, you will each get one minute to examine each girl. You'll hear the timer sound, at which point you will move to the next slave in line. If you do not wish to examine the girl in front of you, please don't jump the line, just wait patiently. You'll get your turn. As always, be mindful of their necklaces and what each signifies. If you have any questions, please feel free to approach their trainers. You can find that information on the table over by the drinks. Thank you and enjoy!"

A few people applauded and the room began to buzz with energy. Sophie pushed forward on her tiptoes, peering around her arm to see if she could get a glimpse of the line. She guessed it was at least sixty men deep, although she couldn't be sure. She was the sixth in line, so it would be at least that many minutes before the first approached her.

She looked back to where Adrien had stationed himself. The chair was now empty. Slight panic set in and she began scanning the tent. She spotted him at the drink table, suddenly wishing he had had the decency to get her drunk for this instead of the previous night's events. Her eyes followed his movement as he was handed a tumbler filled with a decent amount of amber liquid. He made his way back to the table, stopping briefly to talk with a few men, presumably other trainers.

Her view was abruptly cut off by a man in her line of sight. Startled, she stumbled back on her toes, losing her footing for a moment. The cuffs cutting into her wrists, she righted herself.

"Ah, one of Degas's. I can spot an American right away," the man said, nodding to Sophie. His eyes moved over her body as he circled around her. She was reminded of someone considering the purchase of a car. Not soon enough, the timer sounded and the man, smiling politely, moved on to the next vehicle in line.

The next few were similar, and those after that, until Sophie lost track of how many she had encountered. Her arms were beginning to numb and ache, a seemingly paradoxical feat that they had somehow accomplished. Her toes hurt from the constant pressure she was placing on them. She didn't know what was worse, the pain in her toes or the pain from the cuffs if she acquiesced the pain in her toes.

Despite the line of men that continuously blocked her sight,

Sophie couldn't help but look to Adrien every few minutes. He had finished his drink and sat, seemingly assessing the men as they stood in line. Every once in a while, she would catch him glancing back toward her portion of the line to determine which of the buyers was currently surveying her. In a sense, she felt like he was guarding her. Or at least monitoring things. That was, until *she* showed up.

Sophie noticed Adrien's change in demeanor almost immediately. At first, she thought he sat up straight out of concern for her, but as she watched the tall, thin, and ridiculously beautiful brunette sidle up to him and kiss him on the cheek in greeting, Sophie's heart sank. She continued to gawk as the woman placed her hand on the back of Adrien's neck, ever so slightly, allowing her fingers to dip below the collar of his shirt. She watched as Adrien gazed up at her, clearly familiar with this gorgeous Amazon of a woman. And that's when it hit her. They had *fucked.* There was no doubt in her mind that this woman, who was now leaning forward to whisper something in his ear, had been in Adrien's bed. She watched as he smiled at what she said.

Jealousy boiled violently in Sophie's stomach, curling like steam in her chest. *Was this woman allowed to call him Adrien? Had she called out his name while he fucked her?* Clearly, he hadn't rejected her the way he had rejected Sophie. *Was she allowed to touch him without needing permission? Was she allowed to look into his eyes whenever she wanted to? Did he love her?* The last question made her stomach queasy.

"You know, ma cherie, it's impolite to focus on another man when there's one right in front of you who is clearly interested." A thick French accent dragged Sophie's attention away from Adrien. It hurt to look away, yet…she was met with Adrien's eyes staring back at her.

It wasn't Adrien's brother, but this man was obviously related. There was no mistaking those eyes. He was young, maybe the same age as Adrien—late 20s, early 30s at most. He was heavier than both Adrien and his brother. He didn't have the same good looks as either of them, but he was handsome in a different way. In a simpler, boy-next-door sense. He smiled at her, not in the creepy or condescending way that the other men had. In a kind way. "I can recognize a woman scorned from a mile away." He dropped his voice as he continued talking to her. "But you may want to hide the fact that you love him. Buyers won't be kind if they see you have feelings for your trainer."

She blinked. "I don't love him." It was the only response she could think of.

The man placed a finger to his lips. "I won't tell anyone." He winked as the timer buzzed and he moved on.

I don't love him, she repeated, this time to herself.

Adrien unhooked the cuffs from Sophie's wrists. Her arms having gone numb long before and her toes no longer strong enough to support her, she fell forward into Adrien's chest. He picked her up, evidently having anticipated her bodily failure, and carried her back to the room. Once there, he guided her into bed.

"Do you need anything?" he asked. She shook her head. "Good. We're required for dinner. Rest until then. I'll be back. I trust you're too tired to try anything stupid, or do I need to tie you up again?"

She was surprised by his sharp tone, and even more surprised that he was leaving. Of course, she shouldn't have been. "Where are you going?" What she really wanted to ask was, 'Are you going to be with *her?*'

He looked down at her before turning and making his way toward the door, not bothering to answer.

She was left with her jealous thoughts.

◦◦◦◦◦

Sophie heard him fumble with the keys at the door. She hadn't been able to sleep since Adrien left, yet hadn't bothered to move. She still wore only the thong provided to her that morning. Now, she waited in anticipation as he opened the door. She already knew what she would look for. The telltale signs of an afternoon tryst. Was his hair messy from being raked through by her fingers? Was there lipstick anywhere on him? A button missed in a hurried re-dressing? Maybe if she got close enough, she could smell the other woman on him.

The absurdity of her paranoia wasn't lost on her. The knowledge of how ridiculous she was being screamed at her with every jealous thought she indulged in. How could she be angered by his infidelity when he wasn't even Sophie's to begin with? And yet, how could she feel like she belonged to Adrien and the reverse not be true? Despite her reasoning, it was jealousy that won out. Sophie blamed Josh for that. Not once had Sophie questioned his late nights, his refusal to answer his phone when she called, his secrecy about the phone calls he received. Perhaps if she had been a nosy, jealous girlfriend, she would have realized what was happening before it was too late. Now, she had swung wildly to the other side. She was acting like a jealous wife as Adrien came stumbling into the room. Drunk.

She would have laughed had she not been so shocked to see

him in the state he was in. He had always been so reserved, so…
in control. She knew Adrien did not let his walls down very
often. Now, he swayed lightly as he kicked his shoes off, his
arm stretched out to the wall for support. She realized quickly
and with panic that a drunk Adrien would potentially be a
dangerous thing for her. She needed him to be able to play
the game with a clear head. Sophie glanced at the clock. They
would have at least two hours before dinner. Enough time for
him to sober up.

"Do you want some water?" she asked, getting up from the
bed and moving toward the bathroom.

"Why? Do I…look like I need water?" His sentence came
out elongated, slurred, as though he struggled to form the
words. She studied him and he gave her a lopsided grin. Her
heart melted at the sight, his lightheartedness so rare it felt like
she was witnessing a once-in-a-lifetime meteor shower.

She smiled to herself as she filled a glass she found in the
bathroom. She reentered the room, finding Adrien by the bed,
trying unsuccessfully to unbutton his shirt. She walked over
to him, handed him the glass and took over. As he drank, she
deftly moved, button by button, until the front was completely
open, exposing his bare, sculpted chest. She managed to fight
the urge to place her hands there, to follow the hard lines down
his torso, to feel the rippled curves of his muscle. She glanced
up, hoping he hadn't caught her so obviously fawning over him.

Any trace of nonchalance was gone, replaced by something
much more carnal in the glint of his eye. She swallowed, aware
of the growing heat between her legs, her own need begging for
release. She raised her hands, pulling his shirt gently over his
shoulders and down his arms. It was as though the shirt itself
were what had been holding Adrien back. As soon as it hit the
floor, Sophie was being pulled into his arms, pushed back onto

the bed. The backs of her knees hit the mattress and she pulled him with her as she landed on the bed.

His mouth found hers, his tongue exploring, seeking out her need. Her hands did the same, seeking and exploring. She moved over the rough scars of his back, feeling the topography of each lash that had left its mark on him. She wrapped her legs around his waist, pulling him closer. She pushed her hips into his, wanting more. The motion caused a low groan to escape Adrien's mouth, the smell of whiskey still on his breath.

It hit her. He hadn't taken advantage of her when she was drunk. Was she about to take advantage of him? Previously, he hadn't wanted this to happen. For whatever reason, he always seemed to stop things when his inhibitions were compromised.

"Fuck," she whispered as Adrien began kissing and licking her neck, moving down toward her breasts. "Adrien…" *Oh shit. She wasn't supposed to call him that.* He didn't seem to notice. In fact, the sound of his name seemed to spur his need. His hand grappled with her thong, but before he could remove it, she grabbed onto his wrist, preventing his actions. "Listen to me. We need to stop. You're drunk."

That stopped him. He looked at her, bewildered. Then he burst out laughing. "Touché, *Chevrette*." He propped himself on his elbow, Sophie still trapped beneath his body. She could feel his hard-on pressing into her hips. "It's not my fault that I'm drunk, though." His words mirrored hers from the previous night.

She doubted many people could make Adrien drink against his will. Was it that woman from earlier? Had she gotten him drunk? Curiosity got the best of her. "Who made you drink?"

Adrien moved off her, bringing himself to the head of the bed where he lay back on a pillow, utterly exhausted. "You did, *Chevrette*."

24

Sophie knew that Adrien would wake up and pretend nothing had happened. She knew he would revert back to his stoic self, inhibitions restored, as though it had all been a figment of her imagination. He would never acknowledge what had almost happened between them, and most certainly would never admit to his inebriation. The only thing to indicate that he had been drunk at all was his slightly bloodshot eyes, which he quickly masked with some eye drops.

As they readied for dinner, she pulled at the gossamer fabric of the cobalt-blue lace dress she wore. The deep V of the neckline stopped right below her breasts, leaving almost nothing to the imagination. Despite how little it covered, it was elegant in its own way. She actually liked the way it looked, the way the lace covered her, hugged her curves, all while hinting at her tanned skin beneath. It was beautiful.

Adrien led her down to the cocktail lounge from the night before. It seemed the routine was the same: cocktails and appetizers while schmoozing with buyers, then dinner with

Sophie's prospects.

"Degas!" A familiar French accent caught Sophie's attention. It was Adrien's undisclosed relative, the one Sophie had met earlier that afternoon at the showing.

"Daniel!" Adrien broke into a wide smile, a real one, the rare one. It made Sophie grin as the two embraced. Clearly, they were very close. Daniel turned to Sophie, guiding her hand to his lips to place a gentle kiss on her knuckles. She smiled at him, bowing her head in acknowledgment. She felt kindness radiating from him.

"I didn't realize you were going to be here, Daniel."

"Yes, well…I need another one so I figured I'd pop in and see what the goods look like." He winked at Sophie. Again, she didn't find it creepy or demeaning the way it would have felt coming from the other men. There was something about him that felt sincere. "I met yours at the showing earlier. She's quite beautiful. You're sure you don't want to keep her for yourself?" Daniel smiled at Adrien.

Sophie stiffened, her eyes widening. *Would he tell Adrien that she loved him?? What was he playing at? Was he joking?*

Adrien scowled. "You know I don't keep any for myself."

Daniel shrugged. "I know that, but if you were going to change your mind, I figured this one is a good one to do it with. She's a keeper."

Adrien looked suspiciously between Daniel and Sophie. She could feel her face heating and decided it was best to keep her gaze locked to the floor. The next words from Adrien were brusque and in French. She had no idea what he said, but she knew the conversation was over.

Before Daniel walked away, he leaned in to whisper, "Sorry, cherie, I tried." She glanced up and he gave her a half smile.

"Let's go, *Chevrette*." Adrien was irritated, that was for sure.

She followed him through the crowd, keeping her head low and her eyes to the ground as Adrien conversed with various buyers. When it was time for dinner, she followed him in and knelt on the cushion set on the floor next to Adrien's chair. He had chosen a table that wasn't yet occupied and slowly, various interested buyers began trickling in to fill the seats.

"Degas! There you are!" A woman's sultry voice said from over Adrien's shoulder. Sophie adjusted herself on the cushion to sneak a glimpse of the woman up close. It was *the* woman.

"Hello, Victoria." Adrien replied.

Victoria. So, that was the slut's name. Sophie looked the woman up and down, unabashedly in jealous-wife mode now. Victoria was slightly older than she had appeared when Sophie first saw her in the tent that day. Perhaps a few years older than Adrien. But she was definitely as beautiful as Sophie originally thought. The woman had on a skintight black dress that dipped just as low as Sophie's. It wasn't as short, but, nonetheless, the woman was stunning. Her body was toned, bordering muscular. Her dark hair had been pinned up in a high bun with a few wisps gracing the back of her long neck. She wore no necklace like the other girls—clearly she was no one's property. Adrien had mentioned that there were women buyers. Could she be one of them? Maybe Sophie had been wrong about her and Adrien. Maybe this woman was a lesbian looking for a new sex slave to satisfy her needs. Sophie could only hope.

Her dreams were dashed as soon as Victoria invited herself to sit next to Adrien. She turned her body toward him, running her hand lightly along his thigh. Sophie fought the urge to swat it away.

"Maybe when your trainee is busy with the events we can steal away for a few minutes. I can take care of your...*needs,*" Victoria not so silently whispered to Adrien. She emphasized the word 'needs' as though there were some *other* hidden meaning behind it aside from the obvious sexual reference. Sophie was disgusted by the woman's audacity. Evidently, Adrien wasn't amused either.

"You know I don't mix pleasure with business, Victoria. Besides that, *Chevrette* won't be taking part in the events tonight, so I'm going to have to respectfully decline." His response conveyed irritation that Victoria had brought up his personal business in their current setting. Sophie watched as Victoria pursed her lips in apparent disdain at Adrien's response. Sophie hid a smile. It felt like a win to watch Adrien reject her outright.

If Victoria had been thrown off by Adrien's response, she quickly recovered, bringing her wandering hand up to caress Adrien's arm. "Well, let me give you my room key just in case you decide to change your mind later. Once you're done babysitting, maybe you can stop by." She smiled insincerely in Sophie's direction. Sophie glared at her. Victoria's smile faded as she studied Sophie. After a moment, she looked pointedly at Adrien and said, "I think your trainee might have a staring problem."

Adrien's head snapped down to Sophie. Unfortunately, Sophie was still shooting daggers in Victoria's direction and didn't notice Adrien's displeasure until she felt his hand grasp the back of her neck, forcing her to look up at him. He was seething. Sophie's eyes widened.

"Have you forgotten the rules, *Chevrette*?" His voice was low and menacing. She attempted to shake her head, but Adrien's grip prevented it. She chanced responding aloud.

"No, Sir." His grip loosened.

"Good. Then act like it."

Sophie dared one last glance at Victoria, who was currently placing her room key in Adrien's suit pocket, before she decided it was best to just obey. It put her in a foul mood to have to sit there and listen to Adrien and Victoria flirt. The only solace was that Adrien still had a job to do, and he clearly hadn't lost sight of it. Despite Victoria's best efforts at seduction, Adrien was still focused on finding Sophie a buyer.

Still, even though she was the topic of conversation, Sophie felt invisible to Adrien. He hadn't so much as glanced down at her, hadn't acknowledged that she might be hungry or thirsty, and certainly wasn't giving her the attention he had during the previous night's dinner. Sophie had no doubt it had something to do with Victoria's intrusive presence. And it pissed her off.

When Adrien finally began feeding Sophie pieces of the bread that was out on the table, she was determined to make sure he didn't forget about her. As he handed Sophie a piece of bread, not even bothering to look in her direction as he continued his whispered conversation with Victoria, Sophie drew Adrien's hand to her mouth, taking the morsel of food with her tongue and capturing the tip of Adrien's finger in her mouth. She sucked lightly before letting go.

Adrien's conversation skipped a beat like an old record player, only to resume immediately, as though the pause were just a mere fluke in the system. Sophie smiled to herself. She had succeeded in getting his attention. As miniscule as it had been, it had registered. When Adrien made a second attempt to give Sophie some bread, she did the same, catching his finger and swirling her tongue before sucking and releasing it.

There was no mistaking the disruption in conversation this time. Adrien was looking down at her, eyes wild with shock and—

Sophie's stomach flipped. There was no misinterpreting the look in Adrien's eyes. It was pure lust. The type of look that said if they weren't in a room full of people, he would have fucked her right there on the table. She involuntarily bit her lip at the thought and watched as Adrien's eyes darkened further.

Victoria cleared her throat, clearly irritated by the interruption. Adrien peeled his eyes from Sophie, returning his attention to Victoria.

Stupid bitch, Sophie thought. One more chance was all Sophie needed. Maybe she could make Adrien forget about the floozy sitting next to him. That chance came once dinner was served. As Adrien quietly handed Sophie another morsel of food, she closed her mouth around his finger, gliding her tongue down, drawing him further into her mouth.

"Excuse me, Victoria," she heard him say before he turned his body completely to face Sophie. By then, she had freed his finger from her mouth and, using the same hand to grab her wrist while the other simultaneously grabbed her hair, he drew her toward him so that his mouth was next to her ear. Forcefully, he placed her hand on his crotch.

Holy. Fucking. Shit. He was hard as a rock. She could feel the pulse in his hard-on as he pressed her hand into him. "Is this what you want?" he whispered. He was so quiet she could barely hear him, yet the anger in the whisper was apparent. "Because if it is, you should have taken me up on my offer earlier. If you want something to suck that badly, there's a room full of men who would love to indulge you. Just say the words and I'll find one for you." With that, he just as forcefully removed her hand from his hardened shaft and turned back to Victoria. This time, he was the one to place a hand on Victoria's thigh.

"What was that about?" Victoria asked.

"Nothing important," Adrien replied as he leaned in to nip Victoria's earlobe. Victoria smiled triumphantly.

Sophie felt sick. She had turned Adrien on and then inadvertently sent him straight into the arms of *that* woman.

Of course he would choose *Victoria* over Sophie. They had a history together. Sophie and Adrien had…what *did* they have? *Something? Nothing?* She wasn't even sure anymore. Had she ever been sure?

Sophie had lost her appetite. Despite several attempts by Adrien to continue feeding her, this time using a fork, Sophie refused. Finally, Adrien gave up with an exasperated sigh, practically throwing his fork onto his plate, startling more than a few of the buyers. He mumbled an apology.

"Ladies and gentlemen, please excuse the interruption," the Master of Ceremonies came over the loudspeaker. "Would trainers please take their slaves into the play rooms to prepare for tonight's events. Festivities will begin in a few minutes."

"Degas, will yours be joining tonight?" a buyer from the opposite side of the table inquired.

"Sorry, gentlemen, but she's still recovering from a bout of dengue. The showing was as much as she can handle for one day, I'm afraid." As the night before, there was a collective sigh of disappointment.

"Well, at least have her join us to spectate and remain in our company. It would allow us to ask her some questions and observe what she's like, seeing as how we can't have a firsthand taste ourselves," one man suggested. Adrien considered this a moment, then nodded.

"No harm in that, I suppose." He said it more to himself than anyone else.

After a few minutes, the remaining guests were escorted out of the dining area and down a hall into a large banquet room. Trainees were spread around the room, each chained to a different station. It became very clear what Adrien had meant about 'try it before you buy it.'

One of the girls was lying chained to a table. Her back was

flat against the top, her ass was adjacent to the edge of the table with her legs spread and knees bent. It reminded Sophie of a patient at the gynecologist's office, although Sophie knew that the only 'examining' being done tonight would be by her prospective buyers. Across the room, another girl knelt on the floor, her knees cushioned by a soft pillow. There were several more scattered around the room, kneeling, lying down, or bent over, ready to take whatever they were given. These were the girls with the amethyst, or ready-for-purchase, necklaces.

In a slightly darker section of the room, other trainees were chained to the ceiling. This area was adorned with a number of tools that Sophie recognized from Adrien's dungeon: whips, floggers, cat o' nine tails, and some she didn't even recognize. She observed the girls' ruby necklaces, indicating their status as masochists-in-training. Not far from that particular station, Sophie saw several girls with black diamonds twinkling at their necks: sadists. These girls were chained to the floor by their feet, with just enough slack to walk a small circle. In their hands they each held some implement of torture. Sophie wondered what stopped them from just beating their masters to death and escaping. They must have been very well trained. Sophie didn't even want to imagine what their experience must have been like.

Sophie watched as men began lining up in front of the stations like kids at a carnival. She saw a man step up to one of the girls kneeling on the floor and unzip his expensive suit pants. The girl smiled, freeing his erection from his trousers and taking him into her mouth. The man groaned in pleasure, throwing his head back. Sophie looked away, embarrassed, disgusted, and slightly turned on.

"Enjoying yourself?" one of the men from their dinner table asked, his eyes dark with amusement.

No, you sick fuck! She wanted to scream it. But she knew better. Instead, she kept her mouth shut, looking down at the floor. *Where is Adrien?* She looked around only to find him, once again, at Victoria's side. She was whispering something in his ear, her hand on his chest. He, however, was looking directly at Sophie.

She turned away, irritated and hurt by the way he had been treating her. She moved toward another one of the stations, deciding it was best to just stay away from him. She wandered to where one of the girls was lying flat on a table with her legs spread. A woman sat on a stool between them, her face buried in the girl's pussy. Sophie watched as the girl on the table writhed in pleasure while the woman on the stool moved her tongue tortuously over the girl's swollen clit.

"Please, Josh? Just once," Sophie begged, flexing her hips and moving her thumb back and forth over her bunch of nerves. She was wet already, and the thought of Josh taking her in his mouth was only fueling the slickness between her thighs.

"No, Sophie. I already told you. It's gross. It's dirty."

She sat up in the bed, exasperated. "How do you know if you've never tried it?"

"I have tried it, just…not with you."

Her heart sank slightly at his words. She hadn't known he had done it with someone else before. Still… "Well, I'm not her. So, how do you know you won't like doing it to me?"

Josh rolled his eyes, simultaneously rolling toward the side of the bed and sitting up. "Because I just know. A pussy is a pussy. They're all the same. And I don't like eating girls out. Sorry, but that's just the way it is."

She pouted, crossing her arms. She hated the idea that she would never experience a man eat her out. And she would just have to live with it.

"You look like you could use a good licking. Do you need me to take care of that for you?" Mikhail's voice tore Sophie from the memory. She wasn't sure how long she had been staring at the women, but it was clear that the girl was in the throes of her orgasm and Sophie's staring had attracted unwanted attention. She shifted uncomfortably on her feet, unsure what to say to make Mikhail go away. Luckily, she didn't have to think too long.

"That won't be necessary, Mikhail. *Chevrette* was just about to go upstairs," Adrien cut in, positioning himself between Mikhail and Sophie.

"So soon?" Mikhail raised an eyebrow in mock concern.

Adrien didn't bother responding to Mikhail as he placed his hand at the curve of Sophie's spine, steering her from the room. She could feel the tension radiate as they walked in silence back to the room; Sophie out of fear and Adrien out of pure anger.

When he had safely closed the door to their room behind him and locked it, he whirled around. His eyes blazed. "What the fuck was that?!"

She backed up against the wall. "I'm sorry. I can't help them, I couldn't stop it." She was babbling, worried that he was mad at her for something she still couldn't control.

He rubbed the center of his forehead as if trying to will away the anger that boiled behind his skull. "I know…I know. But it can't happen again. What was the memory?"

She flushed, shaking her head. "I don't want to talk about it." It was embarrassing. She was 25 years old and had never had one of the most basic sexual encounters. It dawned on her that she would most likely have her first coital orgasm by her new owner. The thought sickened her, bringing tears to her eyes.

Adrien stepped forward, placing his knuckle beneath her chin to lift her face upward. "Tell me. I need to know so we can make sure it doesn't happen again. What happened?" His voice was soft and soothing. It was the voice of the Adrien that cared, not the one that would so callously flirt with that woman right in front of her.

"I just…I saw that girl who was…um…getting—" How pathetic. She couldn't even say the words.

"Yes?" Adrien raised a brow in amusement. He was going to force her to say it.

"She was getting eaten out," Sophie rushed through the words, causing Adrien's smile to widen. "And I just had this memory of Josh telling me he didn't want to do that because he thought it was gross and all pussies are the same…but it didn't seem like *they* thought it was gross. And I just wondered what—" she took a deep breath, having almost run out of air, "I wondered what it would be like."

She could practically see the wheels turning in Adrien's mind as he put two and two together. He blinked, his head rearing back as he made sense of what Sophie was intimating. "Wait— you've never…" Quickly, she shook her head. Sophie could feel her cheeks flaming. She bit her lip, looking at the floor.

His hand grasped her chin again, steering her gaze to his once more. He was impossibly close, his eyes assuming that darkness again. It was the same look that he wore at the dinner table. "And you were wondering what it would be like…?"

She nodded. His jaw clenched. But it wasn't anger that elicited his reaction. It was restraint. She wondered if he wanted to. If he would. At least then she wouldn't have the experience stolen from her by her new master.

"Please," she whispered.

He drew in a sharp breath. "Tell me what you want. Say it."

"I want your mouth on me. I want you to make me come that way."

In a flash, her back was pressed against the wall, Adrien's body against hers. His hands imprisoned her face as he brought his lips to hers. His tongue licked at the seam of her mouth and she opened, letting him in. His kiss didn't contain its usual ferocity. It was restrained, as though he weren't quite sure he was going to go through with it at all. Her hands reached up to feel the hard planes of his chest, quickly working to remove his suit jacket and shirt. He grabbed at the hem of her dress, swiftly lifting it up over her head. After discarding the clothing on the floor, his body was once again pressed to hers. Gone was the hesitation from the previous moment. The domineering strength and urgency came crashing through. Adrien picked her up, wrapping her legs around his waist as he nibbled and licked along her jawline and down her throat. Her head tilted back to allow him access, goose bumps rising on her arms.

Adrien carried her toward the bed, placing her gently on the edge. He continued his trail of kisses down to her breasts, her nipples peaking at the touch of his tongue. His hand moved to her inner thigh and she opened her legs in anticipation. Groaning, he moved his fingers under the fabric of her thong and along the slickness of her folds.

"Fuck, you're so wet," he murmured, sliding one finger inside her. She gasped at the sensation, arching toward him. He moved his lips down her stomach, taking his time. He lapped at her hips, causing her gasps and moans to crescendo. She hadn't any idea how sensitive her flesh was around her hips.

He knelt before her, trailing his tongue along her inner thigh and up along her creases. Sophie moaned, her hands reflexively grasping Adrien's hair as his tongue slipped inside her. She flexed her hips, wanting more. His hands moved from her thighs to her hips, holding her steady as he began his ascent toward her clit.

"Oh my fucking God!" she cried out as his tongue flicked her clit. His grip around her waist tightened as he continued the motion, alternating between licking and sucking at her bundle of nerves. She pulled at his hair—couldn't help it, and he made no move to stop her. Her hips kept a steady tempo with Adrien's tongue, her orgasm building. He moved his hand lower, this time dipping two fingers inside her. He stroked her as he continued licking.

"God, you taste so perfect," he murmured as he once again took the hood of her clit into his mouth, sucking hungrily. It was her undoing. Her hips bucked wildly as she came, her hands pulling Adrien's head closer to her while concurrently pushing him back. She wanted more and yet her body couldn't handle the intensity. She cried out, her climax coming in waves. Her pussy clenched around Adrien's fingers, grasping and yearning for more.

As she descended from her peak, Adrien's tongue slowed, becoming gentler, mirroring the dissipation of her orgasm. After it had completely faded, Adrien continued kissing her lightly around the swollen area as she caught her breath. She closed her eyes, soaking in the post-coital feeling of bliss. She opened her eyes at the withdrawal of Adrien's mouth. He was standing over the bed studying her.

She smiled up at him shyly. He returned a half-smile, holding his hand out. Sophie lifted herself onto her elbows before taking his hand. He pulled her toward him and she adjusted herself so she was kneeling on the bed, her head level with his own. Wrapping her arms around his neck, she pulled him close. He allowed her, pausing briefly before kissing her. She could taste herself on his lips—sweet and tangy. It was in no way gross or dirty like Josh said, and she hated that she had believed him. And it was Adrien, once again, who had brought her out of the dark. She wanted to show him how much she appreciated him in that moment.

She pulled away, pushing Adrien so that he was forced to move from the edge of the bed. She climbed to her knees on the floor in front of him and began unbuttoning his pants.

His hands closed around hers, impeding her progress.

"What are you doing?" His voice was husky with need. She could see his arousal, wanting nothing more than to be his undoing as he had been hers. Despite his resistance, she continued unzipping his pants to free his hardened cock from imprisonment. "Stop—*Chevrette*—no favors." He said it almost pleadingly.

"It's not a favor. I want to do this. I want to taste you. I want you to come in my mouth."

She could practically see his restraint dissolving, melting away as his last bit of hesitation broke. His breathing quickened and his eyes clouded with lust. His hands, still around hers, loosened their grip. It was the slightest signal, but all the permission she needed.

She took him in her mouth, his hands weaving through her hair. Her lips wrapped around his thick cock, her tongue swirling around the tip before taking him deeper, and then taking him in as far as she could.

"Ah, shit," he hissed as his tip stroked the back of her throat. His grip tightened on her hair. She pulled back, grazing her tongue along his shaft and using her hand to stroke him as she repeated the motion, before taking him in entirely. He flexed his hips with a groan. She began to quicken her pace, stroking and sucking him in a steady rhythm.

"Christ, *Chevrette*. That feels so good." She moaned her response, the vibration from her throat prompting another hissed curse from Adrien. She used her free hand to cup his balls, massaging them as she continued to take him to the hilt. Over and over again she used her mouth as a sheath, taking him completely and then moving back to suck at his tip while she fisted his length. His breathing became uneven and she could feel his cock thickening. She began moving faster, stroking rapidly, sucking harder.

"You're going to make me come." It came out sounding strangled, like Adrien was, as always, trying to exercise some restraint. His hands gripped her hair, encouraging her to take him completely. She moaned once more as she deep-throated him. She wanted it, wanted him to come in her mouth. She wanted him to fall apart for her, the way she had fallen apart for him.

"Fuck!" he cried out as the first spurt of cum hit the back of Sophie's throat. He flexed his hips once more, driving deeper into her throat. She swallowed again and again as he came, his semen thick and sweet on her tongue. He stroked her hair as she began to carefully lap the remnants of his orgasm off his shaft, sucking gently at his tip before sitting back on her heels. Wordlessly, he tucked himself back into his pants and reached down to grab Sophie's elbow, guiding her upright. He leaned down to place a soft kiss on her lips, pressing his forehead to hers.

"What are you doing to me, Sophie?" he whispered.

She tried pulling away to look at him, but his hands were still entangled in her hair. Adrien resisted her, holding her forehead against his. He kept his eyes closed as he steadied his breathing. He couldn't look at her, not yet. He needed a minute to regain control.

What the fuck had he done? He hadn't been thinking clearly, that much was obvious. As soon as Sophie admitted that she'd never been fucked by someone's tongue until she came, he'd made his decision. *That* wasn't what he regretted. He could at least tell himself that he'd done it to get rid of the flashbacks she was having. It was what happened after that he regretted.

For some reason, he'd convinced himself that he would be able to stop the situation from going any further. He had never intended to let her suck him off. It was the rules—rules he had created for himself to avoid this very challenge. But he'd forgotten the rules. Or ignored them. He'd given into weakness, into temptation. Maybe it was the way she gripped his hair, or the way she writhed beneath his tongue. It was as though she were holding on for dear life, as though the very earth was tilting on its axis and would fucking dump her off the edge if she didn't hold on tight enough. Or maybe it was the sound of her moans, the way she cried out as she came—*hard*—that rendered him reckless. The fact that he'd been the only one to do that to her held its poignancy. There was something primitive pulling at him: the idea that Sophie's first experience belonged to him alone. And somewhere in his mind, at some point when her lips had been wrapped around his cock, a shift had occurred. A shift that translated into the notion that Sophie had become *his. But did he belong to* her, *as well?*

And that right there, was the problem for Adrien. Attachment was not something he could afford, and certainly not something that had ever piqued his interest. It was because he'd let his guard down too many times during their time together. In fact, he'd broken a lot of his rules over the past month. He had no doubt what Frederic would do if he discovered how weak Adrien had become.

He let go of Sophie, who stared up at him curiously. He

wasn't sure how long he had been holding her while lost in his thoughts. It didn't matter. He avoided her eyes and stepped back, picking up his shirt. Hastily, he put it on and checked the front pocket for the keycard that had been tucked there earlier in the night. It was still there. *Good.*

He knew what he needed.

25

Sophie had often speculated about whether or not one could feel pain of the soul. Not pain *in* their soul—that was different. That type of pain radiated throughout the soul but didn't originate there. What Sophie truly wanted to know was, did the soul itself ever hurt? Did the pain ever come from within itself, a hurt so deep that it could be felt at the very core of one's being, or was it only ever subject to pain that it allowed to seep in from its host?

She watched Adrien battle with himself in those moments before he left. She watched the unmistakable shadow of regret grab him and hold on for dear life. She wanted to pull him back. She wanted to say something to bring him out of those shadows, but she couldn't find the words. Because what could she say? *It was only a blowjob, Adrien. It didn't mean anything. You don't have anything to regret.* Because deep within her soul, she knew that simply wasn't true. And as she watched him check his pocket for the key that Victoria had placed there and methodically turn to walk out the door, she felt the pain from within her soul.

She realized the soul's pain had its own type of radiating effect. It stole her breath, made her chest hurt. Her knees became weak, her stomach a mess of knots and tumbleweeds. Her eyes stung with the need for tears and her throat constricted with the desire to scream. At the same time, she felt entirely numb. She hardly registered the hard wood against her knees as she crumbled to the floor, absolutely broken.

She was powerless to stop it. When the soul wants something, you give into it. And right then, her soul wanted to bleed out.

It wasn't just about what had happened that night. It was about everything—the loss of her parents, the loss of Josh, the loss of her old life. As she lay on the floor, she began admitting things to herself she never had the courage to admit before. Josh wasn't who she thought he had been. She had lost over a year of her life grieving a man who she now wondered if she had ever truly loved and if he had ever really loved her. Sophie's tears puddled on the cold floor beneath her as she finally admitted to herself that she had fallen in love with her captor. Adrien had brought her out of the worst time of her life, made her feel whole again. And the realization promptly plunged her right back into the cold cruelty that Sophie had come to recognize as life itself. It was unfair. So much had been taken from her already and she was finally feeling as though she had regained some piece of herself. Adrien helped put her back together. But, like any refinished antique, she would be sold. It was the worst type of quid pro quo. She could have her sanity back, but not her life. At least, not the life she had known. A different life lay ahead of her.

There was something else, though, that Adrien had helped remind her of. Her strength. Her determination. Her will to live. She had felt it slowly seeping back in over the past few days. Maybe even weeks, she couldn't be sure. But it was there, growing fiercer each moment. The girl who had picked herself up after her parents' death and moved to Nicaragua to help orphaned children was there, deep inside her, growing stronger every day. She would make it out of this, and she would be better for it. She knew that without a doubt. She could feel it in her soul.

It had been hours, but her tears began to dry. Feeling returned to her limbs, her body aching from lying on the hard floor. She pulled herself up, hugging her knees just as the unmistakable sound of a key turned in the lock. She pulled in a deep breath.

Adrien opened the door quietly and slipped in. He moved stiffly, shuffling toward the bathroom. He passed her, only then realizing that she was sitting on the floor. He looked at her, his face alight with surprise and confusion.

"Why are you still awake?"

Sophie shrugged. She wasn't about to tell him that she had just wallowed in pain for several hours while he was off fucking Victoria. Her eyes raked over his body. His hair was a mess, his shirt more crumpled than it had been. Yes, he definitely had been off fucking Victoria. She swallowed the pain that threatened to rise again.

"Go to bed," nudging his chin in its direction. Sophie sighed at his determined command. She hated that she wanted to submit. She wanted to crawl into bed beside him, despite the fact he'd just come from another woman's bed. She disgusted herself.

He looked down at her, waiting for her to obey. Slowly, she shook her head. "I'll sleep on the daybed."

A flash of anger crossed his features. "Suit yourself." Still, he waited for her to follow his command. She got up from the floor and moved to the daybed. It wasn't until she was lying down that he finally continued to the bathroom. As his back turned, she thought she caught a glimpse of dark lines on his white shirt. She bolted upright just as he shut the bathroom door.

Her heart pounded in her chest. Had she been mistaken? *Was that blood? What the fuck??*

There was no way she could sleep now. She got up and quietly stepped toward the bathroom. She heard the shower turn on as she silently stood outside the door. She contemplated turning the handle, opening it just a crack to see him. But if she were caught, she had no doubt he would be angry with her. Adrien was a private man and spying on him in the shower was the ultimate invasion of his privacy. Still, she listened.

She heard the sound of the shower's spray part to let Adrien in. Heard the unmistakable hiss that escaped his lips, the low grunt that accompanied it. Had she not seen the blood, she might have thought the guttural noises were sounds of pleasure. But she heard an undertone of pain. She stepped back from the door, confused.

Where had he gone? To Victoria's room, she knew that. She saw him check for the key. *But what happened there? What did she do to him?* Sophie was suddenly reminded of the girls trained to inflict pain on their masters. Was Victoria a sadist? Begging the question…was Adrien a masochist? Had he sought out the pain he was in? Had it turned him on? Was that why he left? Because Sophie had turned him on but wasn't able to give him what he really needed?

The thoughts whirling in her head, she hadn't realized the shower had stopped. Adrien emerged from the bathroom, towel around his waist, and stopped dead in his tracks.

"What are you doing?" Annoyance. Sophie swallowed. She had no good answer.

"I needed to use the bathroom." She wasn't about to admit

to spying on him. His eyes narrowed, suspicion clouding the blue rings in his eyes. He stepped back, allowing her to pass. She entered the bathroom and closed the door behind her. Immediately, her eyes fell to the clothing he had left discarded on the floor next to the shower. Lines of blood crisscrossed the white shirt. She gasped, her hand flying to her mouth to hold in the sob that threatened to escape.

He must have overheard her because the next thing she knew, the door flew open. Ascertaining what she had seen, he moved around her, picking up the clothing, anger and pain apparent in his every move. As he bent to retrieve his bloodied clothing, Sophie glimpsed the wounds on his back.

They seeped with fresh blood, long slashes of opened flesh. Newly created, bright red lines overlapped the faded scars of previous lashings. Sophie swallowed the bile that threatened at the back of her throat. He needed bandaging. Badly.

"Adrien…" she began.

He whipped around, his eyes iced with fury. "I told you never to call me that." The sudden movement must have caused him pain. His eyes squeezed shut for a brief moment, his chin resting against his chest as he recomposed himself.

"You need ointment and bandages. Let me help you." She stepped toward him and he countered by stepping back.

"I don't need *anything, Chevrette*," he said flatly, looking at her again.

Her heart hurt for the man standing before her, so unwilling to accept help. "Why?" she whispered. She asked so many questions with that one word.

"What are you asking? Why don't I want to bandage it? Why did I do this?" It was as though he could read her mind. She nodded, wanting to know it all. "Because, *Chevrette*. This is what I need. It's what I deserve."

Sophie blinked. If he had merely said it was what he wanted, she would have let it go. She would have known he was masochistic, and that would have been fine. To each his own. It was the idea that he thought he deserved this that didn't sit well with her. It implied that maybe he didn't really want it, but that he felt compelled to do it.

"You don't deserve this, Adrien," Sophie said quietly. She hoped he could hear the sincerity in her voice. His eyes flashed again at the sound of his name. "I don't know why you think you do, but you don't. You're a good person and good people don't deserve to be hurt like this."

He looked at her as though she had grown two heads. "What world do you live in, woman?! I kidnap and sell girls to *monsters* for Christ's sake! There is nothing redeemable in that. Whatever you've made me out to be in your head, I'm not. There is nothing *good* about me." He clenched his clothing, his fist turning white at the knuckles. Violence was boiling below, Sophie could sense it.

"No, you're right. You do some pretty shitty things to people. But you said yourself that some people don't have a choice, and I think you're one of those people. And even though you have to do some pretty shitty things, you do what you can to make up for it. You let Megan go when I asked. You didn't have to, and we both know that. But you did. And you take care of the girls you train. You make sure we're healthy, you make sure we're strong. You never push us further than we can handle. Everything that I've done, you've asked my consent for first. Maybe I'm the stupid one for saying yes, I don't know. But I do know you check up on the girls you've sold. I saw the way you spoke to *Doll*, making sure she's being taken care of. Whether you realize it or not, you care about us in the ways that you can. And you…helped me…when I didn't know how to help myself.

I feel like *me* again. You helped bring Sophie Kingston back. Yes, the idea of being sold into slavery is a nightmare. But you make that nightmare bearable."

"If you believe that then you're stupider than I thought."

It was a sucker punch. She only let it sting for a moment. "That's fine if you don't believe it, but I do."

They both stood there staring at one another. His face was an impasse, indiscernible. Finally, she decided to break the silence. "At least let me bandage it so you don't bleed all over the sheets. That cleaning fee would be astronomical." She said it with as much sarcasm as she dared.

The corners of his lips twitched as he held back a smile. "There's some ointment and bandages in my bag."

She retrieved the supplies and wet a cloth with cool water to wipe the excess blood that had begun to seep from his wounds. She did it with care, but still, Adrien flinched and growled when she went over the particularly deep lashes.

"Jesus Christ, would you be more careful?" he hissed as she gently began covering the largest gashes with the ointment.

"Stop being a baby," she replied as she focused on her work.

He laughed through the pain. "You're really something else, you know that? I have half a mind to bend you over right here and give you a spanking for that smart mouth of yours."

She felt all the moisture in her body rush below her waist. She was surprised by her reaction—the anticipation she felt at the idea of being spanked by him. No longer did she fear the pain it evoked, rather, she looked forward to the pleasure. *Odd*, she thought. She really had changed, become stronger in a new way.

"Ready for the bandages?" she asked, sidestepping his comment and ignoring the lust that tugged at her. Adrien clenched his jaw and nodded. She began by placing strips of gauze over each lash. He raised his arms so she could work around his torso, her breasts grazing him as she wrapped the cloth bandages around him. It left her feeling heady, being in his proximity again. When she was finished, she tucked in the ends of the bandage and smoothed her hand over the cloth.

She wondered if anyone had ever bothered to help bandage him before. By the scars, it was clear he had endured years of this type of treatment. Yet, by the way things had scarred over, it didn't appear that anyone had ever cared enough to help him afterwards. He had cared for her wounds with so much tenderness, and she was merely a trainee. He had afforded her the care that he had never received. No doubt his father never helped bandage his wounds after he was finished with Adrien. It was sickening to think about.

Absentmindedly, she traced the bandages with the tips of her fingers, wondering about the man who stood before her. He must have known she was finished bandaging him, but didn't stop her from exploring. She couldn't help what she did next. She leaned in and kissed the fabric of the bandages. She wished she had done it before she had dressed him. She wanted to kiss his scars, the same way he had kissed hers.

"That's enough, *Chevrette*." He looked at her through the mirror. She nodded, stepping away. Again, it was there in his eyes. *Regret.*

She watched him as he slept. It was the first time she'd really seen him sleep, exhausted by the physical exertion that accompanies a lashing, as though the whip itself had stolen his energy, licking it away piece by piece. She still wasn't sure what role Victoria played in all of it, but she hated her even more than she had before. *Sick bitch.* Sophie fumed.

Rolling over, she looked at the clock. It was almost 8 a.m. Her stomach growled, reminding her that they would both need breakfast. She looked back at Adrien sound asleep next to her. She didn't want to wake him as he never seemed to sleep this well. She decided she would get up, go downstairs, and get them some food to bring back to the room, unsure if there was room service at a place like this.

She dressed, searched for the room key, and quietly made her way out. She kept her head down, hoping to go unnoticed by anyone who may be passing by. She made it, without incident, to the cocktail lounge. Unsure where else to go, she stepped up to the bar where one of the servers sat. As Sophie approached, the woman raised her brow, looking around to see if she was accompanied by anyone.

"Um…can I order some food?" Sophie asked. The woman raised a brow, staring pointedly at Sophie's necklace. Sophie nervously clasped the diamond between her fingers. "My trainer sent me."

The woman seemed satisfied by this answer, visibly relaxing. "What can I get for you?"

Sophie put in her order and the woman disappeared into a back doorway, presumably the kitchen. Sophie took a seat at the bar, fidgeting with her necklace as she waited.

"What are you doing here by yourself?" A soft, wispy voice asked behind Sophie. She turned in her barstool, awash in tension from the stranger's voice. She was taken aback by the thin, pale girl before her. *Doll* gave her a shy smile before taking a seat next to Sophie.

Sophie looked around for Mikhail. If *Doll* were here, no doubt he wouldn't be far behind.

"Don't worry about him. He's…occupied with other things,"

Doll said. Sophie nodded. Still, she couldn't get her nerves to settle. "You don't say much, do you?" *Doll* asked.

Sophie considered this for a moment. "I thought we weren't allowed to talk to one another."

Doll smiled. "What they don't know can't hurt us." Sophie hated the way she had manipulated the phrase. She kept talking, ignoring Sophie's obvious discomfort. "I miss him, you know." *Doll* looked wistful as she tugged at a strand of pale blond hair.

"Who?" Sophie had an inkling to whom she was referring.

"Master," *Doll* said. The way she said it made Sophie hurt for the girl. She clearly still considered Adrien her master, not Mikhail. "He was so good to me. He was always gentle. Is he like that with you?" *Doll* looked at Sophie then, pain and jealousy swimming in her pale-blue eyes. All Sophie could do was nod.

She practically saw *Doll* deflate. "I figured he would be. I thought maybe I was special to him. He made me feel special anyway. He seemed to care. The way he treats you makes you believe he might keep you. I held out hope right until the end. Even when he was handing me over to *him*," she made a wayward motion toward an invisible Mikhail, "I still thought he was going to stop it. And then, for weeks afterwards, I thought he would come for me," she sighed. "I see now that was pretty stupid of me." Sophie watched as a single tear slid down her cheek. She realized that she was looking into a mirror. This girl loved Adrien, or at least thought she did. Was Sophie falling into the same trap? "I should have known though. He was gentle with me and he cared for me. Looking back it was pretty obvious he was just doing his job. He never felt the same way about me that I feel—*felt*—about him."

"How do you know?" It came out as a whisper. She was desperate to unearth some difference between herself and *Doll*.

"For starters," *Doll* turned to her, all melancholy gone from her features, "he never looked at me the way he looks at you." Sophie saw it then, the hatred that filled *Doll*. She was up to her eyeballs in it and it was seeping out. Sophie straightened in her chair, shivered.

"Here you are." The server was back with her food. She was eyeing the two of them suspiciously. It probably wasn't every day she saw two slaves conversing without their masters present. Sophie quickly grabbed the containers, muttered a quick thanks, and fled. She didn't want to be anywhere *near Doll.*

She was practically out of breath from walking so fast when she barged back into the room, slamming the door shut. Instantly, she regretted it, hoping she hadn't woken Adrien. She looked over. Too late, he was already awake and clearly had been for some time. He sat up in bed, his chest bare except for the bandages wrapped around him. And he was glaring at Sophie.

"Where the hell have you been?"

She raised her hands, holding the containers. "I thought you'd be hungry."

"And so you decided to go wandering around by yourself?" he spat, clearly unimpressed by her thoughtfulness. She decided to forgo telling him about her encounter with *Doll.* It would just set him off further.

She stepped toward the bed. "Bacon or sausage?" she asked holding each respective to-go container out in front of her. He stared at her incredulously.

"Bacon," he mumbled. She grinned and handed him his breakfast before taking a seat at the end of the bed to eat her own. She was right. He was hungry. She had barely gotten through half of her eggs and he had already polished off the eggs, home fries, and bacon. He placed the empty container on the bedside table and leaned back against the headboard, glaring at her as she ate.

Sophie decided that if *Doll* thought that Adrien looked at her in some way that indicated he felt something for her, she had been sorely mistaken. Sophie stifled a laugh at the absurdity of it.

"What's so funny, *Chevrette?*" Adrien was anything but amused.

"Nothing. It's the way you're looking at me, like you want to kill me."

He raised a brow. "And you find that amusing?"

"Apparently, I have a sicker sense of humor than I used to." She finished her breakfast, pushing the empty carton away from her on the bed. "I should probably re-bandage you. Here, let me look." She got up from the bed and moved toward him.

Adrien shook his head. "This needs to stop. Now."

What was *this*? She still didn't know, even after all these weeks. "What?"

"This…taking care of me. The bandages, the breakfast. It needs to stop."

"Why? What's so wrong about it? You need to be taken care of," she defended herself. She defended *him*, really.

"You have no *idea* what I need, *Chevrette*, so don't disillusion yourself into thinking you do." The words stung, stopping her in her tracks. Had she done that? Convinced herself that she knew him, his needs when, really, she didn't have a clue? She felt foolish. She felt how she imagined *Doll* must have felt when she realized Adrien wouldn't save her from her fate.

Sophie turned from Adrien. She didn't want him to see the pain threatening to surface.

"Sophie," Adrien whispered her name. The sound sent a

warm shiver through her body. She wanted to turn to him, but decided against it. "You need to stop. I can't be what you want me to be. You'll only end up broken again."

She nodded through her tears. This time, she wasn't strong enough to stop them from falling.

He hadn't realized tears made a sound until he heard hers echo like broken glass on the floor. He winced, hating the noise they made. Even more, he hated that he was the cause. But she needed to understand that there was no happy end to this story. *Right?* He loathed that it was even a question in his mind.

26

"**P**ack your things, we're leaving today," Adrien told her the next morning. They had spent the remainder of the previous day in relative silence, Adrien providing the occasional command. Sophie obeyed each one wordlessly. Even now, she didn't bother to answer him, just got up and began packing. She felt his eyes on her every movement. He had been doing that, too, watching her silently. She didn't mind it, but speculated its meaning. What was he looking for as he watched?

They hadn't bothered attending dinner the night before. Although curious, she didn't want to ask about it. She was relieved she didn't have to go down there and be paraded in front of all of those men. She was glad they were leaving. It was over and she had made it through, relatively unscathed, aside from the ache in her heart and the pain of her soul. *Minor inconveniences*, she supposed.

It was midday by the time they were ready to leave. Adrien grabbed both of their bags, locked the door behind them, and led her down the stairway to check out.

"Brother!" Adrien's brother jogged toward them as Adrien was placing the key on the front desk. The concierge was nowhere in sight. Adrien turned, and the two greeted each other with a quick hug. "Before you go, I need to update you on a few things." His brother eyed Sophie, clearly uncomfortable with her presence. Adrien nodded, turning to her.

"Wait for me here. I'll be right back." She nodded and he walked away with his brother.

She took a look around, wondering if this was the last time she'd see this place. She hoped so. Despite its elegance and beauty, there was a darkness here that she knew she would never be able to ignore.

"Well, well. Just who I was looking for." Sophie stiffened at the sound of his voice. Scaly, like the man behind it wasn't a man but a snake in disguise. She was turning toward him when he grabbed her roughly. She cried out in surprise but was quickly silenced by his hand over her mouth. "Scream and I'll beat you unconscious, bitch," he hissed in her ear. He reeked of violence and, despite the fact that she had no desire to make any noise, he kept his hand over her mouth. Dragging her down the hall, he continued, "I heard you had a little chat with my slave."

Her stomach dropped. She remembered the way Mikhail had reacted to Adrien making conversation with *Doll* without his consent. At the time, Sophie thought it was just because Mikhail didn't want Adrien talking to *Doll*. She realized now that Mikhail didn't want *Doll* talking to *anyone* without his permission. Had *Doll* ratted her out? Had she known Mikhail would come after her?

It didn't take long to figure out where Mikhail was dragging her. He kicked open the doors to the banquet room, the large space still set up for the pre-auction events. Clearly, staff hadn't broken down the room yet. Mikhail hauled her toward the chains on the walls. She struggled against him, but his arms were wrapped tightly, squeezing the air from her, leaving Sophie effectively immobile. She let out a reflexive scream, muffled behind his hand.

"What the fuck did I just tell you, you little cunt?" Mikhail breathed into her ear. He whirled her around, backhanding her in the process. His knuckle collided with Sophie's cheekbone. The force of the blow knocked her off balance and she stumbled sideways. He grabbed onto her wrists, slamming his knee into her stomach. Doubling over with pain and gasping for breath, Sophie was shoved against the wall so forcefully that her head snapped back, smacking the dry wall behind her. She heard the crunch as her head made contact. She wasn't sure if it was her skull or the plaster that had cracked. She felt dizzy, nauseated from the impact.

She shook her head, regaining her senses, only to realize that Mikhail was in the midst of strapping her into the restraints. She tugged frantically at her wrists, causing a laugh to erupt from his chest.

"What's wrong? You don't like being tied up? Clearly Degas has lost his touch with his trainees." He spit as he referenced Adrien. They clearly had some sort of history. The two did not like one another, that much was clear. Sophie had the distinct impression she would be the one paying for whatever grievances Mikhail had with Adrien. Fleetingly, her mind wondered what *Doll* had to endure under this man's wrath. She almost felt sorry for her. *Almost.*

Sophie flinched when he made impact with her other cheek. Her head snapped to the side, her body going slack from the impact. She was held up only by her wrists, the cuffs so tight that they were cutting into her. She righted herself, regaining her footing.

"Didn't your trainer tell you not to talk with my slave?"

"I'm sorry—" Sophie began to stammer, but her reply was cut short by a slap to the mouth.

"Did I tell you that you could speak? You clearly haven't learned your lesson yet, have you?" His voice was shrill, on the verge of hysteria. Sophie gawked at the violence in his eyes. She swallowed, a shiver rippling down her spine. Mikhail's eyes were two different colors—one brown, the other blue, speckled with greens and browns. On anyone else, it may have been intriguing, beautiful even. On Mikhail, it looked menacing. "Obviously Degas hasn't been teaching you anything. It's about time you suffered the punishment you deserve." He stepped forward, pressing his body against her. He pushed his face into her neck, inhaling. Sophie fought the urge to gag as he snaked his tongue up her collarbone and along her neck. "You're not going to enjoy this," he whispered, stepping back.

He walked toward the tools, left from the previous nights' events. He assessed them, his eyes raking manically over each one before deciding on the paddle. He held it by the handle and walked back to where she hung.

Pure terror coursed through her. He hadn't gone easy on her and she could tell he wasn't about to let up. She had never been paddled before, had no idea how much it was going to hurt. Squeezing her eyes shut, she braced herself for the certain pain she didn't want to see coming.

"Closing your eyes won't make it hurt any less." His breath was on her again. He was close. Could she kick him in the groin? *And then what?* she chastised herself. *Stupid plan.* Keeping her eyes firmly closed, her heart raced in anticipation and anxiety of the first blow. She let out a sob. It escaped her lips before she was aware it had surfaced.

Through the terror roaring in her ears, she heard a familiar sound: a beep. She waited for the click followed by an opening door. But it didn't come. Of course—she was nowhere near the padlocked doors of Adrien's house. *Then why did that sound seem so familiar?*

Sophie's eyes snapped open as relief swept over her. She watched Mikhail's face as he, too, registered the noise. He turned in its direction, only to find himself face-to-face with the barrel of Adrien's gun.

The beep. The safety disengaging. By the look of pure rage on his face, she had no doubt Adrien wouldn't hesitate to pull the trigger. His eyes were blazing fury as Mikhail stood dumbfounded, apparently shocked by the turn of events.

"What are you doing, Degas?" Mikhail inquired, clearly confounded by the sight of Adrien standing there, so ready to shoot him. "She's just a slave. And she broke the rules. She talked to mine." He said it so matter-of-factly, like all slaves should be treated the way he was treating Sophie.

"And you broke the rules by punishing mine," Adrien growled. He turned to the person standing beside him. Sophie hadn't even realized there was someone else in the room. "Get her out of here."

Adrien's brother unfastened the chains at her wrists, eyeing her warily. Her arms dropped like lead weights and, although she tried to catch herself, her knees buckled. It was an odd side effect of fear. He scooped her up and began carrying her out. She watched Adrien, his eyes never leaving Mikhail, his aimed gun never faltering. "Closing your eyes won't make it hurt any less, Mikhail."

She felt his brother stiffen at Adrien's words. They had reached the door, but rather than carry her out like she expected, he set her down, shoving her through the doorway with a whispered command, "Hurry, get out of here. Go to the car. It's out front," before slamming the door in her face.

She would have liked to say that she was brave enough to go back inside. She would have liked to say that she wasn't afraid of the vehemence in Adrien's eyes, the rigid ferocity in his body. She would have liked to witness Mikhail's defeat.

She ran to the car and locked herself inside.

Several minutes later, she heard the brothers approaching before she saw them in the rearview mirror. They were fighting loudly in French. She took a quick inventory. Both were unharmed. Adrien still held his gun. There was no blood on either of them. He couldn't have shot Mikhail. At such a close range, it would have undoubtedly left blood splattered. Sophie let go of the breath she hadn't realized she'd been holding. Despite her abhorrence of Mikhail, she didn't want him dead.

Adrien and his brother stood outside of the car, continuing their argument. She had no idea what they were saying, but it was clearly a heated disagreement. Finally, Adrien opened the driver-side door, climbed in, and slammed it shut. Without a backward glance toward his brother, he started the engine and drove off. Sophie turned to look at the man they had left behind. *Worry.*

Sophie focused on Adrien. He, too, looked tense as he kept his eyes on the road. "Did he hurt you?" he asked without taking his eyes off the road.

"No, not really. Not badly anyway," she replied. "Thank you for stopping him," she began. With a deep breath she asked, "What happened?" She whispered it, unsure if she even had the right to ask. Adrien glanced at her from the corner of his eye.

"I'd like to know the same thing."

She knew that was coming. She swallowed. "*Doll* approached me while I was getting breakfast for you yesterday morning.

She started talking to me. I tried to tell her I didn't think we should be talking but…"

Adrien's fist smashed against the steering wheel. "And you're just telling me this now?!" He was seething. It was the most out of control Sophie had ever seen him and it frightened her. She shrank back against the window. He took a deep breath, conceding that he was swiftly losing his composure.

"I'm sorry," she said. It came out sounding meek rather than sincere. Her body lurched forward as Adrien slammed on the brakes, pulling over to the side of the road as he did. He shoved the car into park. Sophie flinched as he moved to unbuckle her and, before she knew it, he had grabbed her and pulled her over the console to straddle his lap.

He grabbed her roughly by her hair, bringing her face within an inch of his. "I make rules for a reason, *Chevrette*. Rules keep you safe. You can't be safe if you don't follow the rules," he growled. "Do you have any idea what he would have done to you?" He shook her as he said it. She flinched at his roughness, a small gasp escaping her lips.

"Do I scare you like this, *Chevrette*?" His voice was low, menacing. Carnal.

She swallowed, nodding.

"Do I scare you more than him?" Sophie shook her head.

"Why not?"

"Because you would never hurt me." She was sure of that, even now, despite the undercurrent of violence radiating from him. A low growl escaped the back of his throat right before he pulled her to him, kissing her with all of his pent-up ferocity.

He didn't ask, he took, plunging his tongue into her mouth, tasting her. She matched his intensity, all fear dissolving as she let him in. Their tongues licked at one another, his stopping only long enough for his teeth to nip at her lip. It was a brutal rhythm, licking, sucking, biting. She ground her hips in sync with their kiss, rubbing herself against him. It wouldn't take long for her to come that way. But she wanted more. Sophie fumbled to undo the button of his pants and she felt his hands slide under her skirt to shift her panties aside. She moaned as his thumb grazed against her already swollen clit. She was wet, ready for him. She tugged at his pants, adjusting the boxer briefs he was wearing to free his erection. She rubbed her clit against the hardness of his shaft, breaking their kiss to throw her head back and gasp. She repeated the action, reveling in the sensation. Adrien groaned as he watched her, grabbing her by the hips to hold her in place. He moved, matching her rhythm, rubbing himself against her slickness. He allowed his cock to travel from her clit to her entrance, teasing her there for a moment before moving back up to rub against her bundle of nerves. She wanted him to enter her, wanted to feel the fullness of him inside her. But he held her, somehow still in complete control, pleasuring her—pleasuring them both—without allowing her to descend on his throbbing cock.

"Ah," she gasped. Her hands fisted his hair as she continued moving against him. He kissed her again, his breath ragged against her mouth. Her orgasm was building, but it wasn't what she wanted. She wanted him inside her, but the pressure he placed on her hips and his movement beneath her stopped her from getting what she wanted. He was in control, and he wasn't going to give in.

"Come for me." His voice was gruff with restraint. She nodded, bucking her hips rhythmically, bringing herself closer to her peak. His hands tugged at the hem of her shirt, ripping it over her head. He freed her nipples from her bra, taking each one in turn in his mouth. The sensation shot straight to her pussy, pushing her completely over the edge.

"Fuck, Adrien," she cried out as she shuddered and came undone, riding against him, his mouth on her. His hands grabbed at her waist, forcing her to continue her rhythm as she fell apart on top of him. He followed her soon after, a low grunt escaping at the first wave of his orgasm.

"Fuck, yes," he whispered as he continued to come, thick threads of semen pouring from his cock. He kissed her again, moaning into her mouth as the last of his orgasm faded away.

They both slowed their rhythm as they caught their breath, forehead against forehead.

"Why can't I stop myself around you?" he asked. She opened her eyes. Like the other night, he was preventing her from moving her head back to look at him. His eyes remained closed.

"I don't want you to stop," she replied. It was the truth.

"You should, though." He opened his eyes.

"Why?" she asked as he gently pushed her back toward her seat. She climbed over the console as he wiped the cum off himself with his shirt. She adjusted her panties so they were back in place, and located her own shirt.

He paused before replying, "Whatever you're feeling for me isn't real. I've trained you to want me, to feel like you need me. Your feelings for me aren't your own. They're a byproduct of how I've made you."

She considered his words for a second, irritated at their implication. Could he have brainwashed her that effectively? "You have no idea what I *feel*, Adrien, so don't for a second disillusion yourself into thinking you do," she spat his own words back at him. "I know what I feel for you and it's real. So, fuck. Off." She crossed her arms and glared out the window.

He was silent in the seat next to her for a moment before he started the car. As he pulled away from the curb, he said quietly, "You *should* be afraid of me, Sophie. I *will* hurt you."

Adrien tried to ignore the cum that had begun to stiffen his shirt. He couldn't wait to change out of it. His eyes studied the road as he drove, attempting to push his mistakes from his mind. He had made countless numbers of them over the past weeks. Spending time with Sophie outside of her training, allowing her to call him by name, allowing himself to call *her* by name, kissing her, caring about her…it was like watching dominoes fall, one by one, one mistake after another.

And then there was the mistake with Mikhail. He should have killed him. Should have shot that fucker right in the face. He would have, too, had Etienne not come back in the room. *Asshole.* He could never just do what Adrien asked of him. It was like he had some aversion to doing something his younger brother requested. Instead, Etienne had talked things down, managed to reassure a bewildered and pissed-off Mikhail that he, *Adrien of all people*, was the one that was acting irrationally.

You've got to be fucking kidding, Adrien snorted.

It hadn't felt irrational at the time. In fact, it felt totally within Adrien's limits to blow the man's brains out. Mikhail had managed to piss Adrien off one too many times. And this time, Mikhail had really managed to infuriate him. *Chevrette was his.* And Adrien had never liked anyone playing with his belongings. More than once, Adrien had pummeled Etienne for playing with his toys in the sandbox. Only when blood started gushing from Etienne's nose did Adrien let up. But he hadn't wanted to leave a stain in the soft white sand. Had he realized then that stains in the sand could be so easily covered up, he would probably never have stopped.

They had argued about it as they walked to the car. Etienne

had questioned, more than once, what Adrien had been thinking by pointing a gun at Mikhail. Likewise, Adrien had questioned Etienne about what he had been thinking when he stepped in, preventing Adrien from pulling the trigger.

Now, Adrien had a bigger problem on his hands. He had managed to piss off one of the most powerful drug lords, one that held control over most of the drug trafficking routes in Europe and Central America. Mikhail was a man with a lot of power. Most governments knew him and had no way of stopping his hand in the drug trade arena. So, they did what any government would do. They bargained with him. And Adrien and his family had become a big part of that bargaining chip.

They traded women for immunity. Mikhail would keep the drug routes out of France as long as Adrien, Etienne, and Frederic provided him with plenty of women. Adrien had never been a fan of the agreement, and even less of a fan that his own government was the one asking the favor. *The ends justify the means*, Frederic always told him. And so, time after time, Adrien trained girls to hand them over to the type of man he tried so desperately not to do business with.

Adrien had had every intention of killing him, but all he'd managed to do was piss off Mikhail. And a pissed-off Mikhail was dangerous. Adrien pondered what Mikhail's retaliation might look like. Would it be personal? Would he come directly for Adrien? Or would it be through political means, by opening up the drug trade in France? Either way, Adrien decided he would need to change the passcode to the locks at the house. He wasn't taking any chances.

Adrien's cell buzzed in his pocket. He took a hand off the wheel to retrieve it. Frederic's name lit up the screen. *Great.*

"What?" Adrien snapped into the phone. He looked over

at Sophie out of the corner of his eye. She hadn't moved, but he could tell she was listening, could read her body language like an open book.

"I hear you've really made a mess of things, Adrien," Frederic spoke in French, his tone giving away his foul mood. So, Frederic had already heard the news. Was it Etienne or had it been Mikhail himself who'd conversed with Frederic so promptly? Adrien didn't respond. He knew Frederic would get to his point quicker that way. "I'm beginning to question your judgment."

"Really? Because I'm beginning to question Etienne's judgment," Adrien responded, glancing at Sophie. He knew she couldn't understand French, but still, he worried she might pick up on some of their conversation.

"From what I heard, it was a good thing Etienne was there. Otherwise we'd have a bigger mess to clean up than we already do," Frederic snapped. "Is the girl ready?"

Adrien gritted his teeth at the mention of Sophie. "Almost."

"*Almost?* What do you mean 'almost?'"

"Exactly what you think it means," he snapped. He was losing his patience.

"She should have been ready by now, Adrien. It's been almost six weeks. I should be able to sell her as is."

"You think I don't know that?"

"Get it done. Or do I need to start monitoring you to make sure things are moving along?"

"That's not necessary. She's practically ready and there are plenty of buyers interested. We should have no problem selling her."

"I'm not worried about that." Adrien could practically hear the wave of Frederic's hand as he dismissed Adrien's words, swatting them away like an annoying gnat. "It seems Mikhail has taken an interest in her, and I'm inclined to use the girl as a peace offering."

"Absolutely not!" Adrien barked into the phone. Frederic had already hung up.

Adrien should have killed Mikhail when he had the chance. *Should have shot that fucker right in the face.*

———

27

Even without the blindfold that Adrien placed over her eyes, Sophie knew they had neared the training house well before they pulled into the long, bumpy driveway. She could feel it in her bones like an old friend. She never thought she would feel so relieved to be back at her place of captivity. Adrien allowed her to remove the blindfold once the garage doors were closed. He hurriedly collected their bags and began carrying them into the house. Punching in the code and placing his palm on the pad, he held the door open for Sophie to walk through. She waited for Adrien to follow, only to find him fidgeting with the keypad. After a few moments, he came in and moved to the next coded doorway where he did the same thing.

"What are you doing?" she asked, watching him intently from the living room.

"Changing the locks," he replied.

"I know, but why?" she tried again, searching for information. *Was this about Mikhail? Or something else?* Though she hadn't understood his phone conversation in the car, she read body language well enough to know that the conversation had deeply disturbed Adrien. She had caught a glimpse of the caller ID before he picked up. She wondered who Frederic was, still attempting to put pieces of the puzzle together.

"Security measures, *Chevrette*," Adrien evaded. He had finished with the ones in their immediate proximity, and headed down the hallway toward their bedrooms. Sophie followed. Adrien made it to her bedroom door before waving her over. Stepping toward him, he grabbed her wrist and pressed her thumb to the pad, holding it there. She looked up at him, his brows furrowed in concentration as he watched the thumb pad turn green and beep. "There. The code is 7030. Numbers first, then your thumb goes on the thumb pad just like that. You'll be able to get in and out of your room if you need to, but you won't be able to get out of the house or into any of the other rooms. If something happens, your best bet is to stay where you are. No one can get into your room except me. If, for whatever reason, that ends up not being the case, you have the ability to get out. Head toward the ground floor if that happens. Understood?"

"What's going on?" Anxiety gripped. There was no way he would give her access to get out of her room unless something bad was imminent. "Why are you giving me the code? Is something happening?"

"Nothing is happening, *Chevrette*. It's just precautionary. I pissed off the wrong person today and I didn't get a chance to deal with him the way I wanted to. That's all."

His words provided no comfort whatsoever.

⌦⌫

What's wrong? You don't like being tied up?
You're not going to like this.

She couldn't sleep, couldn't shake the malicious look in Mikhail's multi-colored eyes and the hatred in his voice. Her wrists hurt, a phantom pain at the thought of him tying her up. She stared at the door, the coded pad tempting her from its perch on the wall. She could get up, grab a midnight snack. Maybe even sit out on one of the porches while she waited for exhaustion to overtake her. Another scenario played out in her head...rather than turning right out the door toward the kitchen, what if she turned left? What if she made her way into Adrien's room instead? She pressed her thighs together, the sheets suddenly feeling restrictive against her skin.

"Fuck it," she muttered as she hopped out of bed.

7030.

She pressed her thumb to the pad and it blinked green before chirping its confirmation. The lock on the door clicked open and Sophie grabbed the door handle. She hadn't really thought her plan through. She paused at the entranceway, looking down the hallway toward the kitchen, then toward Adrien's room. His light was on and door was ajar. She heard the faint sound of his phone going off, heard him move quickly to the door. *Shit.* At that moment, she remembered what he had said to her about the thumb pads: if anyone beside himself tried to use them, he was immediately notified. She would have felt comforted by this fact were she not frozen with fear that she may have just abused her privilege.

"*Chevrette?*" His voice drifted into the hallway before he appeared in his doorway. He didn't sound mad. Sophie relaxed slightly. "Is everything okay?" She remained silent, didn't know how to answer. He peered at her, his tall, muscular body filling the doorframe. "What's wrong?"

"Nothing. I'm sorry."

He studied her for a moment. "Where were you going?" He

sounded suspicious, like he thought she was scheming some sort of escape attempt.

"Nowhere, I just couldn't sleep. I guess I thought maybe I could...I don't know…grab something to drink or sit out on the porch or...something." It sounded stupid, even to her. He cocked his head, a faint smile playing on his lips.

"It's raining out."

"Oh." She hadn't even realized. Feeling like an idiot, she turned to go back into her room.

"Did you still want something to drink?" His voice stopped her.

She smiled. "Sure."

He led her to the kitchen, where she helped herself to a glass of water. He watched as she drank, his arms crossed, leaning against the counter. Placing the glass into the sink, Sophie let out a shaky breath. She couldn't dispel the tension and anxiety from the whole Mikhail situation. Not to mention the mysterious and anger-provoking phone conversation Adrien had in the car on their drive back. For many reasons, Sophie was on edge. And she couldn't shake the feeling that something bad was about to happen. She looked up at Adrien, wishing she had some answers, or the ability to divine the future.

"Is Frederic your father?" Her question was out before she had the sense to stop herself.

His eyes snapped to hers, alert with alarm and curiosity. "Where did you hear that name?"

"The phone call in the car. I saw the name Frederic on the screen before you picked it up."

"And what makes you think he's my father?" He leaned back in his chair, eyeing her with feigned disinterest.

She shrugged. "The way you got all tense, the same way you did when you were talking to your brother about Henry that first night at the pre-auction. The same way you did when you told me about how your father was the one to give you the scars on your back."

"Playing detective now, *Chevrette?*"

"No...I just...I'm good at listening. And I'm good at picking up on people's body language, that's all. It used to be a part of my job." He didn't respond. "I heard another name, too. Etienne. Is that your brother?"

He leaned forward then, steepling his hands under his chin as he delivered his warning. "You're walking on thin ice, *Chevrette*. Not many people in this world know our real names and those who do don't typically know our profession. The select few who know our names and our line of business are people we know and trust and...well, they keep shut about it because they know my family is not keen on forgiveness."

Her eyes widened at the implications. *Why hadn't he just lied to her? Denied it?* She was holding information she didn't want the responsibility of holding.

"You already know what I'd do if you let it slip. Etienne and Frederic wouldn't be so kind. They would kill you in a heartbeat."

"I won't say anything. But please don't hurt Megan. Please," she pleaded, "I'd rather you hurt me."

He looked honestly perplexed by her words. His eyebrows scrunched together as he asked, "Why is that? Why are you so willing to put your life on the line for her over and over again?"

Could he really not understand why someone would do that for another? She was equally as perplexed as he. "Because I love her. And for me, that means her well-being is more important than my own."

Adrien considered this, as though he weren't quite sure what the definition of love should be. She watched him as he watched her, in silence, neither of them moving. She wished she could ask him what he was thinking but she figured that even if she did ask, he would never answer. It occurred to her how little she actually knew of Adrien.

The shrill sound of Adrien's phone caused Sophie to jump. She saw the tension in Adrien's shoulders as he dug into his pocket to look at the screen. Whatever it said, he clearly didn't like it.

"I don't fucking believe this," he mumbled as he glanced up at the door leading to the garage. Likewise, Sophie followed his gaze, half expecting to see someone trying to break through the security measures. "Get back to your room," Adrien commanded in the acid tone he used when he was pissed off and exasperated. "And don't come out until I tell you to."

"What's going on?"

"*Now, Chevrette,*" he growled. There was something about the tone of his voice that made her turn and run. Having made it back to her room, she slammed the door behind her. Leaning against it, she willed her breath to return to normal and her heart rate to slow. She was safe. Or, according to Adrien, she was in the safest place in the house. She reminded herself that no one aside from Adrien could get in, or at least not without doing some serious damage. There was no way she was going to fall asleep without knowing that everything was okay. *Who was trying to use the keypads?*

Sophie climbed into bed, deciding it was safe enough that she didn't need to hide. Still, she hoped Adrien would come and let her know what happened.

She waited.

The howler monkeys began their morning calls before Sophie's eyes finally closed. She couldn't stay awake any longer. Adrien still hadn't come.

"Good morning, *Chevrette.*"

Sophie bolted upright as adrenaline surged like wildfire through her veins. It fed her, bringing her to her senses, causing a jitteriness in her hands and a buzzing in her ears. *What was it that her body was screaming for her to understand?* As the fog of her poor night's sleep began to dissipate, she remembered the late-night alarm that had sounded on Adrien's phone, alerting him that someone was trying to get into the house. The anxiety in her stomach rolled like a tumbling brick when she realized what had jolted her awake.

It wasn't Adrien's voice that had greeted her.

"You weren't expecting me, were you?" Etienne's eyes twinkled with amusement as he sat perched on the end of Sophie's bed. "Sleeping like a baby. Does my brother always let you get away with this type of behavior?"

Sophie's heart pounded in her chest. Where was Adrien? Why wasn't he here?

"You look worried." Etienne cocked his head, smiling as he studied Sophie. It was his smile that was so unsettling, Sophie decided. He smiled too much, and never really meant it. It made her appreciate Adrien's smiles, so few and far between. At least when he smiled, it reached his eyes.

Etienne moved closer to her on the bed, causing a knee-jerk reaction in Sophie to scramble away toward the headboard. Etienne's smile widened. "Still scared of me, *Chevrette?*" She didn't answer. She wanted to get as far away from him as possible. She looked toward the door in hopes that Adrien would come to her rescue at any moment.

"Is this any way to treat a master, *Chevrette?*" His tone was scathing as he grabbed ahold of Sophie's hair, wrenching her head back to look at him. His smile was gone, though the look in his eyes remained the same as always. Cold.

"You're not my master," she said as evenly as possible. She surprised herself with how confident she sounded. But that smile was back.

"That's where you're wrong, *Chevrette*. I get to be your master for the remainder of your training." He let the words sit in the air, sizzling there before seeping in. "And things are going to be very different." He let his gaze sweep over her as she sat dumbfounded at the news.

"Arrête de la tourmenter." Adrien's command carried across the room. She hadn't heard the keypad or the door click. But he was there. She could feel herself relax. Such an oddity that she now found comfort and safety in the man who was responsible for her hopeless fate.

It seemed even Etienne couldn't disobey Adrien's demands. He released Sophie's hair, her hands instantly replacing his to rub the burn that heated her scalp. "My brother seems to think I'm tormenting you," he snickered. "Isn't it the other way around, though, Brother?" Etienne turned to Adrien who was bringing a tray of food to set on Sophie's bedside table. "You torment your trainees more than I ever have."

Sophie watched Adrien give Etienne a dirty look. She had to hand it to him, the man could shoot daggers. Etienne ignored him. "Am I right, *Chevrette*? My brother trains you to crave sex and then never bothers to give it to you. Must be the worst kind of torture, to want a good fucking and never get it."

"Are you finished, *Brother?*" Adrien's contempt was apparent. Sophie could practically feel it emanating from him. It only egged Etienne on further.

"What? I'm just looking out for your trainees. Right,

Chevrette?" Etienne grinned at her before turning back to Adrien. "The poor girl is probably desperate for a good pussy-licking. We all know you'd never man up and do it."

"I don't have time for your bullshit, Brother. If you're here to check on the progress, then do what you need to do and get out," Adrien snapped. Turning to Sophie, he continued in the same short-tempered manner. "Eat your breakfast and do what he says, unless it directly defies me. Consider him your temporary master. Is that clear?" She nodded.

Etienne smiled triumphantly. "Ready to have some fun?"

"What are you doing here?" Adrien asked as Etienne shouldered past him through the doorway.

"What the fuck, Adrien? Why did you change the code? Did you wipe my fingerprints, too?" Etienne seethed, turning to face him.

"Answer my question first." He didn't have the patience for Etienne's relentless desire to be the dominant older brother at the moment. If he wanted answers to his questions, Etienne would need to answer Adrien's first.

"Frederic sent me."

"Why?"

Etienne glared at him. It had always perturbed Adrien—the way their eyes were the same. It was as though the world had run out of ideas and just decided to make do with what it had already created.

"Because Frederic is starting to wonder if you're up for the job," Etienne finally replied.

"And you? What do you think?"

Etienne took a deep breath before replying, "I'm not sure what

I think. What I know is that you almost messed up back there with Mikhail and I'm not sure what the fuck that was all about. What I know is the girl doesn't seem half as ready as she should."

"What are you implying, Etienne?" Adrien hoped it came across as a challenge. Truly, he was fishing. Had Etienne recognized that things with Chevrette *were not going as they usually did with his trainees? Was it obvious to Etienne that Adrien was a finger's breadth away from shooting Mikhail, not because he was breaking the rules by punishing his trainee, but because of the very fact that he was about to hurt Sophie?*

"Nothing, Adrien." The way he said it suggested he meant the opposite. That he was implying everything, all of it. That he saw right through him.

Last night's conversation replayed in Adrien's mind like a broken record as he followed Etienne and Sophie down to the training room. It left him feeling unsettled that Frederic was monitoring him and that Etienne was playing the part of the judge. There had been a time in their lives when the brothers would have never turned against one another. Adrien thought back to the days when Etienne would plead for Frederic's mercy as he whipped Adrien's back into a bloody mess. His begging fell on deaf ears and, after a while, Etienne stopped asking Frederic to go easy on him. Instead, he watched silently as Adrien endured whatever punishment was bestowed on him. Adrien had never truly understood what had changed between them. Eventually, he settled on the notion that nothing had actually changed between the brothers. It was Etienne alone that had changed.

"Open the door, Brother," Etienne demanded. Adrien felt the muscles in his back tense at the command, his jaw clenching involuntarily at the notion of being subservient in his own home. He shrugged the thought away. The reality was, he had been the one to change all the codes. There was no getting into the training room without his thumbprint. And there was no getting rid of Etienne without getting into the training room. He opened the door.

"On the bed, *Chevrette*," Etienne instructed as he made his way over to the shelves and chests of equipment. Sophie glanced at Adrien. He saw the question worried on her face. *Obey?* Adrien nodded. She would have to obey. Without further hesitation, he sat on the bed and waited. Likewise, Adrien could do nothing but wait for Etienne's deliberation. He stood with his arms crossed watching Etienne pull items from the shelves, considering them a moment before replacing them. Finally, he returned to the bed, placing his items down before turning to Adrien.

"Help me restrain her," Etienne said, grabbing Sophie and shoving her back on the mattress. She cried out as she was forced to lie down. Adrien didn't move. He wouldn't obey this command. Perhaps it was petty, but his authority was being questioned too much for his liking. He wouldn't be bossed around like a little brother in his own training house.

Adrien stood in defiance, arms still crossed, as he watched Etienne grab Sophie's wrists in one hand. Taking the restraints in the other, he began adjusting the cuffs. Adrien knew the exact moment that Etienne noticed the scars on her wrists. His head snapped up to meet Adrien's eyes.

What the fuck? Did you know about this? The question was clear on Etienne's face, both anger and confusion warring across his features.

I know, Etienne. Just leave it. It was a silent conversation, the words expressed with merely their eyes, something Adrien had almost forgotten they could do, it had been so long. But for a brief moment, Adrien's brother was back—the way he used to be *before* it all. The moment passed and Etienne turned back to Sophie, continuing to restrain her, but with a tenderness that hadn't before been present. Adrien observed Etienne step back into himself. The *after*. As though he had shed a layer of unwanted skin, shuddered until it loosened enough to step out of.

Etienne picked up the tools he had selected. Adrien noticed the string of beads in one hand and the remote-controlled vibrator in the other. It was typical Etienne. Bring a trainee to the edge of pleasure without ever letting her go over the edge. Torture. Adrien was familiar with the tactic, had used milder versions of it in his own trainings. The difference between him and Etienne, though, was that when Adrien's trainees were driven to the point of begging to be fucked, Adrien never gave in. He permitted them to come by their own hand, but never gave them what they were really craving. Torturous? Yes, of course. Cruel? Adrien thought it worse to give into their importunities, knowing full well that they would hate themselves for pleading for their own rape.

Sophie's moan brought Adrien back to the present. He watched as Etienne inserted the anal beads, followed by the vibrator. He watched as Sophie's mouth opened in a silent O as Etienne began his ambush. Adrien anticipated every move before it occurred. Etienne would bring her close to orgasm with the vibrator and then turn the volume down before she was able to climax. He would do this over and over again until it drove Sophie mad.

His anger festered in his chest, leaking into his limbs and infiltrating his every thought. Reason should have told him to keep quiet, let Etienne do what he was there to do. Show him and Frederic that Adrien hadn't fucked up, that everything was on track, and Sophie could be sold without a problem.

But resentment and jealousy left him with the acrid picture of an inevitable future: Sophie begging Etienne to fuck her.

———————————————

28

Sophie had heard of people who were able to separate themselves from their bodies, to float above themselves and away from their immediate experiences. It was a form of protection, self-preservation. Sophie had always wondered how one might trigger such a feat. Was it through sheer determination? Or did they stumble upon it by accident? Or perhaps one just willed it to happen. As the waves of pleasure rolled over her again and again, Etienne never allowing her to crest, Sophie couldn't imagine anything better than to be outside of herself.

But her body screamed for release, and throughout the torturous process, her mind could not separate itself from the here and now.

"Do you want to be put out of your misery, *Chevrette?*" Etienne teased.

Yes! God, yes. She needed release. "Please, Sir." She was panting. Yet breathless.

"Do you want to get fucked?" He traced his hand down

the outside of her thigh, ghosting his movements over the top toward her inner thigh. It sent goose bumps down her legs and arms in both pleasure and disgust. The truth was, she *did* want to get fucked. She *needed* it more than her next breath. She squeezed her eyes shut, hoping it would all just go away, knowing that it wouldn't.

Etienne grabbed the hair at the base of her neck, dragging her toward him. She cried out in surprise at his strength and sudden hostility. "Answer me!"

A sob escaped her throat as she opened her eyes. "Y-yes," she stammered. She hated herself for saying it. If she could bear to go without release, she would. But she wasn't strong enough. Despite all she had gone through, she couldn't withstand her body's need. Then again, could she withstand what Etienne would do to her? She looked at Adrien, still calmly standing with his arms folded, watching her. She pleaded with him in that instant, praying that he could read her mind. *Please don't let him do this to me. I've handled everything you've given me, but I can't handle this.*

"Say it! Say you want to get fucked." Etienne shook her, causing a sharp pain to shoot up her scalp where he held her.

"I—" She looked at Adrien again. His face was indiscernible except for a slightly clenched jaw. "I want to get fucked."

Etienne slapped Sophie across the cheek, tearing her gaze from Adrien. Tears stung her eyes as he spoke to her. "There's no point in looking to your trainer, he isn't going to rescue you, *Chevrette*. He doesn't believe in fucking his trainees. But I'm sure you're used to his pussy-teasing by now."

A tear slid out of the corner of her eye. She fought back the urge to let another fall, not wanting to give him that satisfaction. Etienne deserved but one of her tears.

"By the amount of back-handed comments you've been

making today, I'm starting to think this little check-up is less about whether or not *Chevrette* is trained, and more about *how* I choose to do my training," Adrien said evenly from the sidelines. Despite the calm, Sophie could hear the underlying irritation in his tone. "Cut the bullshit, Brother. What is this really about?" He stepped forward, arms still crossed. His coolness was a façade for the anger boiling beneath the surface of his judiciously erected walls. "Would it make you feel better if I put her out of her misery? Train her the way you train yours? Is that what you need to see? Because if that's it, then get out of my fucking way," Adrien's composure was faltering. Even still, his restraint was remarkable as he stepped closer to Etienne, causing his brother to step away from Sophie. She watched as the two seethed in their silent battle.

"You've never done it my way before, why start now?" The sarcasm dripped from Etienne's words.

"And I've never been questioned by my own family before either. Apparently, things change." Adrien's derision matched Etienne's.

Sophie watched the brothers as they warred with one another, a screaming match that played soundlessly in the air around them. She marveled about what it might be like to have a sibling to do that with—to know what they're saying without ever having to use words. She was so enthralled in their feud that she hadn't yet considered what this would mean for her.

Another wave of vibration from the object that still rested inside her rendered her thoughts useless, pulling her away from the men standing before her. She let out a gasp as the sensation caressed her, renewing her need for release. She closed her eyes as she willed herself to peak. She was so close. Just a little bit more...

"D'accord. This should be interesting to watch." Sophie felt her near encounter plummet as Etienne turned off the vibrator and pulled it from her pussy. He laughed as she glared at him, angry with him for interrupting her climax. She was so absorbed in her affliction that it took her a moment to realize that Etienne had stepped back, assuming Adrien's stance, crossing his arms across his chest. An amused smile played at his lips.

Sophie's eyes shot to Adrien. *Was he really taking Etienne's place?* It was what she had been hoping for. She didn't want Etienne to touch her, though she was begging for release. She wanted Adrien. For weeks now, she had wanted to feel him inside of her. She just hadn't pictured Etienne watching their every move.

He leaned over her and began to unclasp the binds around her wrists, growling a low warning in her ears. "I'm untying you so that you can hold onto something. Do not put your hands on me or I will leave you here to suffer. Do you understand?" Despite the harshness of his tone, his fingers rubbed gentle circles around her wrists, restoring their circulation.

She nodded. She understood. There would be no intimacy in this. It was all business and that was fine with her. She needed to come, and at least it was happening with Adrien and not with Etienne.

"Good." Adrien grabbed her by the hips and pulled her toward the edge of the bed. Kneeling before her, he spread her legs, letting out a quiet breath of appreciation at the sight of her wet folds. He blew on her clit, the cool sensation sending bolts of electricity through her. She let out a slight gasp and her heart began to race. Even the tiniest of sensations would push her over the edge in the state she was in. She flexed her hips in invitation.

Adrien took the hint, bringing his mouth to her flesh. In one long stroke, he lapped the sweet silk that had pooled at her entrance from the removal of the vibrator. Once again, her orgasm began to build, bringing her to the edge of the precipice with only a few light caresses of Adrien's tongue. Sophie moaned as her clit began to tingle, the familiar feeling of an oncoming orgasm. As the sensation became more intense, Sophie felt Adrien's hand find the string of anal beads and give a slight tug. She had forgotten they were there, so distracted by the vibrator rubbing against her g-spot. In fact, she had forgotten Etienne's presence, watching them like a hawk that hadn't fed in days.

Adrien licked and sucked at her clit, bringing Sophie what she so desperately needed. Her heart pounded and all thoughts were arrested as Adrien brought Sophie over the edge. And just as she peaked, crying out at the long-anticipated sensation, Adrien began slowly pulling the beads from her, one by one. Her body burst with this new experience, an electric buzzing that fizzled and popped, radiating to every nerve ending from her center to the tips of her limbs.

"Oh my God," she gasped as she clawed at the sheets around her. She fought the urge to grab Adrien's hair the way she had the first time he had made her come undone. Still, she wrapped her thighs around his head, pulling him toward her as her hips bucked uncontrollably under his blissful torment.

Slowly, the tingling began to subside, the buzzing receding to a low hum as Adrien's tongue slowed its rhythm. Still panting for breath, Sophie looked down to the edge of the bed where Adrien knelt on the floor. Her eyes met his. She recognized the darkened look of carnality behind those gray and blue irises.

It sent her stomach into a somersault.

Adrien stood up, finding the hem of his shirt and pulling it over his head, throwing it to the floor. His muscled chest and abs rose and fell with unsteady breath. He wanted her, that much was obvious. His erection strained against his jeans. Sophie pressed her thighs together, craving the feeling of friction she was certain was about to come.

"Bend over the bed," he commanded. Immediately, Sophie flipped herself over, placing her stomach and torso on the mattress and planting her feet on the floor. Her mind flashed to the day he had introduced her to the fucking machine. She told him that she liked it from behind—exactly the position she was in now. *Perhaps he'd been remembering the same moment.*

She heard him unzip his pants, accompanied by his sigh of relief as he freed his hard cock from its imprisonment. His hand rubbed the dip of her spine at the small of her back. Shivering with pleasure, she looked over her shoulder to watch him stroke his thick cock with his other hand, his gaze downcast on her swollen and wet pussy.

"Is this what you want, *Chevrette*?" His voice was husky but still harsh. He didn't bother to look her in the eye when he asked. The lust in his eyes was unmistakable, apparent in every stroke of his thick length. Sophie mewled in response, arching her back. She wanted him. Now.

"Fuck," Adrien murmured as he brought his throbbing erection along her dripping folds. Sophie answered with a moan as the plump head of Adrien's cock rubbed against her already sensitive clit. His hand moved to the curve of her waist. He readied himself at her entrance.

Sophie was momentarily distracted by the sound of shuffling from the far end of the room. She had again forgotten about Etienne, who still stood staring. A twinge of unease spread through her, causing her body to tense.

"Relax," Adrien said softly, all asperity now absent from his tone. He'd misinterpreted her, thought she was tensing at the idea of his entrance. It wasn't that at all. She wanted to say it, to tell him she wasn't nervous, that she wasn't having second thoughts, that she was ready for him. She wasn't afraid. Not of Adrien. It was Etienne who made her apprehensive. Because he was no longer watching Sophie like she expected him to be. He was studying Adrien, scrutinizing him as though on the verge of some sort of illuminative recognition. Her stomach wound itself into knots.

As if one mind, Adrien sensed her unease, drawing slow circles along Sophie's waist with his thumbs, effectively bringing her thoughts away from his brother. She knew this motion. It was familiar, Adrien's way of comforting her, of showing her that he knew she was anxious about something. Every time she had been plagued by anxiety, Adrien had comforted her and told her to trust him. And he had never let her down. He always managed to make things better, or at least not worse. She felt her body relax under his touch, the tension melting from her muscles. She looked back over her shoulder, craving her own silent conversation with Adrien.

I'm ready.

He gave a slight nod and pushed himself inside her. She gasped at the welcome intrusion. Though he wasn't completely inside of her, Sophie wasn't used to his size. She was wet, but she hadn't had sex with anyone since Josh and wasn't sure if she could handle Adrien's girth as her first sexual encounter in over a year. Adrien must have sensed her hesitation because he paused, allowing Sophie to adjust. Bringing his hand around her front, Adrien's skilled fingers began rubbing her clit tenderly. It was just the amount of encouragement she needed and she bit her lip, pressing herself back onto Adrien's cock, taking him the rest of the way. It prompted a hiss of pleasure from Adrien.

She cried out at the feeling of fullness. The vibrator had left her sensitive and now, with Adrien inside of her, the release was thrilling. She looked over her shoulder again to lock eyes with Adrien. Once again, without words, she conveyed her message.

Fuck me.

She watched as Adrien let down his walls of restraint. She watched the look of carnal lust deepen in his eyes. She watched him give in to his desires. It scared her, and it was everything that she wanted.

His grip tightened at her waist as he wrapped her long ponytail around his other hand, while thrusting slowly and deeply inside of her. Her fingers curled around the bed sheets, desperate for something to cling to, something to hold her in place. Her orgasm began to build once again. Her breath turned to short, gasping pants. Adrien's breath matched hers as he changed his rhythm, harder and faster. Sophie propelled her hips to meet Adrien's pace. She let out a low moan as Adrien's thick length filled her to completion, hitting the sensitive area that would plunge her into euphoria. She could feel her body climbing to its peak.

"Don't come yet, *Chevrette*. Not until you're given permission," Adrien commanded through gritted teeth. She hated the command. She wanted release, was aching for it. Why did she have to wait? And yet, she obeyed. Not because Etienne was watching, but because she *wanted* to obey him. She trusted him and knew that following his commands ultimately led to the best possible outcome for her.

Adrien pulled back on her ponytail, allowing her hair to fall from his grip as he pulled Sophie from the bed so that her back was pressed against his chest. His strokes were shorter now as his arms wrapped around her, holding her close. One hand caressed her breasts while the other massaged her clit in a polyrhythmic dance. Sophie arched into his touch as Adrien's thumb and forefinger rolled her nipple causing it to harden in its already budded state. It sent a shiver down her spine, connecting with the building pressure of pleasure that Adrien masterfully infused in her clit and g-spot.

"Do you want to come?" His lips brushed against the shell of her ear causing another low moan to escape her lips.

"Yes, please," she whimpered.

"Yes please, *what?*" he corrected her.

She gasped as his thumb changed direction over her swollen bundle of nerves. "Yes please, Master."

"Good girl," he said as he released her nipples and pushed down on her back, rendering her, once again, face down on the mattress, all while never removing his hand from her clit. He continued weaving quickening circles as the pace of his cock increased, striking deep and hard inside her. It was a punishing rhythm, exactly what Sophie needed. Each of Adrien's thrusts was met by an incomprehensible moan from the depths of Sophie's throat as he brought her to climax, finally releasing her with the words, "Come for me, *Chevrette.*"

She screamed in ecstasy at the permission to claim her release, tipping over the edge as Adrien continued plunging inside her. Her pussy clenched around him, her orgasms taking her in bursts, one pulsing from the inside out, the other from the outside in. They worked in tandem, a perfect synergism that overloaded her system. Amidst her euphoria, she vaguely registered the sound of footsteps, a door opening and closing, as Etienne left the room.

Adrien was slowing his thrusts as her orgasm receded, although he had yet to experience his own release. Wanting nothing more than to give him what he had given her, Sophie attempted to rekindle his rhythm with her own movement. Arching her back and rounding her spine, she pushed her hips into his in a fluid movement, taking him in completely, milking his long length. She was rewarded by his labored breathing, a low groan of approval released from deep in his throat.

"Fuck, yes."

His words drove her further, another orgasm beginning to surface. His rhythm accelerated, his cock thrusting harder, grunting as he did so. She was close again. So close.

"I'm going to come again," she cried the words just as she tumbled over the threshold, her mind numbing and toes curling as she was swept away.

Adrien groaned as he pulled out, leaving Sophie feeling empty. She looked back at him, recognizing the ragged sound of his breathing right before he was about to come. He held his thick length in one hand as his words came out desperately, strained by his effort to hold off. "Come here, open your mouth."

Immediately she was on her knees in front of him. As the warmth of her tongue touched the tip of his cock, he groaned, coming on her tongue, hot and wet, spurting his seed as he milked himself. His cum hit the back of her throat and the roof of her mouth. She swallowed as he continued coming, pumping himself over and over again. As he finished, her tongue darted out to lick the remnants from the tip of his dick.

She looked up from her position on the floor to him peering down at her with an indiscernible look. He cleared his throat as he began tucking himself back in. He gathered his shirt from the floor and put it back on before walking over to Sophie, holding a hand out to her. She took it and he pulled her up to stand in front of him. He reached out to push a lock of hair behind her ear. But that look hadn't left his face.

A perfect blend of awe and regret.

Adrien left her there in the training room. The way she had swallowed his cum and looked up at him so reverently…he would deal with the aftermath later. He needed to deal with Etienne first.

Adrien found him on the main deck sitting in one of the lounge chairs, his face lifted toward the sun. He had poured himself a heavy glass of scotch, which rested on the wooden armrest of his chair. It bothered him how at home his brother seemed to be.

"I see you've made yourself comfortable," Adrien said coolly as he sat in the chair across from him. Etienne's mouth lifted in a sad smile as he turned to Adrien.

"She's ready," he said as he took a sip of his drink. His eyes didn't leave Adrien as he said it.

"I know that. I'm not entirely sure why you and Frederic have been questioning it." Adrien's tone was icy. It was as close to an 'I told you so' as he would ever get. Adrien had never been one for childishness but, in the moment, he felt he deserved to point it out. Etienne was silent. It was as close to an apology as he would ever get. His brother had never been one for apologies, even when he was in the wrong.

Etienne tapped a finger on his glass, a habit that Adrien realized they'd both picked up somewhere along the line. He seemed deep in thought. When he spoke, it was a question and a statement. "You know what has to be done." Adrien bristled at the underlying meaning.

"Of course I do," he spat. He refused to look at Etienne, deciding it was safer to feign interest in the jungle beyond the deck railings.

"You know he wants to sell her to Mikhail?"

Adrien's jaw clenched. "What's your point?" He managed to ask as evenly as possible.

Etienne sighed. "Do you want to make the call to Frederic or should I?"

"I'll do it," Adrien responded.

Shifting in his chair, Etienne downed the last of his drink. "I'll get out of your way, then." He stood up, towering over Adrien before placing a hand on his brother's shoulder. "I'm sorry, Adrien."

Adrien couldn't shake the notion that he was thirteen again, overcome by that feeling of sick shame at having been caught jerking off for the first time.

———————————

29

He was silent. He left her in the training room without explanation, returning sometime later to bring her back to her room. There was no sign of Etienne as they walked through the halls. When she asked where he was, Adrien's reply was simply, "Gone." It was the only word he spoke to her after their session.

Despite his silence, he started her shower and brought her a fresh towel. And when she stepped out of the shower, there was a fresh cup of hot tea on the bathroom counter. She wrapped the towel around her naked body in contentment before reaching for the cup. She dressed, bending over to quickly dry her long hair with the towel before flipping it over her shoulders and looking out the window.

She saw Adrien pacing on the main deck with his phone to his ear. The tension in his body was visible, the irritation palpable in the air around him. She watched as he hung up the phone and shoved it in his pocket before stalking back into the house. Though she couldn't hear it, she could sense the door had slammed shut behind him.

She had the nagging feeling that whatever was pissing him off had something to do with Etienne's visit. She still wasn't sure what was going on. All she knew was that Etienne thought Adrien wasn't training her properly. *Why had he left so abruptly? Did it have to do with what happened in the training room?* The way Etienne had studied Adrien left her with an uneasy feeling. Not to mention the fact that Adrien apparently never had sex with his trainees. In fact, Etienne made it seem like he hardly touched them and certainly didn't allow them to reciprocate sexual favors…and yet he had with her. *No favors,* Chevrette. He had told her that multiple times. His expression of regret after that night at the pre-auction, and again in the training room that day, remained burned in her memory, leaving a sting of guilt on her conscience. *Had he felt forced to do something he didn't want to do?* She discarded the thought. *Adrien wasn't the type to do something he didn't want to do, right?* The more she thought about the situation, the more questions she wanted answered.

Sighing, she continued sipping her tea, deciding to remain in her room while he cooled off. Whatever it was that was upsetting him, she knew him well enough to know that he wouldn't want to talk about it. Better to wait until he was in one of his better moods, when he would be more likely to open up to her.

The questions nagged at the back of her mind as she finished the tea and made her way out of her room. From the main living area, she heard the alarm sound on his phone, alerting him that she had used the keypad. She paused in the hallway, waiting to see if he might tell her to go back in her room. When she didn't hear anything, she decided it was probably fine to proceed.

She entered the large, open kitchen-living room suite in search of Adrien. She found him pouring a glass of whiskey at the kitchen counter. His eyes followed Sophie as she entered the room. Still, he didn't say anything. Awkwardly, she moved to place her empty teacup in the sink. Clearing her throat, she braved breaking the silence.

"Thank you for the tea."

He took a gulp of his whiskey before saying, "You're welcome." His eyes remained transfixed on her. Afraid to break the connection, she decided to barrel forward with her questions.

"Etienne said you don't usually…do that?"

"Do what?"

"You know what I mean."

He raised an eyebrow, feigning ignorance. She fought the urge to roll her eyes. He was going to make her say it. She pursed her lips, mustering the courage to just come out with it. After all, she had done more compromising things with this man than she had with anyone else. Words were nothing anymore. "He said you don't usually have sex with your trainees. He made it seem like you don't lick them, or let them suck you off, and you certainly don't typically come in their—"

"No, *Chevrette*, I don't usually do those things," he interjected, taking another large swig of his whiskey. She watched his Adam's apple bob as he swallowed the liquid.

"Why not?"

"Because it's unnecessary for the purpose of training," he snapped. She blinked at the vehemence in his voice. This last remark made her realize how she must have come across to him—how alike Etienne and Frederic she must have sounded.

"I'm not trying to question you, Adrien. I'm just trying to understand."

He looked away from her, out the window. She followed his gaze until his eyes shifted, meeting hers. "It's not necessary to train someone using sex." His voice was much softer now. Perhaps he realized she hadn't meant to sound like she was siding with his family. He continued. "It only serves to create a power dynamic—a trainee is taught not to say no, so even if they don't want it, they do it anyway. Anyone who's forced into doing something is likely to end up afraid. Fear is necessary for obedience, but Etienne uses it to get his trainees to give into sex. Associating fear with sex is not the point—it actually counteracts what we're trying to accomplish during training." He paused, letting this information sink in. "But Etienne puts them in a position where they think they want sex but ultimately end up regretting it in the end. There's no point, and it's just a useless mindfuck on top of everything else. Sex is supposed to have positive associations. It's what ensures that our trainees don't burn out once their sold. So, no, I don't usually have sex with my trainees, nor do I lick them, as you put it, and I certainly don't make a habit out of sticking my cock in their mouths."

She swallowed. Hearing him say it sent a surge of heat between her legs. Ignoring her reaction, she considered his words. They were pretty basic aspects of human conditioning. She had read about it, studied it. "You're right, I *was* afraid of Etienne. I wouldn't have wanted him to fuck me, even though I probably would have asked for it. In the moment, it was pretty terrifying to feel like my body was making decisions for me. But it didn't feel that way with you. It felt different. It felt… right."

Adrien looked down at her despondently. "That's the other reason I don't usually do that with trainees. The other response, aside from fear, is attachment."

She let the words sink in, drop into her stomach. Of course he didn't want his trainees attached to him. *Look how well that turned out for* Doll, she reminded herself. "So then why didn't you just let Etienne fuck me if you were so worried about these things?" She tried unsuccessfully to hide the hurt in her voice.

A flash of emotion crossed his features but was quickly replaced by his mask of impassivity. "By the way you were looking at me, I thought you didn't want what Etienne was offering. Was I wrong?"

"Of course not. That's not what I meant." So he *had* read the plea in her eyes.

Adrien continued, "Etienne was pissing me off. I saw an opportunity to reassert myself and I took it. That's all."

She hated the tears that stung. Adrien was right, she had gotten attached. She felt things for him that she knew she shouldn't and he had made it clear that those feelings were not reciprocated. Before she made an idiot of herself, she needed to get away from him. She had gotten her answers and there was no need to continue standing there in front of him. She took a step to go, but Adrien caught her arm. She averted her gaze, didn't want him to see the tears that were brimming. But Adrien forced her to look at him, lifting her chin with his finger.

"I can't be the man you want me to be, Sophie."

"I'm not asking you to be anyone you aren't, Adrien. I would never ask that." Still, there was something badgering at the back of her mind. Something that didn't fit. "So, fine, that explains why you had sex with me, but what about our other times together? Etienne wasn't there to piss you off then."

Adrien gritted his teeth, the muscles in his jaw twitching. "What do you want me to say, Sophie?"

"I just want the truth. What was it, Adrien?" She was raising her voice as her irritation with his evasion grew. "You didn't seem to be afraid of any power dynamics when you had your tongue on me, and you definitely didn't seem too worried about attachment when I was sucking your cock to the back of my throat—"

His hand grabbed the hair at the nape of her neck as his body crashed into hers, forcing her against the counter. "You want the truth? Fine, you're right. I didn't give a fuck about those things then because I couldn't fucking think straight! And I didn't give a fuck about those things today because I couldn't fucking stand the thought of Etienne being inside of you. Is that what you need to hear?!" His breath was coming out ragged and strained as his voice broke, "I can't get you out of my head and it's driving me crazy."

His mouth was on hers, her lips parting to let his tongue delve inside to explore, to claim her. *She was his.* Sophie's hands fumbled with his shirt to pull it over his head. Their bodies and lips reconnected and the warmth of Adrien's skin heated her own as she pressed up against him. His hand reached under her ass and lifted her onto the counter. He settled between her legs and placed hungry kisses along her jawline, while his hands worked under her shirt, removing it swiftly.

"Christ, Sophie," he strained as his mouth took her nipple, teasing it into a tight point. Both words and tongue sent a shiver of need down her spine. She wrapped her legs around his waist, pulling him closer. The bulge in his pants pressed against her heated sex, triggering a new rush of wetness between her legs. Adrien moved to her other nipple, giving it the same attention as its counterpart. A ripple of sweet torture spread through her as the tension between her legs grew.

"Please, Adrien. I need you inside of me," she moaned as Adrien ran a finger down the center of her body, stopping when he grazed her swollen bud. She reached for his pants, her fingers unclasping the button and jerking the zipper down. She reached her hand inside and freed his throbbing erection. Scooting down on the counter, she positioned his cock at her entrance, ready to take his length inside of her. She bit her lip in anticipation of the feeling of fullness she knew was coming.

But Adrien brought his hand to Sophie's cheek, angling her so she looked directly into his eyes. The windows to the soul. A muddle of emotions swam behind those blue-rimmed irises— *desire, uncertainty, worry, need…love? Was that there, too?*

"If you don't want this, you need to tell me now because I'm not going to be able to stop myself if we keep going."

"I don't want you to stop yourself. I want this, Adrien. It has nothing to do with how you've trained me and everything to do with what I want. I promise. I need you." She knew he needed to hear those words. He no longer wanted to feel as if the only reason someone was with him was because they *had* to be. Like anyone, he wanted someone to be with him for who he was, despite his flaws. And she did. Because of his flaws, because of who he was and what he did, she had found herself again. And learned to live.

He pushed himself inside of her and she let out a moan of relief as her body adjusted. Adrien's mouth crashed into hers as his hands moved to her waist. She tangled her fingers through his hair and wrapped herself tighter around his body as he began to thrust. She marveled in the sensation that he brought to her body. Impossibly long strokes sent bolts of pleasure through her core and she found herself craving his thickness buried as deep inside of her as possible. She moved to lie back on the counter, to satisfy her craving, but she was stopped by her proximity to the cabinets. Taking her cue, Adrien cupped his hands under her buttocks and lifted her off the counter. He carried her over to the table, laying her out gently, like his most prized possession, across the surface of cool wood. With her legs still wrapped around him, Adrien filled her completely.

"God, you feel so good," he murmured as he continued to move inside her. "So. Fucking. Good." He punctuated each word with the push of his hips, the skin above his shaft kissing Sophie's clit with every pump. Her breasts bounced with the force that Adrien exerted, and she gripped the edge of the table for leverage.

Her back arched upward, a low moan escaping her throat. Sophie watched as Adrien fucked her, his eyes hooded with lust as they followed each retreat and subsequent penetration of his cock into the wet and aching need between her legs. Sweat glistened along his forehead as he worked both of them toward their peaks.

"Oh my God, Adrien, I'm going to come," she exclaimed, her voice rising in sync with her orgasm. "Don't stop. Please, don't stop."

Her begging was met by a low groan, an accelerated tempo, and Adrien's thumb massaging the sensitive nub at her center.

"That's it. Come on my cock, Sophie," he said between gritted teeth. It was enough to push her over the edge. She called out his name as she pulsated around him, hips rocking and muscles squeezing. He followed her to his own climax, her sex still milking his cock as he erupted inside of her. She could feel the warmth of his seed as it filled her, his cock jerking inside of her with each spurt. He stilled inside her before letting himself fall forward on top of Sophie. Instinctively, she wrapped her arms around him as he pressed his forehead into the dip at her collarbone. Their breath matched one another's, coming out in rapid, uneven, yet contented pants.

"What now?" she asked. It was a loaded question. *How do we move forward? Does this change anything? What happens next?*

"Dinner." Adrien shifted to kiss the well between her breasts before pulling himself off of her. She knew he knew that wasn't what she was asking. Still, she could appreciate his desire to preserve the moment, not mar it by trying to figure out the future. She wanted to bask in the here and now, allow herself contentment with what was happening rather than worry about tomorrow. It was a simple pleasure she hadn't indulged in for the longest time.

"Well, I usually have guys make me dinner *before* I let them fuck me," she quipped.

Adrien failed to hide his smile, raising an eyebrow at her crass humor. "Well then, I guess I owe you, don't I?"

"I need to get some work done," Adrien said as he put his plate in the dishwasher. Sophie stood at the sink rinsing hers. It was such a strangely domestic thing to be doing with him, but it felt natural. His words, though, caused her to falter. *Work* to Adrien meant…what exactly? Selling her?

"It's not that kind of work," he clarified. He must have sensed her tension, as miniscule as her reaction had been.

"What kind of work is it?" Curious. She hadn't realized Adrien had *other* types of work. She was again reminded of how little she really knew of him. She awaited an answer as a smile played on his lips.

"I'll show you," he replied, grabbing her hand and leading her toward the wing of the house opposite their bedrooms. She followed, her hand clasped in his as he opened the door at the end of the hall. This room mirrored his bedroom in its size and layout, but had been set up as a home office. He led her over to his desk where an open laptop sat. Swiping his finger over the keys to wake it up, he navigated a few things before turning the screen so that Sophie could see.

There was a blueprint on the screen, a design she recognized immediately.

"The thumb scan?" she asked, confused as to why he was showing it to her. And then, it slowly sunk in. "Wait…did you *make* that?" Her eyes widened in amazement. She looked up to see Adrien grinning, the pride gleaming in his eyes.

"Etienne and I have been working on the design for a while. Obviously, it's working, so we're thinking of getting a patent for it."

"Holy shit, Adrien—that's amazing!" She remembered the applied security measure to his gun and reveled at how many lives just that tiny measure could save. "Have you thought about marketing it to gun manufacturers?"

He nodded. "Yeah…definitely. The thing is, gun control already exists in France, so this type of design is only applicable to places like here or the United States. International patent laws are a little sketchy, and since we're getting our patent out of France, we need to do a bit more research to be able to market to countries where it would make a bigger difference."

She beamed at him in absolute awe that he had created something that could impact the world so positively, despite the fact that he had been using the technology in such a destructive way. It was essentially the driving force behind her captivity, the very reason why she couldn't escape. But then again…

"So…what does this mean for your current…uh…job? Are you going to quit doing this once you have the patent and start marketing the thumb scan?"

He busied himself clicking around on the computer, avoiding her eyes. "I've never really thought about it," he replied as he set the laptop on the desk. He looked up at her, no longer finding an excuse not to. "I've never had any reason to quit before."

Before. She wondered about his choice of words. He had said it as though they had entered the *after.*

❦

Sophie fell asleep to the faint clicking of the keys on Adrien's computer. She had opted to stay in his office with him while he worked but soon fell asleep in the overstuffed armchair on the opposite side of the room. The truth was, she wasn't sure where else to go. Would she be expected to go back to spending her free time in her room? Or had some barriers been broken down, permitting her some freedom to move around the house? A part of her was afraid to ask, afraid to hear the answer.

As she dozed, she felt Adrien's muscled arms scoop her up, carrying her against the planes of his chest to bed. In her light sleep state, she was vaguely aware that this would be the answer to her questions but was too tired to care at that point. She slipped back into a deep sleep before she could determine which bed he had placed her in.

She awoke sometime later, recognizing the soft bed as Adrien's. She smiled to herself and rolled over. Despite the internal warmth she felt at waking in his room and not her own, she was met by cool sheets from Adrien's empty side of the bed. She sat up, eyeing the clock. It read close to 3 a.m. Looking around, she caught sight of Adrien out on his balcony. He had left the door to the room cracked, a cool breeze drifting in through the opening.

He stood staring out into the forest beyond the property, something Sophie had seen him do on more than one occasion.

He had changed from his earlier jeans and t-shirt, now wearing only his sweatpants. Sensing her eyes on him, he turned. Had they perhaps become so connected that it was possible he could feel her wakefulness, as though it had somehow caused a change in the air around them?

He stepped back into the room, closing the door behind him.

"You're still awake?" she asked, cocking her head to the side. He walked toward the bed and lifted the sheet to climb in beside her.

He smiled sadly as he sat with his back against the headboard, using the pillow as a cushion.

"You're always awake. Don't you ever sleep?"

"Could you sleep soundly if you were me?" He smirked as he placed one hand behind his head and looked up at the ceiling. Sophie stayed silent. It wasn't necessary to admit that she wouldn't be able to sleep if she did the things Adrien had done to people. And she was certain she didn't know the half of it.

"Why do you do this?"

"I thought I already answered that question."

Her fingers traced the contours of his chest. "I know. I just thought maybe you'd tell me the whole truth this time." Her hand rose and fell on his chest with his steady breaths. "I know you said you're good at it and you didn't really have a choice. But why?"

"Does it matter? It doesn't change anything." His fingers wrapped around hers, ceasing the pattern she was drawing on his chest.

"It matters to me," she mumbled. It stung to know that even after she had opened herself to him he still wouldn't share anything about himself.

"I'm not used to explaining myself to anyone," he replied, tracing his own pattern along the ridge of her knuckles. He cleared his throat before continuing. "My father is a dangerous man. I learned at a young age that those who defy him pay a price. It didn't matter what it was—if Frederic wanted something, he would find a way to get it. I grew up watching him dispose of anyone who tried to get in his way."

"What do you mean 'dispose of?'" Sophie asked, although she had an inkling what he meant.

Adrien chewed on his bottom lip before answering. "When Etienne and I were kids, we used to wonder what happened to all of our father's business associates. We would watch them go into his office with him, but a lot of times they never came back out. I was ten at the time, Etienne was twelve, maybe thirteen by then. We were curious, thought maybe our father had a secret passageway or something in his office that his business associates would exit through, and that was why we never saw them leave. So, we snuck in, searching for it. Looking back, it was a stupid idea. I think we just wanted to see if we could get away with it. We were never allowed in his office, so the idea of getting to see it was tempting." He glanced toward Sophie who was listening intently. It was more than Adrien had ever shared with her. *With anyone, probably.*

"I think we must have gotten distracted, but we heard Frederic and someone else approaching from down the hall. If he caught us, we knew we would be punished, so we hid. My father had a cabinet in his office that we climbed into. Etienne hated small spaces so we kept the door cracked.

"Frederic and one of his runners—" Adrien paused, "—that's what we call the men who kidnap the girls we train—they were arguing about something. I don't remember what, but it's not important. The runner was disagreeing with him and things got heated..." Adrien trailed off. "The letter opener must have been lying on the desk. It happened so fast. I don't think the man even realized what was happening until the thing was lodged in his windpipe. He panicked, tried to take it out." She watched the ghosts of his memories floating in his eyes, invisible scenes of things he wasn't telling her. "I knew the moment life left his body. He was on the floor by that time, just lying there. But it took a minute longer for him to actually die. It was like a sigh of relief. You could feel it. The room changed, like the air around us knew there was one less person in the world." He shook his head, dispelling the image from his mind. "Anyway, it turned out Frederic knew we were there the whole time."

Sophie's heart skipped a beat. "Did he punish you?"

Adrien looked down at her and replied despondently, "He made us bury the body."

It was the first time he had told anyone that story. As he told it, he wondered if he might feel a difference afterwards. Would telling the story somehow reduce its power over him? Would the world feel lighter? Warmer? Less fucked up? But the only thing he felt when he'd finished was disappointed. Because saying it aloud didn't make one bit of difference.

Adrien watched Sophie sleeping next to him. He had spared her most of the more gruesome details that had flashed across his mind. The *pop* of the runner's punctured windpipe as the letter opener hit its mark. How Etienne and Adrien found Frederic's *other* business associates while digging the runner's grave. The smell of rotting flesh that caused Adrien to vomit on his shoes. There was no point in filling her mind with the images that he himself wished he could get rid of. There was no point. So, what *had* been the point of telling her?

He would never expect her to forgive him. But maybe by telling her, she could understand.

———————————

30

Sophie had learned a lot about Adrien's moods since that first night together in his bed. Most of the time, Adrien was quiet, contemplative. But Sophie found that a genuine smile from Adrien wasn't as rare as she first thought. They were fleeting, however, often replaced with a frown or an irritated sigh. At times, he would just get up and walk away, leaving Sophie confused by the sudden and drastic change in him, leaving her with the feeling that he was upset with her for making him smile. Or perhaps he was just upset with himself.

Today was no different. Adrien was brooding again. He had spent a lot of time on the phone over the past few days and it always seemed to send his mercurial mood into a tailspin. So, when she heard his phone ring, Sophie decided to step out onto the deck and enjoy the warm sun. She heard him answer the call in his clipped French, an instant indicator that it was a conversation that would likely ignite Adrien's short fuse.

She knew how it would go. It had been the same every time for the past couple of days. The phone would ring, Adrien would pick up, there would be some heated discussion in languages that Sophie couldn't understand, and he would either hang up with a furious press of a button or just throw his phone to indicate he was finished. A silent ruminating would ensue while Adrien attempted to reign in his emotions. After Sophie witnessed the first phone call, Adrien went down to the home gym and didn't reemerge for several hours. But after the second phone call…

Sophie pressed her thighs together at the memory. She approached him with every intention of having a conversation, to ask him if everything was okay, but Adrien wasn't in the mood to talk and Sophie let her intentions drop. He took her hard and fast against the wall, her orgasm a trigger to his own. Afterward, as if in apology for not doing so prior, he carried her to his bed and caressed her with his tongue until she fell apart in his mouth. The third phone call ended similarly to the second, with the exception that Sophie had no interest in trying to talk to Adrien before they fucked. She hoped this phone call would end the same.

She looked in through the glass door of the bedroom, hoping to catch a glimpse of Adrien. *Odd*, she thought. She couldn't see him any longer. Had he gotten off the phone? She decided to go inside to find him. Though she still couldn't leave the house, she walked through the hallways, moving freely with her newly-granted access to the keypads.

She stepped into Adrien's room where she had left him, looking around until it was apparent the room was empty. She figured he must have gone to the gym. Swiftly, she made her way down the hallway and stairs to the ground floor. Punching in the key code to the gym, she opened the door to find that room vacant, too. Confused, she turned to go back upstairs.

She took a quick peek in the kitchen and living area before

deciding to head back to Adrien's room and just wait for him there. As his door unlocked with the familiar click, she heard the beep of a keypad down the hall. Turning to see Adrien emerge from her old room, he caught her eye as the door shut behind him. She smiled, cocking her head inquisitively.

"What were you doing in there?"

He returned a half smile and replied, "Nothing." He paused before deciding on a different answer. "I was looking for you."

Her smile broadened. "I was looking for you, too."

He stepped toward her, his half smile turning full. "Were you?"

"I thought maybe you were done with your phone call, and…" her voice trailed off as Adrien pulled her against his chest. The air caught in her lungs as his arm nestled firmly in the dip of her back while his free hand traced a delicate path down her jaw. His eyes searched hers before brushing a delicate kiss across Sophie's lips. Her hands cradled the back of his neck to pull him closer. He took the invitation, deepening the kiss. Her lips parted in welcome and Adrien's tongue stroked lightly against hers. It felt different, this kiss. It was soft and slow. Like being in a china shop, too afraid to move amidst the delicacy, for fear of shattering its contents into a million pieces.

He pulled back, whispering into her mouth. "Do you trust me?"

She nodded, kissing him again. She didn't have the time or desire to wonder why he asked. He stepped forward, causing her to step back, dancing backward until the edge of the mattress hit the back of her thighs. She let her legs buckle, pulling Adrien down with her. He broke their connection only to remove her sundress and discard his own clothing on the floor. Sophie moved back on the bed as Adrien knelt in front of her.

"God, you're so beautiful," he said, positioning himself at her entrance. She mewled in response, the anticipation sending a wave of heat through her center and a pool of moisture between her legs. Grabbing her hips, Adrien pulled her close, her legs wrapping around him as his thick length entered her.

"Ah," she gasped. Despite the past few days, she still felt tight against him. She wondered if she would ever get used to him being inside of her, if she would ever feel less full when she was wrapped around him.

Adrien moved slow and hard at first, taking his time to fill her completely. It wasn't long before Sophie's orgasm began to build with Adrien's cock deeper inside of her than it had ever been before. His hands moved over her, tweaking her nipples until they budded into little peaks. She moaned at the sparks of electricity igniting her.

"I want to watch you," Adrien said breathlessly, pulling Sophie up to sit on top of him, her legs still wrapped around his waist. "I want to watch you come." His voice was strained, his breathing short and heavy. She realized how close he was to his own orgasm. She wrapped her arms around his neck, their foreheads pressed together. She nodded as she matched his tempo, moving her hips on top of him.

"Oh my God, Adrien!" she cried out as her climax took her and sent her flying over the fringe. Her movements became erratic as she broke rhythm, consumed by the jolts of ecstasy pulsing through her. Her sex squeezed around Adrien's cock, her fingernails digging into his back. She could feel his eyes on her as he watched her fall apart with him inside of her. He groaned in restraint, waiting until Sophie's orgasm had completely faded before burying his face in her neck and grunting as he released his seed. He stilled, allowing Sophie to feel his cock jerk inside of her.

Their breathing was harsh and jagged as they sat entwined. Sophie realized it was the first time she felt like Adrien had made love to her, not just fucked her. Sure, previous times with him had been amazing—passionate, needy, laced with desperation. This was something else.

Adrien kissed Sophie lightly along her collarbone, drawing her from her thoughts.

"Shower?" he asked. She nodded, disentangling herself.

He took her again in the shower. His fingers held onto her hips for dear life as the hot water cascaded around them.

Humming absentmindedly to herself, Sophie pulled her wet hair into a bun before stepping out of the bathroom. She noticed two packed duffle bags on the bed and Adrien nervously pacing by the large windows.

"What's this?" she asked.

Adrien turned to her, taking a deep breath before answering, "We're leaving."

She was taken aback by the response. She considered it a moment. Of course they had to leave here. They couldn't stay—not with everything that had happened. She just hadn't expected it to be so soon. She hadn't expected it to be *now*. Adrien had never broached the subject of leaving with her before. They had no plan. Unless…he already had one.

Discerning her worried expression, he instructed, "No more questions, *Chevrette*. Trust me." She blinked at the use of the moniker. *Odd,* she thought. He hadn't called her that since Etienne left. *Was it a fluke?* A feeling of unease crept in, but she pushed past it.

She nodded. She trusted him. *Of course I do,* she reminded herself. He grabbed the duffle bags and led the way to the garage. Throwing the bags into the back of the Jeep, Sophie climbed into the passenger seat next to Adrien. She half-expected him to blindfold her, smiling to herself as she toyed with the thought. As they pulled out of the driveway, Sophie's eyes took in her breathtaking surroundings.

She had never seen this side of the house before. It was as beautiful as its opposite, the façade built with wood and a sandy-gray stone. It felt odd saying goodbye. She wondered if she would ever return. The thought of not setting foot in it again caused a slight twinge in her heart. It was the place where she was held captive, yes, but it was also the place where she learned to live again. She took one last look at his home, committing every inch of it to memory as they wound down the driveway through the forest. Sophie never wanted to forget it.

They drove for hours, taking mostly single-lane roads that were bumpy and unpaved. Conversation was minimal. Sophie could feel the tension emanating from the driver's seat. She knew better than to ask him about it. He wouldn't give her a straight answer anyway. She was just going to have to trust him.

The car slowed as Adrien put his blinker on to turn onto a long road where trees gave way to an open field. Sophie squinted into the distance, making out what she believed to be a building. *An airfield.* As they approached, she saw a small jet set on the tarmac. They were leaving the country.

"Where are we going?" Sophie asked as Adrien put the car in park. He didn't bother to turn it off as he opened his door.

"*We* aren't going anywhere," he replied.

Her stomach sank at the coldness in his tone. She watched

as he methodically removed the bags from the backseat and walked around the vehicle to open her door. She looked toward the jet where a man stood waiting at the bottom of the stairs leading up to the doorway. At the top of the steps was another man holding a machine gun.

She was being *sold*. This was it. This was what was always meant to happen. *The way he treats you makes you believe he might keep you. Doll's* words echoed in her mind, a warning that she had not heeded. Like *Doll*, she, too had fallen for the comfort that Adrien provided. She believed he wouldn't sell her.

"Let's go," Adrien barked, holding the door open. Sophie could feel her body beginning to tremble with…what? Fear? *No,* she decided. She had entered this whole mess without fear. She wouldn't indulge in it now. Taking a deep breath, she unbuckled her seat belt and stepped out of the car, looking straight past him. She avoided Adrien's eyes. Likewise, he avoided hers. *It's better this way.*

She walked toward the plane, holding her back straight and her head high. She faltered, feeling faint as she recognized the man awaiting her. *Those eyes were unmistakable.*

Sophie clenched her jaw, forcing herself forward. She didn't look back—refused to give him the satisfaction.

So much of Adrien's life had occurred within the confines of Frederic's influence. Adrien always had free will, that he could admit. It was choices that he lacked. And what choice did he have but to sell her? It was too dangerous not to. Frederic would find her and kill her if he didn't go through with it. Once again, Frederic left him without an option. Still.

She never looked back. Of all of them, he figured she might have. Only in his disappointment did he realize that he hoped she would. *Odd,* he thought, *the human capacity for hope.*

―――――――――――――――

A Note From the Author

Dear Reader,

First, I would like to thank you for reading *The Holding*. Whether you loved it or hated every word, I am humbled and grateful to you for taking the time to read this book. You, the reader, are what make the words in my mind more than just the imaginings of a slightly off-centered artist. Thank you, from the deepest part of my being.

This story was inspired by what I like to call "the chiaroscuro of life"—that juxtaposition of light and dark that makes up the complexities of what it means to be human. I found myself writing this story with the intent of portraying these characters as neither entirely good nor wholly bad, but as the complicated mix that tends to define us all.

Though Sophie and Adrien's story is indeed fictional, I wanted to acknowledge the very real world of human trafficking. As someone who identifies as a humanitarian, I struggled with bringing the theme of sex slavery into this story, as I would never intend to glorify or minimize the very serious nature of the topic. It is estimated that there are over 40 million people living in slavery across the world today and as many as 80% of those people are being sexually exploited. And, unlike Sophie, these victims are not a part of a fictional story whose pages can be closed at will. There are numerous resources available if you are interested in learning more information and finding ways you can support anti-human trafficking efforts.

You may be wondering, "So, is this it then? Is this the end?" The answer is both yes and no. It is the end of the novel, yes. But the story is never truly over. I hope I have given you enough and too little at the same time. I hope it is the type of story that keeps you wondering about all of the possibilities of fate. I hope you enjoyed reading this book as much as I enjoyed writing it. Perhaps you will finish Sophie and Adrien's narrative in your own imagination. And, perhaps someday, I will share with you the rest of their story.

Sincerely yours,
M.A. Newhall

Acknowledgments

I would like to give a huge thank you to everyone at Ormus Publishing for taking a chance on this project. Bill Cordaro and Michelle Burinskas: I am forever appreciative of your guidance and wisdom throughout the process. Without you, this story would have stayed in the quiet depths of my C: drive. I would also like to thank Eddie Vincent at Encircle Publications for stepping in, saving the day, and seeing this project through to completion. To Michelle, Maylene, and my other beta readers—your feedback means the world, without which I wouldn't have had the courage to put this story out into the universe. I would like to give the biggest thank you to my editor, who I also get to call my best friend. For all of the short stories, essays, and school papers I have asked you to edit over the years, I am so grateful that you are still by my side (and still willing to edit for me!). This project wouldn't have been as much fun without you. Thank you, ShellBelle. Finally, a huge thank you to my husband for encouraging and supporting the oddities in me.

About the Author

M.A. Newhall is an avid reader, multimedia artist, and writer. Though she enjoys any form of art that allows her creativity to escape the confines of her mind, her passion for the written word began at a young age. Her first experience with publication came in the fifth grade when her writing was selected for a book of children's poetry. Since then, it has been her dream (and one of many bucket-list items) to publish a full-length book. *The Holding* is M.A. Newhall's first novel. When she isn't writing, M.A. Newhall can be found with a coffee in hand, pursuing her other bucket-list items. She resides in the quirky town of Salem, Massachusetts with her husband and cats.

9 780099 743623